KEEPER OF THE FLAME

Other Crang Mysteries

Crang Plays the Ace
Straight No Chaser
Riviera Blues
Blood Count
Take Five

JACK BATTEN

KEEPER OF THE FLAME

A CRANG MYSTERY

DUNDURN
TORONTO

Editor: Dominic Farrell
Design: BJ Weckerle
Cover Design: Laura Boyle
Image credits: © Noppol Mahawanjam/123RF.com
Printer: Webcom

Library and Archives Canada Cataloguing in Publication

Batten, Jack, 1932-, author
Keeper of the flame / Jack Batten.

(A Crang mystery)
Issued in print and electronic formats.
ISBN 978-1-4597-3322-0 (paperback).--ISBN 978-1-4597-3323-7 (pdf).--
ISBN 978-1-4597-3324-4 (epub)

I. Title. II. Series: Batten, Jack, 1932- . Crang mystery.

PS8553.A833K44 2016 C813'.54 C2015-904914-8
C2015-904915-6

1 2 3 4 5 20 19 18 17 16

Canada Council for the Arts

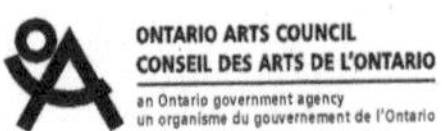

We acknowledge the support of the **Canada Council for the Arts** and the **Ontario Arts Council** for our publishing program. We also acknowledge the financial support of the **Government of Canada** through the **Canada Book Fund** and **Livres Canada Books**, and the **Government of Ontario** through the **Ontario Book Publishing Tax Credit** and the **Ontario Media Development Corporation**.

Printed and bound in Canada.

VISIT US AT

Dundurn.com | @dundurnpress | Facebook.com/dundurnpress | Pinterest.com/dundurnpress

Dundurn
3 Church Street, Suite 500
Toronto, Ontario, Canada
M5E 1M2

FOR PETER AND ALBERT

CHAPTER ONE

The man on the other end of the phone was saying in a brisk voice that I shouldn't leave my office in the next fifteen minutes. He wasn't asking me. He was telling me.

"Aren't you the pushy one," I said to the man, speaking on my brand new iPhone.

"You're the right guy?" the man said. "By the name of Crang?"

"The very same," I said.

"I'm calling for Roger Carnale," he said. I could hear traffic sounds in the background of wherever the guy was calling from. "Mr. Carnale's on his way to your office. Right now, I'm talking about. I need to guarantee him you'll keep yourself available."

"Guarantee to your heart's content," I said. "Do I assume your Roger is in the market for my sharp criminal representation?"

"No way," the man said, brisk as ever but giving his best to add an acerbic tone. "Mr. Roger Carnale is executive director of the Flame Group. He's going to talk to you about something big that has to do with Flame. This is serious for Mr. Carnale. You don't have to know anything else."

He hung up.

I got out of my chair and walked over to inspect the view from my window. A couple of weeks earlier, I'd changed offices, moving down two flights in the same building to a space on the third floor. This office had a better view. Upstairs, the angle I had on midtown Toronto and the world beyond had been limited, nothing past the south side of the condo next door. My new window gave me a prospect looking east across Spadina Avenue, which was all abustle. That was Spadina's permanent state. On the far side, two pretty girls sat on a grassy hillock in the little park at the corner where Spadina met Bloor Street. Matt Cohen Park it was called — a tribute to a deceased novelist who once lived in the neighbourhood. Both girls were wearing baggy tan shorts. One completed her outfit with a pink T-shirt, the other with a halter top. Closer inspection from a distance told me both had superb legs.

The brisk guy on the phone had said "Flame" in a manner that made me think it referred to a person. Who was he? Or maybe she? I had no idea.

I went back to the iPhone sitting on my desk and punched up Annie's number.

"You heard of anybody possibly by the name of Flame?" I said when Annie came on the line. Annie B. Cooke was my go-to person for information on a far-flung variety of topics. She was also my live-in sweetie.

"Canadian rap singer with a tilt to mainstream," Annie said. "And how are you this fine September noon, old sport?"

"The better for hearing your voice," I said. "Are you speaking of Flame along the lines of the other rap guy from around here? Drake?"

"Similar careers up to a point," Annie said. "The major difference, compared to Drake or practically any other rapper, Flame projects profundity, relatively speaking. The thinking fan's idol. It's earning him oodles of cash."

"He's new on the scene?"

"Been at it awhile, but gotten big only the past three, four years. I'm speaking of filling the Air Canada Centre. That kind of big."

"I don't recall you mentioning the guy before."

"Good heavens, Crang, I've never listened to Flame's records or watched his videos or anything else fan-like."

"Your record-collecting days ended with late Marvin Gaye, if I remember?"

"Actually, I've always been a Stevie Wonder girl."

"Wait a minute, if you've never heard or seen Flame, shouldn't you have added an 'apparently' to what you just told me about profundity?"

"Not really. I get the inside dope from impeccable sources."

"Maybe you could just divulge the sources? Let me weigh the impeccability?"

"The magazines in Loblaw's checkout line," Annie said. "Waiting to pay for groceries is when I study up on my pop culture."

"I'm more a *Vanity Fair* browser."

"He's a handsome-looking devil, Flame. Judging from photographs."

"What's your frame of reference?" I said. "Evaluating handsomeness?"

"Compared to you, sweetie," Annie said, "I have to admit Flame comes up short."

"You think I was angling for a compliment?"

Annie moved past my question and got back to Flame.

"The magazines," she said, "treat him with something like reverence."

"Should I be impressed?"

"Probably depends on why you're asking about such an unlikely person," Annie said. "Unlikely for you, I mean."

"His executive director is going to walk through my door any minute now."

"That's odd." Annie said. "My sources don't suggest there's a whiff of scandal attached to Flame."

"Solid as your sources are."

"Flame's reputation, the point I'm trying to make, he's a spotless guy. No scandals, no sexual harrassment, not even tats."

"And he earns oodles, you say?"

"So my sources report."

"I'll let you know at dinner how much of the oodles he might care to share with me."

"And why he would," Annie said.

CHAPTER TWO

When Roger Carnale arrived at my office, he wasn't alone. He introduced his companion as Jerome Suggs, Flame's vice-president of operations and chief of security.

Carnale was a tall, slim, thirtyish guy with good looks of a bland sort. Making his entrance, he seemed a touch wary. A lot of my clients, meeting a criminal lawyer for the first time, get that way, but most of them face criminal charges and have reason for wariness. As far as I knew, Carnale was clean of problems with the law and the guardedness that went with them. Maybe he came by circumspection naturally.

He was turned out in a lightweight, pale-brown suit, blue shirt, and striped tie. In one hand, he carried a slim, black leather briefcase with metal rims around the edges. In the other hand, he clutched a fedora and a walking stick. The fedora, in the same light brown shade as his suit, was folded and creased the way Superintendant Foyle wore his hat in *Foyle's War* on Masterpiece Theatre. The walking stick was made of black wood, and since neither of Carnale's legs appeared to suffer from gimpiness, the stick must have been strictly for effect.

Jerome, the security chief, was a very large black man. He had on jeans and a black summer windbreaker, which he wore over a black T-shirt notable for the symbol in its centre consisting of a single red and yellow flame. Jerome had a shaved head, a bemused expression, and he carried a briefcase in plain brown leather. He and Carnale sat in two of the three client chairs on the other side of my desk.

"You come highly recommended, Mr. Crang," Carnale said.

"By who?"

Carnale nodded in Jerome's direction.

"By Philip Goldenberg," Jerome said to me in a deep bass voice — a voice with a strong New York accent.

"As compliments go, that's not bad at all."

"The other dudes in Goldenberg's law office called him 'Fox.'"

"That's because he's smart like a fox. Does cross examinations that sneak up on witnesses."

"He said you took jobs that were off the reservation," Jerome said.

"He probably phrased it 'off the reserve,'" I said.

"Could be, man."

"What Americans call a reservation, Canadians call a reserve."

"You do things different up here."

"Other than that," I said, "those were Fox's words?"

"Exact quote," Jerome said.

"If you gentlemen didn't retain him," I said, "I take it whatever brings you to my office doesn't involve a criminal charge."

"Quite right, Mr. Crang," Carnale said. "Our objective is to head off an offender. Almost as essential, we need to keep the matter we're about to discuss out of the media."

"What kind of situation is it that hasn't happened yet?"

"I describe it as robbery, plain and simple," Carnale said, turning once again to Jerome.

"The situation is where a man wants money from us to keep his mouth shut," Jerome said.

"Your guy, Flame, he's the one on the wrong end of this shot at extortion?"

"Sad to say, man, he is," Jerome said.

"This fine young man's future could be destroyed," Carnale said. He sounded outraged.

"To state the obvious, you want me to head off the extorter," I said.

"That's why we're here," Carnale said.

"Got any idea how I might learn this man's identity?"

"We know very well who he is, Mr. Crang," Carnale said, leaning even heavier on the indignation. "And we can tell you where to find him."

"This whole deal sounds like the equivalent of a stickup in broad daylight," I said. "Not your run-of-the-mill extortion."

"Very brazen, indeed."

"Let's start with the guy's name."

Carnale nodded to Jerome.

"Goes by the name, Reverend Alton Douglas," Jerome said. "The dude runs Heaven's Philosophers on St. Clair Avenue West. I got the information off the business card he gave me."

"Imagine that," I said, "a person of the cloth dabbling in criminal pursuits. How much is he asking?"

"What he wants, man, that's no dabbling," Jerome said. "Eight big, big ones."

"Eight million dollars?"

Jerome nodded.

I made a little whistling sound. "What's he know about Flame, asking for money like that?" I said to Jerome.

Carnale stood up abruptly. He was even taller than I first thought. I was an inch short of six feet, and if I were standing, Carnale would tower over me.

"I need to keep a luncheon appointment, Mr. Crang," he said to me. "One of our bankers downtown. I take it we've now got you on retainer?"

"Sounds like my kind of job," I said.

Carnale said he'd leave Jerome to get into the details with me.

"Jerome will be your contact person until you tidy things up for us," Carnale went on. "I trust that will be a matter of days. As few as possible."

Carnale turned, carrying his briefcase, walking stick, and *Foyle's War* fedora, and was out the door before I could rise from my chair.

I looked at Jerome. "Your boss is a man in a hurry."

"Got a car waiting downstairs," he said.

I went over to the window and watched Carnale as he came out of my building, now wearing the fedora. A large shiny black SUV was parked at the curb. A chauffeur climbed out of the front seat, and held the back door open for Carnale. I could tell he was a chauffeur from the dark suit and the hat he wore. The guy was almost as tall as his boss, slim, probably in his late twenties, judging from my view three floors up. He slammed the car door shut firmly.

"Expensive looking car," I said to Jerome.

"Brand new Escalade," Jerome said.

I couldn't tell an Escalade from an Eskimo Pie.

"Chauffeur's the guy who phoned me earlier on?" I asked Jerome.

"He's the one," Jerome said. "Serious young dude. Tries hard to look cool."

"Looking cool probably comes out of the chauffeur manual."

The Escalade pulled away from the curb, and when I turned from the window, Jerome was checking his watch.

"Where do you feel like discussing the Reverend Alton Douglas?" I said to him. "Over lunch maybe?"

"It's one o'clock, man," Jerome said. "I always feel like lunch at one o'clock."

"Follow me," I said.

CHAPTER THREE

"Damn," I said, "I hate it when they do that."

"Who does what, man?" Jerome said.

We were sitting at a table in the window of Freda, an intimate, stone-floored restaurant around the corner from my office specializing in pasta dishes.

"They changed the menu," I said. "I always have the chicken sandwich. Now it's gone. Eliminated. Disappeared."

A young waitress appeared. Like all Freda's waitstaff, she looked crisp and smart in white shirts and black pants. Our waitress had exquisite features and a slim build. She left us with two menus and two glasses of water.

"Chicken sandwich, man?" Jerome looked aghast. "You come to an Italian restaurant and you order a chicken sandwich?"

"It's organic chicken!"

"Chicken sandwich ain't a manly dish, man."

The waitress returned, and Jerome asked for spaghetti Bolognese and a glass of red wine.

"Spaghetti Bolognese is manly, Jerome?"

"The thing speaks for itself, man."

"You're kidding, Jerome, right?"

Jerome smiled at me.

"I'll have the same as my friend," I said to the waitress.

She wrote my order and went away.

Jerome said, "What's your opinion so far about the problem with Flame?"

"Back in the office," I said, "I couldn't help noticing your Mr. Carnale didn't always have the answers to my questions on the tip of his tongue."

"That's 'cause he's the big picture man."

"Give me an example," I said. "I assume you're talking about the big pictures in Flame's career?"

"Roger Carnale's the man that spotted Flame's talent in the first place. This was before the kid was called Flame, back ten, twelve years when he was, like, fifteen, just doing his thing in some little neighbourhood ice cream soda club."

"Very astute of Roger," I said. "But it's ancient history. Not directly related to the present problem with the clergyman. What's a more recent big picture item Roger's promoting?"

Jerome waggled an index finger at me. "Now we getting to the reason you been hired."

The waitress came back with our glasses of red wine.

"The big step Mr. Carnale's rolling with," Jerome said, "Flame's gonna become a movie star."

"There's a market for rap movie musicals?"

Jerome leaned over the table. "See, man, that's where Mr. Carnale keeps his eye on the big picture before the average guy does."

"I'm all on tenterhooks."

"Listen to this," Jerome said. "Flame's the next great romantic movie idol."

"Not just a singer, but an actor too?" I said, probably sounding skeptical.

"Flame's got the acting chops, man. You heard of the Stella Adler Acting Studio in New York?"

"Very leading edge, I believe. Or maybe it once was."

"Flame's been studying there the last year."

"But you said something about Flame being the next romantic idol. What's that mean? He's going to pick up where Denzel Washington's leaving off?"

"Don't think colour, man."

"What am I missing?"

"Flame's destiny, he'll be the Cary Grant of his generation. Flame's post-racial, man. Doesn't matter to the audience he's black. They never notice he's black, white, whatever. Flame's romantic in the eyes of the whole spectrum, you understand what I'm sayin'?"

I didn't respond right away.

"You *have* heard of Cary Grant, man?" Jerome asked, persisting.

"Jerome, it's people of the present I've never heard of," I said. "People from the past, they overlap with my past. Cary Grant was tall and handsome, cleft chin, made the ladies swoon, filled the men with envy even though they admired him as much as the ladies did."

"Cleft chin, man," Jerome said. "Flame's got one of those."

"Now that I think about it," I said, "there's nobody among today's Hollywood leading men who's Grant-like in looks or style or wit."

"Those guys need a shave, got their little goatees. You're right, man, they ain't got the touch old Cary had. Maybe George Clooney, but otherwise no way, man."

The waitress arrived with our main courses. While she went through the routine of serving us, offering fresh pepper, a sprinkling of cheese, I wondered about Jerome's estimate of Flame's future.

"A young black guy as the next Cary Grant?" I said. "Hard to see it."

"Puts you in the minority, man," Jerome said.

"Who's in the majority?"

"We got a finished script. Got a big-name director signed on. And, listen up here, Crang, we got a contract with a Los Angeles studio. Major studio, man. People're putting fifty million into our project."

I stopped chewing. "I'm impressed, Jerome. Practically speechless."

"Gonna be a big public announcement the end of September," Jerome said. "Providing there's no setback before then."

"Like the blackmailing minister of God? That kind of setback?"

"Like him, like the Reverend Alton Douglas. Only, the thing about Alton coming along at this particular moment, it's coincidental."

"He's not attempting his Flame shakedown because he knows the movie contract is going to put Flame in the chips any minute now?"

"Not possible, man," Jerome said. "Number one, he couldn't have heard about the movie. We got the cone of silence workin' for us till the minute we go public. There's been nothing about the movie on Twitter, nothing in what they call the trade papers, *Hollywood Reporter* and such like. The Reverend'll learn about it the same time everybody else does."

"So, you're telling me Flame's worth eight million without introducing the movie money into the mix?"

"Mr. Carnale say he could snap his fingers at the bankers, man, and they'd send over ten million, twenty, in a Brinks truck, all cash money, do it in a flash."

"I follow you, Jerome," I said. "But the coincidence of the Reverend Alton Douglas coming on to the scene right now means that whatever he's got on Flame could blow up the movie."

"That's the problem in a nutshell, man."

"So tell me this," I said, "what information has this Reverend put together on my new client, Flame?"

"Now," Jerome said, "we at the ugly part."

"We are?"

"Very ugly, man. Very."

CHAPTER FOUR

Jerome stopped eating his spaghetti and meat sauce.

"Goes back a long way, the thing I'm about to tell you," he said.

I stopped eating too.

"Before Mr. Carnale discovered Flame," Jerome said, "he was an unknown kid, like I said earlier. So, up in his bedroom, this one day a lotta years ago, he wrote the words for nine songs. Didn't put them on a video, didn't tape himself singing them. They were just words on nine sheets of paper, and these lyrics, man, they *disgusting*. They anti-gay, they against woman, they racist. I'm telling you man, these songs were so gross you couldn't imagine them in your worst nightmares."

"The little I know about rap customs," I said, "putting down gay people is a popular theme in the lyrics. Right up there with denigrating women. Faggots and whores — two universal rap themes."

"Not like these ones of Flame's," Jerome said.

Both of us paused, then resumed eating.

"What Flame did all those years ago," Jerome said, "he put away these nine sheets of paper in the drawer in the place where he lived with his mama, the words for each one of the songs written down on the sheets. Flame's mama saved all that shit to the present day. At her house, she's stored away every single song

Flame ever wrote. That includes these nine sheets causing the problems, man."

"And that's what the Reverend Alton Douglas now has in his possession?"

"Everything on the song sheets is in Flame's own handwriting, his signature on every sheet," Jerome said. He reached for his slim black briefcase on the floor beside his chair, and took out a handful of white pages held together with a paperclip.

"These here," Jerome said, handing me the sheets, "are copies the Reverend handed me the night before last. Monday that was. You can keep the damn copies for the time being, man, while you're workin' on the case. Personally, I don't care if I never see this stuff again. But here's the crux of the situation, man. The Reverend told me he gonna put these nine pages on the Web in two weeks' time unless we pay the man eight million dollars."

Under the paperclip holding the nine pages, Jerome had fastened the Reverend Alton Douglas's card and his own card. I removed the paperclip, put the cards in my inside jacket pocket. And then I started to read the first page of Flame's song lyrics.

"Hold up, man," Jerome said in a peremptory tone. "Don't read them right now, not when you're eating your nice pasta. I'm warning you."

"I've got a cast-iron stomach, Jerome," I said, "if that's what you're concerned about."

I read down the page. It appeared to be a song about two men making love with one another. And as they got intimate, one man used a very sharp knife to cut off the other man's testicles.

"Oh dear Jesus," I said.

"Brace yourself, man," Jerome said. "There's much worse in there, man. One's about people pooping on other people."

I was still on the first song, the one that mixed semen and blood. It got very specific in its descriptions. Even as a kid, Flame seemed to have a talent with words. Waxing lyrical about one guy torturing another guy. The spaghetti lurched in my stomach.

I looked at Jerome, and my face must have reflected what was going on in my belly.

"Cast-iron, man?" Jerome said. "The way you appearing right now, it's more like a leaky tin foil."

The waitress came to our table.

"The spaghetti Bolognese not agreeing with you, sir?" she said to me, her expression showing concern.

"Nothing an espresso won't fix," I said. "Double, if you don't mind."

I didn't speak until the espresso arrived, and I took a sip.

"I assume the other song lyrics are in the same spirit as this first one," I said to Jerome.

"Worse, if anything," Jerome said. "Two women dancing with no clothes on get their boobs shot off by a dude with a rifle watching them. Another song does what you might call variations on the n-word."

I read my way through all nine pages of lyrics. Two of the songs did imaginatively sick things with urine. All of the songs, taken together, added up to the most repulsive catalogue of written work I might have ever read.

"If these see the light of day," I said, "Flame can kiss away his chances of succeeding to the Cary Grant mantle."

"Those damn songs would definitely smear my man's image."

"It would be hard to look at him as a mature and profound performer."

"Not a chance. Everybody'd stop thinking of him that way, man."

"All because of a youthful indiscretion."

"You might say so."

"I'm assuming the words Flame wrote all those years ago don't reflect the big-time songwriter and singer he grew into today. What I'm asking, Flame's not popular because he's a musical master of misogyny and homophobia?"

Jerome put down his knife and fork, and gave me a long look.

"I wouldn't be working with the dude these last six years if I thought he was the kind of guy you see in those words," Jerome said. "He's a very fine and decent and thoughtful young man, Flame is."

"The ugliness was some kind of youthful abberation?" I said. "It's all gone now?"

"You got my word on that, Crang."

I nodded, and both of us took a moment to reflect on where the two of us stood on the matter of Flame's problem.

"As I see the situation," I said, breaking the silence, "my assignment for you and Roger comes in three parts. Get back the original sheets of lyrics from the Reverend Alton Douglas. Be as sure as I'm able that the Reverend isn't hanging on to more copies of the lyrics. And avoid paying the eight million or a large part thereof."

"You save any of the eight million, man," Jerome said, "Mr. Carnale no doubt gonna give you a nice little bonus. But that's not at the top of the damn list. We want the original song sheets back. All of them, man."

"You'll probably like to know how the Reverend got his hands on the originals in the first place," I said. "How did the sheets of lyrics get to him from Flame's mother's house?

"Definitely that'd be of interest."

"The mother doesn't know how that happened?"

"We're keeping her in the dark about the blackmail, man. All she knows, from me asking her, is that the originals of the nine sheets don't seem to be where they supposed to."

My stomach had settled, and the espresso brought a fresh jolt of energy.

"Let's see if you can give me more of a handle on the Reverend," I said to Jerome. "He approached you Monday night. Where did this momentous meeting take place?"

"Air Canada Centre, right here in your town, the place where Flame was doin' a concert," Jerome said. "A couple hours before the concert happened, I'm outside the Centre, just getting the feel of the crowd that's showing up. So, there I am, tending to my duties when this dude comes up to me in a grey suit and blue shirt, nice tie. Dude's about fifty-five, thereabouts, and he all business."

"Not wasting any motions."

"He hands me the sheets of paper. He tells me he wants eight million dollars two weeks from that day — Monday like I say. He says he be in touch with me before then, say where he wants the eight million sent. Gonna be some place offshore is what he says. Then he's gone."

"Gone," I said, "but not far. The religious institution he's connected with? Heaven's Philosophers? You and Mr. Carnale said it was on St. Clair West? That's a few blocks north of where we're sitting right now."

"I assume you're gonna find him there, man."

"I'll make it my first stop," I said. "Maybe it'll be my only stop if the Reverend is co-operative."

I swallowed the last of my double espresso, and Jerome signalled the waitress for the bill.

"You don't mind my saying," I said, "the Reverend — this particular Reverend, I mean — makes a curious shakedown artist."

"Him being a reverend and all?"

"There's that, but he's also going about the blackmail in a fashion that seems to me the last word in transparent."

"Transparent or opaque, man, it don't matter," Jerome said. "Just get back the sheets of the damn lyrics like you been hired to do."

"I'm your guy, Jerome."

CHAPTER FIVE

When I got back to the office, Gloria was setting up a new coffee maker. It was a replacement for the older model that the moving guys broke during my shift in quarters from the fifth floor to the third.

"Goodie," I said. "A fresh source of caffeine."

"It's a De'Longhi," Gloria said. "Not absolutely top-of-the-line, but quite fine."

Gloria was my part-time researcher, bookkeeper, and all-round smoother of troubled waters. Part-time because I shared her services with two other criminal lawyers. Gloria was sixtyish, ten years older than me. She was tall, with silver hair that she grew long and free. She liked to wear baggy blouses and long, flowing skirts. I suspected a spectacular figure lurked under the billowy garments, but I'd never know unless we were invited to the same swim party.

Gloria and I admired the sleekness of the De'Longhi for a minute or two. Then I went down the hall to the washroom and filled my office jug with water for the coffeemaker.

When I came back, Gloria was examining a package of coffee I'd bought earlier.

"'Kicking Horse'?" she said, reading from the label. "'Hoodoo Jo blend? Made in Canada'?"

"Not *made* in Canada, if you look closer," I said. "*Blended* in Canada."

"Were you feeling nationalistic when you bought this?"

"There's a lot to be said for throwing one's business Canada's way."

When I got the coffee machine started, I sat down to discuss lawyerly matters. Gloria was sitting in one of the client's chairs, her iPad in front of her hooked up to a portable keyboard. The whole apparatus, iPad plus keyboard, probably weighed no more than a few ounces, which was a lot less than the thick file of hard copy documents in her hands. The digital age had its advantages.

"This one," Gloria said, raising the file in the air, "you put back in the cabinet and forgot to bill the client."

"It wasn't tucked in there too long, I trust?"

"Month maybe," Gloria said. "It's the murder case where the Crown dropped the charges a day into the trial."

"Yeah, my client was the nice girl from Sobey's meat department," I said. "It started out murder one. I got it reduced to manslaughter a couple months before trial. Then the Crown threw up their hands. One of my better results this year."

"All the more reason for being generous to yourself on the fees," Gloria said.

The coffee machine burbled to its conclusion. I got up and poured coffee into my two best mugs, both deep Matisse blue in colour and purchased at the Levin Ceramics Museum. Gloria and I took our coffee the same way — black, no sugar.

"Hmm," Gloria said, sipping and savouring. "It's surprisingly fabulous, Crang."

"More specific, if you don't mind?"

"Hardy, an oaky taste, and a touch mysterious. That good enough for you?"

"Label says it's organic and fair trade."

"Okay, okay! It makes me feel on the side of the angels as well as caffeinated," Gloria said impatiently. "Now can we get to the fee for the Sobey's meat girl?"

I sipped some more of the Hoodoo Jo, confirmed it was damn good, and said to Gloria, "Forget about the fee thing for a minute while I tell you about the juicy new file we got."

"Okay," she said. "Juicy always thrills me."

I told Gloria all about Flame and the Reverend Alton Douglas's machinations. She jotted notes in her iPad, and held back whatever comments she had until I finished.

"You kind of skated over what this person Flame wrote in his songs that was so almighty horrible," Gloria said as soon as I stopped talking.

"Homophobically ugly, racially horrific, and so on, accept my word for it," I said. "The point is, Flame's people think the song lyrics are bad enough to take the Reverend Douglas's intentions very seriously."

I got the pages with the lyrics out of my jacket pocket, neatly folded, and handed them to Gloria.

"Read them if you want," I said. "But if I were you, I'd give the whole thing a pass."

Gloria took the pages, not wasting so much as a glance at the words on them. "Why don't I just open a file," she said. "Put these pages in the file for future reference."

"Which may not be necessary," I said.

"So," Gloria said after she'd filed the pages, "the alleged bad guy is a church minister?"

"Seems that way."

"So what you'll want from me is everything I can find out about Reverend Alton Douglas," Gloria said as she typed. "Background, financial situation, all that. And the building where his church is on St. Clair, if it really is a church. Who owns it, so on, so forth? And what in god's name, if you'll pardon the phrase, are Heaven's Philosophers? I'll see what gives with them."

Gloria stopped and looked at me.

"That ought to do it," I said.

"I'll get on things as soon as I leave here," Gloria said. "But first, suppose you take a look at this butcher-girl file and tell me how much to bill her."

She handed me the file, and while I flipped through the notes and documents inside it, and wrote numbers on a separate sheet of paper, Gloria tapped on her iPad.

After a few minutes, she said, "It appears your minister guy got kicked out of the Catholic Church."

"You mean it's *Father* Alton I'm dealing with?" I said. "I assumed he was a plain old fundamentalist Christian fanatic."

"Maybe he is now, but a Catholic priest is how he started."

"What was it, doing terrible things with little boys got him in trouble?"

"Just the opposite," Gloria said. "His sexual contacts appear to have been with mature ladies of the parish."

"All of this, you got in fifteen minutes?"

"Tricks of the Google trade."

"Nice start, kiddo."

"An old photograph of him is in here. He's about late thirties at the time. Actually comes across as kind of cute."

Gloria turned her iPad around to give me a peek at the screen.

"Got the collar on and his numbered St. Michael's sweater over the religious blouse, whatever they call it," I said. "Juggling a football in his hands. Athletic guy. Nice big smile. Probably knew how to sing the 'Too Ra Loo Ra Loo Ra' lullaby."

Gloria switched off her iPad. She packed it and the keyboard in her red leather handbag.

"Friday afternoon," she said, "I'll come back here and shed more light on the Reverend and his establishment, though I think we both smell fishy things already. In the meantime, how about the nice butcher girl?"

I shoved the file across the desk to Gloria who gave a quick look at the sheet of paper I'd written the numbers on.

"This is a ridiculously tiny fee," she said. "You realize that?"

"It's what she can afford," I said. "But I know I'll be charging the Flame people a ridiculously enormous fee, which is what they can afford."

"Crang," Gloria said, shaking her head a little, "this isn't the billing system that helps big businesses stay big."

"I'll take that as a compliment."

CHAPTER SIX

Annie and I lived in a house on a north-south street called Major, two blocks due west of my office. Like just about all the other houses on Major, ours was three storeys of brick, narrow and semi-detached. Major ran south from Bloor, in a neighbourhood named, prosaically, Harbord Village. The name came from Harbord Street, the main east-west street to the south. Lately, Harbord had been attracting a lot of trade in upscale dining establishments. I was still throwing most of my eating-out business to the older restaurants on Bloor.

When I got home around seven, Annie was sitting at the dining room table, staring at our garden through the floor-to-ceiling window. A novel by someone named Jane Gardam lay open on the table in front of her, but she wasn't reading it. She looked distracted, or maybe something worse. I put my arms around her from behind.

"Sweetheart," she said to me, "I've been feeling so rattled I almost did something drastic a few minutes ago."

"How drastic?"

"I was on the verge of making a martini."

"Your martinis are undrinkable," I said. "You never get the balance right."

Annie turned in my arms and looked up at me. “See what I mean?” she said.

“It’s still almost a whole week before the book launch,” I said, “and already you’re a nervous wreck?”

Annie straightened up, pushed the Jane Gardam novel to one side, and folded her hands on the table.

“Crang,” she said, “just make the martinis. Please.”

Three steps up from the dining room was the open kitchen. I hustled up the steps and mixed two vodka martinis, made with Polish potato vodka from the good people at Luksusowa. One martini on the rocks with three little olives on a toothpick for Annie, the other straight-up with a twist of lemon for me. Both with a whiff of vermouth.

I carried the drinks to the dining room table. Annie and I clinked glasses in a small toast.

“Here’s to your book,” I said. “Reads like a smash hit to me.”

“Ha,” Annie said, “you’re the only one who’s read it except for the publishing people.” She took a sip of martini. “But thanks, fella.”

Annie’s book, her first, covered a small corner of the movie world. Movies were her business. She talked about them on CBC Radio, blogged reviews twice a week, wrote occasional magazine profiles of movie people, and now she had written a biography of Edward Everett Horton.

Edward Everett was never a movie name on everybody’s lips, but his acting won him semi-fame in the 1930s and ’40s when he worked as a character actor in musical comedies. He was a tall, funny flibbertigibbit of a guy who played second banana to Fred Astaire in a dozen films. Horton, now long deceased, grew up a New York kid and attended Columbia University. That was no doubt the reason why the university signed on to publish Annie’s book.

They were throwing a launch party for her at a theatre somewhere in Columbia’s complex of buildings. That was the following Tuesday. The plan was I’d fly down with Annie for a day and a half, then come back after the launch. Annie would stay longer to do publicity for the book. The prospect of the launch was what got her in a tizzy. She was relaxed and funny on radio, but when she was in front of a real live audience, like the one she'd have at Columbia, she got the heebie-jeebies.

"I heard a bit of good news today," Annie said, sipping her martini.

"'We pass this way but once,'" I said, quoting.

Annie looked at me, "Where's that from?"

"Old *New Yorker* cartoon. Guy beaten down by life arrives home to his beaten-down wife. Guy says to wife, 'Heard a bit of good news today. We pass this way but once.'"

"I'm going to be on the *Charlie Rose* show next week," Annie said.

"Well, look at you," I said. "Big-time Annie."

"Charlie Rose reaches people who buy books."

"Not to mention his show gets rerun at all hours of the day and night."

"Maximum exposure," Annie said.

"Are you cheering up?" I said.

Annie polished off her martini.

"I've still got to give the goddamn speech at the launch," she said.

I made Annie another martini, same way as before. She carried it with her on a stroll through the back garden while I organized the collection of salads Annie had planned for dinner.

Around the house, we referred to the garden as the Eighth Wonder of the World. We had it designed and installed by a woman known by her clients as the Garden Goddess. Annie and I figured she deserved the GG status. Guests to our place exclaimed over all the greenery out there. "Greenery" was missing the point. There were greens aplenty, but they shaded deceptively into greys and maroons and deep purples. We had a birch tree, a Japanese maple, a ginkgo. We had hostas and a couple of berms. The foliage, bushes, and trees were so dense at this time of year that they blocked all trace on the horizon of the architecturally offensive buildings over on Spadina, including the one housing my office.

I arranged place mats, dinner plates, napkins, and cutlery on the dining-room table along with enough different salads in bowls to feed the whole neighbourhood. Salads of chicken, tuna, potato, and plain greens, plus coleslaw. I opened a bottle of Pinot Grigio and fetched two white wine glasses.

Outside, Annie was nowhere in sight, concealed among the foliage. I sat at the dining-room table and sipped my second martini. A minute or two later, I caught glimpses of Annie's white blouse and tan slacks. The entire Annie soon emerged from among the garden's thick pleasures. Annie was a petite woman, beguilingly so to me and all other admirers of feminine beauty. She had a triangular face, thick black hair, large brown eyes, and all kinds of shapeliness.

"I've finished with moping," Annie said after she sat down at the table. "At least for tonight."

"The miracle of a martini," I said.

"Not to mention the soothing effect of the Eighth Wonder."

Annie dressed the green salad in a concoction of her own invention. She was world-class in salad dressing. We helped ourselves to salads and started to eat.

"Want to hear about Flame and his problems?" I said.

"He's really got oodles of do-re-mi?"

"And then some."

Annie made a circular motion with her left hand. "On with it, pal," she said.

I told her the whole story just as I'd told Gloria, soft-pedalling the lyrics to Flame's songs but adding the Google scoop about the Reverend's history of Catholic disgrace.

"You know what I'd do if I were you?" Annie said when I finished.

"You'd phone the Reverend," I said. "Make an appointment and call on the man."

"Take the direct approach." Annie said, nodding in agreement with herself. "Works every time."

"I prefer to take the direct approach indirectly." I said.

Annie made a small harumphing sound.

She said, "What's the word you use to describe what you do when you are, as I more accurately call it, stalling?"

"Reconnoitre."

"Baloney by any other name," Annie said.

We were making steady inroads on the salads. My favourite was the one Annie put together with the potatoes and just the right balance of mayonnaise, yoghurt, and green onions. The Pinot Grigio wasn't bad either.

"By Friday noon," I said, "I'll have Gloria's report on the target guy."

"The Reverend who's an alleged scoundrel," Annie said.

"Also by then," I said, "I'll have nosed around Heaven's Philosophers on St. Clair. Taken the measure of the sort of people who go there for their spiritual needs. Chatted up the more amenable among them about the Reverend. Observed the man himself from a bit of distance. Taken the lie of the land." I hesitated. "Or is it the lay of the land I'm taking?"

"To lay is to place," Annie said, "To lie is to recline."

"I recall that from your previous wordsmith seminars."

"How that works out in practice is a horse of a different colour."

"How so?"

"In Canada," Annie said, "it's 'lie of the land.' In the U.S.A., it's 'lay.'"

"Where the Reverend Douglas is concerned," I said, "I'm taking the lie of the land."

"That's what I was afraid of," Annie said. "The part you're ignoring, historically speaking, is that something always goes wrong on your misbegotten reconnoitre excursions."

"Where's the threat on this one? From a possibly nutty clergyman?"

Annie shook her head, looking momentarily doleful.

We ate more heaps of the salads, but didn't come close to polishing them off. Annie took her Jane Gardam novel up to bed while I put the leftovers into containers in the refrigerator. I loaded the dishwasher and followed Annie upstairs.

She seemed to be getting a kick out of Jane Gardam. I got in beside her with my copy of Gary Burton's autobiography. How a kid from a small Indiana town made musical history as the world's greatest jazz vibraphone player, and discovered he was gay. We read for an hour, and just after we turned the lights off and just before we drifted off to sleep, Annie snuggled up to me.

"Promise you'll be careful, sweetie," she whispered in my ear.

"Mmm," I murmured.

It was an ambivalent murmur.

CHAPTER SEVEN

The quarters for the Reverend Alton Douglas's church were on the north side of St. Clair near Jane Street in a stretch of buildings that had seen better days. A scrappy-looking bingo hall, a shut-down McDonald's, a discount gas station. The church was the exception. Was it proper to call Heaven's Philosophers a church?

It was early afternoon as I coasted past it in my trusty 1983 four-door Mercedes. The building didn't really have the air of a house of worship — not from the outside, at least. No steeple, no cross. In height, it stood three storeys, with the ground floor much larger in width and length than the two storeys above. Unlike the upper floors, glass enclosed the first level on all sides, giving it an airy look. On floors two and three, the exterior was all brick with just two tall narrow windows at the front. They weren't stained-glass windows as best I could make out from down below.

I steered the Mercedes north on the street running along the west side of the church building, parked, and got out. I was dressed in casual but respectable looking duds. Two-hundred-dollar jeans from Rainbow on Yorkville, black Nikes, buttoned-down navy blue shirt, summer jacket in a shade Annie called wheat. Clothes fit for a religious experience if that turned out to be on offer. I walked back to the Heaven's Philosophers front entrance.

Inside, the floor of the lobby was done in sleek grey marble. On either side, curved staircases, likewise marble, led to the second floor. Straight ahead, three shops ran in a line against the north wall. Left to right: a travel agency, a coffee bar, and a copy shop. Each was modest in dimensions; none of them was thrumming with commerce at the moment.

A fortyish guy in a suit and tie sat alone at a desk in the travel office, leafing through a brochure without much enthusiasm. The young guy in the copy shop was likewise on his own, sitting at a computer with a super-large screen and playing a game that involved blasting dragons to smithereens. The coffee bar was more my speed. It was the only place doing what might be called business. I ambled in its direction.

Behind the counter, a dark-haired kid in his late teens had two kinds of coffee on sale, espresso and an unidentified blend. The counter also sported a plate of glazed doughnuts in a round glass cage. The doughnuts gave signs of having been encased for more than a couple of days.

Three customers standing in a group were holding heavy, white china mugs of coffee, probably the unidentified blend. Everything about the physical appearance of two of these guys was thick. Thick bodies, thick voices, possibly thick heads. The third guy was just as tall as the other two but slimmer and less rackety. Grey haired and in his early seventies, he looked to have two or three decades on them.

What the first two guys reminded me of were people I saw in the hallways outside the criminal courts at Old City Hall waiting for their cases to be called. They looked like guys who could have been my clients. For a startled moment, I thought one of them was the real article, somebody I represented within living memory. Was that possible?

This particular guy was thick and meaty and loud. He wore jeans, a lightweight black sports jacket, and a tie with a design you couldn't miss, something featuring large black balls against a deep maroon background. When the guy spoke, it was in a high-pitched voice that didn't go with the rest of the package. I'd heard and seen the guy before, but not, I realized, as a client of mine. He was Fox's client in a fraud case a couple of years back. I'd acted briefly for one of Mr. High-Pitched Voice's co-accused. The representation was brief because the Crown severed the charges against my guy, and sent him to trial on his own. Before we got started on the new trial, the client fired me in favour of a lawyer his mother liked better.

I was pretty sure I'd nailed the identity of the guy with the voice, but to make it rock solid, I needed to check with Fox. If I was right, it'd be swift progress to get the identification thing squared away. Then I could put my mind to the reason why a possible bunch of heavies were hanging out in the halls of Heaven's Philosophers.

I stepped up to the counter and asked the dark-haired kid what he was peddling besides espresso.

"Today, sir," the kid said, "I'm featuring a blend from Paraguay."

"You recommend it?"

"First day I've gone with the Paraguay, sir," the kid said. He had the barista patter pretty much under control. "But my customers tell me they're cool with its flavour."

"Get many of them around here? Customers?"

The guy let his cheery barista manner slip a notch.

"Enough," he said after a few seconds. "It, like, depends."

"On what? Sundays better than week days?"

"I'm not open Sundays."

"Aren't you skipping a potential bonanza? Think of all those thirsty parishioners coming out of an uplifting sermon in the room at the top of those stairs."

"Mister," the kid said, a touch exasperated, "I do what I'm told, okay?"

"I'm assuming there is Sunday church, sermon included?"

"Yeah, Sunday afternoons, but the coffee bar is closed then, like I said," the kid answered. "You want to order something or not?"

I asked for a Paraguay, paid three bucks, and carried my heavy, white-china mug to another counter where milk and sugar were available. It wasn't because I wanted either milk or sugar but because I needed to take up position where I could surreptitiously snap a photo on my cell of the guy with the high-pitched voice.

I took a sip of the Paraguay and savoured it for a moment. This was good stuff. From Paraguay? That made it a first for me.

I put my mug down on the counter with the milk and sugar. I was standing in a position that placed me at an angle facing three-quarters away from the trio of gents. The guy I wanted the photo of was in the middle of the three. He was turned my way, though his head was slightly inclined allowing him to pay attention to the older guy on his right who was speaking. The third guy in the trio, the one on the left of the guy I was interested in, was notable for his aggressively jutting jaw.

I got the iPhone out of my jacket pocket, gripping it in my right hand as if I was raising it to my ear. When the phone reached waist level, aimed past me in the general direction of the three guys, I pressed the shoot button of the camera function. It went off without any flashing lights or any sound beyond a subdued click.

I have minimal skills at photography. Generally, I steer clear of taking photos of loved ones, never mind strangers. I'd used the iPhone as a camera just once. My subject was Annie. She said the picture added ten years to her age. It made her look like she was wearing a bad wig. She told me to delete the photo. I did as I was told.

Putting the phone to my ear in the Heaven's Philosophers lobby, I pretended I was listening to a message. There was no message, and I wasn't listening to anything except the three guys behind me. If they stopped talking, it might mean they'd caught me snapping the picture. If they shouted, "Hey, asshole!" it would mean for sure they'd caught me.

I relaxed when they carried on with their loud chat as before.

I carried my mug with the nice brew to one of the benches along the lobby wall. I flicked the screen on the iPhone to the photo I'd just snapped. The picture was half okay. The not-okay half showed nothing except the left sleeve of my wheat jacket. The close-up of the jacket eliminated from the photograph the guy with the jutting jaw. In the other half, I had a profile of the older guy and a pretty clear full-face view of the guy I figured for Fox's former client.

I pressed a bunch of buttons to send the photo and a short note to Fox winging their way to Fox's office. While I was winding up my communications, someone beside me cleared his throat. I jerked my head up in automatic surprise.

"Pardon me, friend, I didn't intend to sneak up on you." It was the older guy of the trio, the one with the grey hair. He had his hand stuck out. "Willie Sizemore, investment advisor."

I stood up, still a little shaky from the guy's stealth arrival. "Crang's my name."

"Just thought I'd introduce myself," Sizemore said. He had a salesman's manner, the kind of guy whose big smile and unctuous tone came as part of the package. "You're new to Heaven's Philosophers if I'm not mistaken. And I rarely am about new visitors."

"First time I've dropped by."

"May I ask what attracted you to us?"

Sizemore was nosy, though so far not offensive about it. He was pretty good-looking for an older guy except for the deep gouge on the right side of his head running from the temple down to a spot behind the ear. The gouge looked as permanent as the Grand Canyon.

"I might be keen on exploring ecclesiastical issues," I said. "Maybe your Reverend Alton Douglas has something to offer in that line."

"Indeed he does," Sizemore said, apparently thrilled with my explanation. "But keep in mind there are members of our group who offer advice and services of many sorts."

"In your case, it's financial investments, I take it."

"Fifty years in stocks and bonds," Sizemore said. "Haven't lost a client yet."

He gave a little chuckle, and handed me a card from a small leather case.

"If you ever feel dissatisfied with your present investment strategy," Sizemore said, "all you need to do is give me a ring."

We shook hands again, and Sizemore returned to his meaty buddies.

The three of them got refills and carried the cups of coffee up the curving staircase on the left side of the lobby. Their heels on the marble made storm-trooper clicks in the lobby's emptiness. When they reached the top, I heard the opening and closing of a door. Then all went quiet.

In the silent lobby, I got off my bench and walked over to the coffee shop.

"It's nice the way you brew the Paraguay," I said to the barista. "Very tasty."

"Yeah, thanks," the kid said, looking modest about it.

"The Reverend Douglas in this afternoon?" I asked. "You happen to notice?"

The kid gave me a blank look.

"Alton Douglas?" I said. "The minister who runs Heaven's Philosophers?"

The kid brightened up. "Oh, you're talking about Al?"

"I guess I am if that's how you address him."

"He's, like, relaxed as far as religion," the kid said, a big smile on his face.

Geez, that irritated me, the verbal construction where the speaker didn't complete the phrase. Should I correct the kid's grammar? Or just let it go? I opted for straightening out one possible casualty to improper verbal constructions.

"You mean," I said, "'as far as religion is concerned.' Or 'as far as religion goes.'"

"Yeah, that's what I said," the kid said, looking like he was addressing a person of limited comprehension. "Al is relaxed about that."

I abandoned my educational efforts. "Al's in, is he?"

"In his office upstairs," the kid said, "but, like, most afternoons, meetings go on up there."

"Meetings with the three gentlemen who just went up?"

"Them and probably others, but what happens and who meets I don't know anything about," the kid said. He was growing cautious. "What's it to you exactly?"

"Maybe I'm thinking about discussing ecclesiastical issues with the Reverend," I said. If the explanation worked with Willie Sizemore, it ought to go over with the kid.

He shrugged, but otherwise had nothing more to offer. I put my empty mug down on his counter, nodded, and walked out to my car.

According to my just conceived plan, I figured to wait in the Mercedes until the population in the church building had thinned, then I could carry out some creative snooping. I sat behind the wheel, noticing something I'd missed earlier. The church had a fairly large parking lot behind a row of thick trees separating the lot from the building. No attendant was on duty in the lot, and no machines for payment were visible. Four cars occupied slots. That could be one for Reverend Al and one each for the three guys who were having coffee in the lobby. But that was only a guess.

While I was pondering vehicles and parking, an American-built car, big but not an SUV, pulled into the lot. Two guys got out, one extra-large in size, but neither of them running to the type of the two big lobby guys. The extra-large specimen was shaped like John Candy, and wore a white summer suit. The other much less hefty and had on an unbuttoned cardigan in an unappealing maroon shade. Both passed my car, presumably on their way to the meeting in the church. I snapped photos of the two. I was getting good at the surreptitious paparazzi thing.

In the next ten minutes, two more cars and six more guys of different variations of extra-large arrived. Counting the three guys who were on the premises when I arrived, that made a total of eleven people meeting upstairs in the Reverend Al's quarters.

That seemed to be the end, and then things got quiet in the parking lot.

I clicked open my iPhone. A text from Fox had arrived.

> You poaching my clients now, Crang? The one you're asking about you're welcome to take. You might remember him from the case you were briefly involved in. The guy's mouthy. Thinks he knows more law than his counsel. Good riddance if you want him. Name's Robert Fallis, known to one and all as Squeaky. He's the guy on the left in your picture. The older guy is unknown to me though I suppose he could be Squeaky's type.
>
> Fox
>
> P.S. I walked Squeaky on the fraud charge. Your guy in the case got convicted under other counsel, if memory serves.

Fraud? Could something of that nature be the subject of the meeting in the Reverend Al's office? Was it what Squeaky Fallis and his colleagues practised under religious cover provided by Heaven's Philosophers? Was it all that simple? Fraud had a close relationship to extortion. Was the Reverend blackmailing Flame as the front man for the heavies he could be closeted with at that very minute?

I texted my thanks to Fox, got out of the car, and walked down to a variety store on St. Clair. I bought the *Toronto Star*, the *National Post*, and a Mars bar. Back in the car, I ate the Mars bar and read the *Star*'s four sections, skipping nothing except the woman columnist on the op-ed page. She was a scold. Scolding is not a good attitude in a columnist. I looked at my watch. An hour had gone by.

I got into the *Post*, all the way to their own op-ed woman scold, when the guys from Heaven's Philosophers began strolling down the street from their meeting. I counted all eleven of them. They cleared out the parking lot, and I opened my car door.

It was time to do something sneaky.

CHAPTER EIGHT

I was a half-dozen strides from the entrance to Heaven's Philosophers when the Reverend Douglas came out the front door. It had to be him. He was a trim guy, youthful for someone past fifty. There was an all business cut to him, but with the sleeves of his shirt rolled up, he wasn't sweating it any. He headed east on St. Clair, the direction that took him away from me.

I waited until he got a block up the street before I tried the door. It wasn't locked. I stepped into the lobby. Both the copy shop kid and the barista had closed operations and departed. The travel guy was still in business, talking on the phone and consulting something on his computer. I chose the flight of marble stairs on the right side of the lobby, out of the travel guy's line of vision, and climbed the stairs silently, going over the marble at a good clip, feeling like a fleet fellow in my Nikes.

At the top, a balcony was designed to lead people around to the right. I went that way, and arrived at a pair of double doors. Inside, rising two storeys, was a church — the kind of church imagined by Ikea. The benches and walls were done in light brown–finished wood, each seating place on the benches equipped with a fitted cushion in red and yellow. The rows of seats would accommodate at least a couple hundred worshippers. Or maybe "students" was the correct term for adherents to Heaven's Philosophers. Up above, two large skylights flooded the room with bright good cheer. Down below, there were no crosses, no listing of hymns, no conventional Christian symbols of any sort; there was no pulpit at the front, though there was a lectern with a mic in the middle of what might otherwise be called the altar.

The only decor, conventional or otherwise, consisted of two extra-large painted portraits hanging on the back wall and looking down on the congregation. On the right, the subject was a tall, slim, Christ-like figure with long hair, a beard, and an expression somewhere between melancholy and caring. The man in the portrait may have resembled Jesus, but he wasn't quite Him. Maybe one of the disciples? He wore a contemporary suit, off-white shirt, and no tie. In the other portrait, the subject was definitely Buddha, plump and bald, looking jolly and aware, wearing a white T-shirt and grey track pants.

Below the portraits, there was a door in the wall. I walked over and gave the knob a twist. The door opened, and I stepped into the room on the other side. It was good-sized, with a conference table close to the wall on the left. At the moment, ten or eleven chairs stood at odd angles around the table, and several empty white china mugs from the coffee bar downstairs sat haphazardly up and down the length of the table. At the table's far end, there was a MacBook just like mine.

The room's other major piece of furniture was a desk. It took up position beyond the conference table and closer to the centre of the room. A matching MacBook sat on the desk along with a small Canon printer, some scattered papers, and a pair of ballpoint pens. This had to be the Reverend Al's working centre. On the chair at the desk hung a jacket, also no doubt the Reverend's. The jacket told me I had no time for dilly-dallying.

The floor was covered in thick Oriental carpets. I stepped across a couple of them to check behind the two doors in the wall to my right. One was a closet, the other a bathroom complete with walk-in shower. The bathroom had a stark look, done in black and white: white fixtures, black everything else — black towels, black toilet cover, black glass at the sink, black plastic curtain drawn across the shower. I went back to the desk and tried the drawers. Nothing of recognizable interest in any of them except possibly in the one on the upper left. It was locked.

Sitting at the Reverend Al's desk, considering all options, I opened the Mac laptop. It was in sleep mode. The Reverend was making it easy for snoopers like me. I passed up on his emails and went straight to Documents. There were dozens of them. I clicked on the most recent, and found myself reading something that had the feel of a sermon but wasn't exactly what I would call a sermon. More like a dissertation. It came with a title, "The Teaming of Buddha and John of the Revelations." John must be the other guy in the paintings on the wall of the big room next door. That solved one small mystery. I sped through a few of the dissertation's pages, just enough to tell me I'd learn nothing about the Reverend Al's connection to the Flame Group and the eight million bucks. I put the computer back in sleep and moved to the computer on the conference table.

It was in sleep too. I went to Documents. There were eleven of them, all titled with somebody's name. Two names I recognized, Robert Fallis, old Squeaky himself, and William Sizemore, the investment advisor. I opened the Fallis document. The screen flooded with rows of numbers, with dates and other names listed beside each number. Some names were corporate, some individual. The entries made no sense that I could fathom. I thought about printing out the document, but it ran to twenty-two pages. The Reverend Al might interrupt me in mid-printing. I clicked back to the names on the other documents. Sizemore and nine more people, all guys. These were probably Squeaky's colleagues at today's meeting, but beyond that hunch, I didn't have enough information to make a stab at identifying the gentlemen.

I put the MacBook back in sleep and got more comfortable in

the chair. Looking across the room, I noticed a small window at shoulder height, opening into the audience side of the auditorium. I walked over and peeked through the window. The Reverend Al probably used this peephole to check the crowd before he made his entrances for the Sunday services that the kid barista mentioned. Peering out the window, my mind mulled over the possibilities for Heaven's Philosophers liturgies.

In my dozy meditation, it took an extra millisecond to register the swinging open of the auditorium's main door. Reverend Al had returned for his jacket. He was now striding down the centre aisle at a crisp pace. I got on my tiptoes and shot across the office into the bathroom. I closed the door gently and put my ear to it.

In a whole minute of listening, I didn't catch a sound. For all I knew, the Reverend could be walking across the floor as I strained to listen. He might be headed for the bathroom. He might open the bathroom door while I was standing there.

I moved deeper into the bathroom, back on tiptoes, and slipped behind the black shower curtain. Ideas filled my head about techniques for silent breathing. Was I doing that now? I couldn't tell. I imagined that I could hear my heart pounding. I concentrated harder. Damn, it was my heart. I was sure I could actually hear it. Would the Reverend hear it too? Did he take regular showers in here? At the moment, the shower was bone dry.

The bathroom door opened. Apparently the Reverend needed the facilities. But which one? Dear god, surely not the shower.

The toilet seat went up. The going-up sound seemed to have a quick double click, as if the two seats went up, top and bottom. Two seats meant a piss. Or was I imagining things? Wishful thinking?

The next sound was of urine hitting water. I hadn't been thinking wishfully. The Reverend was taking a piss.

It was a hell of a piss. A powerful shot into the bowl. The guy really needed to relieve himself, his prick projecting what sounded like a rope of urine.

Prick, pecker, dink. The penis had a lot of synonyms.

The Reverend pissed on.

Cock, dong, schlong, wang, wiener, member, Johnson, Peter. I thought of other possibilities among given male names. Rod was one, an upper-case Rod or a lower-case rod.

Maybe Reverend Al had downed a gallon of the barista's Paraguayan. His urine was still going at full strength. Or maybe he had a doctor who prescribed pills that bring on several pisses a day, part of the treatment for a disease. I couldn't remember which one. But Reverend Al, the little I'd seen of him, didn't look like a guy with a disease. Whatever the reason, he kept on firing pee.

Shaft, wand, love stick. Those names implied an erect penis. Lot of naming possibilities there. Third leg, one-eyed monster, soldier, dagger....

All of a sudden, it was quiet on the other side of the curtain. The Reverend's piss didn't just dwindle to an end. It stopped dead, from a tumult to zero in an instant.

The toilet flushed. The toilet seats clunked down. Water ran in the sink. Reverend Al was washing up. The water ceased running. The bathroom door opened and shut.

Reverend Al had vacated the bathroom. Was he leaving the entire premises? I waited fifteen minutes, then came out from behind the curtain and eased open the bathroom door a crack. The office looked empty enough to encourage further inspection. I pushed the door all the way back. Nobody in sight. The jacket was gone from the Reverend's chair. I hustled over to the peephole and looked through it. Not a soul to be seen.

I took time to relax my shoulders. They'd been tensed up during the pissing escapade. I stretched my arms, and congratulated myself on the run of good luck.

I reached for the knob on the door that led into the church's main auditorium. The knob didn't budge. My luck had hit reverse. Reverend Al had locked me in the office.

CHAPTER NINE

I got out my iPhone and punched Maury Samuels's number.

It gave four rings before Maury picked up.

"This isn't a good time, Crang," he said. Maury never bothered with hello when the name on his phone's screen was somebody he knew.

"You're the man for a rescue job I need done, Maury," I said.

For decades, Maury made his living as a break-and-enter specialist, the guy who went into hotel rooms while the guests were asleep in their beds. But three or four years earlier, crowding seventy, Maury hung up his Bally shoes. Bally, he once told me, was a brand that practically guaranteed no squeaks in the leather. Sound-free footwear was essential to a B&E practitioner. Maury quit the business, but retired or not, he could still pick the lock on any door.

"I'm making my shrimp dish," he said on the phone. "It's special for my friend Sal."

"Tell him he can come with you," I said. "Probably find it educational."

Maury's sound of small disgust came down the line. "You're thinking I got a guy named Salvatore over here for a shrimp dinner?"

"It's somebody with a different given name?"

"It's a different sex, for crissake," Maury said. "I'm cookin' for my lady friend, Sal, which is short for Sally."

"Okay, let me pitch the job to you in different terms," I said. "During all your time breaking and entering, did you ever go into a building given over to religious observance?"

Maury paused. "You talking about a cathedral?"

"Smaller size but same principle."

"No, I never did a church," Maury said after another pause. "This place of yours, it's got gold, art work, frankincense and fuckin' myrrh?"

"Couple of original oil paintings."

"Not that I'm thinking in terms of loot."

"You're retired," I said. "But consider the challenge."

"If I had a résumé, it'd look good to put a church on there."

I told Maury my situation in a short and quick version.

"Crang," he said, "when this is done, you're gonna owe me."

Maury hung up.

The sun had dropped out of the sky. The only illumination in the place came through the two skylights in the church's main room and another window at the back of Reverend Al's private quarters. Turning on lights in Reverend Al's office wouldn't be a smart move. Neither would anything else that might draw attention to any part of the Heaven's Philosophers building while I was locked inside.

In the gloom of the office, I opened the Reverend's computer. It was shut down. I tried the computer on the conference table. It was still in sleep mode. Whoever regularly used the machine had forgotten to turn it off. Or just didn't give a damn. I went to Documents. Getting out my iPhone, I typed in the names of the eleven guys who appeared on the Document titles. Robert Fallis, who was the guy nicknamed Squeaky, and the rest of them, William Sizemore and so on. When I finished, I strolled over to the peephole and watched for Maury.

Twenty minutes later, I caught the faint sound of somebody tinkering with the lock on the door into the auditorium. In no more than ten seconds, the door swung open. Maury's large but trim figure stepped in. Maury always dressed in tweed jackets and nice pleated slacks from Harry Rosen, and he was attired as usual tonight. He was using a small flashlight to guide his way down the church's centre aisle.

"Back here, Maury," I said, my voice pitched no higher than a conversational level. Sound carried easily in the room. Reverend Al could whisper his sermons, and nobody would miss a word.

Maury needed ten more seconds to unlock the office door.

"A blind guy could pick his way into this joint," Maury said. "Or out of it."

"I'm grateful to you, Maury," I said. "Your friend Sal waiting in the car?"

"She's carryin' out a diversionary tactic downstairs."

"The travel agent's still in the building?"

"I sent Sal in first," Maury said. "Keep the guy's eyes involved on her while I slid past. But I don't want to leave her with him too long. Sal's new at this."

"Just one more detail I need you to look at," I said.

I led Maury to Reverend Al's desk.

"You mind opening the top left drawer?" I said.

Maury handed me his little flashlight.

I aimed its beam at his fingers while he sorted through a ring holding many picks. He chose a particularly slim one. It fit the lock first try, and Maury slid out the drawer. I ran the flashlight over the contents, which appeared to be a stack of paper for the printer

"Nobody keeps printer paper under lock and key," I said.

"Look some more," Maury said. "And will you for crissake make it fast."

I riffled through the stack, and a third of the way down, sheets covered in typing turned up. Two repeated words stood out on the first page. "Semen" and "blood."

"This is what I came for," I said to Maury. "Among other things."

I folded the pages with the song lyrics into my jacket pocket, nine pages in all. Unless there was something wrong with my math, I now had the only two existing versions of Flame's hateful song lyrics. The copy that the Reverend had given to Jerome was in a file at my office, and this one, the original, from Reverend Al's drawer, was in my jacket pocket.

Already, by recovering the Reverend's nine pages, I'd completed a large part of my assignment for the Flame Group. But the way I saw things unfolding, I could maybe use my possession of the pages to pressure the Reverend into spilling the beans about how he got his mitts on them in the first place. I gave myself a mental pat on the back.

Maury and I left the Reverend's office, and eased down one of the curving staircases to the lobby. The travel agent had his back to us. He looked intent on Sal. I'd be intent on Sal if I were him. She had a lot of blonde hair and an outstanding set of knockers. Maury and I crossed the lobby and waited on the sidewalk a half block east of the church's front door.

When Sal came out of the building a few minutes later, she was carrying two file folders. She had on a flowery summer dress, the neckline cut low and the hem ending halfway down her thigh.

"How old is she?" I asked Maury as Sal sashayed up the street toward us.

"Could be my daughter," Maury said. "Granddaughter even."

"Is this a Viagra situation?"

"Sal admires my stamina."

"That's not answering the question."

"Hey, you guys," Sal said, holding up the file folders. "Look what I got."

Maury introduced me to Sal. Sal's last name was Banfield.

"What've you got?" I asked her.

"Jimmy in there's my new personal travel consultant," Sal said. She had a surprisingly cultured voice with a tone usually heard in the tonier Toronto neighbourhoods, notably Rosedale. "He drew up two ten-day winter holidays for a couple. One to Naples, Florida, the other to the island of St. Kitts."

Sal turned to Maury. "Which one do you like, my friend?"

"St. Kitts," Maury said, sounding definitive.

Years back, Maury and a friend got busted in Columbus, Ohio, on an illegal boondoggle I've never understood. Both guys skipped out on their bail. That made Maury a wanted man in the entire United States of America.

"You want a taste of island life?" Sal said to Maury.

"Much better than mainland U.S." I said. "Less *confining*."

Maury looked a dagger at me.

"Listen you two," I said. "Can I buy us all a drink before you go back to the shrimp dish? I got an identification parade to run by Maury."

We went into a bar another half block up the street. It was called Faith and Begorra. Inside, the decor ran to paintings of maidens with harps, signed photographs of the Chieftains, and arrangements of crossed hurling sticks. Everything was painted in shades of green.

A waiter wearing a light green shirt and dark green pants pointed us to a table and took orders. Double Stoli on the rocks for me, beer for Maury, white wine for Sal.

"Does the white wine come in green?" Sal asked with a teasing smile.

"For you, darlin'," the waiter said, addressing Sal's chest, "anything's possible."

The waiter went away, and I pulled out my iPhone.

"I got ten guys in different photos on here," I told Maury. "Tell me if anybody looks familiar. These people are all connected to the church back there. I also got eleven names, but I don't know how the names go with the photos."

I showed Maury the list of names on my iPhone. Sal watched the name parade over Maury's shoulder.

"So one guy on your names list, you don't got a picture to go with him?" Maury said.

"No photo for one out of the eleven, yeah," I said.

"Let's stick with just the photos," Maury said. "Show them to me."

"You're on."

I started from the beginning with the picture of Squeaky Fallis and the investment consultant I knew as Willie Sizemore. I wasn't counting the guy blocked out by my jacket.

"That's your friend Fox's old client on there, Squeaky," Maury said. "Don't remember his last name."

"Fallis," I said. "His buddy's named Sizemore. You know him?"

"No idea who he is," Maury said. "Listen, Crang, why don't you run through the whole collection you got, and I'll tell you at the end who I know? Be faster."

The waiter distributed the drinks. Sal's wine was green.

"That's cute," Sal said.

The waiter thanked Sal's chest, and left.

I flipped slowly through the rest of my photos. Maury was silent.

"You don't know any of these guys?" I said to him.

"Go back four pictures," Maury said.

When I flipped back, the photo on the screen included the John Candy look-alike in the white suit.

"That's Jackie Gabriel's kid," Maury said.

The guy didn't look like anybody's "kid." He was middle thirties at least.

"Who's Jackie Gabriel?" I said.

"Five, six years ago, you wouldn't have had to ask," Maury said. "He was the king of poker games in the city. A little blackjack too. Jackie ruled the card games."

"An ace card player is what you're telling me?" I said.

"You're not getting the concept," Maury said, impatient again. "Jackie was the guy that set up the games. He'd work out of somebody's basement, a vacant apartment over a store, a bunch of places like that. Guys came and played. Hundred or more players scattered around these different places every weekend, not so many during the week. Very systematic operation. Jackie took a piece of the action, and with him, the house never lost."

"Isn't that why people go to casinos?" I said. "To lose their money at gambling games?"

"Casinos grabbed a chunk out of Jackie's business," Maury said. "But he still has a nitch. The serious card players prefer Jackie's games."

"Niche," I said.

"Like I said," Maury said.

"So Jackie's son is George Gabriel, correct?"

"Georgie," Maury said. "You know him already?"

"I saw his name on some documents belonging to Heaven's Philosophers."

"That's Jackie's beef right there, this Heaven's Philosophers," Maury said. "He wants Georgie to get back in the family business. He thinks the religious thing, whatever Georgie and the other guys are runnin' in there, it's too big and risky. Jackie says outfits like that attract the cops sooner or later."

"Jackie knows what Heaven's Philosophers are all about?"

"He hates their guts, if that's what you mean."

"You think Jackie would talk to me?"

"He approves of anybody who might throw a wrench in the church bunch," Maury said. "I'm assuming that's what you got in mind."

I turned to Sal. "You have a view on any of this, Sal?"

Sal said, "You mean, as a contributor to this evening's break-in, my opinion now counts for something?"

"What do you do with yourself when you're not facilitating illegal entries?"

"I work on my Ph.D.," she said.

"Really?" I said, not quite sure whether she was joking. "What school?"

"English Department, University of Toronto," Sal said. "I'm

writing my thesis on the novels of an American writer named Richard Russo."

"*Nobody's Fool*," I said. "I loved it."

"That's the same as Maury," Sal said, a big smile on her face. "All you guys did was see the movie because Paul Newman was in it."

"Yeah, but I read the novel, too," I said. "And a couple of his other books. *Straight Man*, *The Old Cape Magic*."

"You read those?" Sal said.

"*Empire Falls*."

"Crang, wow, I salute you."

"You want any tips for your thesis," I said, "keep me in mind."

Sal turned to Maury. "Give this man whatever he wants."

"I'll phone Jackie soon as I get back to my place," Maury said to me. "Ask him about having a meet with you."

We finished the drinks and walked back to our cars. Maury was parked on the same street as I was. He opened his passenger door and ushered Sal into her seat. After he closed the door, Maury gripped my arm and steered me a few steps up the street.

"No," he said with great emphasis, "I don't need fuckin' Viagra."

Maury got in his car and drove away.

CHAPTER TEN

When I arrived home a little after ten, Annie was in her office on the first floor writing in longhand on a yellow legal pad.

"Wouldn't it go faster if you went straight to your computer?" I said. "Type whatever it is you're writing there?"

Annie held her left hand in the air while she continued to write with her right, meaning I should wait till she finished. I waited.

In a couple of minutes, Annie stopped writing.

"Have you heard," she said, "that writing something by hand facilitates the memorizing process?"

"I learned that for myself at exam time in high school," I said.

"Exactly," Annie said. "Write out stuff about the hard subjects and memorize it long enough to pass the exams."

"Physics and chemistry for me."

"What I'm doing here," Annie said, nodding at the pad, "I'm memorizing the speech I'll give at the book launch."

"Reading the speech to the audience might be easier."

"Yeah," Annie said, "but then they'd see my shaking hands, and that's probably all they'd remember — the nervous woman from Toronto with the rustling pages. They'd forget everything else about me."

"Including the subject of the book you're promoting."

"I'm going to look the Columbia people right in the eye," Annie said, "and sell them on Edward Everett Horton."

I gave Annie a pat on the back and a kiss on the lips.

"You've had a bite to eat already?" I said.

"At this hour, of course I have," Annie said. "But consider yourself welcome to yesterday's leftover salads in the fridge."

Out in the kitchen, I made myself a martini and arranged a selection of the salads on the dining room table.

My iPhone rang. I looked at the screen.

"Fast work, Maury," I said on the phone.

"Jackie'll see you Saturday morning around ten-thirty," Maury said. "He wants you to know he's very keen."

"But not keen enough to see me tomorrow?"

"He'll be at the hospital, which is one of the things I should brief you concerning."

"Brief me concerning?"

"Jackie had a stroke last year."

"The poor guy," I said. "He's not disabled?"

"His left side doesn't operate so good," Maury said. "And his speech gets kinda shaky. But nothing's wrong with Jackie's brain."

"Or memory?"

"That either."

"What about this hospital visit tomorrow?"

"He has one of those every three months, just in case," Maury said. "Saturday morning, I'll pick you up at Kennedy subway station, ten o'clock. You wait out front."

"That's the far east end of the Bloor line, right?" I said. "Jackie lives in Scarborough?"

"North York."

"I can never figure out the damn suburbs."

"Why else do you think I'm driving?"

Maury hung up.

I took my time over the martini, and still hadn't started on the salads when Annie came out to the kitchen. She poured a glass of Chardonnay, and sat down across from me.

"What trouble did you get into today?" Annie asked.

"I met a girl who's writing her Ph.D. thesis on Richard Russo's novels," I said.

"Truly?" Annie was smiling, "That's not the kind of person a criminal lawyer encounters every day."

"Practically never."

"What's the catch?"

"She's Maury's girlfriend."

Annie registered a moment of authentic surprise, but recovered in a hurry.

"For one thing," she said, "that must mean the girl has attributes other than intellectual."

"Remarkable knockers."

Annie smiled a different smile, one of the rueful sort. She shook her head.

"My conclusion, you meeting the girlfriend and so on," Annie said, "is that good old Maury is already involved in the Flame case, if I can call it that."

"I think of it as a file."

"In the past, "Annie said, "whenever you've gotten yourself into a piece of illegal behaviour, your buddy Maury was somewhere on the scene."

"You know what we should do?" I said. "You and I should go out on a double date with Maury and his girlfriend. Sal's her name."

"'Double date?'" Annie said. "Honest to God, Crang, where are you? Back in high school?"

"This girl, she's different. From the sound of her voice, she must've grown up in Rosedale. But speaking of high school, Sal probably went to Branksome Hall."

"Got the Rosedale honk, has she?"

I nodded. "So there's the Rosedale background and the Richard Russo thesis," I said. "You'll find her interesting and kind of amusing. We all go out together, you might get a more balanced slant on Maury."

"Nice try, fella," Annie said, She got up and refilled her wine glass from the Chardonnay in the fridge.

She sat down again. "Tell me how far you got with the Reverend on St. Clair."

"You're going to think about the double date?"

Annie hesitated for a minute. "If you're really serious, I promise I'll think about it," she said. "Now, what about the Reverend?"

I patted my jacket pocket. "I obtained irrefutable evidence that Reverend Alton Douglas was in possession of the blackmail document."

"'Obtained?' That's a weasel verb if I ever heard one."

"Further," I said, plowing ahead, "I have an appointment on Saturday morning with a man who has contacts inside the Reverend's operation that he wishes to share with me."

"More weasel words. 'Inside contacts'? That must mean the guy with the contacts has his own criminal status."

"That was before his stroke."

"I bet this guy's a friend of Maury's."

"Good bet there, sweetie," I said. "But bear in mind, I'm merely at the information gathering stage."

"I wish no ill to the man with the stroke," Annie said, "but you're skirting dangerous territory."

"That's the trick," I said. "I stay on the edges, getting all the dope that's available, then make my move on behalf of the client who is paying me."

"Do I gather you weren't actually in the Reverend's presence today?"

"Not that anybody would notice," I said.

"You know, sweetie," Annie said, "it'd be a comfort to me if you spoke to Reverend Alton Douglas before we go to New York. Get it out of the way. Put my mind at ease for when I'm not around to keep an eye on you."

"That's exactly my intention," I said. "I'll have a sit-down with him after church on Sunday."

"He gives sermons? This part is on the up and up?"

"Just like ordinary clergymen, which proves my point," I said. "The guy's harmless."

"Maybe this isn't going to be the disaster I've been thinking it'll be."

"My opinion entirely."

Annie stood up. "I'm going back to the speech," she said.

"After two glasses of Chardonnay? Won't your memory be impaired?"

Annie shook her head. "I'm just going to read it out loud for timing. The aim is not to exceed twelve minutes."

"That's the same way a defence lawyer thinks in a jury address," I said. "Nothing to be gained from boring the folks with too many words."

Annie carried her glass to the office. I transferred some of each salad on to a dinner plate, and started to eat.

"Ladies and gentlemen," I head Annie say from her office, "courage is not a quality…"

Courage? Edward Everett Horton?

This was sounding like a speech I needed to hear.

CHAPTER ELEVEN

Early Friday afternoon, waiting for Gloria to get to the office, I got launched on a research project. If I was representing Flame in a legal matter, shouldn't I get myself halfway up to speed on the kind of music he was famous for? It might help in making strategic decisions. On the other hand, the music stood a better chance of boring the pants off me.

I Googled hip hop. In no time, I was semi-immersed in Jay-Z. Naturally, he pronounced his name the American way. Jay-Zee. It sounded sleek. Pronounce it the Canadian way, Jay-Zed, it was about as sleek as Diefenbaker. I read on my screen that Jay-Z was a singing, composing, and producing hip hop billionaire. He was married to Beyoncé, though the latest rumours on the couple suggested that they were separated. Her I knew a thing or two about. She was the one who sang "At Last" to Obama and Michelle when they danced at the inaugural ball in 2009. That was as close as I could place Jay-Z to a real song.

I played a YouTube video of Jay-Z singing his anthem, "Empire State of Mind." Macho guy Jay-Z rapped while Alicia Keys sang the soprano part. His style was insistent, like a kid saying, "Pay attention to *me*!" What he sang was more a chant than a melody. The guy was arrogant. Just like Sinatra, except not one ounce as musical.

I checked out more Jay-Z YouTubes. Did he write love songs? I played a number of his titled "99 Problems." It seemed to make the point that whatever problems Jay-Z had, a girlfriend wasn't among them. Only he referred to them as "bitches." Jay-Z was no latter day Cole Porter. I played a little more of the number. Girlfriends were also "hoes" with "pussies." Jay-Z's concept of romance reached dimensions unknown to square parties like me.

I stood up from my computer, stretched my arms, and sat down again, turning to the business of checking out Flame. I learned right off the bat, listening to the first Flame YouTube, that Flame's voice was the opposite of Jay-Z's — a baritone rather than a tenor. On recordings and YouTubes, Flame worked to the usual staccato background of beats and vocal groups. Almost all his numbers were love songs. Nothing profound that I could hear, lyrically speaking, but the words took a more generous attitude to women than Jay-Z's "pussy." "Tender" and "soft" kept turning up when Flame sang of his girlfriends. He got "crushes" on women and asked them to be "huggable." He came across as the earnest guy where Jay-Z played the cynic. Did that make Flame unique? I couldn't tell. Jay-Z was my only source of comparison so far, and I wasn't in the mood for sounding out Kanye West or any of the other hip hop guys I had sort-of heard of.

Me, a fifty-year-old white guy who grew up on rhapsodic Bill Evans records, I'm hardly hip hop's target audience. My interests could branch out from jazz, but it would be more in the direction of something orderly, Bach for instance, rather than something unruly by people with names like Snoop Dogg.

Another Flame YouTube came up on my screen. It joined Flame's name with Billy Strayhorn's. What was this? Billy Strayhorn was from my world of music. He'd been Duke Ellington's right-hand man for years, a composer of memorable songs. I punched up the YouTube. The film quality was terrible, but the sound was clear, and I had no trouble recognizing the baritone voice. It belonged to my client.

Flame was singing Billy Strayhorn's great ballad "Lush Life." The song went back almost eighty years, all the way to a time when "gay" meant light-hearted and carefree. How did the kid come across it? His version sounded like the one Johnny Hartman recorded with John Coltrane in the early 1970s. That was the definitive interpretation of "Lush Life." Flame singing the song was a revelation, the young guy doing justice to a tune that was a standard by my definition.

I played the YouTube again, this time concentrating on the visual. It showed Flame as he sang the song, a very young Flame in a tuxedo, and the figure of this boyish version of the man was superimposed over four people acting out the song's lyrics. Three males and one female gathered around a table, all of them dressed in evening wear, tuxs for the men, though they were really boys, and a long gown for the girl. The four of them held champagne flutes in their hands, and they affected a languid air. As an actor, Flame was absolutely convincing in his world-weary pose.

This was all surprising, Flame's voice and his play-acting. Just his choice of "Lush Life" as a song to perform was persuasive for me. I turned off the MacBook, and leaned back in my chair, feeling warm and fuzzy about representing the guy.

Five minutes later, Gloria came through the door carrying her familiar red leather bag and smiling her familiar smile. She began the ritual of unpacking the bag. Then she stopped to give me closer inspection.

"You're looking blissed out," she said.

"I think I'm a little crazy for our client."

"Flame?"

"Don't get the wrong idea."

"I haven't got any ideas."

"Put it this way, kiddo. Listening to some of his music, I feel more involved in acting on behalf of Flame's interests."

"Glad to hear it," Gloria said. "Now what's with the coffee? I don't smell anything brewing."

I got out of my chair, and took charge of the coffee-making. In ten minutes, I set full cups in front of each of us.

"Okay, shoot," I said to Gloria, "tell me what I don't already know about the Reverend Al."

Gloria opened her iPad and began scrolling through the pages.

"Not much on him personally," Gloria said. "I concentrated more on Heaven's Philosophers and the origin of the building they're in."

"You still got a little about the Reverend?"

"His annual income is sixty-two thousand bucks plus a clothing allowance."

"Not bad for a disgraced clergyman," I said. "Who's his employer?"

"A numbered company," Gloria said. "The same one that owns the church building."

"No names that go with the numbers?"

"For pete's sake, Crang," Gloria said. "Give me a little more time."

I held up my hands in a peace gesture.

"Care to hear the background of the church's building?" Gloria said. "Probably doesn't pertain to your problem, but it's kind of entertaining."

"Go ahead," I said, "Entertain me."

"Another conceivably unorthodox religious bunch put the place up twelve years ago," Gloria said. "It went by the name Steady for Jesus. Apparently made up of stout Protestants who regretted the way Anglicans and Presbyterians and such like were drifting. So they formed their own church."

"This group later morphed into Heaven's Philosophers?"

Gloria waved both arms in a gesture that let me know I'd wandered way off track. "Different personnel entirely. Steady for Jesus was funded 100 percent by Stewart Sclanders. That name ring a bell?"

"Sclanders Lumber?"

"You got it in one," Gloria said. "Sclanders is still Canada's number one supplier of two-by-fours and whatever in wood products. Young Stewart is third generation and the scion of the family fortune."

"Steady for Jesus was his hobby?"

Gloria shook her head. "It was his commitment until he fell hard for a lovely girl named Julie Fineberg."

"Love trumped all?

"Stewart converted to Judaism, married Julie, and left Steady for Jesus to wither on the financial vine."

"That's the end of those guys?"

"More or less," Gloria said. "The Steady for Jesus property sat vacant until three years ago when the numbered company I mentioned scooped it up at a bargain price and began operations."

"What's with them financially?"

"The question gets us right to the crooked flim-flammery."

"You base this on what?"

"First, a question of my own. You've been out to the Heaven's Philosophers? The physical operation?"

"Studied it intimately."

"Do I gather there are three other businesses on the premises in addition to the religious component?"

"After a fashion, yeah, three others."

"In the last taxation year," Gloria said, her eyes on the iPad screen, "the numbered company shows income of four-point-four million bucks from an international travel agency, six million from a dining lounge, and five million from an IT centre."

"Jesus, the gall," I said. "The international travel agency consists of a guy and his computer. The dining lounge is good for a cup of coffee and a week-old doughnut. And the IT centre features a kid and a computer with an over-sized screen. Where'd you get these numbers?"

"Don't you want to know how much income the church shows all by itself?"

"How much?"

"Twenty-nine million," Gloria said. "And where I got the numbers was from their income tax returns."

"But if it's a numbered company, ipso facto its tax records aren't public."

"Right, for ordinary people," Gloria said. "But I've mentioned my friend Nikki to you from time to time?"

"She comes to town from the Maritimes and stays with you for a couple of weeks every summer, your oldest friend since school days."

"Since good old Allenby Public School up on Avenue Road," Gloria said. "Nikki, I once told you this, she moved down to Prince Edward Island because of a guy from there she was seeing. The guy didn't last, but her job in the Revenue Canada offices did. Nikki's department — now, get this — it's called the Taxpayer Relief Intake Centre. That's the one where taxpayers go begging permission to pay late because of serious physical or mental illness and, please, can they be excused from paying a penalty on top of the tax."

"A department like that really exists?"

"Nikki works night and day to keep up with the sob stories."

"But she still has time to poke around for her old pal Gloria?"

"Her job gives her access to the entire country's tax records," Gloria said. "That's where I got the Reverend Al's annual salary, clothing allowance included, and all the financial figures for the so-called church."

"Not that I'm not grateful," I said, "but isn't Nikki risking her livelihood?"

"Nikki kind of relished it when I asked the favour," Gloria said. "She said people at Revenue Canada are forever in one another's pockets. Nobody blinks an eye when somebody from another department asks for numbers that might be none of their business."

"Huh."

"*Huh*? Is that all you can say?" Gloria said. "Think of the implications in these clearly made-up income numbers the people at Heaven's Philosophers are bandying about."

"What it means, "I said, "they must have a money-laundering scheme going on."

"That's what Nikki thinks."

"Don't tell me she's going to get Revenue Canada involved?"

"Nikki's merely a dispassionate observer giving her oldest friend a helping hand," Gloria said. "Honestly, Crang, relax and show some gratitude for the gifts I'm laying on you."

Gloria was right. I was the guy who didn't think twice about invading the Reverend Al's inner sanctum. So why should I come over all moralistic about somebody else, Nikki in this case, playing fast and loose with confidential government documents? It was all in the interests of aiding my client Flame, who happened to be the good guy in whatever was going on. He could possibly turn out not totally good in the long run, but he was likely better than everybody else.

"Sorry, Gloria," I said. "I got to keep my eye on the ball."

"What does your eye see?" Gloria said. "Besides a ball?"

"The guys at the church rake in millions in illegitimate enterprises of a kind unknown for the time being," I said. "Then they scrub the money clean by declaring it as income in barely existent businesses headquartered in the church building."

"Nikki reads the situation the same general way."

"These guys are probably raking in ten times the figures they show on the tax returns. The numbers are just for the tax people's benefit. My opinion, they're hiding tens of millions more in laundered money."

"Nikki thinks the bad guys will likely bail out in a couple of years," Gloria said. "The fraud involved is too out front to keep pulling it off indefinitely."

I gave Gloria a long look that I meant to be thoughtful and meaningful.

"What's with the dippy expression, Crang?" she said.

"The question is this," I said. "Are the eight million dollars the Reverend Al's trying to squeeze out of the Flame people part of the

Heaven's Philosophers operation? Are they bucks that'll undergo the usual money laundering process?"

"Sounds to me like a good guess."

"That would mean Heaven's Philosophers are involved in the blackmail, and I need to pin down the names of the guys behind the church."

"You keep saying names," Gloria said. "And I keep saying I haven't had the time to uncover any."

"No fear," I said.

I got out my iPhone and clicked a few times until I pulled up the names of the eleven guys I took off the computer in the Reverend Al's office.

"See what you can find out about these guys," I said. "Hold on a second and I'll send them to your iPad."

"And what are you going to be doing while I run down the list of rascals?" Gloria said.

"Chatting with a guy who's got a contact inside Heaven's Philosophers," I said, completing the business with my iPhone.

I seemed to be on a roll.

CHAPTER TWELVE

Maury picked me up outside the Kennedy subway station Saturday morning. In a few blocks, we were driving north and east through Scarborough. Or maybe it was North York. Clusters of high rises, built in the last twenty years in an uninspired style, alternated with streets of houses that had been around since the early 1950s. The houses were mostly bungalows on large lots. In a few places, the bungalows gave way to the tear-down treatment, replaced by giant, mock-Tudor residences that muscled up to the lot lines on either side. They looked like houses that natural-born bullies would go for.

Maury parked outside one of the old bungalows. It was surrounded by mature but healthy trees that must have been planted at the same time the houses went up. The effect was kind of charming.

"Jackie's lived here fifty years," Maury said.

"Here being where exactly? North York?"

"Markham," Maury said. "Everybody else on the block moved in from China the last few years. Jackie's the last holdout from the old days."

Maury rang the bell, and a short, cheerful-looking woman in her seventies answered the door with a warm smile. She gave Maury a kiss on the cheek and shook my hand firmly. Maury introduced her as Irene Gabriel.

"Jackie loves company these days," Irene said.

Jackie was sitting in the living room, watching television with the sound on mute. The screen showed five guys and a dealer playing cards. Poker, I thought. Jackie, also in his seventies, had his left foot tilted over on its side at an unnatural angle, and his mouth took a slight leftward slant. Otherwise he seemed free of visible stroke indications.

"You want to hear about my kid and these Heaven's Philosophers?" Jackie said to me. His speech, as Maury had warned, sounded clumsy, but the words were entirely decipherable.

"And about where the Reverend Alton Douglas might fit into the picture," I said.

"When he was our priest out this way," Jackie said, "Father Al got a raw deal."

"Couldn't keep his hands off the ladies of the congregation?"

"Off one broad," Jackie said. "It was only one woman Al got tangled with, but what a broad."

"Hot stuff?"

"Ever heard of Chuckie Domenico?"

"The condo developer?"

"Biggest builder of condos anywhere in North America," Jackie said. "Not bad for a guy from right around here. But it was Chuckie's wife, Audrey, who happened to be the broad in question. Chuckie was so crazy about putting up his condos he never noticed his gorgeous wife was sleeping around."

"And the Reverend Al was one of her lovers?"

"Audrey got a kick out of seducing guys. With her, it was like a game, getting guys in the sack who weren't supposed to be there."

"That's what cost Al his job?"

"It was a political error on Father Al's part, if you follow me," Jackie said. "Al was the priest of our congregation, here in Markham, very popular guy with everybody. Audrey kept making eyes at him until he tumbled, and that's when he committed what I call his political mistake. Church politics I'm talking about."

Irene Gabriel came into the living room carrying a tray with a teapot, three cups and a plate of digestive biscuits without any chocolate or other sugary trimmings. I wondered about the tea. I read somewhere it had as much caffeine as coffee did, not necessarily a good thing. Or so I understood.

"This is herbal tea," Irene said. "No caffeine."

Maury looked like he wasn't enjoying the herbal tea experience. I, on the other hand, felt I might dedicate myself to healthy practices.

"What Father Al didn't know but everybody else did," Jackie said after his wife left the room, "was Audrey had been banging Father John Capelletti for a couple of years."

"Another man of the cloth?" I said unnecessarily.

"Father John'd been the big priest over in Woodbridge for somethin' like twenty years," Jackie said. "He had the ear of the archbishop, major contacts inside the hierarchy, all that, and he was so pissed off about Father Al doing his dalliance with Audrey he pulled the strings to get Al tossed out of the church."

"Father John, have I got this straight, was having sex with Audrey Domenico at the same time as Father Al?"

"But he started way before Father Al came along, which was why Father John took his revenge."

"How did Al end up in Heaven's Philosophers?"

"That was Georgie's idea," Jackie said. "My son."

"Ah," I said, "I'm beginning to follow the chain of connections."

"Georgie was always nuts about Father Al," Jackie said. "Most of the young people back then felt the same. So what happened, all these years later, Father Al gets bounced, and Georgie gives him a helping hand. I got no quarrel with that. My objection is I want Georgie to come back into business with me."

"Running card games?" I said.

"Look at those guys on TV," Jackie said, pointing to the figures slumped over their cards on the television screen. "Poker's hot as a pistol right now."

"George's running gambling for Heaven's Philosophers?"

"That goddamn church outfit."

"My contacts," I said, not mentioning the contacts consisted of my office researcher, "tell me Heaven's Philosophers are laundering tens of millions of dollars every year."

Jackie nodded. "Georgie would pull in a nice chunk of that from the gambling."

I reached into my inside jacket pocket, and got out the list of names from the Heaven's Philosophers computer. I handed the list to Jackie and asked him which names he could tell me anything about.

"I know that loudmouth Squeaky Fallis," Jackie said after a minute or two. "Smart enough, but not a man I trust. The only other guy whose name means anything to me, apart from my son, is Willie Sizemore. He once made me a lot of money on the stock market. Other times, he lost me some."

"I met Willie briefly," I said. "A guy with a slick line of patter."

"I gotta tell you a story about him," Jackie said. "Willie comes from a rich family that sent him to Upper Canada College. Private boys' school, you heard of the place I'm talking about?"

I said I knew the school.

"They played cricket there instead of real sports," Jackie said. "This one time, in a game Willie talks about, a kid from the Eaton family swung his cricket bat and whacked Willie in the head by accident."

Jackie leaned forward. "You know who I'm referring to? The Eaton family?"

"Everybody in Toronto knows the Eaton family," I said. "They had department stores going back to Timothy Eaton in the nineteenth century."

"Crang," Jackie said, "I heard my grandson saying to his friend the other day, 'The Eaton Centre? Who the fuck is Eaton?' He's sixteen, my grandson. My point, not everybody knows about Timothy Eaton and all the rest of the Eatons since him."

"Point taken, Jackie. What about the Eaton at UCC smacking your stock broker guy with the cricket bat?"

"Right in the temple," Jackie said. "Willie describes it so graphic he makes you want to inspect his head up close, check out if it's got a dent."

"You can't miss the dent," I said. I still didn't see the relevance of the cricket incident, but I imagined Jackie would get back to it somewhere in his narrative.

"Willie's been in the stock market his whole life," Jackie said. "Most of the time, he makes money for his clients without either him or them getting caught in what I might call shady shit."

"But not all the time?"

"Willie's been known to take his own clients for a ride," Jackie said. "What happens, the client suddenly loses his whole investment. Willie says, too bad, it's just a case of he got a bad tip on a stock or the market did something nobody expected. Willie's always got a sorry excuse. But the truth is the poor schmuck's money ended up in Willie's pocket, and usually there's nothing the schmuck can do about the loss."

"You're not going to tell me this happened to you?"

"Something like twenty years ago. Willie lost me one hundred grand. A misfortune was what he said. I told Willie it'd better be *your* fucking misfortune because I'm calling in somebody not so friendly as me. I was talking about a muscle guy who would beat the shit out of Willie. I named who I had in mind — a guy from the mob in New York City. Willie knew I meant businss, and the very next day, he brought me back my one hundred grand. That was when he told me the story about the Eaton kid and the cricket bat. He said every now and then he had an episode where he did something crazy, something out of his control, and it was all on account of the crack in the head."

"Are you saying Willie is never purposely crooked? But he gets a little addled from time to time?"

"That's his line," Jackie said. "Just a couple years ago, a good friend of mine was out two million bucks on an investment he made with Willie. I went to Willie and asked him if he was having one of his cricket bat episodes. Willie knew this was code for he better rethink the situation of the lost two million bucks. The result was my good friend got his money back, just like I did twenty years ago."

Jackie seemed to have gone as far as he cared to with Willie the stockbroker. But taking Willie and Georgie as examples, I thought there might be a discernible pattern of specialization going on at Heaven's Philosophers. Maybe each guy on my list brought a particular criminal activity to the table. Willie did crooked things on the stock market. Georgie looked after the gambling side. Other guys tended to other money-making criminal ventures. There had to be somebody in the group lending money at exorbitant rates. And who knew what other scams and shakedowns the Heaven's Philosophers guys carried on.

"Any of the other names on my list mean anything to you?" I asked Jackie.

"Ring no bells with me," Jackie said. "But I'll tell you an educated guess I can make."

"What's that?"

"At least one of the guys on the list is gonna be an enforcer. Maybe two."

"I assume that's like in hockey?" I said. "The enforcer's the guy who scores no goals but runs up an hour in penalties every game."

"Close to the same thing," Jackie said. "Heaven's Philosophers need at least one or two guys in charge of collecting money from people who're slow payin' what they owe the group. These enforcer guys keep the customers straight, making them toe the line. You see what I mean?"

"Got you, Jackie," I said. "One or two goons."

"They're the guys you need to worry about most of all."

"Because they're tough?" I said.

"No," Jackie said. "Because sometimes they need to kill people."

CHAPTER THIRTEEN

Late Saturday afternoon, I was sitting in the office resisting another cup of coffee and fretting about Jackie Gabriel's warning. The fretting was low-grade, not enough to distract me from the Flame assignment but enough to think I ought to advise Jerome Suggs what was afoot. As a matter of straight facts, Jackie hadn't done much more than confirm the sort of information that Gloria's research had aready unearthed. But coming from Jackie's mouth, the situation of the Reverend Alton Douglas vis-à-vis the Heaven's Philosophers people seemed more vivid and threatening.

The Reverend's connection to Squeaky Fallis and the others meant he was tight with authentic villains. These included one or two guys who specialized in violence, possibly up to and including homicide. Whether any of the eleven Heaven's Philosophers guys had a hand in the eight-million-dollar blackmail scheme remained up in the air. Now, more than ever, my intention was to move fast, and hope the schmoes on St. Clair didn't catch on to my activities until after I squared around with the Reverend on all matters relating to the nine sheets of song lyrics.

I punched in Jerome's cell number.

"I've been thinking, Jerome," I said when he came on the line.

"I been thinking too, man," Jerome said in his deep voice. He sounded enthusiastic about something. "I been thinking Scarlett Johansson."

"I assume this is for the movie Flame's supposed to be making and not just some free-form daydream you're experiencing."

"*Supposed* to be making, man? There's no doubt he's making it. And Scarlett Johansson, man, she's the one can carry the load in a romantic thriller. Got some nice comedy too, this movie."

"Uh-huh," I said.

"Don't you think so, man? About Scarlett for leading lady?"

"Tell me the storyline. Maybe that'll help me with an opinion."

"Flame plays a young guy just out of law school. Can't get a job doing defence work, so he starts a blog to keep his hand in. Blog he's doing, it's all about cold cases, murders never solved. One day, this nice girl comes to him and says she likes his blog, but she says sooner or later Flame's gonna stumble on her name in a case he's blogging about. There's people think she's the killer. She says to Flame's character, man, she never killed the victim in question, and she and Flame spend the rest of the movie finding the real killer and falling in love."

"Not bad, Jerome," I said. "Who came up with the story?"

"It's mine, man. Original story by me."

"You wrote the script too?"

"I wrote a script, man, but it's been worked over by real professional Hollywood screenwriters since I did mine a couple years ago."

"Let me get something straight, Jerome. The script idea for this movie of Flame's is yours. You're the guy with all the enthusiasm about it. Now you're casting parts for it. So how come you tell me that Roger Carnale, Mr. Big Picture Man, deserves the credit when it somes to Flame as the new Cary Grant?"

"Man, that oughta be obvious," Jerome said. "Mr. Carnale's the boss of bosses. He hands out the money on Flame's side of things. Mr. Carnale's the man who meets with the Hollywood moguls. When he gets together with those dudes, man, I'm not even allowed in the same room. You see what I'm talking about?"

The conversation had wandered into the subject of a possibly internecine struggle at the Flame Group. This wasn't anything I wanted to get myself involved in, though my natural inclination was to take Jerome's side over Carnale's. Still, no matter what else was going on, overall it was best for me me to stick to the blackmail scheme I was being paid to squelch. Leave the movie ambitions to the other guys.

"I'm with you on Scarlett Johansson, Jerome," I said. "She's a natural for the role."

"But that's not why you're phoning me, man," Jerome said, speaking without as much oomph as at the beginning of our conversation. "You're calling because of what? You made contact with the Reverend Alton Douglas?"

"I expect to talk to him in depth tomorrow," I said. "But in the meantime I've put myself in a position I like for future negotiations with the Reverend."

"How'd you manage that, man?" Jerome said.

Should I tell Jerome about retrieving the Reverend's no doubt illicitly obtained copy of the song lyrics? On the whole, I thought not. It might alarm Jerome who would pass on the word to Roger Carnale who'd be likewise distressed. No need to tell the client that stealth filching of documents was part of my repertoire.

"What's more, Jerome," I said, skipping over the answer to his question, "a bunch of certified criminals are part of the Reverend's circle. I've got as far as identifying these guys. The next step is maybe I should think about using their connection to the Reverend as a plus for our side."

"You're losing me, man," Jerome said. "Criminals and whatnot, what do you think's going on anyway?"

"Just to keep it simple," I said, "could you pass the word on to Roger that I'm meeting the Reverend tomorrow with expectations of knocking the man for a loop. You should preferably do that right away. Let him know I'm on top of things."

"Tell Mr. Roger immediately, you say?"

"Please, Jerome."

"Easier said than done, man."

"Why's that?" I asked. "The image I have of the Flame operation, it's you and Carnale and the rest of your team in the penthouse suite of some midtown Manhattan tower."

"Oh, man," Jerome said, "Mr. Roger don't even have a cubbyhole of an office in New York City. He got nothing down here at all."

"Where does he work out of?"

"Toronto," Jerome said. "But don't ask me what street, what address, what neighbourhood, 'cause I haven't the faintest idea, man."

"The rest of the team is up here with him?"

"There isn't what you call a team," Jerome said. "We contract out the booking work, the publicity, security for concerts, all that. Everybody's independent except me, and a guy name of Arthur Kingsmill who does the accounts. The two of them run their shop out of Mr. Carnale's house somewhere in Toronto. They handle the money, pay the bills and such like. I'm on the road with Flame or else back here at my apartment on 125th Street. I'm taking care of our boy, Flame, and Mr. Carnale rings me on his cell five, six times a day. Tells me what he wants. Then I do it. You with me, Crang? That's how the business runs."

"You don't phone him?"

"Now you're beginning to understand what I'm talking about."

"Have you even got a number for the guy?"

"Mr. Carnale says he changes his number a regular number of times, and that's a person who don't make jokes, man."

"Tell me, Jerome, does everybody in the music industry keep themselves as elusive as Roger does?"

"I just know two things, man," Jerome said. "Mr. Carnale pays everybody top dollar, me included, and he hasn't ever stepped wrong these last few years in what's called positioning Flame's career."

"An unorthodox business model is what I would say, Jerome, but I gather it's been smooth sailing, glitch free and all of that?"

"Very steady as she goes, man."

"Except for the episode with the Reverend."

"Crazy thing like this never happened before. Nothing even close, and I ought to know. I been around Flame a long time, man."

"Just one more question, Jerome," I said. "If I absolutely need to reach Roger, what's my procedure?"

"This is hypothetical, I'm assuming, man?"

"Let's say so."

"You call my line," Jerome said. "Then I pass along the word to Mr. Carnale the next time he phones me."

"A stately process."

"One might call it that, man."

"Speed is never of the essence?"

"Mr. Carnale's made his choices," Jerome said.

I thought about that for a few beats.

"Anything else, man?" Jerome asked.

"Not at the moment."

Jerome clicked off his phone.

CHAPTER FOURTEEN

When I arrived at the auditorium in the Heaven's Philosophers building a little after three Sunday afternoon, John Lennon was singing "Imagine." The Reverend Alton Douglas was standing behind the lecturn at the front of the room. A laptop sat on the lecturn, and two large speakers flanked either side of centre stage. It looked like the Reverend ran the show on his own — he was the only performer and he was his own personal DJ.

All but a very few seats had people in them. They were mostly guys in their late twenties and early thirties. Some were accompanied by lady friends. Most weren't. Everybody seemed alert and attentive. I was the only older party in the room, apart from the Reverend. He was giving the congregation a bright smile. I tried for my best imitation of a sympathetc parishioner.

John Lennon sang about imagining a world without countries and nothing to kill or die for, a world without religion. When the recording finished, the Reverend went into a five-minute riff on the song's lyrics. He thought Lennon was on to something.

"What we shouldn't demand is a heaven or an afterlife," the Reverend said. "This is the time for us to live the generous life here on Earth today, to live according to the ideas and philosophies of two men who walked the planet centuries ago, Buddha and John of the Revelations."

The Reverend pushed a couple of buttons on his laptop, and something lively I recognized from Vivaldi's *Four Seasons* filled the room. Everybody sat a little straighter. People nodded at one another. The Reverend beamed on us all.

After the Vivaldi, the Reverend talked about Buddha, about karma, about cause and effect. If we did good things, the Reverend said, quoting Buddha, then good things would happen to us in the future. Alas, he said, it worked the other way too. If we did bad things, we could expect to get bad things back one day.

Joni Mitchell came on singing her song about paradise and parking lots.

The Reverend had a persuasive presence. He never pressed a point too hard. He smiled and was agreeable. He looked good, his face unlined, his body erect, his grey suit fitting just right. He read some more from Buddha, offered a thought or two from John of the Revelations. Then the collection was taken.

It was the guy from the travel agency downstairs who was passing the collection plate. He worked his way from row to row, finally reaching the very back where I sat. He gave me a slow once over. Did my face ring a bell for him? Had he spotted me in the building on the night Maury Samuels sprang me from the Reverend's office? I put a five spot on the plate.

The Reverend delivered a few more homilies. He played a tune by a folk singer with a nasal problem. Or was that redundant? The Reverend made a couple of announcements and suggested readings for the next week's service.

To wind things up, a recording by a pianist I couldn't identify played a couple of Bach's *Variations*. A jazz pianist once told me that if a person could play Bach, he could play bebop. And the other way around. That gave me an idea I might mention to the Reverend.

When the last of the *Variations* faded away, a dozen of the young men gathered around the Reverend, asking questions, eager beavers looking for guidance from John of the Revelations, Buddha, and the Reverend Al.

The Reverend was patient, even erring on the side of longwindedness in his answers to the questions, though I noticed him flicking a look at me a couple of times. I was the guy waiting in the back row, looking a little too old and out of place for services at Heaven's Philosophers.

Finally it was just the Reverend and me in the room.

"My name's Crang," I said, approaching the Reverend. "I'd like to talk with you if you can spare a few minutes."

"I was expecting you," he said, reaching out to shake hands.

"Expecting me by name?"

The Reverend shrugged. "Let's just say I've been expecting someone on the errand you're on, if I'm not mistaken."

"How about we sit in your office?" I said. "You can listen to me while I ask you to give back Flame's sheets of lyrics?"

"It would come as a relief to me, Mr. Crang."

CHAPTER FIFTEEN

In the Reverend's office, I couldn't help revisiting in memory the scene of my recent embarrassment. For an irrational moment, looking across the room to the bathroom door, I felt tempted to tell the Reverend about me lurking behind the black shower curtain during his marathon piss. But I resisted the temptation. Why make myself look like a nut before we'd even begun our chat?

I chose another conversation starter.

"You ever think of playing a Bud Powell track during the services?" I said.

"Excuse me?" the Reverend said.

"Greatest of the bebop piano players. You could program a tune of Bud's called 'Glass Enclosure.' Sounds like Bach, only it's bop."

Even as I spoke, I knew my Bud Powell tangent was sewing confusion.

"Put that one aside for now," I said. "What about the nine sheets of Flame lyrics? Offensive as hell, I know they are. Sickening. But Flame would like them back."

"You are a lawyer, Mr. Crang?" the Reverend said.

"How could you tell? Is it the clear look in my eyes when I stare down your answers to my questions? The quick mental processes?"

"Mr. Crang," the Reverend said. "I want you to tell your clients I profoundly regret my role in this enterprise, which is clearly criminal."

"Let me get this straight, Reverend," I said after a small moment of silence. "You're going no further with the half-baked blackmail scheme?"

"I'm returning the sheets to you and performing whatever other duty you require, short of turning myself in to the authorities."

"And you're not going to hold back any copies?"

"I just want to get the one set of sheets I have in my possession out of this office and back to the rightful owner. I guarantee I will be retaining no copies."

"Have you *made* more copies?"

"Just the one I handed to the security man."

"Jerome?"

"Yes, Jerome Suggs."

"You'll sign an affidavit saying as much?"

"I'll sign it, of course, but what exactly do you want me to say in this affidavit?"

"That's my department. I'll go back to the office after we're done with our heart-to-heart here, draw the affidavit, and bring it around for you to sign."

"I'm most grateful," the Reverend said.

"Tell me this," I said. "How did you get your hands on the music sheets in the first place?"

The Reverend shook his head slowly and a little sadly. "I can't answer that," he said.

"You can't answer it because you've no idea how the sheets came into your grasp or you can't answer the question because somebody else will give you a hard time if you do?"

"Can't we just close the book on the whole wretched thing, Mr. Crang? You get the sheets back, and I get something that's even more valuable."

"And what would that be?"

"Peace of mind," the Reverend said.

Now that I looked at the Reverend from closer range, I could see the signs of stress in his face, the beginnings of purplish bags under his eyes, the lines in his cheeks a little deeper than maybe I expected of a guy in his line of business.

"Why did you pull such a crazy stunt in the first place, Reverend?" I said.

Douglas sighed and leaned forward in his seat, resting his elbows on the desk before he spoke.

"Mr. Crang," he said, "you would have to understand my present situation and some of how I arrived at my current employment before I could explain why I committed what you call a crazy stunt."

"Your present situation?" I said. "Let's see, Heaven's Philosophers pays you sixty-two thousand a year plus an allowance to buy nice suits like the one you're wearing today. Before you came to this place, you had a Catholic parish up in Markham, but you lost it when Father John Capelletti caught you making time with his squeeze, who happened to be Chuckie Domenico's wife, Audrey, who I understand is stacked. Jackie Gabriel's son, Georgie, lined you up for the job here at Heaven's Philosophers on the rebound from the parish that Father John got you kicked out of."

The Reverend looked shell-shocked.

"This is an invasion of everything I thought to be my private life," he said. His voice had a quiver in it.

"Don't worry, Reverend," I said, "I'm not telling anybody what I know. I just want you to understand we should go along with one another, and pretty soon this mess we've got on our hands will be more or less tidied up."

There was a sharp rap on the door. Before the Reverend could issue an invitation, the door swung open, revealing the travel agency guy. He was carrying a large-sized, plain brown envelope that appeared to be stuffed with something, probably money.

"The collection's ready and counted, Alton," the guy said to the Reverend.

The Reverend stood up.

"Thank you, Jimmy," he said, reaching for the brown envelope.

"Seven hundred and forty-eight dollars today," Jimmy said. "That's the highest total since you began."

Jimmy had an understated air about him. His clothes looked like they came from The Bay — no style to them, clothes a person barely noticed. The same went for his all round demeanour.

"This is Jimmy Wain," the Reverend said, introducing the guy and me to one another. "Jimmy, this is Mr. Crang. He's interested in my work with Heaven's Philosophers."

Jimmy paused a moment, staring at me, then said, "It's good work Alton does."

With that, he left the room, closing the door smartly. I had the feeling Jimmy had stored my name away.

"Speaking of money," I said to the Reverend, "what were your plans for the payoff you expected to pry out of the Flame Group?"

"I expected no payoff, as you call it, Mr. Crang."

"This was a freebie job you were taking on?"

"I was promised a substantial donation for my little church here," the Reverend said, waving his arm to include the office and the formal church beyond it. "Whatever the sum, I would apply the money first to a library. I want more reference material to help the young people you saw at our service this afternoon master the ideas I'm putting in their minds."

"Eight million bucks would buy enough books to restock the entire Vatican library."

The Reverend looked annoyed. "Nothing like the entire sum was ever intended for the donation," he said.

"Who's supposed to get the big bucks?" I asked. "Or is that another question you can't answer?"

"Please, Mr. Crang, don't ask me more," the Reverend said. "I admit my responsibility in the whole misadventure, but I can't go beyond myself in accepting blame."

"Here's my problem, Reverend," I said. "You're tied up in this building with a lot of guys who operate in different worlds of crime. How do I know they won't scramble whatever arrangement I make with you?"

"The people you're speaking of employ me in the church," the Reverend said. "But that's the end of my relationship with them."

"Give me a break, Reverend," I said. "These guys meet in this office of yours two or three times a week. That makes a prima facie case for your involvement with their shifty enterprises."

For the first time in our conversation, the Reverend smiled. It was a nice smile.

"Come with me, Mr. Crang," he said.

I followed the Reverend out of the office, down the church's centre aisle to a desk at the back of the auditorium. I hadn't noticed the desk before. It was close to the north wall, and on the desk's top, there was nothing except textbooks with covers that indicated they dealt in theological subjects.

"This is my second office," the Reverend said, indicating the desk and the books on it.

"If I'm guessing correctly," I said, "when Squeaky Fallis and company convene a meeting in your office, they ban you to the particular Siberia this desk represents?"

"They don't care to share reports of their activities with me."

"And you don't share yours with them?"

"If I'm out here and they're in the other office," the Reverend said, "it's pretty obvious that no exchange of any sort gets transacted."

Should I believe him? His explanation seemed logical enough, and despite his other flaws, a taste for blackmail being one, the Reverend didn't strike me as a natural born teller of untruths. I thought I'd probably accept his version that he had no connections to the Fallis group's criminal stuff. But I wondered what the bad guys would say about that.

The Reverend motioned for me to sit down with him, side by side in the back row of the auditorium.

"This affidavit you mentioned," he said, "can you bring it here for me to sign tomorrow at about this time?"

"How about a quicker turnaround?" I said. "I can leave now and be back in ninety minutes with the affidavit hot off my drawing board."

The Reverend shook his head. "I need one more day to tend to a certain matter."

"Tomorrow I'm out of town," I said. "I'll come at one o'clock Wednesday. Deal?"

He nodded. "That would work. We have one problem with Wednesday, but I know a way around it."

"The problem being ...?"

"Wednesday noon, Mr. Fallis and the other associates will be gathering downstairs for their weekly social time."

"How about you come to my office?" I said. "Or else we can meet in neutral territory?"

Reverend Douglas shook his head slowly. "They like to keep track of me during the hours we're open here at Heaven's Philosophers."

"Come on, Reverend. Let's get the paper work done. It can't be that hard to decide on a place."

The Reverend stopped shaking his head. "Here's my solution. What we do, or rather what you do, is use an entrance to the building that none of the others are aware of."

He stood up and took a few steps to the north wall behind his desk. A thick, dark curtain hung on the wall. He pulled it back, revealing something that looked like a wooden door but had no knob or keyhole that I could see. What it did have was a lot of intricate carving in the wood.

"You want me to come in through here?" I asked the Reverend.

"A secret entrance and exit," the Reverend said, looking very pleased with himself. "It was installed by Stewart Sclanders himself. You know who he is?"

"Lumber baron and founder of Steady for Jesus."

"Exactly."

"And I'm imagining he put the secret door in place for his girlfriend, Julie Fineberg, to slip in and out. Or for him to do likewise in reverse."

The Reverend looked a trifle miffed that I was taking the edge off his revelations.

"I went to see Stewart Sclanders to confirm that this was indeed a door," Reverend Douglas said. "He was most obliging. He supplied me with two sets of keys to the doors up here and down at ground level."

"I can't spot the keyhole," I said, looking at the door.

"You see the unicorn among the door's carvings? Right there at waist level? The keyhole is in the unicorn's horn."

The Reverend took a key from his jacket pocket, and fit it into the unicorn's horn. Then he used the key as a leveraging tool, a substitute doorknob, to open the door. What I saw now was a ladder attached to the wall leading straight downwards in an enclosed and very dark space.

"There's a light switch up here and another at ground level," the Reverend said, flipping on the switch. I leaned over, and in the glare of a set of light bulbs running along either side of the ladder all the way to the ground, I looked down two long flights.

"The climb up looks like a cardiovascular challenge," I said.

"You seem in good health, Mr. Crang."

"And I have motivation."

"To get the affidavit signed, exactly. That makes you ideal for using the ladder."

The Reverend handed me two keys. Then he closed the door, and drew the heavy curtain that hid the door from view. He went back to his desk in what he called his second office and took a daybook out of the middle drawer.

"I'm inking you in for one o'clock on Wednesday," he said.

"It's a date."

Together the Reverend and I walked out of the auditorium into the open area at the top of the marble stairs. Jimmy the travel guy was nowhere in sight. Neither was anyone else.

"I'll be happier than you can imagine to end this sad affair," the Reverend said.

"You didn't mention the copy of the song lyrics that you somehow acquired."

"Oh yes, yes," the Reverend said. "I know that's important to you and your people, and I can assure you it'll be in your possession when you leave here on Wednesday."

"That's one thing I'm absolutely certain of," I said, knowing that I already had the song sheets in my office files. Clearly the Reverend hadn't yet checked his desk drawer for the sheets. He'd get a shock when he finally opened the drawer, but better from my point of view he should suffer a jolt than I should let the dratted sheets out of my control.

My business with the Reverend done for the day, I trotted down the winding staircase. I paused to check the first floor. Nobody was in sight, nobody lurking on the sidewalk out front. I left by the building's main door and drove away, feeling pleased with myself.

CHAPTER SIXTEEN

An hour later, I phoned Jerome.

"The Reverend Douglas has folded his hand," I said to Jerome.

"He's backing off?"

"The Reverend says, in so many words, he's ashamed of what he did."

"Man, what happened to the guy?" Jerome said. "He's had a vision from some higher power?"

"He'll sign an affidavit swearing he's got no more copies except the one he used for the blackmail."

"And that one, he'll give back to us?"

I hesitated, once again, considering whether I should tell Jerome I'd already taken possession of the copy. I came up with the same answer as before; no, I wouldn't tell him.

"Not to worry, Jerome," I said. "I'll have the Reverend's one and only copy."

"When's this happening, doing the affidavit and whatever else? Later today?"

"Wednesday at one o'clock, it'll be signed, sealed, and delivered."

"Why's he stalling, man?" Jerome said. "You heard Mr. Carnale last week, him saying he wants this done pronto."

"It's my own call on the timing, Jerome. I'm going to be in New

York from late tomorrow until Wednesday morning. It's something I can't avoid. Don't want to avoid it either."

"This ain't on Flame business?"

"It's not even on my business," I said. "This is the woman in my life launching a book she wrote. The launch happens to be at Columbia University."

"Columbia? Do tell, man. The campus is only ten minutes from my place, walking time."

"A movie book, Jerome. Might be right up your alley. It's a biography of an old-time comic actor named Edward Everett Horton."

"Man, Edward Everett was my kind of guy," Jerome said, sounding as excited as I'd heard him. "He made movies with Cary Grant. *Arsenic and Old Lace.* I love those old movies, man. Edward Everett gets me laughing every time."

"You should come to the launch."

"It's not one of those where you get in by invitation only?"

"Consider yourself invited, Jerome. At the Miller Theater on the Columbia campus. Five o'clock, Tuesday afternoon."

"Your girlfriend wrote the book? Would I have maybe heard of her?"

"Annie B. Cooke."

"Oh dawg, this is too much," Jerome said. I thought he might swoon on the telephone. "Annie B. Cooke, she wrote the article about Jamie Foxx in *Premiere.* This was even before Jamie won his Oscar for *Ray*. Man, I loved that article."

"Back in the day when *Premiere* was still around."

"She's retired from writing about movies? It's a lot of years since I read her name."

"She's still in the game. Mostly in Canada, but she blogs. You can find her online."

"Man, if I meet her at this book launch, I gotta tell her about Flame's movie."

"She thinks Scarlett Johansson makes workable casting for the female lead," I said.

"I'm going Scarlett all the way."

"Scarlett's perfect, but Annie and I were talking movies last night, especially your movie. Annie said Scarlett's fee may too high for a production like yours."

"Annie really got into it about my movie, man?"

"She likes the potential of the whole concept."

"That's very nice, man," Jerome said. "But you talk about money, me and Mr. Carnale been around the floor a few times about money lately."

"He doesn't want to budget at the Scarlett Johansson level?"

Jerome seemed to be taking his time about what he said next. "There's a lotta things I can't talk about, man."

"Concerning money?" I said.

"Money seems to be at the root of it, yeah."

"You're sounding cryptic, Jerome."

"That's because I don't know what's happening, man."

"If money's the issue with Carnale, the news about the Reverend caving in ought to put old Roger in a more amenable mood. This is eight million dollars saved in one fell swoop."

"Yeah, well, man, the swoop shoulda fallen faster," Jerome said. "That'll be Mr. Carnale's point of view."

"Forty-eight hours from now, it'll be a done deal," I said.

"You want me to tell Mr. Carnale about all of this right away?" Jerome said. "Or wait till you got the affidavit you talkin' about signed?"

"Cheer the man up," I said. "First chance you get, spread the good word."

"But I don't know whether cheering up gonna occur to Mr. Carnale, the way he's carrying on this last while."

On that pessimistic note, Jerome rang off.

I opened my MacBook and drafted the affidavit I wanted the Reverend to sign. I liked what I wrote, but at just two pages, it ran a little thin. I added some boilerplate paragraphs that beefed it up to five pages. The extra stuff was meaningless, but it gave the affidavit more heft. That was the practice of law in a nutshell, a business that offers the world more meaningless heft.

I printed out two copies of the affidavit and went home to Annie and a martini.

CHAPTER SEVENTEEN

I was back in the office just after nine the next morning. Annie's and my plane to Newark didn't take off from Billy Bishop Airport until mid-afternoon. We'd take a cab from Newark into Manhattan. In the meantime, before we left, I figured to shuffle a little paper at the office. I unlocked the door, picked up the empty water jug on my desk, and walked down the hall to the men's room. I filled the jug with enough water for one cup of coffee, no more. When I came back, two guys were sitting in the clients' chairs and a third guy, the largest of the trio, was leaning against the wall just inside the door.

"Good morning, gentleman," I said. "New clients are always encouraged."

I could put a name to one of the seated guys. He was none other than Squeaky Fallis. He had on the same lightweight black sports jacket I'd seen him wear at Heaven's Philosophers, but a different noisy tie, this one featuring an assortment of lollipops in orange, pink, and yellow against a medium blue background. The other two guys I recognized from my photo sessions at Heaven's Philosophers, but I couldn't identify either by name. The guy sitting beside Squeaky had a placid expression and a hairline that had receded all the way to the centre of his skull. The guy doing wall duty was working hard on a ferocious mien. He might be one of the enforcers Jackie Gabriel warned me about. He had the extra-large size going for him and the guileful look of someone committed to a career in bullying.

"Clients?" Squeaky said. "Do we look stupid enough to hire you, Crang?"

The line drew chuckles from the other two guys.

"Care for coffee, Mr. Fallis?" I said, looking at Squeaky, then at the other two. "Either of you gentlemen?"

"No coffee, goddammit," Squeaky said. He was apparently the trigger-tempered type.

"I'll just help myself," I said. "But if you've got time to sit awhile, I'll fetch the water for three more cups in case the aroma wins you over."

"Sit the fuck down," Squeaky said. First I started the coffee machine, then I walked around the desk to my chair. My moves were unhurried and deliberate. No sense letting Squeaky think he was intimidating me.

"You been annoying Reverend Al," Squeaky said. "I want to know why."

"Did the Reverend say I was annoying him?" I said.

"What I say is what counts, Crang," Squeaky said. "And I say you been an annoying son of a bitch."

"I attended the Reverend's service yesterday afternoon." I said. "He's a loquacious speaker, don't you think?"

"You got no business I know of around the goddamn building."

"Everyone can use a little spiritual reinforcement," I said. "Isn't that reason enough to visit the Reverend?"

The coffee machine signalled that it had finished its business. I got up and poured myself the one cup it produced.

"You were hanging around the place one morning last week," Squeaky said.

"I had a coffee in the lobby," I said, sitting down again.

"You were asking questions about the Reverend."

"Damn," I said, "that barista is a real Chatty Cathy."

"Sunday afternoon, you went into the Reverend's office after his bullshit service."

"Jimmy the travel agent spilled the beans about that one, am I right?"

"I'm telling you, Crang," Squeaky said. "Answer the questions or I'll tell Ernie to pop you."

I turned to the guy holding up the wall.

"How do, Ernie," I said.

Ernie didn't answer. He was busy practising his malevolent stare.

"What'd you want with the Reverend?" Squeaky said. "You're running out of chances here."

I sipped from my cup of coffee.

"Client confidentiality applies to my conversation with Reverend Douglas," I said.

"Bullshit," Squeaky said. "You're not his lawyer."

"The Reverend is someone my client has dealings with," I said. "I can't tell you what Reverend Douglas and I talked about because my professional relationship with him is covered by the confidentiality I owe my client. If all of this is too deep for you, Squeaky, I'll reduce my explanation to words of one syllable."

Squeaky slammed his fist on my desk. "Call me Squeaky one more time, and I'll tell Ernie here to toss you out the window."

"Windows in this building are built not to open," I said.

"Then *through* the damn window."

"Whatever you say, Mr. Fallis," I said. "It's Mr. Fallis from now on."

"You got something going with the Reverend," Squeaky said. "What the fuck is it?"

"I've already covered that question." I said. "Now let me ask you one: are you and the other ten guys at Heaven's Philosophers engaged in a transaction with the Reverend that has a non-ecclesiastical slant?"

Squeaky didn't say anything for a few seconds. I assumed he was pondering whether to answer the question or call on Ernie's services.

"We hired the Reverend for one reason, you dumb fuck," he finally said. "He runs our church. None of us give a damn how he runs it. Just so he makes things smooth, and keeps the place looking like a church."

"Nice of you to fill me in, Mr. Fallis," I said. "Let's go for another query on my list. You ever heard of a guy named Flame?"

"What the fuck?" Squeaky gave my desk another crack with his fist.

If I read things correctly, I'd gone too far.

"Perhaps we've reached a finale here," I said, "unless you gentlemen have changed your minds about coffee."

"Crang," Squeaky said, "if I hear you been talking to the Reverend one more time, if I learn you been coming into the church again, I'm getting Ernie to put the boots to your ass."

Squeaky stood up. The other two followed Squeaky's lead. The guy with the receding hairline pushed out of his chair. Ernie straightened himself off the wall.

"Sure about the coffee, guys?" I said, a thoughtful host to the end.

Squeaky gave a slight nod. It wasn't to me. It was to Ernie.

When I turned to face Ernie, he had grabbed the cord on my De'Longhi machine, and yanked it out of the wall. With one hand, he lifted the machine over his shoulder. The idiot was going to bust the De'Longhi.

"I'll make you a bet, Ernie," I said.

"Screw you, Crang," Squeaky said.

"Let me fix you a cup of coffee with that machine you're holding, Ernie," I said, "and you'll love the taste so much you'd never dream of wrecking the thing."

"Give it a heave, Ernie," Squeaky said.

Ernie did as he was told. His target was the far wall of my office, but his aim was a little off, and the machine smashed into the floor just short of the wall. A broken handle flew off the main container, some glass broke, other metal parts came out of the crash in jagged pieces.

For a moment, there was no sound in the room except the noise of Monday traffic drifting up from Spadina. Ernie and his fellow idiots seemed to be feeling the momentary shock of the crashing coffee maker. I was busy talking myself into not taking a swing at Ernie. The guy outweighed me by about seventy-five pounds. If I threw a punch at him, I'd end up in approximately the same shape as the coffee maker.

Squeaky, Ernie, and the bald guy broke into laughs.

"Next time, Crang," Squeaky said, "it's not gonna be a coffee machine that gets smashed. You understand what I'm saying?"

All I could do was stare at the wreckage of my nice De'Longhi. The three guys left the office. They didn't shut the door, and I could hear their footsteps echoing down the hall all the way to the elevator. The three idiots were still laughing.

CHAPTER EIGHTEEN

I was on my knees and elbows on the office floor, picking up tiny pieces of glass with one hand and dropping them into a paper cup in my other hand. My back was to the open door. Somebody rapped on the doorframe.

I turned my head, but not far enough to confirm who I thought was at the door.

"If you knuckleheads are back for a return engagement …" I said. I wasn't sure how to end the sentence.

"I don't guess I'm one of the knuckleheads you were expecting," a woman's voice said.

I recognized the Rosedale honk in the voice. It belonged to Maury Samuels's girlfriend.

"Sal," I said. "Sorry, I had a bad experience in here a few minutes ago."

I climbed to my feet, careful not to spill the broken glass out of the paper cup.

"Somebody busted your coffeemaker?" Sal said. She looked clean and fresh, wearing a black blouse buttoned to the neck, jeans, and a tailored, white linen jacket. "Was it the knuckleheads who did the busting?"

"Yeah, it was them," I said. I didn't feel like talking about it right then.

"Maury isn't with you?" I said to Sal.

"I'm here for a reason I don't want Maury to know about."

"A secret meeting?" I said. "I'm always partial to secret meetings."

I dumped the paper cup in my wastepaper basket, and Sal and I sat down at the desk.

"I went by your house," Sal said. "Annie told me you were over here."

"You spoke to Annie?"

"We had a coffee in your gorgeous dining room," Sal said. "She's so nice, Annie."

"She's a natural, all right."

"She said we should go on a double date, you guys, Maury and me."

"Annie said that?"

"What is it anyway, a double date? Some old-timey social ritual?"

"That's as good a description as any I've heard," I said. Then I moved the conversation along. "What is it Maury isn't supposed to know?"

"I realize you're his good friend and everything, but this is something you got to promise me not to tell. Maury'd get pissed off."

"I'll put it in the vault."

"The vault? What do you mean?"

"It's a term from *Seinfeld* for keeping a secret."

"It must be another generational thing, but honestly I don't get *Seinfeld*."

"How do you feel about Laurel and Hardy?"

"That's different. Laurel and Hardy are classic. Something classic is easy to grasp. It's timeless."

"Wait twenty years and you'll feel the same way about *Seinfeld*."

Sal sighed. "Liking *Seinfeld* is probably one more old-timey social thing," she said.

"Tell me," I said, "what might piss Maury off?"

"Porn films."

I paused for a minute. "Are you implying you have something to do with them? Appeared in porn maybe?"

"Almost."

"Almost? That's like a woman saying she's a little pregnant."

Sal made a motion with her hand that said we should wipe the slate clean on the subject, and start all over.

"When you were showing Maury the names and pictures of the guys in that phony church on St. Clair the other night," Sal said, "I recognized one of the names. Frederick Chamblis."

"But you didn't see him in the photographs I took?"

"I thought he must be the one guy you said didn't get on camera. People call him Freddie the Champ."

"And you know him through your connection to the porn movie business?"

Sal shrugged. "Well, I don't know how much of a connection you'd call it."

"Take your time, Sal," I said. "Go back to wherever this begins."

"It begins with this very attractive girl I know who lives in my apartment building," Sal said. "Franny's her name, and her ambition since she was a little kid is to be an actress."

"Is she getting anywhere with that?"

"Oh, you know, bit parts in TV movies. She had a speaking role in a play at the Fringe Festival last year."

"Struggling. But she's very attractive?"

"Which is what got her in the porn game."

"Ah, a plot takes shape."

Sal nodded. "Franny needs the money, and porn, the kind she's involved in, it pays good bucks."

"How good, roughly?"

"Five or six thousand per movie, and it generally takes three days to shoot one of the films."

"Makes for an impressive pay package."

"Franny approached me around this time last year about doing porn with her, even though she knows I'm the last girl in the world who needs the money. The thing is, I got this inheritance from my grandpa. It paid for my apartment. My place, this is kind of interesting, is right around the corner from here, St. George and Lowther. The inheritance paid for that, paid for my Volvo, and it covers tuition at school, and there's still lots left over."

"What's in you that makes Franny think you'd get into porn if the money's irrelevant?"

"I'm a free spirit where relations with the opposite sex are concerned."

"To wit," I said, "Maury."

"To wit, him, totally."

"In no time at all, if I follow where your story's going, you were naked in front of a movie camera."

"Three cameras," Sal said. "I'll explain that in a minute. First, I should tell you I made it clear to Franny I had conditions."

"Like what?"

"I don't mind getting nude with guys who are nude, and I don't mind fooling around with them in front of a camera. But the conditions I had, one for example, I wouldn't do blow jobs."

I went silent, thinking to myself, as far as I knew, blow jobs were a staple of porn videos.

Sal broke into my silence. "You do know what a blow job is, Crang?"

"Of course."

"Where the guy sticks his dipstick in the girl's mouth?"

"Dipstick?"

"It's just another word for penis."

"I know," I said. "Dipstick just slipped my mind when I was making a list recently. But never mind that. So you say you'll do porn as long as blow jobs aren't included?"

"They make me gag."

"But don't the porn producers object? I sort of imagined blow jobs are a big attraction."

Sal shrugged. "I got a lot of other attractions to offer."

"Right," I said. "Suppose you just tell me more about you and Franny and the porn business."

"Franny said these movies were different from 99 percent of porn films. Not sleazy or cheap. These had money put in them. Three cameras, professional cameramen, a director, a lighting guy, a girl who does the art direction and designs the set and chooses the actors' clothes. Everything like a real movie with a budget."

Sal gave me a big smile. I tried to smile back. But Sal could read the skepticism in my face.

"Let me show you what I'm talking about and you'll be convinced," Sal said. She reached for my MacBook, turned it around to face her and began tapping into some Google pages. "The things Franny told me were no lie. You'll see."

Sal tapped some more, then turned the computer toward me so I could follow what the movie she'd brought up was all about. On screen, a very pretty blonde girl ambled into the frame from off stage. The scene was brightly lit, had pricey looking furniture, everything in good taste. The girl had on a white dress and sat down on a sofa. The sofa was white too. So were the walls and the thick carpeting and most of the décor I could see.

"White is the visual theme of all the films these people make," Sal said.

The girl sat on the sofa and soon removed her clothes including her underwear. It was white. She began to masturbate. She was vigorous about it. Another girl entered the room. She was dark and voluptuous. Seeing the first girl in action, the second girl took off her white clothes, displaying her spectacular breasts, and joined in the masturbation. Also vigorous. Soon the two girls were helping one another in mutual pleasuring. Both girls had had Brazilians recently.

"You get the idea about the production values?" Sal said.

I coughed and said, "Yes." My voice seemed unusually high-pitched.

"In this movie we're looking at here, a guy comes in before too long, gets into it with the two girls, and la-di-da-di-da," Sal said. "But let me show you one thing more."

She began to fast forward through the rest of the film.

"The brunette girl in the movie?" Sal said as she ran the fast-forward. "That was Franny."

"Your Franny?" I said. "Great heavens!"

I thought of telling Sal that I was a lawyer gathering facts for a file, and I needed her to go back for a lengthier examination of Franny's person. But I resisted. Instead I asked a question.

"What type of guy do these films cast in the male roles?"

"The type who looks at a naked girl and gets a stiffie in about five seconds."

"Stiffie?" I said.

"It means an erect penis."

"Another one that slipped my mind recently."

Sal looked at me for a moment, shrugged and moved on.

"The point with the male actors," she said, "is the director doesn't want to wait around with everybody else while the guy takes forever to get it up."

"It would be an unfortunate expenditure of resources."

Sal had fast-forwarded the film all the way to the end of the credits.

"Look at the very last name," she said.

I looked. The last credit read, "'Producer: Freddie the Champ.'"

"That's our guy from Heaven's Philosophers?" I said.

"Not only that," Sal said. "What you'd also be interested to hear is that he was the guy, when I agreed to get involved. He drove Franny and me to the studio. And it, the studio where the movies are shot — get this — it's in his house, which is a mansion practically."

"What's this guy look like, Freddie the Champ?" I said.

"He's not heavy, but he's got a body like he lifts weights, and he's scary in a smooth way," Sal said. "His hands, when Franny introduced me to him and we shook, were like a couple of power tools. My impression, he could have crushed me if he wanted to. He could crush Mike Tyson."

I thought about the guy in the first photograph I took at Heaven's Philosophers, the one where I got Squeaky Fallis, but the sleeve of my jacket covered up one of the other guys in Squeaky's group. That guy had a jutting chin.

"Anything distinguishing about Freddie's face that you noticed?" I said to Sal.

"Just that it was sort of lean like all the rest of his body. The guy comes on like a regular joker, but he's actually very forceful. Totally a threatening guy."

I decided to forget Freddie's description for the time being, and move on with Sal's story.

"Freddie drove you and Franny to the mansion where the filming was going to take place," I said. "Where was the mansion?"

"Out in the east end, in the Beach, but a part of the Beach I'd never been in before. It's a very hilly neighbourhood, lot of trees and very big houses. None was quite as big as Freddie's place. It's huge, and he's got the living room made over into a movie set where the porn films are shot."

"And he's the homeowner, you know that for sure?"

"He acted like he owned it, and nobody that I saw called him on it. The only people in the place that day were connected to the movie, and they seemed to think Freddie was the homeowner. One other guy, not with the movie crew, he came into the room a couple of times, but he seemed more like a servant type of person."

"What was it about him that persuaded you he was of the below-stairs class?"

"The guy was deferential," Sal said. "I didn't pay much attention to him. My impression was of a very tall, not bad looking guy, well-dressed, quiet and polite. That was all."

"Okay, you're in the house to shoot a film. Then what happened?"

"The first day is always a sort of audition day for everybody: the actors, the cameramen, the director. It seems to be the custom, audition happens on a Sunday, then a day off on the Monday, and everybody gets down to shooting the whole movie on Wednesday, Thursday, Friday. Audition day, it's when we get a script, which mostly just says what sex acts happen in what order.

"So on this day I'm telling you about, when Franny and I were there, we took off our clothes and moved around, did poses whatever way the director told us. The cameramen shot our bodies from different angles, tits, ass, pussy, whatever, while we just more or less ran through the whole storyline without actually doing any of the sex acts."

"What about the guy in the male role?"

"That guy was perfect," Sal said. "Franny and I gave him a flash of our legs wide open and it was an instant hard-on for the guy."

"But something must have gone wrong," I said. "You dropped out of the movie, right? Was it sudden second thoughts or what?"

"A mix of reasons. I didn't go for the type of guy I'd have to screw in the movie. This particular guy had these godawful tattoos. The atmosphere didn't feel right. Maybe I just got plain chicken about the whole idea of the porn thing. Anyway, I turned down the job even though they were begging me."

"A sound decision," I said. I gave Sal's hand a squeeze of a reassuring nature.

"Except," Sal said, her voice bright, "I'm ready to do an audition with Franny one more time."

"Really?" I said. "Why so?"

"It's a plan to help you."

"*Moi*?"

"You want to know more about Freddie the Champ and Squeaky what's his name, and all those other guys out at Heaven's Philosophers, am I right?"

"Given recent events, the need for information might have lost some urgency," I said. "But, yeah, I wouldn't mind getting a better handle on the crowd from the church."

"That's where I come into the picture," Sal said. "The point is I've got an open invitation to do a film whenever I feel ready. The director and the cameramen, these guys told Franny they had a high appreciation of my body. They keep mentioning this to Franny. So, really, all I need to do is go along with her on an audition day, and you come with me."

"I'm not a five-second man," I said. "That might restrict my value to the film. Why else would I be there?"

"As my lawyer is why you're there," Sal said. "I've got it all figured. When they hand out the contracts to everybody at this audition, I tell them I've brought my lawyer to read mine. They already know I'm not a dummy, so arriving with a lawyer won't surprise anyone."

"That puts me on site for a legitimate reason," I said. "But what do you imagine in your plan I would do with my time in the house?"

Sal shrugged. "It gives you pretty much free rein on your own in the mansion."

"That might work," I said. "I could poke around for whatever information about Freddie the Champ and his associates that's on offer. Kind of vague, but what the heck."

"It's pretty clever, don't you think?" Sal looked pleased with herself.

"And I'm grateful to you for the thoughtfulness," I said. "I should tell you, if things break the way they're supposed to, I may be free of Heaven's Philosophers and related parties by Wednesday afternoon. But it's best to prepare for all eventualities, and if Squeaky and Freddie the Champ continue to be bothersome, I'll call on you."

It seemed a long shot that I'd need to perform a sneak job in the mansion where porn movies were filmed. But Sal was so earnest that I didn't want to disappoint her completely. Besides, the conversation with her had chased away the small case of the blues I'd developed over the episode of the smashed coffeemaker. I owed her something for that.

"Done," Sal said.

She kissed me on both cheeks by way of goodbye, and went out the door.

I needed another ten minutes to clean the debris off the floor. Then I left for home. Annie and I had a plane to catch.

CHAPTER NINETEEN

At four o'clock next day, on the Tuesday afternoon of Annie's book launch at Columbia University, the two of us were standing on the west side of Fort Washington Avenue on a corner way up at 190, just south of the Cloisters. We were waiting for Manhattan's M4 bus. During Annie's six or seven days in New York, and my day and a half, we were borrowing a co-op apartment owned by a friend of Annie's who worked for the UN. The friend was currently doing good works in Darfur, and we had the run of the place. The address placed the co-op in Hudson Heights at the very top of Manhattan. Go any further north and you'd soon be off the island and into plain old New York State. The good news was that from our remote location, it was a straight run on the M4 to Columbia University.

"We could take a cab," I said.

"No cab," Annie said. "I don't want to rush things."

"You've seemed remarkably calm the last twenty-four hours."

"Even serene?" Annie asked. "Would you say I've been serene?"

I nodded. "Serene is *le mot juste*."

"I think it's the preparation I've done. Memorizing my speech. Going over it dozens of times. I've got what I'm going to say to the audience under control."

"The heebie-jeebies have vanished?"

"Let's say they're in abeyance."

The M4 bus came, and we got on it.

"Jerome wants to take us to dinner afterwards," I said to Annie. Not many people were riding the bus at that hour, and we had good seats. "That okay by you?"

"Flame's coming too?"

"He'll join us later," I said, "when he's done for the night in the recording studio."

"Hanging with those guys seems like a nice way to come down after the speech."

"You know what I was thinking?"

"That I could talk to Flame about himself and his movie, and bank the material for an article I'd write when the movie actually gets made."

I smiled at Annie. "No moss grows under this girl's feet."

Annie's elbow jabbed me in the ribs.

We got off the bus at 116th Street and stepped into the middle of the great university. Architecturally speaking, Columbia's buildings made a hodgepodge. Most were done in high Gothic. One was state-of-the-art modern. The latter turned out to be the law school. There were marble statues scattered among the buildings and many sculpted archways. Most buildings were worn by age but still regal, even in some cases authentically majestic.

The address for the Miller Theater placed it on Broadway. The theatre was three storeys high, built of dark cement blocks, and squeezed on either side by nondescript apartment houses. The Miller wasn't much to look at from the outside, but when Annie and I stepped inside, we arrived in a small gem of a space. The orchestra level seated about five hundred people, and a steep balcony took in another couple of hundred. The theatre's feel was elegant and intimate.

A small crowd of editors, publishers, and sales people from Columbia's book department surrounded Annie the minute we came through the Miller's front door. I slipped past the throng, and pushed open a door to the auditorium. Jerome was already there, a large presence in the front row.

"Very classy, this is, man," he said to me. "In the record business, we launch a new disc, it's usually in a smelly nightclub. We serve a lotta drinks, and people sneak some weed in the alley out back."

"In here today," I said, "Annie's speech rates top consideration."

"Sorta the same as at record launches, except with them, all the speakers are drunk or stoned. They talk too damn long."

"Annie's sober," I said, "and she's timed the speech for twelve minutes."

"They gonna sell books today, man?" Jerome asked. "That the etiquette? Or they give them away, one to a customer? Something like that?"

"Strictly for sale, Jerome. Book launches are where a lot of authors move more books than at any other time. Annie'll throw in an autograph for free."

"I'm getting four books, man, and I need them all signed."

By five o'clock, there were about three hundred people in the seats. Annie arrived on stage with a young man and a middle-aged woman. The woman was her Columbia editor. The guy stepped to the microphone with a big grin on his face. He said he was the president of Columbia's book division. The young president told the audience Annie was a Toronto movie critic, and she'd written his favourite book of the season. That drew a big round of applause.

Annie took her place at the mic. She had on one of the outfits she bought for the book tour — a black suit, a beautifully tailored jacket and skirt. The jacket was cut low in the bodice, and the skirt fell to just above the knee. The combination did the job of looking simultaneously chaste and sexy as hell. Annie gave the crowd her million watt smile, and began the speech.

"Courage is not a quality that comes first to mind in describing an actor famous for his double takes," Annie said, "but Edward Everett Horton was a courageous man."

Where the courage came in, Annie said, was him being gay but sticking it out through a long career, all the while knowing somebody might out him and blackball him from the business. Horton was hardly alone as a gay guy in film, of course. Annie described the lives of gay actors like Eric Blore, Franklin Pangborn, and Clifton Webb and gay directors like George Cukor and Edmund Goulding. There were gays in the makeup departments and in set design and costumes, too. All of these people looked out for one another in Hollywood. But of the gay actors, of all the gays in front of the camera, no one flourished as grandly as Edward Everett. He wasn't just a supporting actor; in most of the movies through his prime decades, he played the sidekick to the lead, giving him plenty of space to strut his stuff. He held his own with everybody, often as second banana to the incomparable Fred Astaire.

Annie broke down Edward Everett's talent, and spent the last minutes of her speech analyzing his finesse with double takes, which frequently morphed into triple takes and even quadruples. By way of illustration, she referred to a scene from a 1937 Astaire–Ginger Rogers movie called *Shall We Dance*. In the particular scene, Horton arrives at a New York hotel where he's met by the establishment's manager, played by Eric Blore. The two characters introduce themselves to one another, becoming instantly embroiled in a case of misidentification. Horton is the one who does most of the misidentifying, and as the truth of his errors is exposed to him, though he is never going to admit to so much as a tiny faux pas, his face registers dawning realization in a double take, followed by a hint of a triple take and finally a climaxing quadruple take. It was all accomplished in a matter of a few brilliant seconds, and as Annie B. Cooke on the stage of the Miller Theater did her impersonation of Edward Everett in the scene, her beautiful face going all rubbery in the Horton manner, her reworking of the comic actor's catalogue of embellished takes brought the house down. Nobody had seen loveliness and comedy in such a winning combination for such a long time. The audience went bananas.

CHAPTER TWENTY

Annie and I were sitting with Jerome at a table against the wall in a basement club in SoHo called Right Now. It was just past eleven. We'd had dinner at an Italian restaurant a couple of blocks away, near the Holland Tunnel. Then we walked to the club for our rendezvous with Flame. Jerome told Annie and me that Right Now was the current trendy spot for the hip hop crowd.

"How many books did I sell tonight?" Annie asked, not for the first time.

"Three hundred and twenty-four," Jerome and I said in unison.

"Just making sure you guys were on your toes," Annie said.

She was beginning to come down from the stratosphere she'd been flying in after the triumph at the Miller Theater. She was tired, but still raced up on adrenalin and high spirits.

A waitress with a blonde bob and a black miniskirt took our orders. Annie, scaling back, asked for soda water. Jerome and I ordered Budweisers.

"Isn't that cousinQu in the crowd over there?" Annie said, waving her hand in the general direction of an area where five or six tables were pushed together to accommodate about twenty-five people. "The guy with no shirt and the pants riding way below his hips?"

"You know about cousinQu?" Jerome said to Annie. Jerome still hadn't got over the thrill of meeting Annie.

"Annie studies at Loblaw's," I said.

"What's that, man, a website?"

"His table, cousinQu's," Annie said, "it looks like they're unhappy with the people at the table on the other side of the room. See what I mean, a lot of rude gestures going back and forth?"

"That's Big Mose over there," Jerome said, talking about another table as crowded as cousinQu's. "Bad blood between those two boys over dAruba."

"Do I need to know all this?" I asked.

"I read about what's happening," Annie said to me. "CousinQu and Big Mose are two major rappers, both in love with dAruba. So, right now, in front of us, we have the two rivals in the same room, their entourages gathered round. It's like a rap summit at the club where all the rap greats congregate. Who's going to win dAruba, the queen of hip hop? Crang, sweetie, we're present at a moment in pop cultural history."

"Just answer one question," I said. "What are they drinking? You'll notice it's dozens of the same bottles at both tables, those opaque ones, kind of metallic looking, got an emblem on them, an ace of spades, it looks like."

"That there's Armand de Brignac Brut Gold champagne," Jerome said. "Ace of Spades is what the rappers call it. Runs a thousand bucks a bottle in a club like this."

"Ever since Jay-Z put Ace of Spades in his song 'Show Me What You Got,' it's been *the* drink," Annie said. "People quit Cristal and started drinking the new stuff."

"Isn't this getting silly?" I said.

"History, Crang," Annie said. "Didn't I just say that?"

"Where does Flame fit in this?" I asked Jerome. "Has he got a stand on dAruba? What's he think about Ace of Spades?"

"He doesn't drink much of anything, man," Jerome said. "But that Ace of Spades, he's got bottles of the stuff in his mother's nice cool basement. Rap people are always giving one another gifts of Ace of Spades. Flame been saving his."

"I'm getting the impression of a cautious person. That about right?

"Ask Flame himself whatever you want to know, man," Jerome said, turning toward the rear of the club. "There he is over by the door. He always comes slipping in the back way."

Flame was shorter than I expected, about five-nine. His head seemed a little too big for his body, but the head size gave an effect of strength and command. His skin colour was what was once called café au lait. Maybe that was still the accepted description. Flame was a handsome guy, and as advertised, he had the Cary Grant cleft in the chin. His body was of the lean and athletic type, and he wore much more conventional clothes than the two other big shots of rap in the room. Flame had on a loose olive shirt, buttoned up all the way to the neck, medium brown, pleated trousers, and dark brown, all-weather loafers.

Flame walked to Big Mose's table. Big Mose rose to greet him, and the two guys hugged one another and chatted for a couple of minutes. That done, Flame strolled across the room to cousinQu's table and went through the same routine. CousinQu's pants slid down another inch into very dangerous territory.

At our table, Flame shook hands all round, beginning with Annie. Up close, he seemed even more of a star-quality kind of guy. He sat in the empty chair next to mine.

"An old recording of yours I'm curious about," I said to Flame once we'd settled in together.

"I'll help if I can," he said.

"A song that seems out of sync with the rest of your work."

Flame smiled. "'Lush Life,' I'm betting."

"How old were you when you discovered the song? And why?"

"Age was the point," he said. "I was seventeen at Harbord Collegiate. I got to be buddies with a guy who was big on jazz. He played me somebody's record of 'Lush Life,' and he said the guy whose song it was, he wrote both the melody and the lyrics when he was eighteen. I thought, *Whoa, eighteen?* So I taught myself the song and made a video of it just to see if some of that might rub off on me."

"You wanted a little Billy Strayhorn in your music?"

"Strayhorn, right, I forgot his name."

"I don't hear much of him in your own songs of today."

"It was the idea of him that influenced me," Flame said. "A guy only eighteen could write like that? Maybe I could too. Not write exactly his kind of music, but write music I was serious about. You follow me?"

I wanted to push Flame further on the subject of Billy Strayhorn, but an escalation in the racket coming from the other tables drew our table's attention.

"What's going down with those two?" Jerome said to Flame, nodding in the general direction of cousinQu, then of Big Mose. "They gonna get nasty?"

Flame looked at his watch. "I give it another half hour."

"Then what?" Annie asked.

"They'll probably start throwing bottles at one another."

"Full or empty?" I said.

Flame shrugged. "I'd say whatever each person happens to pick up."

"Are you serious?" I said. "At a thousand bucks a pop, they're going to toss champagne around?"

"People, at a certain level, they stop thinking about the cash side of things," Flame said. "There's just so much available money, you get what I'm saying, it isn't even a factor."

"But wait a second," I said. "Only one guy at each table actually earns the big dough. All the other people, apart from Big Mose and cousinQu, are just guys in the entourage. They do chores, right? Drive the cars and pour the champagne? But essentially they're hangers-on?"

"It's all part of the mystique," Flame said. "Money, bodyguards, entourages, expensive cars. Their fans expect it of guys like Big Mose and cousinQu."

"But not of you?"

Flame laughed. "If I showed up with a dozen guys opening car doors for me, fetching me some Ace of Spades, my fans would consider it a betrayal."

"That was your strategy from the beginning?"

"Not mine, Mr. Crang," Flame said, bending a little closer to me. "It's all Mr. Carnale. He's the one who shaped my image." Flame hesitated for a moment. "That sounds pompous, right? But it's true, the part about Mr. Carnale."

The waitress with the blonde bob reappeared. Flame asked for a cup of coffee. Nobody else wanted anything more. Annie and Jerome were laying plans for Jerome to drive Annie around the city to her book promotion interviews over the next few days. Otherwise, the publishing people at Columbia were leaving the transportation arrangements to Annie and whatever cabs she could flag down.

"It was Roger's plan that you'd be the rapper on the tight budget?" I said to Flame. "Give the appearance of not being a spendthrift?"

"That's no appearance, Mr. Crang," Flame said. "That's the reality. Mr. Carnale, he's kept me on an allowance from day one."

"No penthouse in Manhattan, cottage in Muskoka, those kinds of addresses?"

"I've spent big just once, comparatively speaking," Flame said, "I bought my mother a house near Dundas and Bathurst back home. It's close to our old apartment in the projects where I grew up, close to Mum's friends from when she started in nursing. But it's a nice old house."

"Where's your own principal domicile?"

"I got a room in my mother's house. The rest of the time down here in New York, I live in a hotel a few blocks from here. Nice funky place, like the Chelsea used to be, so I'm told."

"That sounds modest," I said. "What's happening to the millions I assume you bank with concerts and videos and the rest?"

"Mr. Carnale keeps me invested," Flame said. "I get quarterly statements, shows where my money is. Steady growth, the arrow pointing up in every statement."

"The Carnale long-term idea is when guys like cousinQu over there and Big Mose eventually lose their fans or go out of style," I said, "they'll discover their money's all disappeared on entourages and Ace of Spades. You, on the other hand, will have investments, not to mention a movie career. That's your profit curve?"

"Jerome told me he filled you in on me and the movie," Flame said.

Even though the club's din put us all in the market for hearing aids, he dropped to *sotto voce* when he mentioned his movie. Straining to listen to him, I made out what he was saying mostly in fragments.

"And Annie too," I said, close to shouting.

"I appreciate the discretion from both of you," Flame said. "And whatever it is you're doing about this Reverend who's running the blackmail thing, I'm grateful for that too."

"You have any idea how the Reverend got his hands on the song lyrics?"

Flame shook his head. "Those sheets of paper were always in either my mother's apartment or her house depending on the year. Mum's a saver. Everything that concerns me, school report cards, newspaper reviews, all of that, she hangs on to the paper stuff. Put it all on shelves at the house the last few years. I suppose anybody who came through our place could have messed around in my things. Taken what they wanted."

"Wouldn't that be a time-consuming chore for anyone, going on a hunt through years of material to find the song lyrics we're talking about?"

"Not necessarily," Flame said. "My mother's an organizer as well as a saver. She's got all the papers arranged chronologically, year by year, different files for each year. All a person would have to know is what year he's looking for. Start from there, and it's a quick process."

"Any suspects come to mind?" I said. "A person with a motive for thieving?"

"I hate to name a name," Flame said. "It would probably have to be somebody I regarded as a friend."

"Not a nice dilemma."

"Could be a musician I worked with or anybody else who came over to rehearse with me. Lots of people visited at my place for different reasons. Music or business or a media interview or just socializing."

Jerome interrupted Flame.

"Heads up, everybody," he said.

"What's going down, man?" Flame asked.

"The major thing that happened," Jerome said, "Big Mose sent the blonde waitress to cousinQu's table with a bottle of Ace of Spades and a note. See that over there — cousinQu's still reading the damn note."

"Might be a clothing tip," I said. "Big Mose is warning cousinQu to pull up his pants."

"Likely it's something about dAruba," Flame said. "Mose is telling cousinQu that dAruba may be the love of cousinQu's life, but she'd rather have sex with Mose."

"That'd get the man going," Jerome said.

"I beg to differ," I said. "Shouldn't it get us going? Vamoose out of here before the bottles start flying?"

Everybody at our table was looking over at cousinQu. He held the paper close to his eyes, and he was staring at it, his face more or less a blank.

"Man looks like he's gonna blow his top any minute now," Jerome said.

"The concentration he's needing to absorb the damn note," I said, "it might be the Gettysburg address written on there."

"Okay, people," Flame said. "The back door."

Flame went around the table and held Annie's chair while she stood up. He offered her his arm, and the two of them led

Jerome and me on a path through the tables, Jerome bringing up the rear.

We had just passed one end of Big Mose's table on a beeline for the back door when a bottle crashed into the wall at the other end of the table.

I stopped to take a look. The bottle that hit the wall must have been the one Big Mose sent with the note.

"My god, Jerome," I said, "that bottle was full!"

Jerome pushed me in the back. "Keep moving, man," he said. "Next bottle's liable to hit you in the head."

"Think of the wasted bubbly," I said.

Jerome gave me another shove. This time, I went where I was shoved.

The four of us headed out the club's back entrance, but that didn't take us into the outdoors. We were in a long, dimly lit subterranean passageway. Flame, our leader, knew where our destination lay. We followed him through the gloom to a flight of stairs. Up we went, then a quick left turn through another door. That put us in a back alley half a block removed from Right Now. The air felt fresh and invigorating after the club's muggy atmosphere.

"Thanks, guys," Annie said to Flame and Jerome, "never a dull moment in your company."

Jerome left the alley to find a cab for Annie and me.

"I expect we'll be getting together some time soon," Annie said to Flame.

"Count on it," Flame said. He kissed Annie on both cheeks.

Jerome came back with a yellow checkerboard cab.

"I'll pick you up at ten in the morning," Jerome said to Annie. "Your apartment."

"Ten o'clock?" I said. "Jeez, I'll be landing in Toronto about then."

Annie slipped her arm in mine. "In that case, you'll need a little shut-eye, sweetie."

She and I got in the cab for the long ride uptown.

CHAPTER TWENTY-ONE

My plane was an hour late getting in to Billy Bishop. I took a cab to my office, and told the driver to wait while I picked up a couple of items. One was the affidavit I wanted Reverend Douglas to sign, and the other was the copy of the lyrics I freed up from the Reverend's desk drawer. I was thinking about using the copy to pressure the Reverend into telling me how he, of all unikely people, got his hands on the damn things in the first place.

I felt tired, hungry, and irritable, but I had enough wit to direct the cab driver on a route that led us through streets behind Heaven's Philosophers. Steer clear of St. Clair, I thought. Cut down on the chances of getting spotted by Squeaky Fallis's crowd. Play sneaky the way the Reverend asked me to.

The cab driver let me out half a block up the street back of the church parking lot. I walked the rest of the way, carrying a crisp, sealed, brown envelope with the affidavit inside. The swiped copy of the song lyrics were tucked in my jacket pocket.

The church parking lot was empty of cars. Maybe Squeaky and his guys were late to their weekly social gathering. I walked along the alley in back of the church, and using one of the keys the Reverend had given me, I opened the door into the passage with the hidden ladder. So far, everything was proceeding smoothly.

Too bad I looked on myself at that moment as a world-class ass. Skulking in a narrow passage and climbing a ladder two storeys high seemed an embarrassment. Maybe I should charge my client extra to cover the humiliation factor.

I started climbing. After a few steps, it began to feel a little more like fun. I stepped up the rungs in steady form and with no apparent danger to my cardiac system, arriving soon enough at a tiny platform next to the door into the church's auditorium.

I got out the Reverend's second key, and fiddled it into the door's keyhole. The key turned easily, and I gave the door a shove. As it opened, I got tangled in the curtain that covered the door from the inside. I'd forgotten about the curtain. It was heavy, and I thrashed around with the thing for a few seconds. When I pushed past it, I faced two men who were looking at me with expressions that went beyond hostile.

Both men held guns in their hands. The guns were zeroing in on my chest.

One guy was wearing a grey windbreaker, and the other was in a Toronto policeman's uniform.

The two were shouting at me to hold my hands over my head. I hated the shouting. Cops always shouted. They shouted on TV crime shows, and they shouted in real life. I raised my arms.

The cop in the windbreaker was someone I recognized. His name was Wally Crawford, and he'd been in the Homicide Squad for almost as long as I'd been a criminal lawyer. He and I had faced one another in court a dozen times over the years, me asking him questions on cross-examination, him dancing around the answers.

"Who's dead, Wally?" I asked, my hands still in the air.

"How do you know somebody's dead?" the uniformed cop shouted. "Answer me! How do you know? Did you do it?"

"Cool it, Gordie," Wally said to the uniformed cop. Wally put his own gun back in its shoulder holster under his grey windbreaker. Still speaking to the uniformed cop, Wally nodded toward me. "This guy's name is Crang," he said, "and he knows I'm in Homicide."

"So what?!" Gordie shouted. He was still aiming his gun at my abdomen.

"So it's logical for Crang to conclude somebody's dead," Wally said.

"Wally," I said, my hands still in the air, "could you tell Wyatt Earp to down weapons please?"

"Gordie," Wally said, "do like Mr. Crang asks."

Gordie complied, but he didn't look happy about it.

"Is this a professional visit, Crang?" Wally said to me. "And what the hell kind of way is that to get in the building?"

"It's the screwball route the man I have an appointment with told me to take," I said. "The man's name is Reverend Alton Douglas, and I hope to hell you're not going to tell me he's the one who's dead."

"Hold on, Crang, I hope you're not the type to go all weepy on me," Wally said.

"It is the Reverend who's bought it," I said.

Wally looked down at the floor, then up at me. "He was killed in his office sometime last night. Sorry, Crang, it looks like you lost yourself a client."

"If you think I'm here on behalf of a client, you're right," I said. "But the Reverend, dead or alive, isn't the client."

Wally took a moment to process what I'd said. He gestured me to sit in the back row of the auditorium's seats. It was the same spot where the Reverend and I had our sit-down three days earlier. Wally plunked himself beside me. Gordie, the uniformed guy, hovered.

"You came here to see this guy Douglas?" Wally said. Wally wore a bushy moustache going a little grey. He had a large gut and a sharp brain. "I suppose your next line is going to be something about client confidentiality preventing you from telling me what the meeting was about?"

"That's my line, Wally," I said. "But if we keep things between the two of us, I'll take a big chance and tell you my client's name."

Wally turned to the uniformed cop. "Gordie, see if you can check out when the doctors are going to do an autopsy on our body."

Gordie looked offended, but he left on his assigned errand.

"Is it going to help me, knowing who your client is?" Wally said to me.

"You ever heard of a hip hop singer named Flame?"

Wally gave me a wide smile. "I got two teenage daughters. So I'll tell you how well I know Flame. He's the guy I hear night and day on the girls' sound systems. I see posters of him all over their bedroom walls. Last week, I took them to the ACC and listened to goddamn Flame for a couple of hours. Have I *heard* of him?"

"You're practically a fan."

"I hate to admit it, the guy's not bad," Wally said. "He's your client for real?"

"Spent last night with him at Right Now in New York City."

"Jesus, Crang," Wally said. "I tell this to my girls, I'll be their hero for at least a half hour."

"That's only two degrees of separation between Flame and their dad."

"Okay," Wally said, sounding like he was getting down to business, "you had an appointment with the deceased Alton Douglas for today?"

"I talked to him on Sunday after he conducted his afternoon service in this room where you and I are sitting right now," I said. "After the service, we went into his office back there, and made the arrangement to meet up today."

"The guy was an actual minister?" Wally said. "Gave sermons, a few hymns, the whole nine yards?"

"The content of the sermons and the type of music, both of those you might not have recognized from any church service you've been to in your life," I said. "But, yeah, essentially the Reverend Douglas was close enough to legitimate."

Gordie, the uniformed cop, returned. "Autopsy's not till tomorrow," he said to Wally. "They'll let you know the results soon as possible."

Wally said thanks, and the cop resumed his hovering duties.

"What about this appointment you say you had today?" Wally said to me. "That's the goods?"

I held up the envelope. "I got an affidavit the Reverend was going to sign," I said. "That was the purpose of the meeting. He'd sign the thing, and the small dealings between my client and him would be wrapped up."

"You got anything besides your word that says it was going to happen, this meeting that the Reverend now can't keep with you?"

"That piece of furniture over there," I said, pointing to the Reverend's desk against the back of the auditorium. "If you've searched it, you'll have found the Reverend's daybook. I saw him ink me in for one o'clock today."

"Gordie," Wally said to the guy in uniform, "what's the report on the victim's desk?"

Gordie blushed pink. "I don't believe we've got to the desk yet," he said, "sir."

"Anybody even noticed the goddamn desk before now?"

"Sir!" Gordie said. He made a smart about turn and set off on another chore.

Wally walked over to the desk.

"Which drawer?" he asked me.

"Middle."

Wally put on a pair of latex gloves from his windbreaker pocket, and slid open the middle drawer.

"*Voila*!" he said, lifting the Reverend's daybook from the drawer.

Wally flipped through the pages until he stopped, presumably at the page recording the Reverend's plans for today.

"Another *voila!*" Wally said. "You're down for one o'clock on this day's date."

"In ink?"

"Crang, you're coming up roses."

"Okay, if you don't mind, Wally, it's my turn to ask questions," I said. "How did the Reverend get killed?"

"A smack on the side of the head," Wally said.

"The proverbial blunt instrument?"

"Roughly speaking, yeah."

"Baseball bat, a billy, something like that?"

"But not a baseball bat or a billy or anything resembling either one."

"How can you tell?"

"The medical officer who attended here an hour ago, very sharp guy I've worked with on a bunch of cases, he said the wound was done by a weapon with edges. That's on the basis of his eyeballing the victim. It could have been a metal instrument, but whatever it was, it was something that left straight lines in the Reverend's skull. This MO said he'd let me know more detail later, him or somebody else on Grenville."

Grenville Street, in midtown, a couple of blocks from police headquarters, was home to medical and technical personnel who specialized in DNA, fingerprints, and other forensic solutions of mysteries.

"Who found the body?" I said.

"Kid in the little coffee shop downstairs," Wally said. "He told us he came up here around nine this morning. It was his routine, fetching Douglas his morning coffee. Instead, he found the man dead."

"Here's a tip for free, Wally," I said. "Take a look at the eleven guys who run their businesses out of here. You and your people might recognize a few names."

"These eleven guys are in illegal enterprises?"

"Such genteel phrasing, Wally."

"With the eleven of them," Wally said, "what's the fastest way I can find names?"

"You notice a computer on the conference table in the office?"

Wally thought about it. "Two computers in there, one on the desk, the other on the big table. It was the late Reverend's office, right? So both are his computers?"

"More complicated than that," I said. "The Reverend ran the church as a kind of front for the gang of eleven, but they didn't let him sit in on their meetings. That's why he had the other desk out here. It's where he retired to at meeting time."

"Crang," Wally said, giving me a beady-eyed look, "you know a hell of a lot for a guy representing a rap singer in what you call small dealings."

I shrugged, something I was getting not bad at. "I like to give my clients thorough representation. It keeps them coming back for more."

Wally turned and headed for the Reverend's former inner office. I followed, then hesitated.

"The deceased's no longer with us?" I asked. "By which I mean, not still lying on the floor in there?"

"Ought to be laid out on a slab downtown right about now."

I went into the office a couple of paces back of Wally. The first things I noticed were the sheets of paper scattered on the floor behind the desk. The desk's left hand drawer, which was locked the last time I saw it, hung open. It wasn't hard to reason what must have happened. The Reverend and his visitor got into a squabble over the whereabouts of the sheets with Flame's scurrilous song lyrics on them. The Reverend opened the desk to show the visitor the lyrics hidden in the stack of copy paper. When he couldn't find the sheets with the lyrics, either he or the visitor scattered the paper in a fit of pique. Not long after that, if I my reasoning was correct, the visitor whacked the Reverend with a weapon that was built on straight lines.

"The pieces of paper on the floor," I said to Wally, "they all blank?"

"Far as I know," Wally said. "Why do you ask?"

"Just getting the whole picture in my mind."

"Don't forget to include in the picture some tiny traces of blood on the pieces of paper."

"I noticed."

The blood on the papers looked more rusty brown than red. The papers themselves were scattered across the rug behind the desk. Probably, I thought to myself, the Reverend was standing back of the desk when the killer whacked him. The spray of blood from the blow seemed to be confined to a small circumference, reaching only a couple of feet beyond the place behind the desk where the Reverend had taken up position. That was just before the other guy in the room let fly with his whack.

"One thing I should have told you," Wally said. "Don't move anything around in this room. Don't touch any of the stuff in here."

"The forensics people haven't finished?"

"Done as far as I can see," Wally said. "But with those guys, they're kind of fussy about what's a complete job and what isn't."

I told Wally I'd keep my hands to myself. While he looked over the computer on the conference table, I scanned the room for any telltale signs of my previous presence. Nothing looked like a giveaway, though I couldn't remember what I might have touched in the bathroom when I was concealing myself behind the black shower curtain.

"Any of the eleven names mean much to you?" Wally asked me.

"Squeaky Fallis is a guy I encountered on a fraud case," I said. "Aside from him, I'm only aware by second hand about shiftiness among the other ten."

"What kind of name is Squeaky?"

"An accurate kind once you've heard his voice," I said. "In the computer, you'll find he goes by Robert Fallis."

Wally was tapping on the computer's keys.

I walked over to the Reverend's desk chair, planning to sit in it.

"What'd I tell you, Crang?" Wally said. "About touching things in here?"

"Not even sitting down?"

"You got tired legs from climbing that ladder?"

I stood around for a few more useless minutes before I decided the chances were slim I'd pick up any fresh revelations from the scene of the crime.

"You mind if I leave now, Wally?" I said. "Preferably by the front door."

Wally turned. "Go ahead," he said. "But we're gonna talk again. To my way of thinking, you know too damn much about whatever's going on in this building."

"The result of intense study, Wally," I said. "All of it done on behalf of my client, and your girls' hero, the one and only Flame."

I went down to the lobby, which was busy with cops carrying out cop jobs. The coffee kid seemed to be doing good business with police customers. Neither of the other two shops had opened, and I saw no sign of anybody from the Squeaky Fallis crew. I pushed through the front door, and went looking for a cab.

CHAPTER TWENTY-TWO

At home, I made a tuna salad sandwich on twelve-grain bread, poured a glass of orange juice, and phoned Jerome. I needed to keep the Flame group notified of developments. The Reverend's murder was a hell of a development. But if Jerome was chauffeuring Annie to interviews around New York City, I didn't want her to get the idea from what I was about to tell Jerome that I might be under siege from different quarters. This was going to be a tricky conversation, and I hadn't thought it through. Maybe I should hang up before Jerome answered. I could start all over again after I came up with some tactics.

"Crang, my man, what's happening?" Jerome said on the phone.

Too late to revise my tactics, not that I had any tactics.

"Just reporting in, Jerome," I said. "There's been a significant turn of events up here."

"Lot going on down here too, man," Jerome said. I could hear the honks of car horns from his end. "And all's positive man. Capital P."

"With Annie, you mean?"

"She's got news for you, man, gonna blow your doors off."

"Annie's right there beside you, wherever you are?"

"Parked in Queen's, man," Jerome said. "Your girl's inside

a studio across the street doing somebody's afternoon radio show."

"Jerome, be careful what you do with the information I'm about to give you."

"Don't tell Annie, that what you mean?"

"Somebody murdered the Reverend Alton Douglas."

"Sheesh, man," Jerome said. Then he went silent, no doubt mulling over the implications of the Reverend's demise. "Isn't that a good thing?" Jerome said. "Good except for the poor man's near and dear. I'm supposin' he's got some of those."

"There are complications, Jerome."

"The matter of who killed the man, that's one of them?"

"At the moment," I said, "the police haven't a clue."

"The way you're talking, *literally* they don't have a clue, or that's just a figure of speech you're using?"

"The one clue they may think they have is my arrival on the murder scene in an unorthodox fashion."

"Whoa there, Crang," Jerome said. "Police got you connected to the murder? Man, that's some serious shit."

"Two things I want from you, Jerome. Don't say a word to Annie about this part of our conversation. She'll worry at a time when she needs a clear head."

"What's the other thing?"

"Get the news to Carnale. Tell him somebody killed the Reverend at Heaven's Philosophers last night. The extortion plan died with the Reverend."

"What about the song sheets?"

"No problem there either."

"That's what I tell Carnale?" Jerome said. "'No problem'?"

"Let him know he should phone me if he wants more of the inside dope."

"You got nothing personal to do with the Reverend's murder, am I right to assume that, man? Just ease my mind. You definitely don't seem the murdering type."

"Thanks for the vote of confidence, Jerome."

"What about our Miss Annie, the new star of New York City?" Jerome said. "You got a message for her?"

"Tell her I love her to pieces."

"To pieces?"

"That'll do it."

"If you say so, man," Jerome said.

He hung up, and I got back to my tuna salad sandwich.

CHAPTER TWENTY-THREE

Maury phoned at the wrong time. The sun was just beginning to fade over the horizon, and my thoughts were turning to the first martini of the day. I answered the call anyway.

"Get your ass out to the Kennedy subway station," Maury said.

"This is another command performance for Jackie Gabriel?"

"He says he needs to see you, a life or death thing."

"I got the impression last time that Jackie's already told me everything he knows about Heaven's Philosophers."

"Another guy'll be there besides Jackie."

"Somebody who might get my wheels turning?"

"Georgie's the other guy," Maury said.

Right away I was interested. This was a chance to talk to one of the eleven Heaven's Philosopher people on more or less neutral grounds. To me, neutral meant any place where Squeaky Fallis wasn't within shouting distance.

"Also, you probably know this, somebody murdered the Reverend," Maury said. "Jackie's got his shorts in a knot about what it might mean for Georgie."

"Is Georgie given to violence?"

"Maybe in a card game that goes south," Maury said. "Otherwise, he's a very laid back kind of guy."

"I'll see you in three quarters of an hour."

I hustled up to the Spadina subway station, and was right on time for Maury and me to again penetrate the deepest northeast suburbs. As before, Jackie's wife, Irene, met us at the door. But the note of grace she showed on our first visit was somewhere under wraps. This time, Irene invited us in with an abrupt gesture. The expression on her face was sour.

In the living room, there wasn't a cup of tea in sight. Jackie and his large son were sitting in armchairs, both with glasses holding an amber coloured liquid and a lot of ice cubes.

Georgie Gabriel was as John Candy–like as I recalled from my glimpse of him in the church parking lot a few days earlier. But for a guy with such a bulging midsection, he managed to look natty in a tan-coloured summer suit. With the suit, he wore a navy blue shirt and a red-and-white striped tie. He gave me a sweet smile, and we shook hands.

"You want a drink, Crang?" Jackie said.

"Vodka on the rocks would be nice."

"In this house, we drink scotch," Jackie said. "Or my wife can fix you a coffee."

"Or tea," Irene said, sounding disgruntled. "Which is what you especially should be drinking, Jackie."

"This is a special occasion," Jackie said.

"That's always your excuse when you want a drink," Irene said.

"I'll have a scotch," I said.

"Your son possibly going to jail?" Jackie said to his wife. "That ain't a special occasion?"

"Scotch for me, too," Maury said.

Irene fired a dirty look at her husband before she left to fetch the drinks.

I turned to Georgie. "What do you think you might be going to jail for?" I asked.

"It's Pop who figures I'm on the way to the clink," Georgie said. "That's somewhere I've never been before, and the way I intend things to work out, I'm not gonna spend time in the place in the future either."

"Crang," Jackie said, "didn't I tell you that an outfit like the goddamn church was too big for its own britches? I said it was for sure gonna attract the cops' interest. And it damn well did."

"Heaven's Philosophers wasn't what got the police up to the place," Georgie said. "It was this thing with somebody killing Father Al."

"Where do you see me fitting into the picture?" I asked Jackie.

"Right beside Georgie. I want you for my son's goddamn lawyer."

"That's not possible, Jackie," I said.

Jackie looked like the stroke, the scotch, and the turndown he got from me were about to come together in one shock wave.

"Relax, Jackie," I said. "I can explain. Take a deep breath."

"The hell with the deep breath," Jackie said. "I'm taking a deep scotch."

He drained his glass down to the ice cubes. "Your excuse better be good," Jackie said to me.

I said, "I already have connections to the Reverend that make it improper, if not illegal, for me to represent anybody in the case involving his murder. I might even be called as a witness at the trial if a charge gets laid."

Irene returned to the living room carrying drinks for Maury and me.

I took a sip from mine, the first scotch I'd had in something like a decade. It tasted alien and thrilling.

"The murder case isn't what Georgie needs to worry about anyway," I said, directing my remarks to Jackie. "But I agree he needs a lawyer on call. The cops, as a kind of by-product of the murder investigation, they could decide to take a look at whatever hanky-panky Georgie and the other guys at Heaven's Philosophers have been up to. The gambling, the stock market manipulations, all the scams they've pulled off."

"So you'll be Georgie's mouthpiece on this stuff?" Jackie said.

"I'll get Georgie representation from a colleague of mine," I said. "His name is Philip Goldenberg, better known among his admirers as Fox."

"He's as good as you?" Jackie said.

"Better," Maury said.

"Ah, the voice of experience speaks," I said.

Part of me was kidding. The other part was wondering if Maury was pissed off at me. Was it all about my recent connection to his girlfriend, Sal? If that was the problem, it would mean Sal had revealed her secret porn life to Maury sometime in the last twenty-four hours. I had no way of knowing, though it seemed unlikely Sal had confessed. Damn, learning a deep, dark secret meant I had to carry around the baggage that the secret dragged in with it.

"Good to hear, Maury," Jackie said. "Very reassuring."

"You'll be impressed with Fox, Jackie," I said. "Both you and Georgie."

I sipped some more scotch, and directed a question to Georgie.

"Have I got it right, you're the one who introduced the man you still call Father Al to Heaven's Philosophers?"

Georgie shifted his shoulders a little. "Father Al deserved a break," he said. "And I knew he needed a job."

"Once you set up the Reverend at the place on St. Clair, did he become pals with Squeaky and the rest of them?"

"Not with Squeaky." Georgie laughed. "Nobody's an actual pal with Squeaky. Not me anyway."

"How about the others?"

"Everybody appreciated Father Al being around as kind of the visible guy at the church. You've probably heard all this, about him making the whole place look respectable."

I nodded. "But what I'm wondering, did anybody in particular hang with the Reverend?"

"None of us went to his Sunday services, if that's what you mean. Mostly what it was, we'd see him around the building and say, hey, Reverend Al, how's it going?"

"Nobody you know of went for a drink with him? A coffee downstairs maybe?"

"Like who?"

"That's what I want you to tell me, Georgie," I said. "Ernie? What about him? Did he in particular get along with the Reverend?"

"Ernie Weyburn?" Georgie said. "Nothing against Ernie, but he's not Father Al's type."

"What's Ernie's particular line of activity?"

"He's in what's called the protection game. He goes, for instance, to a contractor type of person working on something like a new subdivision up near Concord where there's a lot of building going on. Ernie tells the contractor he can guarantee there won't be any damage done at the subdivision on nights or weekends when nobody's around if the contractor pays a certain fee. The guy usually pays the fee."

"And if he doesn't?"

"Ernie sets a fire and burns down a couple of the half-built houses."

"Then the subdivision man comes up with the fee?"

"Probably has to add in a penalty for late payment."

"That was what Ernie has been doing on behalf of Heaven's Philosophers?"

"Plus," Georgie said, "he might handle muscle work for other people in our group if they need to straighten out somebody that's giving us any kind of trouble."

"Ernie's an enforcer?"

"Nobody at Heaven's Philosophers ever uses that word. But enforcer is probably accurate when you're talking about what Ernie does."

"Are there any other enforcers at Heaven's Philosophers?" I asked. "Maybe, for example, Frederic Chamblis? Also known as Freddie the Champ?"

Georgie let out a loud laugh. "Freddie the Champ. What a joke. The only guy who ever calls him that is Freddie himself."

"But he's an enforcer too?"

"I know a couple people in our group, they've used Freddie for muscle. He can be as mean as they come, and he's got the punch to back it up. But mostly he makes porn movies. He's always inviting the rest of us up to his house to watch the movies...."

Georgie stopped and looked across at his mother in the chair near the door. "Sorry, Ma," he said. "I only went to Freddie's movie nights the one time."

"That's not something your friend Father Al would have approved of," Irene said. "God rest his soul."

"Did the Reverend have any special connection to Freddie that you noticed?" I said to Georgie.

"Like, you mean did they have some special deal on the go?"

"Since I may not know what I'm talking about, your interpretation of my question sounds good enough."

"Then the answer's no," Georgie said. "Reverend Al probably felt about Freddie what a lot of us feel who are supposed to be his friends."

"Which is what?"

"That he's an asshole?"

"Georgie!" his mother said sharply.

"Sorry, Ma."

"Where we getting to in this conversation, Crang?" Jackie asked, sounding out of sorts. "I mean, what's the purpose?"

I wasn't going to tell Jackie or anyone else in the room that I thought I had moved an inch or two forward in my informal investigation into the Reverend's murder. My chat with Georgie had placed someone with a penchant for violence, namely Freddie the Champ, on the outer fringes of the Reverend's life. Was that worth following up? Maybe, but for now, I'd place my investigation into Freddie's career further down on my to-do list.

In the meantime, sitting in the Gabriel living room, I needed to wind things up with Jackie and his family, preferably on a friendly note. I owed Jackie that.

"Let's talk about what might lie ahead for Georgie and the other guys in Heaven's Philosophers," I said.

"Yeah," Jackie said. "But first, how come you call Georgie's lawyer Fox? He ain't Philip Goldenberg?"

"He's both, Jackie," I said. "But before I explain, why don't we get fresh beverages in front of us." I turned to Irene and gave her one of my most winning smiles. "I know I could use a nice cup of tea."

Irene beamed back at me.

"How about you, Jackie?" I said. "Herbal tea's great for the blood pressure."

"So I keep getting told," Jackie said.

"It could also be a good mood setter for what I can tell you about Fox, the guy who's going to take good care of Georgie."

"Tea for everyone?" Irene said, once again the gracious hostess.

It was the Gabriel family I wanted to get on side. The tea order seemed to be doing the job, and it didn't really matter for the moment that Maury was the only holdout.

He wanted another scotch.

CHAPTER TWENTY-FOUR

Next morning at the office, I told Gloria about the smashing of the coffee maker and the death of the Reverend.

"Our Reverend? Alton Douglas?"

"The very same."

"He's dead?

"As a doornail."

"I hope it was natural causes."

I shook my head. "Blunt force smack to the head."

"Definitely unnatural," Gloria said. "I wish it had been a heart attack or anything else that wouldn't bring some after-effects on you."

"On me?"

"Whoever killed him, they probably did it because they knew he was talking to you. So now …"

Gloria let the rest of the sentence trail off.

"Aren't you just spreading the good cheer," I said.

Gloria got the iPad and cellphone out of her bag and placed them on her side of the desk.

"Let's go at these things in order," she said.

"Good thinking," I said. "What have you got on this guy by the name of Frederic Chamblis?"

"If we're going at things in order, he isn't what comes first."

"Something's ahead of Freddie?"

"Coffee," Gloria said. "Be right back."

While Gloria went on the coffee run, I walked over to the window and studied the Matt Cohen Park. I checked up and down the park's length, short as it was, but there was no sign of the two girls with the great legs. Probably too early in the day. The food wagon on the sidewalk at the Bloor end was open for business. I forgot what it sold. Falafels? Foot-long hot dogs? Anything healthy? Rice and beans? I couldn't remember, and thinking about possible menus was making me unnaturally hungry for that time of day.

Gloria came back holding two cardboard cups of coffee from the Second Cup on Bloor. She handed me the smaller of the two, smaller but bigger than a cup I'd normally pour for myself. Gloria's was extra large.

She sat at the desk, sipped from her humungous coffee, and opened up her iPad. While she tapped keys and checked through new files, she asked me about Annie's adventures in New York.

"She just got asked to go on the *Ellen DeGeneres Show* next week," I said. "I was talking to her this morning. Out of the blue, Ellen invited her on."

"Wowie, first the *Charlie Rose Show*. Now *Ellen DeGeneres*."

"The girl is scaling the show-biz heights."

"You realize something, Crang," Gloria said. "Ellen broadcasts from Los Angeles?"

"Annie flies out there Sunday, does the show Tuesday, fits in some interviews on the coast and heads home."

"She'll sell a gazillion books."

"That's the possibility."

"Frederic Chamblis, right?" Gloria said getting back to her iPad screen. "I put together files for all the guys in the eleven."

"At the moment, I'm hot for Chamblis."

"Sometimes identified as Freddie the Champ."

"The identification is mostly by Freddie himself."

Gloria stopped typing and gave me a look that had a big question mark in it.

"Who might you have been talking to?" she asked.

"Georgie Gabriel."

"You're on to one of the other eleven even before you get my research? Are you trying to make me redundant?"

"Never," I said. "Tell me about Chamblis."

"He's got a record. One for assault sixteen years ago. Didn't do any time on it, but two years later, he went to the slammer for an aggravated assault. Since then, he's avoided the courts and presumably the cops."

"Doesn't mean he's given up the rough stuff."

"Means he's just got smarter."

"What about associations?" I said. "Any idea who Chamblis runs with?"

"You mean apart from the Squeaky Fallis people?"

"Apart from them, yeah."

"A bunch of hookers."

"Pardon?"

"Freddie's in the management end of show biz," Gloria said, a big smile on her face, pleased she'd surprised me. "But as far as I can make out, all his clients are girls who specialize in taking their clothes off."

"Requires a special talent on the girls' part."

"This is really interesting, and it's also gross and offensive in the extreme," Gloria said. The screen on her iPad filled with a video not unlike the one Sal Crosby showed me a few days earlier. Two pretty girls in white underwear on a white sofa, part of a set where everything else was likewise white, the curtains, the rugs, the whole works.

"Take a look at the girl on the right," Gloria said.

"Piles of black hair." I said. "Doesn't look like a wig. Brown eyes. Breasts not especially large but gorgeously shaped."

"I'd say you've got her fixed in your mind."

"It appears she's getting ready to remove her bra and thong."

"We don't need to hang around for that," Gloria said. "Just remember what she looks like. The name she goes by is Sissy Diamond. The producer of the movie happens to be the one and only Freddie the Champ."

"Why doesn't that surprise me?"

Gloria tapped some more keys, and the images of Sissy's porn video gave way to a series of Internet advertisements placed by women offering their bodies for hire in a variety of sexual activities, all described in lascivious detail. All the ads came with photographs of the women — wearing miniscule thongs in some cases, absolutely nothing in others.

"See these ads?" Gloria said.

"Prostitution in the digital age?"

"Exactly," Gloria said. "You'll notice the women look attractive enough but definitely a little used up."

"I can understand why," I said. "The services they're offering, that'll wear down any woman."

"Take for example the girl in the upper left corner."

I leaned closer to the screen. "Hey, it's Sissy Diamond. Or maybe her older sister."

"It's Sissy, but the photo was taken five years after the video."

"Sissy's had a breast job. Those things look like weapons."

"She's also got a lot of miles on her."

"The face, lordy" I said. "Woman's gone all gaunt. Maybe from drugs. Definitely, I'd say, from drugs."

"Poor thing."

Both of us took a moment to worry over Sissy's downward cycle.

"How did you do that?" I said to Gloria. "Trace Sissy's career curve this way?"

"Girls who want to work on the videos need to join the performers' union," she said. "ACTRA. Alliance of Canadian Cinema, Television and Radio Artists. I phoned the people at ACTRA and got the dope on Sissy. I found out that Freddie Chamblis came into the picture at every turn in the girl's performing life. He was the producer on her movies, her manager for everything she's ever done."

"Including the part where Sissy's a prostitute?" I said. "Bet you didn't get information on that from ACTRA."

Gloria shook her head. "But I phoned the number listed in Sissy's ad. Asked a few questions. Got passed along to a guy with a deep voice. I'm pretty sure the deep voice belonged to our man Freddie."

"The guy's a major league pimp?"

"My theory about Freddie," Gloria said, "he employs the fresh young girls for his high-end porn videos, and then when the girls age a little, begin to show signs of too many hours frolicking with guys under the camera's lights, he gives them a cosmetic fix-up and shuttles them into the call girl side of his operation. Fiendish, don't you think?"

"You got more examples than just Sissy?"

"I quit when I reached five girls total," Gloria said. "By then, it was getting too easy to mix and match. And too depressing."

"Fantastic work, Gloria."

"I also got Freddie with the deep voice on the line in some of my further explorations."

"You think he caught on to what you were up to?"

"I doubt it. He just seemed pissed off in general."

"Don't phone again," I said. "You've made your case as far as I'm concerned."

"So what have we got?" Gloria said. "A violent guy who runs strings of women. In my opinion, he needs to be kicked off the street. Am I right?"

"You're right," I said. "A source tells me Freddie lives in a mansion in the Beach. Does that square with your research?"

"The Beach isn't a mansion type of area," Gloria said, once more hitting her iPad's keys. "What does your so-called source say about that?"

"She says it's in a hilly neighbourhood with a lot of trees."

"What I say," Gloria stopped typing and directed me to the screen, "is Freddie the creep lives in Scarborough, and the house is nice but no mansion."

On her iPad, Gloria was showing me a shot of a three-storey detached house, all brick, a garage wide enough to accommodate three cars, no flowers but the lawn green, smooth, and boring.

"You find that on Google Maps?" I said.

Gloria nodded. "It's definitely Freddie's abode. But the other house you're speaking of, this so-called mansion in the Beach, Freddie could own it under a corporate name."

"The one in Scarborough, that's the only house listed in Freddie's name?"

"Absolutely," Gloria said. She paused and looked at me. "You're not doubting me, whether I got the Freddie residence right?"

"I'm doubting my other source," I said.

"Glad to hear it," Gloria said. "Is the other source super confidential?"

"Sal Banfield."

"Should I know the name?"

"Maury's girlfriend."

I told Gloria the entire story of Sal, Maury, Franny, the house in the Beach, porn videos, and Freddie the Champ.

Gloria put her elbows on the desk and dropped her head into her hands. She peered up at me.

"Crang, honey," she said, "you've got your work cut out for you."

"Get Sal out of Freddie's clutches."

"And the other girl," Gloria said. "Franny."

I devoted a couple of beats to thinking about Gloria's suggestion.

"Yeah, get Franny out, too," I said finally.

Gloria gave me a hug. If the hug was one of congratulations, I thought it was a lot premature.

CHAPTER TWENTY-FIVE

It was seven in the evening, and I was lying on top of the duvet on Annie's and my bed, doing my best not to think about Sal and Franny. Or about the Reverend's murder. I didn't have a plan, and if I worried too much about formulating one, I'd never come up with a solution. I needed to relax, and let the ideas flow naturally.

Annie had left five of the Jane Gardam novels on the floor on her side of the bed. Two were library books; the others were actual purchases. Annie got a big kick out of Gardam. Maybe I would too. I began to read the one titled *Old Filth*. It was set among a group of English lawyers decades earlier who took their legal talents to the Far East. The *Filth* in *Old Filth* was short form for this kind of English lawyer: Failed In London Try Hong Kong. One of the Hong Kong lawyers, a character called Edward Feathers, was known by the nickname Filth. Old Filth in his later years. The book was funny, clever, and beautifully written.

I read the book for a while then I dozed off.

My iPhone woke me.

"Hello," I said, woozily, not feeling organized enough to look at the screen and check who was calling.

"That you, man? It's Jerome."

"Nobody'd ever mistake your voice for Mickey Mouse's, Jerome."

"I catch you at a bad time, man?"

"Just musing over my next line of activity. Musing can be enervating, you know."

"Well, man, I can save you from some of that," Jerome said. "Your services are no longer required in the matter of Flame, who has ceased to be your client, effective forthwith."

"I'm fired?"

"Would you please submit your account."

"Forthwith?"

"Imagine so."

"Why do I see the fine hand of Roger Carnale in the language of my dismissal?"

"No doubt because he's the only person in the organization who hires and fires."

"There's that."

"In one way," Jerome said, "I can see the point in letting you go."

"Yeah," I said, "the guy I was hired to deal with is now permanently out of the picture."

"On the other hand, the picture ain't none too clear."

"Are you preparing to convey a particular message, Jerome?"

"This is something nobody's ever gonna authorize me to tell you, but since you and me and Annie are now good friends — don't you think so? — I'm gonna tell you anyway."

"Yeah, Jerome, I'd say the three of us have been through a lot together. A big-time book launch, a riot in a hip hop club. Events that bind a relationship. Not to mention you're chauffeuring my sweetie all over the Big Apple."

"The part about me not being authorized to inform you of something, you know what party I'm talking about who ain't gonna do the authorizing?"

"Our mutual superior, Roger Carnale," I said. "But the natural question that springs to mind: What is it Roger doesn't wish me to know?"

"There's another blackmailer doing the same dodge tried by the late Reverend."

I let out a long stream of breath I didn't realize I was holding in. "This person," I said, "wants money, and if he doesn't get it, he's apparently in possession of a copy of Flame's nasty song lyrics that he'll go public with?"

"That's what Mr. Carnale say to me."

"How much does he want, the alleged new extorter?"

"Eight million."

"Everything's the same as with the Reverend, dearly departed as he is?"

"Everything's the same, except one thing."

"I can't wait, Jerome?"

"He's been paid his money."

"Roger forked over the eight million?" I said. "Just like that, he caved?" My voice was rising in indignation. "No wonder he's fired me. He didn't want anybody stepping in the way."

"It's a confounding development, man," Jerome said. "That's why I'm spilling the beans, even though Mr. Carnale told me to go silent on you."

"Doesn't make sense, Jerome. None of this adds up. Where did the third set of song sheets come from? There were only supposed to be two of them. And why did Roger deliver instant payment? He made a major fuss over the Reverend's blackmail, but gets blown over like a house of cards on this second one."

"This is all late-breaking developments, you get that, man?"

"The Reverend's not been buried in the ground yet, as far as I know, and already a second extorter has made his move, and gone away with eight million of Flame's money."

"No time wasted, man," Jerome said. "Mr. Carnale only told me a couple hours ago about how it went down. By then, it was what they call a *fait accompli*."

"Is Flame aware he's just been suckered out of the eight million?"

"Mr. Carnale spoke to my boy Flame this afternoon. I don't believe the word 'suckered' came into the conversation, but Flame, you know, he believes whatever Mr. Carnale lays out for his consideration. The boy's always confident it's all gonna work out in his favour in the end."

"Sounds like you discussed this with Flame pretty thoroughly."

"For just long enough, man, a few minutes." Jerome said. "But let me get back to what Mr. Carnale asked me to tell you."

"That I go away quietly?"

"That's what it boils down to, man."

"My answer, in a nutshell, is I intend to find out who killed the Reverend and who squeezed Carnale for the eight million dollars this second time."

"You know I'll have to deliver the message about your intentions, what you're telling me, to Mr. Carnale?"

"If you do that, Jerome, Roger's going to know you're the one who revealed all to me."

"A lot of times, my big mouth gets me in trouble, man, but I'm gonna live with it this time 'round. Maybe something good'll come out of it. It's not fair on Flame, man, him losing eight million."

"Stir the pot," I said. "Go to it, Jerome."

When Jerome hung up, I went downstairs and made a martini. I had leftovers in the fridge, some takeout noodles with all the Vietnamese extras from a restaurant on Bloor. I sat at the dining room table, looking out at the darkening garden and thinking about the mess of the entire Flame affair. It seemed to me that a connection of some sort probably existed between the Reverend and the second extorter. The Reverend had tossed in the towel in his shot at taking Flame for the eight million. That cost him his life. Then the second guy assumed ownership of the blackmail operation, and scored a big win right out of the box. Ergo, the second guy carried more heft than the Reverend, the kind of heft that might even lead a man to kill somebody.

My bet was that the second guy was likely Freddie Chamblis. At the very least Freddie made a believable candidate for the role. He had an insider's track on events through his connection to Heaven's Philosophers. And killing, as in whacking the Reverend, wasn't beyond him. Chamblis had already established himself in my mind as an all-round nasty piece of work. Anybody who ran a porn and prostitution operation wouldn't draw the line at blackmail. Or at murder either.

I took the leftover noodles out of the fridge, decided against heating them, got a fork, and began to eat the noodles cold and straight from the container. They tasted delicious, aided by a second martini.

Freddie Chamblis was my choice for villain of the story. But how was I going to build my case against him?

Little by little. Piece by piece.

I'd go at this carefully but swiftly, starting next day.

CHAPTER TWENTY-SIX

The part of Palmerston Avenue I was pointed toward ran north from Dundas a couple of blocks west of Bathurst. It was a pleasant walk from my house to that part of lower Palmerston on a sweet, late-summer morning. I took a route by way of the back streets, slicing through a corner of Kensington Market. Only a few establishments had opened this early in the market's business day. A couple of Polish butchers and the Italian restaurant with the big picture windows were in business, but not the vintage clothing stores. Kensington Market had been peddling old clothes since long before anybody thought of labelling them vintage.

I had phoned Flame's mother first thing in the morning, and now, getting on for 10:30, I stood on the doorstep of her Palmerston Avenue home. It was semi-detached, and had a small open porch with room for three wicker chairs. The lower half of the two-storey house was made of reddish-brown brick, the upper half of wood, which was painted a merry shade of yellow. The wicker chairs on the porch had cushions covered in fabric with stripes of green, mauve, and deep blue, colours that reminded me of the back garden at home on Major.

The front door was opened by a slim woman with brown skin and a warm smile. She had an easy, natural beauty, telling me in one glance where Flame got his movie star–ready good looks. The woman was Alice Desmond. She pulled the door back all the way, and invited me in.

"You're the man hired to help David," she said. It was a statement, not a question.

"First time anybody's mentioned Flame's real first name," I said. Ms. Desmond and I were standing in the front hall as we talked.

"Flame doesn't really suit David for a name, Mr. Crang," Ms. Desmond said. "He never gets burned up about anything." She paused. "Well, hardly anything."

"As I mentioned on the phone, Ms. Desmond," I said, still in the hall, "I need to find out how the person blackmailing Flame got his hands on the particular song lyrics. Or should I call him David?"

"David," Ms. Desmond said. "And call me Alice."

"I'm plain Crang."

"You like some coffee, Crang?" Alice said. "It's just been made."

She showed me into the living room while she disappeared down the hall to the kitchen. The living room's walls were plum-coloured. The sofa I sat in was in an off-green shade. In front of it was a coffee table with a stack of magazines that appeared to deal in rap subjects.

Alice came into the room carrying a wooden tray large enough to hold two mugs of steaming coffee, a bowl of sugar, and a small jug of milk.

"How do you take your coffee?" Alice said.

"As it comes."

Alice handed me one mug, put two spoonfuls of sugar and a hit of milk in the other. I took a sip of my coffee, and pronounced it very tasty, which it was.

"I guess what you want," Alice said, "is some kind of record of who came through the house and when."

"You can provide that?"

"Not quite, but enough to be helpful, the way I figure it."

"You figure it how?"

Alice swallowed some coffee. She made a face, as if the coffee was still too hot for her taste. She placed the cup on the coffee table, and leaned forward, clasping her hands together.

"You must understand that David shares most of his life with me," Alice said. "Tells me what's up with him, especially the parts where he might be worried."

"So you're aware of the two different attempts at blackmailing him?"

Alice nodded. "I think I'm also aware of how you're proceeding."

"Uh huh," I said, intending to sound like a wise and interested fellow.

"You're hoping you can pin down this second blackmailer by working backwards from the stealing of the song sheets out of this house."

"You suppose I'll get anywhere with the idea?"

"I'm laying all of this out just so I'm sure you and I are on the same page."

"One thing I wonder about before we get any further," I said. "How do you think David came to write the unpleasant lyrics in the first place?"

"*Unpleasant!* That's rich, Crang!" Alice let out a whooping laugh. "How about deeply disturbing?"

Alice paused long enough for her words to sink in. "But, sure," she said, "I got a theory. First of all, remember he had just turned sixteen when he wrote the damn things."

I nodded.

"Two years earlier," Alice said, "his father walked out the door of our apartment, and never came back. He didn't say a word before he left, and he's never said a word to either of us to this day. A few months after he was gone, we learned through the grapevine that the man — I'm talking about my husband and David's father — he was back where he came from, namely Jamaica. He had ditched us, and it was as if his life with his wife and his son didn't exist and never had. It probably sounds trite to say so, but that's the motivation David had to write the lyrics. He was very upset about the abandonment and the lack of communication from his father, and all the upset came tumbling out in this one batch of songs."

"He showed the lyrics to you early on?"

"Soon as he wrote them," Alice said. "I read the lyrics. Right away I told David this was a brilliant use of words, but unless he intended to commit professional suicide, these songs should never be heard or read anywhere beyond the walls of our apartment. For a day or two, David didn't let out a peep what he thought about my warning. Then he came back to me, saying he agreed with me all the way. That was the last time the subject of the lyrics was ever brought up that I know of until all this trouble descended on us last week."

"But you've kept the lyrics in a sort of home museum?"

"Them and every other piece of paper or vinyl or tape or whatever that touches on David's career," Alice said. "What else would I do with the stuff except save it? I'm a proud mother. Unfortunately, as it turns out, this habit of mine, a mania you might say, took in stuff that I ought to have destroyed. But that's in hindsight."

She stood up. "Bring your coffee, Crang. We're going on a little tour."

Alice's shape, as I followed her up the stairs, could have belonged to a teenager. She was probably in her early fifties, but from the rear I saw no sign of middle-age spread. Her dark grey slacks fit her just right. She had on a plain white T-shirt and a blue-and-grey scarf tied lightly around her neck.

The second floor was divided into three rooms. The one at the front, large and bright, was the master bedroom. The middle room, with the door closed, must have been Flame's bedroom, and at the back, we reached the Flame museum collection.

The only furniture in the room was a pair of armchairs in brown corduroy covering. There was a light brown carpet on the floor. Everything else in the room had some connection to music; stacks of CDs, a couple of retro LPs, magazine photographs of Flame, mostly in full colour, pinned on bulletin boards, and shelves of magazines. Most of the magazines were hip hop magazines that were unknown to me, but I noticed a *Maclean's* in the mix, *Rolling Stone*, *Newsweek*, and a bunch of other mainstream magazines.

Against one wall were shelves in rows, running four levels from the floor up. Each group of shelves had a tab with the year marked over it. As the years went on, the notations were broken down to months and dates. I checked the shelves marked 2011 just to get a representative feel for what I was examining. The notations listed documents for three consecutive dates in January, one date in February, four in March, and so on through the entire year. Adding the numbers up told me that 2011 had a total of forty-four entries.

"In these shelves," I said to Alice, "you've listed the songs that David composed in each month of each year?"

"Busy little beaver, isn't he?" Alice said.

"He wrote forty-four songs in 2011?"

"Some were dogs," Alice said. "Or I should say in David's view, they were. Most of them he never performed. Others got to be hits. Or they were at least good enough to sing at his concerts."

I moved around the shelves until I got to the year when David was sixteen. Comparatively speaking, the number of songs he composed was slim, not close to the later output of 2011 and David's other senior years.

I took out the sheets for the entire year.

"This is what he wrote in the year of the songs that are causing all the grief?" I said to Alice.

"Yeah, but you won't find *those* lyrics in there."

I flipped through the songs. Alice was right, as I expected she would be.

"Somebody removed the lyrics we're interested in," I said to her. "But we don't know when the theft took place."

"I've never made a habit of going through the pages on those shelves," Alice said. "Except when a visitor asks me about specific songs. In that case, I dig the songs out. The whole thing makes me quite proud, like I'm aiding a scholar in his work."

"But nobody ever asked to look at the songs that came to be blackmail material?"

Alice shook her head. "I guess that's because the person who wanted the lyrics just went ahead and took them without mentioning what they were interested in."

"Sounds about right," I said. "Now, tell me about keeping a list of the people who've been through the collection?"

"I did that," Alice said. She was sitting in one of the armchairs, holding a three-ringed notebook she had taken off the last shelf in the row against the wall. She motioned me to sit in the other armchair.

"Here in this notebook is where I wrote names," Alice said.

"This is from the very beginning?"

Alice nodded. "I started writing down visitors' names when we still lived in the apartment buildings a couple of blocks from here, south of Dundas and the other side of Bathurst. Then we moved here. In all this saving of stuff, it wasn't that I was a doting mama, though I suppose I was. But really it was more that I knew David would become a star one day."

"And you were going to keep a record of his ascent?"

"That was the idea. But I had a second motive, and that was to get the addresses of all the visitors, so I could send them notice of David's appearances in different clubs around town. What I mailed out wasn't quite a newsletter, not as grand as that, but it kept people informed about dates and places they could hear David."

"How many not-quite-newsletters did you send out?"

"Only a dozen altogether. That was because I was just getting the hang of the thing, how to write a proper notice, when Roger Carnale came along. He took over everything involved in David's career."

"But you kept the museum open for business and recorded the visitors' names just like always?"

"I went a little overboard," Alice said, smiling at her foolishness. "I wrote down every name of every person who came through the door. Even kids who'd be knocking on my door two, three times a week. I wrote down their names all the times on all the days they showed up. It was crazy at the start."

She handed me the three-ringed binder. The first pages were thick with the same names over and over.

"Then what?" I said.

"Then I started writing people's names and addresses only on their first visit," Alice said. "And since the visitors started to step up several levels in importance, it wasn't just David's kid friends. Musicians came here, talented people who were looking to make a mark in hip hop. Some of them became well known, not at my son's level, but successes. Anyway, I wrote their names and addresses the first time they came, and I made a note of each person's credentials."

I turned the pages in the binder. "Here's Roger Carnale in 2004," I said. "You describe him as 'manager.'"

"He was in and out of here damn near as often as I was," Alice said. "But you'll only find his name written down that first time he came calling. That was my system, first visit the only one I noted."

"Roger detected star quality from the get-go," I said. "That much I understand."

"He told some fabulous stories about what he saw ahead for David. They were too flattering for David or me to resist, so we signed up with him, binding us to him for practically ever. It may sound extreme, but the thing is, Roger has backed up everything he promised."

"Roger still comes by your house?"

"Only sometimes when David's in town," Alice said. "But Roger also takes me out to dinner alone a couple of times a year. We go to Canoe, places on that level, ritzy. Nothing but the best for Roger, which I must say I don't mind at all."

"Any idea where Roger lives?"

Alice shook her head. "Roger's cagey about things like his address, his phone number."

"What do you chalk that up to?"

"My theory is he's avoiding people who want him to do for them what he's done for David."

"You ever try the theory on Roger?"

Alice gave another shake of her head. "Roger doesn't encourage personal stuff of any type. The last couple of years, it's been especially awkward dealing with the man. What I mean, he makes it awkward, the way he holds back information that maybe my son and I should know."

I turned again to the three-ringed binder and flipped through its pages. "Am I likely to find anybody besides Roger in the same category of frequent visitor?"

"Jerome. Whenever business brings him up here."

"Who can resist Jerome?"

"Not me," Alice said, giving me a wink.

"How about a man named Frederick Chamblis? He ever ask to see your archives?"

"Who's he?"

"I think he's the Reverend Alton Douglas's killer."

"Oh my, Crang." Alice raised her hand to her mouth. "You're not fooling me?"

"It isn't a certainty, but let's say he's my suspect number one at the moment."

"The name means nothing to me," Alice said. "I'll bet money this guy's not in my binder."

I thought about her answer for a moment, then I pulled a folded piece of paper out of my inside jacket pocket and handed it to Alice. "Anybody on the list ring a bell?"

"What's the story with these guys?" Alice asked.

"The entire eleven of them were associated with the Reverend in a place called Heaven's Philosophers."

"I know for sure this Reverend Douglas never came here,"

Alice said. "Nobody who even dressed like a church minister dropped by."

"What about the people on my list?"

Alice ran her finger down the names, "I see you got that guy Frederick Chamblis written on here," she said.

"The man gets around."

Alice took her time reading through the names.

When she finished, she gave the paper back to me. "I'm sorry to say none of these guys crossed the entrance to my house, at least not under these names," Alice said. She paused for a moment before she went on. "You know, Crang, as far as suspects go, if somebody was going to steal something, they could always give a fake name, and it would fool me."

"You never ask for ID?"

"My little museum, why should I check on the identity of anybody who wants to visit?"

I reached into the side pocket in my jacket and took out my cellphone. "One more item for your eyes, Alice," I said. "Look at the ten photographs on here. They show ten of the guys in Heaven's Philosophers, all except Chamblis."

Alice flipped through the photos, needing no more than a glance at each guy.

"Not a single soul looks the least bit familiar," she said. "But they look like kind of a thuggist group, you know what I mean?"

I switched my own attention to the names of people in the binder who had visited Alice's house in the previous year. One name I recognized, a *Toronto Star* reporter. I gave her a pass. Journalists in my experience, Annie being a prime example in such matters, are honest souls. No other name made me pause and reflect. I thought about all the visitors whose names Alice had collected over the years. Was it worth my time getting Gloria to run a check on the whole lot? I didn't need much thought to answer my question in the negative. I already had a list of prospective villains. It was better to concentrate my time and energy, and Gloria's, on them. If none of them panned out, then I might turn to the grind of tracking the visitors to the Flame museum.

"You look like you're done here," Alice said.

"Coffee was nice though," I said.

"Come out on the porch," Alice said. "We'll have another cup."

The coffee was losing its heat, but it was pleasant sitting on the porch with Alice watching the passing parade. Many of the people moving slowly down the street in cars were looking for a parking space while they visited the hospital two blocks east on Bathurst.

"I've been working over there for almost thirty-five years," Alice said. "Toronto Western Hospital."

"A nurse, right?"

Alice nodded. "I went all the way up the ladder to the operating room in the cardiac department."

"Cardiac must be tough."

"Long hours," Alice said. "And sometimes patients' hearts give in. They die."

"And you're still over there?"

"Part-time. But I tell you, Crang, if some other interesting job comes along, outside of nursing I mean, I'll snap it up."

"You like me to keep my eyes open? Positions come open in my line of business all the time. You'd be game for that?"

"Do I look like a woman who's finished with the working life?"

"You look like a woman in the prime, Alice."

Both of us smiled.

CHAPTER TWENTY-SEVEN

At home, I made two chopped-egg sandwiches for lunch, and ate them while I finished *Old Filth*. The novel was so good I was already working up a taste for the next Jane Gardam book in Annie's pile upstairs. The slip of paper I used for a page marker in *Old Filth* was the Toronto Public Library notice with the date for the book's return. It was three days overdue.

I wiped the chopped-egg remnants off my chin, put the book under my arm, and walked up Spadina to the library branch half a block north of Bloor. Inside, it smelled of books. Had the digital age produced a distinct odour for its own forms of communicating words and sentences? Not that I was aware of. Maybe the warm smell of pages and glue and bindings from real books would survive into a future when books existed only in Kindle and other e-forms.

I paid *Old Filth*'s late fine, and stepped outside. At the same time, an SUV pulled up at the curb. A tall, slim guy in a cap got out of the driver's seat, and walked around the car to the door at the right rear. He opened the door, and made a motion indicating I should climb in. The SUV was Roger Carnale's brand new Cadillac Escalade. The tall, slim guy was Roger's chauffeur.

"I'm here to drive you to your meeting with Mr. Carnale," the chauffeur said. It was the first time I'd seen him up close. He wasn't a bad looking guy, maybe trying a little too hard to come across as more authoritative than he was capable of conveying.

"Didn't know I had a meeting scheduled," I said.

"Mr. Carnale says so. That good enough for you, smart guy?"

"You talked me into it."

I slid onto the rear seat.

Before the chauffeur shut the door, he leaned closer to me, and said, "First we're making a stop at your office for a little pick up."

"Let me make a stab at this," I said. "Roger wants me to return the sheets of Flame's lyrics, the copy that Jerome entrusted to me."

"I'll let you off at your place, and wait for you in the car while you get them."

"Good man."

The chauffeur leaned closer to me and put his hand on my shoulder, gripping it as hard as he could manage. "Don't make me come in after you," he said.

"You think you can take me, big guy?" I said, faking a show of bravado.

For an instant, the chauffeur looked puzzled.

I smiled. "Relax, fella. I'm as keen to talk to Roger as he is to talk to me."

The chauffeur climbed behind the wheel, drove a block south, parked, and let me out.

It took only a couple of minutes up in my office to make sure my two copies of the song lyrics were identical. I hadn't thought before to check for marks, secret or otherwise, that might tell someone which pages were the authentic Flame originals and which were the copies made by the blackmailer, whoever that may have been, the Reverend or some as yet unidentified party.

Detecting no marks of any partcular indication on either set of the sheets, I put those intended for return to Carnale in a large brown envelope, and placed the other sheets back in my files. I was supposing the second sheets were the ones I'd retrieved from the Reverend's desk. But, wait, I thought to myself, if the two sets of sheets were identical, how could I tell the version Jerome gave me from the ones I'd retrieved? And did it matter? I had no time to waste on questions. My ride was waiting. I locked the office door, and hustled down to the car and chauffeur.

"Now we're off to Roger's office?" I said. "Or maybe his abode?"

"Dream on, if you think I'm gonna tell you where his house is," the chauffeur said.

He drove south on Spadina, made a left turn at Harbord, and headed east toward Queen's Park.

"I've heard of guys keeping a low profile," I said. "But Roger's going for complete invisibility."

The chauffeur said nothing. He looped part way around Queen's Park until he was pointed north. We passed the Royal Ontario Museum on the left and the Gardiner Ceramics Museum on the right. The Escalade stopped for a red light at Bloor.

"Throw me a tiny scrap," I said to the close-mouthed driver. "Does your boss live in a grand neighbourhood? I'm guessing, say, Forest Hill?"

"Give it a rest," the driver said. He turned around and directed at me one of those looks you see in crime movies, the old hard-and-silent stare. With the driver, the look didn't quite come off, but he continued with the tough guy chatter. "You don't want to push me too far. What I might do, believe me on this, I wouldn't want to predict."

I decided not to say a word for the rest of the trip.

The traffic light turned green, and the driver returned to his driving business. He signalled for a right turn off Avenue Road at Cumberland, drove down the block to Bellair, a left turn, then a short block up to Yorkville. We were in very pricey territory. Forty years earlier, long before my time, Yorkville was synonymous with hippies and dope and folk music. Neil Young came from out of the neighbourhood. Now it was couture boutiques and three-million-dollar condos.

The Escalade looked right at home in these surroundings. The driver stopped the car beside the Four Seasons Hotel patio. Roger Carnale was sitting at a table with a bucket of ice holding a bottle of something that looked to me from a distance to be Veuve Clicquot. The chauffeur opened my door, and I stepped out.

Roger was equipped with what I was now thinking of as his sartorial trademarks. He wore a beautifully creased fedora, this one a shade of dark blue to match his summer suit. Beside his chair, a walking stick leaned against a briefcase. Both the stick and briefcase were different from the ones I'd seen in my office. The stick was an ivory colour, and the briefcase had no metal fittings.

Roger rose from his chair and shook hands.

"Crang," he said, "nice of you to make time."

Since I had no choice in the matter short of a donnybrook with the chauffeur I might conceivably lose, I let the remark go. Besides, I had questions of my own to ask good old Roger.

"Some champagne?" he said to me.

"You ever try a brand called Armand de Brignac?" I said. "Very chic in some circles."

"Ace of Spades?" Roger said, suave about it. "An expensive but vulgar choice, Crang."

He made a motion to the waiter who had been standing by during my arrival. The waiter lifted the bottle from the ice bucket and poured me a glass. It was the Veuve Clicquot. I took a sip, showed the waiter my expression of pleasure, and turned to Roger.

I said, "Jerome has already told me I should lay off the Reverend's murder and everything else untoward that followed."

"Poor Jerome," Carnale said, "you and I insist on putting him in awkward positions."

"I'm assuming he told you that he told me you didn't want me to know about the second blackmailing?"

"Jerome has warmed to you and your friend Ms. Cooke," Carnale said. "So has Flame for that matter."

"One more name you might put on the list," I said. "Alice Desmond. She was most accommodating this morning."

This revelation got a narrowing of the eyes from Carnale.

"Listen, Roger," I said. "I know you want me to go away. What I don't understand is, how come? If you allow me to hang around a little longer, I might find the answer to big questions. Who killed the Reverend? Who's the second blackmailer? Are they the same guy?"

"I don't expect you to just go away, in your phrase," Carnale said. "I'm prepared to pay you handsomely for the excellent work you've done on my behalf. Then I expect you to retire from the field, and let me get on with Flame's business."

As he spoke, Carnale reached into his jacket's inner pocket. He pulled out a long white envelope out of the pocket, and placed it on the table beside my champagne glass.

Throughout this small display of Carnale's riches and power, I'd been holding the brown envelope containing the song lyrics in the hand that wasn't engaged with the glass of Veuve Clicquot. I held out the brown envelope to Carnale.

Without making any comment, he stowed the brown envelope in his briefcase.

"I'll tell you what's in the white envelope," Carnale said to me. "Then you can just slip it in your pocket, and we can enjoy our champagne together."

"How much?" I said.

"A certified cheque for twelve thousand dollars."

"That's just about right."

"I'd say it winds up our business, wouldn't you."

"Not quite," I said. "How about you tell me something about the second blackmailer?"

"You're becoming tiresome, Crang."

"You paid him off, correct?"

"Jerome has already told you I did," Carnale said. "I thought it was necessary to pay this fellow in order to free myself of extraneous worries as we went forward with the movie plan."

"And the blackmailer returned to you the originals of the song lyrics?"

"Of course he did," Carnale said, sounding peeved to be going over familiar ground. "That was the term I insisted on when I made the payment."

"Where do you suppose the blackmailer got the sheets of lyrics?"

"That's obvious, isn't it? From the late Reverend Alton Douglas."

"Is that what the blackmailer himself told you?"

"He confirmed that set of circumstances."

"You think the second guy was partners with the Reverend?"

"He didn't say he was in so many words," Carnale said. "But it wasn't hard for me to draw the conclusion he worked with the Reverend. It's even possible the second man killed the Reverend in order to keep the blackmail money all to himself."

Carnale was making a lot of sense except for the major detail that the Reverend wasn't in possession of the sheets of lyrics, not from the instant I liberated them from the his desk drawer. Carnale didn't know that I knew he was lying.

"You've thought the whole thing through?" I said to Carnale.

"That should be obvious, even to you, Crang."

"When you paid this guy, was it in person or by way of a deposit in a bank account in Zurich or Belize or some other foreign spot with loose banking regulations?"

"Since my dealings with the blackmailer were via a series of cell conversations, I've no idea what he looks like," Carnale said. "I've never met him and almost certainly never will."

He seemed close to the blow-up stage. Did I dare ask one more question? Yes, I dared.

"Where do you live anyway, Roger?" I said. "Man of your grand taste and, if I may guess, your impeccable breeding? On the old family estate on the Bridle Path? Something of that nature?"

"Crang, let me just say I don't think any rational observer would doubt that I've been patient with you beyond all tolerance. It's none of your concern where I live, how I conduct my business, who I deal with, what form the dealings take. And quite frankly, I've reached my limit in tolerating your intrusion into these areas.

As far as I'm concerned, you and I are now finished with our conversation."

I looked at my watch.

"Yeah," I said, "I've got a PVR I want to watch this afternoon."

Carnale stood up from his chair.

"But hold on, Roger," I said, "you're leaving a bottle of Veuve Clicquot still a quarter full."

Carnale's chauffeur held open the back door of the Escalade. The car had been waiting on Yorkville during Carnale's chat with me. Carnale got into the back seat.

"Hey Roger," I called before the chauffeur shut the door. "I suppose a lift to my place is out of the question?"

The chauffeur shut the car door. Roger hadn't acknowledged my request. The chauffeur gave me another of his attempts at the hard stare before he got behind the wheel. The Escalade pulled away.

I checked my watch again. I had set the TV set to tape Annie on *The Charlie Rose Show* on the PBS staton. Annie had phoned me late the night before with the news that she'd done her interview as part of a program where Charlie focused on movies. There were three separate interviews with different people: a Czech director, the American screenwriter and playwright John Patrick Shanley, and Annie. She wasn't sure of the programmed order of the interviews, which meant I had to watch the show from the beginning and maybe do a little fast-forwarding. I figured to watch the whole thing.

Annie had interviewed Shanley years earlier and liked the guy. He told Annie about his father's death. The old man had loved playing his accordion so much that when he died Shanley and his siblings buried their father with his accordion in the casket. It was the kind of story you didn't forget.

I sat on the patio allowing the waiter to pour the rest of the champagne into my glass. I finished it, put the envelope with the twelve grand in my jacket pocket, and walked home to the television set.

CHAPTER TWENTY-EIGHT

The Czech director was first up on Charlie Rose's guest list. He sat across from Charlie at the large round table, the backdrop on the set in the deepest black. Charlie and his questions gave the Czech guy all the space in the world to pontificate. The guy took advantage. "Existential" turned up in his conversation more often than it did in the entire works of Jean-Paul Sartre. And I caught at least a half-dozen invocations of "the zeitgeist."

John Patrick Shanley came next, talking about his scripts for *Moonstruck* and *Doubt* and some other, more recent movies. He didn't mention the accordion in his father's casket, but he had other anecdotes that were just as funny and touching.

Then came my very own true sweetie. Annie had on her tailored jacket that showed a tantalizing hint of décolletage. I expected Charlie to get into a discussion of Edward Everett Horton's sexuality, but all the way through Annie's eighteen minutes, Charlie stuck with questions about the Horton comedy style. Annie hauled out material I recognized from her speech at the Miller Theatre, but she expanded on the points she wanted to make. Charlie sat back, and let her fly. Annie was smart and engaging and gorgeous. Television was made for her. Or maybe the other way around, she was made for TV.

Not more than ten seconds after the program faded to total black, my phone rang. It was Annie.

"You were sensational with Charlie," I said. "But I don't think I need to watch the Czech guy again."

"He actually said existential and zeitgeist about a dozen times while we were still in the green room waiting to go on."

"I miss you, sweetie," I said.

"I miss you, too," she said. "But, listen, I'm worried about the trouble you're getting into up there."

"Oh," I said, trying for a tone of innocence, "what trouble in particular?"

"A murder, the porno business, a bunch of guys who broke your new coffee machine. Just for starters."

"Gloria phoned you?"

"I phoned her," Annie said. "I grilled her, so don't blame Gloria if you feel she betrayed you. I was tough on her, like the way a criminal lawyer would cross-examine a witness. I did my best imitation of your friend, Wolf."

"Fox."

"Huh?"

"The man's nickname is Fox."

"That's beside the point," Annie said. "When I come home, I want to find my guy all in one piece."

"No danger, sweetie. Honestly."

"You're mixed up with guys who're paid to maim people. That's what I call a dangerous situation."

"Listen, sweetie," I said, "I don't know when it was you gave Gloria the third degree, but it sounds like she wasn't entirely up to speed on the whole Flame deal at the time. Things have evolved since then."

"What horrors did she miss out on?"

I told Annie about my interview with Georgie Gabriel at his father's house and about my champagne meeting that afternoon with Roger Carnale.

"That's good news, getting together with this Carnale guy," Annie said. "The way I look at it, if he says you're off the case, then you have no client. So no need to press on further."

"Yeah, but he's lying about the set of Flame lyrics he got from the second blackmailer."

"You've lost me," Annie said. "Explain it all once more. But keep to the salient material."

"Why you're confused is you need to know one detail I haven't mentioned until now. It's about the set of lyrics the Reverend supposedly had in his office drawer. After I left his office on the first day I visited his church, I knew that the set of lyrics was no longer in the drawer. It was gone. So when Carnale told me he paid eight million bucks to get possession of a set of lyrics that came originally from the Reverend, he was misrepresenting the existing state of affairs. The sheet of lyrics was, let's say, elsewhere."

Annie took a little time to think about what I'd said. I had of course left out the part about me swiping the song lyrics from the Reverend's office, which was how I knew he no longer had his hands on the damned things.

"What makes you so sure the lyrics weren't in the Reverend's drawer?" Annie asked.

"Information received."

"Oh, sweetie, come on! I've heard that line in dozens of BBC procedurals." Annie didn't care for my answer. "It can mean one of umpteen different explanations, most of them disreputable."

"How about I learned it from a reliable source?"

"I'll ignore for the moment your possible evasion on this particular issue, and ask a different question."

"Which is?"

"Why does that necessarily mean Carnale was lying when he said he believed the set of lyrics he received from the second blackmailer had previously been in the Reverend's possession?"

"Because what he said couldn't have been possible."

"Sure, it could," Annie said. "Suppose the Reverend made an

extra copy of the lyrics. He concealed the copy from everybody except his confederate in the blackmailing scheme. Then the Reverend broke the bad news to the confederate that he was backing out of the whole scheme. That got the confederate so hot and bothered that he murdered the Reverend, took the extra copy of the lyrics, and used that copy to blackmail Carnale to the tune of the eight million bucks. How was Carnale to know there existed three sets of lyrics?"

"That's not bad reasoning, honeybunch," I said.

"Do I have to do all the analytical work around here?"

"Who do you suppose the confederate might be?"

"Crang, my dearest," Annie said, speaking slowly and spreading out her words, "there is no need to worry over such matters now. Why? Because you are off the case. You get that? Off. The. Case."

"I think Freddie Chamblis aka the Champ fits the role of confederate to a T."

"Fine," Annie said. "Tell that to the Homicide cop. Wally you said his name is?"

"Crawford."

"Tell him."

"You know I always like to weigh my options."

"That's another of your old euphemisms for stalling," Annie said. "Come on, sweetie, retire from the darn field on this one."

"Plus, I got to unhook Sal Banfield from her porn connections."

"You're right on that one," Annie said. "I can just imagine the swell double date if you and I were lugging around the information that Sal and a bunch of other naked persons have been making out with the cameras rolling. We know all about this while her boyfriend of the moment, namely your friend Maury, remains in the dark concerning the nude gamboling."

"You're OK with the double date otherwise?"

"I agree it might be fun to have dinner with her."

"And with Maury."

"Maury included."

"When do you figure you'll be back?"

"Middle of next week, Thursday at the latest," Annie said. "I'm turning down a bunch of the New York people who've come into the picture in the last few days asking to do interviews."

"Turning down?" I said. "Aren't authors on tour supposed to ride the waves of publicity for all they're worth?"

"Sweetie, I'm so sick of hearing my own voice," Annie said. "*Blah, blah, blah*. All day long, the only person talking is me telling the same anecdotes again and again."

"The limelight's not all it's cracked up to be?"

"If it wasn't for Jerome offering a little conversation between interviews," Annie said, "I might have lost my mind already."

"Jerome's good company?"

"He talks mostly about Flame's movie. That's entertaining, though it gets repetitive, all about him originating the movie's storyline, casting, choice of screenwriter and director, and so on. Plus the part about Carnale keeping him out on the fringes on the money side of the movie."

"Yeah, I've heard those tunes before."

"But, listen, Jerome's actually pretty savvy about moviemaking. He had some kind of job in Warner Brothers' New York offices before he joined Flame."

"But what is it that's making Jerome uneasy?" I said. "Carnale's money matters in general? Or strictly money on the movie project?"

"He seems to sniff something fundamentally amiss," Annie said. "I pushed him on it, and he seems okay as far as receiving his own pay is concerned, and he says Flame still gets regular reports about his money investments. Jerome just senses a certain fishiness in the air. That's as far as he's willing to go."

"Carnale paying me a reasonably healthy fee to go away raises a red flag in my own mind."

"You've got a fee from the man?"

"By certified cheque."

"How much?"

"Twelve grand."

"Crang, that's the bottom line in more ways than one," Annie said, hectoring me just a little. "Put the money in the bank unless you've done the sensible thing already."

"I just got the dough this afternoon," I said. "The bank's closed till Monday."

"You can deposit it in your bank's machine."

"I'd rather wait for the tellers to get back to work."

"Crang, you've got to adjust," Annie said. "Tellers are so twentieth century."

"Yeah, but machines don't smile and say hello to me the way tellers do. They don't ask if I'd like a cup of the coffee."

"Sweetie, really, come on."

"Do you know about the coffee? Banks serve it these days. Tellers make it themselves for us account holders."

"Is the coffee any good?"

"They haven't got that part under control yet," I said. "But I still like watching when the tellers deposit the money in my account."

"Crang, the ATM does the same thing," Annie said. "Or you can make your deposits online."

"The machine doesn't give me a pretty smile after the transaction. Plus the tellers will probably get better at making the free coffee."

"I love you, Crang," Annie said. "But keep in mind banking in the twenty-first century is working quite well, thanks."

"Sweetie, I'm going to take that last part under advisement. You may be right."

Annie made spluttering noises on the other end, but that gave way to a few minutes of long-distance billing and cooing before we signed off.

CHAPTER TWENTY-NINE

First thing Saturday, the morning was soft and still. Leaving the house, I walked up Major to Sussex Avenue, and turned right toward Spadina. No cars moved on the side streets; not even Spadina had much traffic. I noticed just one other person on foot. Half a block up ahead of me on Sussex, a bulky guy was walking in the same direction. He had on a dark windbreaker and baseball cap, which I judged from behind to be Yankees gear. The bulky guy crossed Spadina to the other side. I turned north to the office.

I sat at my desk, typing notes about Georgie Gabriel and his connection to Heaven's Philosophers. Fox had told me to drop by his office that morning, and fill him in on the criminal charges that could possibly be coming Georgie's way. Just as I had figured, Fox said he'd get a kick out of acting for a Squeaky associate but would never again represent Squeaky himself.

When I finished making the notes, I printed out a copy and put it in the inside pocket of my ancient seersucker jacket. Before I left the office, I wandered over to the window to think about the rest of the day. Right away, I spotted the two girls with the great legs. They were wearing their tan shorts and their T-shirts. Both carried large-sized containers from Starbucks. Personally, I made a point of boycotting the place. The Starbucks idea of price gave me a case of outrage. Their coffee quality wasn't so great either, in my opinon — on about the same level as the stuff my friendly bank tellers made.

Standing in the Matt Cohen Park, the two girls looked confused about where to settle. I could understand the dilemma. Their usual spot on the little hill was occupied. The occupant, his head down as he flipped through a newspaper, was the bulky guy I'd seen on Sussex an hour earlier. The dark windbreaker and the baseball cap were the giveaways, now revealed as Yankee gear for sure. The overall effect of the guy seemed kind of familiar, but his cap and his head's downward angle, buried in the newspaper, meant I had no straight-on view of his face.

I checked back for the two girls. It took a minute to locate them. They'd retreated to a bench at the far eastern side of the little park. From the distance, I got not much more than a faint glimpse of the spectacular gams. There seemed no point in me hanging around any longer.

Locking the office door, I set off on foot for Fox's office. He worked out of a building on University Avenue just north of the courthouse. I walked over to the University of Toronto grounds, and turned south past my favourite building on campus, Convocation Hall. I liked the hall for its domed roof. The glass that wrapped the dome made it the most gloriously bright public hall in the city. Annie once took me to hear John le Carré do a reading in the hall on an early summer evening. I spent so much time marvelling at the light that I hardly heard a word le Carré spoke. Annie told me later he was brilliant.

For the rest of the route to Fox's office, I cut east to University Avenue then turned right, going straight south, past Mount Sinai Hospital and Toronto General and Sick Kids. Name your ailment, and University Avenue had the treatment centre. Cancer? Princess Margaret was the hospital for you.

I stopped at a fast food place near the corner of University and Dundas, and bought a medium-sized coffee to go. The coffee was so hot I knew I could never carry the cardboard cup as far as Fox's office without baking my fingers. I took a handful of the restaurant's paper napkins and wrapped them around the cup for extra protection.

Fox's building was twelve storeys high. He had an office on the top floor. I rode up the elevator, got off, and walked halfway down the hall. The outer door to Fox's office, which opened onto the main hall, was ajar. His inner office door was shut. That was a signal. When Fox shut his inner door, he didn't want to be disturbed until he finished writing his address to the jury or his list of questions on a cross examination or whatever chore needed his uninterrupted concentration. When he was done, he would open the inner door, and make himself available.

I was a big fan of the twelfth floor in Fox's building. Two doors led from the main hall out to the bare roof, which took up the twelfth's rear quarter. This was the only downtown building I knew that offered an open-air view of the surrounding neighbourhood of high-rises and skyscrapers. The roof had a covering of pebbles and tar that got sticky in the summer sun. The idea for people venturing out there to do some sightseeing was to stick to the narrow wooden walkways that criss-crossed the pebbles and tar.

While I waited for Fox, I strolled across the first walkway that led to the edge of the roof. It was a spot where the surrounding wall reached no higher than my upper thighs. The wall's miniscule height probably broke construction regulations, but I wasn't in a mood to worry about that. I just liked the way the view bucked me up. I stood there, holding my coffee cup gingerly, looking out over the city, feeling like the king of all I surveyed.

I pried the lid off the coffee. Steam flowed out of the cup. The coffee had cooled. Though it would no longer scald, it still felt like it could raise a blister. I was thinking of trying a sip when I felt a motion behind me. I didn't hear anything, not a footstep or any other identifiable sound. But I sensed somebody moving.

I turned halfway around to my left.

A guy in a Yankee baseball cap was about three strides back and coming at me fast. It was the guy I'd seen on Sussex Avenue and in Matt Cohen Park. This man's chin jutted out. I knew the chin. I'd seen it in the lobby at the Heaven's Philosophers building. The chin belonged to Freddie Chamblis.

Freddie Chamblis?! Dear god, he was the guy with all the muscles and the power. Sal Banfield said Freddie could crush Mike Tyson. I had no doubt Sal was right, and now the guy who could squeeze Mike Tyson had me in his sights.

At the moment I turned on the walkway, Freddie was pushing off on his left foot, his outstretched arms lunging at my shoulders. He looked like a guy hell bent on shoving me off the roof.

Off the roof!? The man had to be a maniac!

In the moments after I turned, Freddie's left foot drove him forward. His right was in the air, prepping for the next push. His arms were closing in on my shoulders. In the instant I took in what was happening, I thought Freddie might be slanted marginally too far to his own left to catch me at an angle that would jack me over the little wall.

As Freddie came at me, I brought my right hand around on a line directed at his head. My right hand was holding the cup of coffee. When I turned, my right had the momentum to generate good speed toward Freddie as he prepared to smack me.

In mid-swing, I tilted the cup and let the hot coffee fly into Freddie's face. The direction of my swing was perfect. The coffee splashed against Freddie's cheeks, nose, and chin. His mouth opened as if he were screaming at the burning sensation of the hot liquid. I heard nothing. The scream was silent.

Freddie's fists thudded into my left shoulder, but by then the combination of his off-kilter aim and his drenching in hot coffee had sapped the guy of most of his drive. I gave Freddie a small body check as he passed into my range. He shoved back at me. By then, neither of us could hold our balance.

I fell backward. My bum bounced on the wooden walkway. My upper back hit squarely on the pebbles and tar.

I lay where I had settled, my eyes staring up to the sky. After a moment, I lowered my sightline back to roof level.

Freddie was nowhere in sight.

Jesus, did he go over the guard wall?

I tracked in my mind Freddie's possible path, and waited for the noises he would make if he had taken a flight downward. He would scream as he fell. His body would go *boink* if he bounced off the roof of a parked car. Pedestrians would yell and shout. Ambulances would arrive with sirens at top volume.

I lay on my back and considered the possible sounds.

It took a handful of seconds to realize I wasn't hearing anything in the way of distinctive noises. No screams, no *boinks*, no shouts or sirens.

I straightened up from the walkway, out of the tar and pebbles. When I got upright, I needed a moment for some dizziness to settle. My head cleared, and I looked over the edge of the wall, not allowing much of me to show. I didn't want witnesses to spot me from the street. They might get the idea I was the guy who tossed Freddie to his death. It was self-defence, but who was to know that?

The street came into view down below. It was Centre Street. I walked it regularly on my way to and from the courthouse. The street looked the way it always looked. No body lay on the pavement or on the sidewalk or on the roof of a car.

Where was Freddie?

I got out of my crouch and leaned further over the wall. The first piece of news I registered was that Freddie wasn't dead. He hadn't gone splat on the street. One storey directly below me, the eleventh floor had a wide balcony with a yellow canvas covering. Freddie had plunged through the centre of the covering. He and a piece of ripped yellow canvas lay on the balcony's floor. Freddie was on his right side. His left arm wasn't moving. It was twisted at an angle that wasn't usual for an arm. A lot of Freddie's other bodily parts looked like they might be busted. But he wasn't dead. The mean bastard had lived through the experience.

I knew he was alive because his eyes were open and blinking madly in all directions. Some of his other parts were fluttering, the ones that weren't fractured or otherwise out of commission.

As I leaned over the wall, watching in something like amazement and relief, Freddie stopped blinking his eyes. He fixed his gaze upward. I leaned a little further over the wall, studying the direction of Freddie's eyes. What was he staring at?

It took me a whole five seconds to wise up that Freddie was eyeballing me. He probably couldn't fathom how a guy like me — smaller, lighter, and not as destructively inclined as someone in the enforcer racket — had got the better of him, him being a prince of assassins.

I stared back until I heard a small commotion from the balcony. Whatever was happening, whoever was coming on to the scene, involved the balcony door. The door was out of my range of vision. I waited a bit longer.

Three women emerged one by one on to the balcony. They surrounded Freddie. One flapped her arms in what I assumed was shock. All three women let out whoops of surprise. None of the three did anything that indicated they had medical training. One pulled out her cellphone. Her voice carried up to me as she asked for an ambulance. Cops and fire engines would also no doubt answer the call. The woman on the cell didn't seem certain of the building's address. She worked that out with the operator. The other two women were kneeling on either side of Freddie. Both were murmuring at him. He didn't seem capable of speech, not yet anyway.

It was past time for me to beat a retreat. Any moment now, the women would look up at the torn awning over their heads. If I stood there gawking, they'd take note of me.

I turned and picked up the empty coffee cup and the napkins I'd used for protection against the coffee's heat. I shoved the paper stuff into my pockets. The roof looked tidy except for small splashes of spilled coffee. Nothing I could do about them.

I trotted down the hall. Fox's inner door was still closed. I gave one rap, and threw it open. Fox wasn't alone. Another guy sat across the desk from him. I knew the other guy: Archie Brewster. He was in his mid-sixties, balding, chubby, and amiable, a wizard neurological technician. A dozen years earlier, he made himself incredibly rich by inventing a device for use in brain surgery. With the windfall, Archie built his own lab where he did DNA tests and indulged in other forensic messing-around. Since the place was only semi-legal, Archie operated it more or less under the radar. Criminal lawyers like Fox and even me on occasion made up most of his clientele.

"Hey, Crang!" Fox said. "The door was shut for a reason."

"The cops ought to be heading up here in five minutes," I said. "We need to beat it."

Without a hint of hesitation, allowing no time for second thoughts, Fox grabbed two briefcases from the floor, and began stuffing the papers from the top of his desk into the cases. Archie had a slim briefcase of his own. He put some documents in it, looking at me with a half-smile on his face. He seemed to be enjoying the experience, even if he hadn't any idea what kind of pickle I was in.

"These police," Fox said to me, "they're calling for a reason that might be inconvenient?"

"More than inconvenience where I'm concerned."

"I'll take your word for it."

Fox snapped shut the bulging briefcases, handed one to me, and carried the other himself. "Don't want to leave stuff lying around that might get clients in trouble," Fox said. He led the way out the door, Archie and I following.

In the hall, Fox punched a button for the elevator.

"You want to give me the short version of what's up?" he asked, looking at me as we waited.

"I helped Squeaky's pal Freddie Chamblis fall off the roof," I said.

"That'll be a mess."

"The way things worked out," I said, "it could have been a lot worse."

"What? Freddie happened to be wearing a parachute?"

The elevator arrived. It was empty. The three of us got on, and Fox pressed the indicator for the building's parking garage in the basement. "We'll get my car," he said.

"Freddie landed on the balcony one floor below."

"Nice aim, Crang," Fox said. "Those balconies run down the side of the building almost the entire length, eleventh floor to the second, but I imagine it takes a certain skill to dump a guy in one of them."

"The whole deal was self-defence on my part."

"If that's your story, stick to it."

"Sticking to it shouldn't become an issue," I said. "If we get out of here without a cop busting me, I don't plan to tell anybody what happened."

"How about the victim? Aren't you concerned Freddie might talk?"

"First, Freddie is not anybody's victim. Second, he knows he'll only get himself jammed up if he tries to pin his injuries on me. He's not that dumb."

Fox nodded. "Anybody who hangs around with Squeaky is, by definition, a person who rates low on the scale of human values."

"You ever acted for Freddie?"

Fox shook his head. "The time I defended Squeaky, the one I mentioned in my email the other day, that was when Freddie started hanging around. He spent his time with Squeaky and me whether I liked it or not. The fact was I didn't take to him any more than I took to Squeaky."

"Let's just clear the building," I said. "Then we'll talk about the situation."

Archie spoke for the first time. "I love it when you get in a scrape, Crang," he said. He was still wearing the half-smile. "It's pretty damn entertaining."

The elevator stopped at the ground floor.

"I didn't press for the ground floor," Fox said, looking surprised.

The elevator doors slid open. Two uniformed cops stood waiting in the lobby. One male, one female.

"You going up?" the female cop asked us. She seemed pleasant. Neither she nor her partner had their guns drawn.

Fox shook his head at the female cop's question. "To the parking garage."

"Sorry then," she said, "we need this elevator."

Archie, Fox, and I stepped off. Fox put a firm hand on my shoulder, positioning me so that I faced the cops as they got on the elevator. All the cop gear strapped to their waists — guns, flashlights, batons, other stuff — made creaking noises as they moved.

"Which floor is it, Bobby?" the woman cop asked her partner.

"Eleven," Bobby said.

The female cop reached for the button.

"Wait a minute, Grace," Bobby said. He turned to Fox, Archie, and me. "Which floor were you guys just on?"

"Twelve," Fox said. He still had the guiding hand on my shoulder.

"You hear any noise coming from down below?" Bobby asked. "From the eleventh?"

"The way this building's constructed," Fox said, "it'd have to be a bomb going off before you'd hear anything a floor away."

Bobby turned to me. "How about you?"

"We were together," I said, indicating Fox and Archie as the other parties I was talking about. "It was a business meeting. We were concentrating on what was in front of us."

"What kind of business?" Bobby said.

"Two of us are criminal lawyers," I said.

Bobby got a sneery expression. "Push eleven," he said to Grace.

The elevator doors closed.

"What was that all about, the thing where you steered me with the hands on my shoulders?" I asked Fox. "Is this your new affectionate side?"

"Take a look at the back of your lovely old seersucker."

I took off my jacket. The back was freshly decorated with pebbles and tar.

"The police officers might have wondered," Fox said.

I let my shoulders slump. "You mind dropping me off at my house?" I said to Fox.

"That's my plan," Fox said. "But we'll stop at Archie's first. It's closer."

Archie got in the back of Fox's car. I sat up front.

"How's business?" I said to Archie, talking over my shoulder. I wasn't especially interested in Archie's answer. I was talking more to ease my case of jittery nerves.

"Business is just right," Archie said."How about you, Crang? You worried about the guy who went off the roof?"

I turned to look at Archie. He still wore the half-smile, looking more amused than alarmed by the events I'd described.

"Nothing a good martini won't fix," I said.

Fox looked at his watch. "Kind of early for a drink. Not even 11:30."

"The morning I've put in," I said to Fox, "you don't think I deserve a martini?"

"Crang makes a very good point, Fox," Archie said. "Why don't you step on the gas and get us all where we're going."

Fox stepped on the gas.

CHAPTER THIRTY

When Fox pulled up in front of my house, I invited him in for a drink. He said he'd give it a pass. He needed to get home and finish his paperwork. The mention of paperwork reminded me why I'd called on Fox in the first place. I reached into my seersucker jacket pocket and handed him my notes about Georgie Gabriel. Fox drove away, and I went inside to assemble the ingredients for the martini I deserved.

I poured the vodka, making the kind of martini I once heard a guy describe as a silver bullet. It ran to five ounces of vodka. I carried the glass to a chair in the dining room facing into the garden. My shoulders felt sore where I'd crashed on the tar and pebble roof. I flexed the muscles in the upper back, trying to loosen them up, and wondered what in heaven's name Freddie Chamblis's attack had been all about. That might take some thought. I raised my glass and took a generous swallow. A feeling of warmth spread across my chest. This was a silver bullet that hit the spot.

I sipped some more, and developed thoughts about Freddie. The guy had been stalking me from early morning. That was obvious. He waited for me outside the house, and stayed on my tail all the way to the twelfth floor of Fox's building. He must have been looking for the right place to give me the business. The roof made sense because he could toss me over, and everybody would assume I had been alone out there, and got a little too frisky with the roof's edge. They'd say I miscalculated, and fell twelve storeys to the street.

All of that was plausible enough, but the tougher question came next. Why? Why did Freddie set out to knock me off? Why kill me of all people?

I drank more of the silver bullet, and sorted through the puzzles. I'd been thinking for days that Freddie was probably the Reverend's partner in the first attempt at blackmail, the one that the Reverend bailed out of. The way I reasoned things, Freddie bumped off the Reverend, which left him all alone to get on with the business of taking the Flame Group for the eight million. So Freddie was left sitting pretty, collecting all the blackmail money for himself. That seemed to make sense. But apparently he wasn't sitting pretty enough for his own complete satisfaction.

The fly in the ointment, as Freddie probably saw things, was me. He got the idea I might pull something that would separate him from the eight million. Chances were pretty good that Wally Crawford was already nosing through the Heaven's Philosophers people, asking questions about the Reverend's murder. Freddie might have found out it was me who pointed Wally in Freddie's direction as the suspected killer. That was one piece of damage I'd done the guy, and he probably wondered what other problems I might cause if I kept messing around with murder and blackmail and the Reverend. Freddie didn't know what I might pull. Hell, I didn't know either. The bottom line was that Freddie needed to put a stop to whatever he imagined I might discover. That was why he tried to heave me into Centre Street.

The ring of my cellphone interrupted my ruminating. Did I need to pick up? The phone was in my seersucker's right hand pocket. The jacket was folded over the chair in the kitchen. I didn't feel like getting out of my seat, and walking up the five steps to the kitchen. The mood I was in, I wasn't keen on talking to anybody at that moment. The phone rang on. I didn't budge. The rings fell silent, but the clicks from the cell told me whoever called had left a message.

I sat in the dining room until my silver bullet had almost dwindled away. It had certainly eased the tension of the morning's events. I felt closer to a sense of calm. Should I make another drink? Probably not — it being the middle of the day for one thing. Something to eat and a short snooze seemed more in order.

I slathered some organic peanut butter on two slices of multigrain bread, and ate the sandwich, followed by an apple and an oatmeal and cranberry flaxseed cookie from the good people at Voortman's. All of the nourishment taken care of, I checked the phone message. It was from Sal Banfield. She and her friend Franny wanted to meet me later that afternoon. Sal said the subject to be discussed was the last chance they were offering me at digging into Freddie Chamblis's private papers in the house where the porn movies were shot. Sal and Franny suggested they meet me that afternoon for a coffee and a discussion of their proposal. I was to choose a place off the beaten track. That was how Sal phrased it.

I phoned Sal's number, got her voice mail, and told it I would be at the Sovereign Coffee Bar on Davenport east of Dufferin at four o'clock. That gave me two hours.

I sat at the computer and Googled the Toronto General Hospital for its ER number. When I got through to ER, the person who answered said nobody named Frederick Chamblis had been brought in.

I tried Mount Sinai.

"You're lucky," a woman in Mount Sinai's ER said. "Mr. Chamblis's papers happen to have been placed in front of me just now. You're a relative?"

"Half-brother," I lied. "Same mum, different dads."

"Name?" the ER woman said. "I need it for Mr. Chamblis's chart."

"Crang."

"Good news and bad news for you, Mr. Crang. Your half-brother's right side is intact. His left side is broken up pretty badly."

"Is Freddie more or less disabled?"

"Broken foot, knee, hip, wrist, and shoulder."

"All on the left side?"

"Plus a skull fracture over the left ear."

"No internal injuries? No vital organs endangered?"

"Your half-brother seems to have been spared any of that."

"What's Freddie got to say about his wounds?"

"Quite a lot," the ER woman said. "But the doctors can't understand most of it. The trouble is with Mr. Chamblis's tongue. When he took the fall, his teeth clamped down on his tongue. Now it's swollen twice the normal size."

"Makes communicating awkward, I imagine."

"He's Mister Mumbles."

"How long do you plan to keep Freddie down there?"

"A week. Maybe more. You can visit any time."

The ER woman hung up.

I put down my cell, and went upstairs for a nap before meeting with the only two porn movie actresses I'd ever met in my entire, excitement-packed life.

CHAPTER THIRTY-ONE

I arrived at the Sovereign ahead of my two dates. The place wasn't large but it was classy. Its location situated the Sovereign in the neighbourhood labelled Little Italy. It had been called that for as long as I could remember and probably a lot longer. Two local young guys had started up the coffee shop a year or so ago, and by my lights, they were doing everything the right way.

The interior ran to dark wood panelling, with the same shade in the tables and the counters. I sat at a table for four, and while I waited, I admired the movie poster on the wall over the table. It was for a Fellini movie, but not an obvious one, not *Dolce Vita* or *Ginger and Fred*. The one in the poster was called *Il Bidone*. I needed to check it out.

Sal and Franny came in, making cooing sounds of appreciation for the layout. Both were dressed in T-shirts and jeans, attracting immediate approval from the clientele, which was young, male, and Italian.

Since I'd never met Franny in person, Sal performed the introductions.

"I've heard a lot about you, Crang," Franny said. "I like it that you're on our side, you being a lawyer and all."

"I've seen a little of your work," I said to Franny. "Very, ah, impressive."

The ladies sat down, and all three of us ordered cappuccinos. The barista assembled the coffees with panache. I felt like breaking into applause. The barista had black hair and the looks of a young Mastroianni. He served the cappuccinos from a tray, giving the placing of each cup on the table a small flourish. The girls and I tasted the coffees, and murmured our pleasure.

"Oh my god," Franny said, *sotto voce*, "the coffee guy's so totally gorgeous."

"He should be in movies," Sal said.

"Probably is," I said.

"You think so?" Franny said.

"Nobody works in a coffee shop," I said, "unless they own it or are pausing between roles on stage or screen."

"You would know things like that," Sal said to me.

"Because I'm so overwhelmingly handsome myself?"

"No," Sal said. "Because you've been around for a while."

I wasn't sure whether I had just been insulted.

"This place far enough off the beaten track for you girls?" I asked.

"That was just Sal being paranoid when she told you about meeting at a sort of secret place," Franny said.

"Listen," Sal said, "the type of guys we're dealing with, it pays to be cautious when you're going to make a major move."

"What's the major move?" I asked.

"Franny and I are quitting porn," Sal said. "No more movies."

I didn't point out to Sal that, technically, she had never entered the porn industry. She'd done multiple auditions but no movies.

"What persuaded you to quit at this particular moment?"

"It's only these last few days I've appreciated how demeaning the business is," Sal said. "For women, I mean."

"Also," Franny said, "how demeaning one particular man in the business is to the women."

"Freddie Chamblis?" I said.

"You noticed it too?" Franny asked.

"If you two stay with him long enough," I said, "his idea is to nudge you into prostitution with him in the role of pimp."

Franny gave me a surprised look. "Have you been going undercover or something? I only found out about that slimeball's operation a couple of days ago. It was from a girl I ran into who I used to make movies with, and now she does escort work. She hates it, naturally. But Freddie won't let her out. It's like he's got a lock on her."

"What we want to do before we quit," Sal said, "is bring Freddie down."

The handsome barista reappeared at the table.

"Would you ladies like some of our homemade biscotti?" he said. "On the house for customers as lovely as yourselves."

The girls giggled, and the barista placed a plate on the table. The plate held three biscotti.

"I'm included in the biscotti giveaway?" I said to the barista.

"Of course," he said, shrugging. "The ladies are our guests, and you're the ladies' guest."

Each of us munched a biscotti and agreed it was delicious.

"Your idea," I said to the girls, "is to resurrect the plan involving me on a sneak job at the porn mansion?"

"Correct," Sal said. "But it's got to be during tomorrow afternoon's audition, because after that Franny and I are so totally out of there."

"One thing," Franny said to me, "you better be super careful where Freddie Chamblis is concerned. You might not appreciate what a menacing bastard the guy really is."

"Freddie won't be on the premises tomorrow," I said. "Or any time soon."

Sal and Franny looked at one another, then back at me.

"What do you know that we don't?" Sal said.

"Freddie's in Mount Sinai," I said. "He took a bad fall this morning and suffered enough damage to make him no physical threat to anybody in the near future."

"Wow," Franny said, "that gives you practically a clear hour to search his office for whatever proof you need that he did what you think he might have done."

"Murder for one thing," Sal said to me. "Maury says you think Chamblis is behind the death of the Reverend at that phony church on St. Clair."

"I don't remember discussing murder suspects with Maury," I said.

"Nothing much gets past Maury," Sal said. "You must have noticed that."

"Speaking of his close observations," I said, "you think the porn auditions have slipped by Maury?"

"That's another reason I'm quitting," Sal said. "I want to get out before he discovers I've ever been involved."

"From my point of view," I said, "it'd be better if you were square with Maury right away, no matter what your status is in the business."

"I know," Sal said in a smaller voice. "It's not fair that you have your normal interactions with Maury, and all the time, you know something private about me that he isn't aware of."

"Annie knows too," I said.

"You told her?" Sal said. Her voice rose to mild hysteria.

"I tell her everything," I said.

"That's so sweet," Franny said. "I hope I meet a guy who feels that way about me."

"To be accurate, I tell Annie everything *eventually*," I said. "The moments of major threat to my personal safety I usually withhold until after I survive the threat."

"I'll tell Maury about the porn stuff," Sal said. "*Eventually.*"

I drank a little more cappuccino. It was so good I was trying to make the first cup last. If I ordered another, I'd soar over a healthy caffeine limit.

"Let's assume I gain easy access to the Freddie mansion," I said to Sal and Franny, "what's the layout in there?"

"Like I told you," Sal said, "the living room is converted into the set for the actual shoots. There's a door between the front hall and the living room, but it's kept strictly shut and locked while we work. No admittance whatsoever except for people who've got business on the set."

"Where's Freddie's office in relation to the living room and the movie set?" I asked.

"On the next floor up," Sal said. "You get to it by way of stairs behind a door at the far left of the front hall. At least, that's where we always see Freddie and a couple of other people heading after the shoot."

"Who are these people you're talking about?" I said. "The couple of others?"

"It's not as if we've ever made a close study of who comes and goes upstairs," Franny said, getting into the conversation.

"Give me a little taste of what you're reasonably sure of," I said.

"One's the guy I mentioned to you, the servant-type person," Sal said. "You know, polite and well-dressed, very tall, that guy. He goes upstairs."

"And the other?"

"He's sort of a weird dude," Franny said. "Also tall, in good shape. He's always hanging around, hoping to get cast in a video."

"Really?" Sal said, turning to look at Franny. "I know the guy you mean. Watching most of the time, that guy was, but he didn't do any audition I was part of."

"He was in one of my actual movies." Franny said. "Very eager guy. And so totally serious. You'd think his role was out of a Shakespeare play. I'd look at his face when he was getting himself ready to, you know, go down on me, and I'd get the impression he thought he was playing Hamlet. And I was Ophelia, except with no clothes on."

"How was his, ah, performance?" I said.

"Adequate," Franny said.

"This thespian you're talking about, the Hamlet guy, he has access to the mansion's upper floor?"

"He hangs with Freddie and the servant guy," Fanny said. "Which means he goes where they go."

"So they're on the set during the filming," I said, finishing the last of my cappuccino. "And then afterwards, they drift upstairs. Okay, I get that."

"Keep in mind tomorrow's an audition, not a shoot," Sal said. "That means we'll only be on the set an hour and a half at most."

"That ought to be long enough for me to check out the upstairs quarters," I said, standing up. "All in all, I think we got a plan."

Neither Sal nor Franny made a move that suggested they were thinking of leaving in my company. They seemed to have mutually agreed to stick around without saying anything to one another in front of me.

"You ladies are having another cappuccino?" I said.

"We're mostly curious about the barista's social attachments," Sal said. "Like, if he has one that's serious."

"If you mean sizing him up as boyfriend material, you've already got a boyfriend, Sal."

"Franny hasn't," Sal said.

"Good point."

Franny said to me, "It's too forward of me, that's what you're thinking."

"What I think," I said to Franny, "the barista may be about to become a very lucky man."

The two girls smiled at one another.

CHAPTER THIRTY-TWO

It was mid-afternoon on Sunday, and Sal was at the wheel of her Volvo with Franny riding shotgun up front. I had the back seat all to myself. We were on Kingston Road east of Woodbine Avenue in the part of the east end known as the Beach, still a few blocks from the neighbourhood identified by the girls as the location of Freddie Chamblis's home of impressive luxury.

"You and the barista make a connection yesterday?" I asked Franny.

"I hardly slept ten minutes last night," Franny said.

"The way I'm supposed to interpret that, you were carrying on all night with the barista?"

Franny turned in the front seat to look at me. "It was the caffeine that kept me awake, Crang," she said, sounding indignant. "I drank three cappuccinos yesterday afternoon."

"You weren't carrying on?"

"I don't sleep with people on a first date, if that's what you're implying."

For a moment, I was at a loss about how to answer Franny on that one.

Franny said, "Just because a girl makes porn movies doesn't mean she has loose morals in her real life."

"Of course," I said, "but are you going to be stepping out with the barista any time soon?"

"Well, he hasn't got a girlfriend, and he invited me back to the Sovereign for another cappuccino."

It seemed best to drop the subject. "That sounds like progress," I said to Franny before I went silent.

Sunday afternoon traffic on Kingston Road was heavy and noisy, but two blocks further along, after Sal turned right and steered down a street just past a store with a big Häagen-Dazs sign out front, a calm seemed to come over that part of town. It felt tranquil, a neighbourhood that promised peace and quiet. Soon, the houses grew larger, and the land began a long slope down to Lake Ontario. Our view of the lake was blocked by the neighbourhood's heavy forest of trees, but we could feel the fresh breeze off the water. The street we were on became twisty and winding, and the houses on the hillside lots escalated in size to a category that rated mansion status.

"See the place down the block on the right, Crang?" Sal said. "That's where we're headed."

The house was sprawling, the largest residence on the street, occupying the biggest parcel of land. Judging from the glimpses I got of tall fencing at the back, the house came with a swimming pool, no doubt Olympic-sized. The house itself was only two storeys, but it covered so much horizontal area that it probably had five or six bedrooms, maybe even a bathroom for each.

"This has got to be a seven- or eight-million-dollar spread," I said.

"Did we exaggerate?" Franny said to me.

"If anything," I said, "you understated."

Sal was coasting, taking her time to let me size up the layout at my leisure. The house was made of stone and had a large porch across the front. As we got closer, I could see two men talking on the porch.

Sweet Jesus! I recognized both guys. If they spotted me, they'd know who I was. Neither of them would send any love in my direction.

"Drive past the house, Sal," I said, speaking as authoritatively as I could manage while at the same time ducking below the car's window level.

"There's a space in front of Freddie's place, Crang," Sal said. "What's wrong with parking there?"

"Keep going!" I said through clenched teeth.

"Hey, Ernie and Lex are on the porch," Franny said.

"Who's Lex?" I said from my undignified position on the car's floor.

"The guy we told you about," Franny said. "Thinks he's doing Hamlet in every scene."

"Totally a weirdo," Sal said.

The girls might know the man as Lex, but to me, he was Roger Carnale's chauffeur.

"It's pretty usual for those two guys to be around, Crang," Sal said. She had pulled up at the curb a half block from the mansion. "Why are you freaking out?"

I straightened up in the back seat. "Ernie's the guy who smashed my coffee maker," I said. "Ernie's a guy I understand to be active in the protection racket and available for enforcer duties."

"On purpose, he smashed your coffee maker?" Franny said.

I nodded yes.

"What's Ernie doing at the porn shoot?" I said.

"Whenever Freddie can't show up for whatever reason," Franny said, "Ernie fills in."

"Freddie figures muscle needs to be on the job at every video session?"

"I never thought of it that way," Franny said. "But, yes, I suppose it may be his approach."

"As far as you know," I said, "neither one of them, Freddie or Ernie, has been called on to do any rough stuff?"

"They just stand around checking out girls' tits and whatnot."

"What's the plan now, Crang?" Sal said. "You can't come inside if there are all these people who'll know you."

"Let's just go ahead as we discussed," I said, "except you bring the contract out to me in the car. I'll bide my time till the auditions get under way."

"That'll work," Sal said.

She and Franny fussed with their handbags in a small display of what I took to be pre-performance nerves.

"Think of this as your last hoorah in the porn industry, girls," I said. "And it's all for a good cause."

"What's the good cause again?" Franny asked.

"Bringing down Freddie," I said, "the exploiter of helpless females."

"Oh yeah," Franny said.

The girls walked back to the mansion, and it wasn't until twenty minutes later that Sal reappeared. She was carrying her contract, and her clothing appeared to consist solely of a lightweight white gown that ended mid-thigh.

"What's happening in the house?" I said.

"That creep Lex is doing an audition scene with me," Sal said.

"Want me to write a clause in the contract that you never perform with people whose given names include an X?"

"Like I'm X-rated?" Sal said, smiling.

"They're set to start?"

"Soon as I go back," Sal said. "They'll be locking the door into the set in a couple of minutes."

"If I give it five minutes, I can make my move?"

Sal nodded. "I'll leave the front door unlocked. That gets you in, and when you're finished with your poking around, put the contract on one of the tables in the entrance hall."

Sal handed me her contract, and walked back up the sidewalk. Halfway to the house, she flipped up the thin white gown and wiggled her bare bum in my direction. The reaction this little display generated in me was mostly embarrassment. I didn't want to see the girlfriend of my friend in a state of clotheslessness. For that matter, now that I knew Franny a little, I didn't care to be around when she was naked either. The way I was now feeling, I intended to keep Annie the sole woman I would study in the nude for the rest of my life. Maybe I was experiencing an attack of puritanism, but if so, so what?

The contract Sal had handed me read like routine stuff for any performer in movies or TV shows. Conracts were never my long suit, but for something to make me feel like I was earning my lawyer's fee, I wrote in a clause about the Party of the First Part, namely Sal, refusing to appear in scenes involving oral sex.

Since I couldn't spot a reason for making any other corrections or additions, I folded the contract, and slipped it into my jacket pocket. I got out of the Volvo, all set to do my sneak job on Freddie Chamblis's porn mansion.

CHAPTER THIRTY-THREE

The mansion's front hall would dwarf the living room in Annie's and my house. It was more exquisitely furnished too. It featured two love seats with midnight blue satin covers and a scattering of small carved wooden tables. Next to one of the love seats, a plant with exotic green leaves sat in a white container. If I correctly remembered one of the Garden Goddess's informal lectures, the plant was a schefflera. Commonly called an umbrella plant for a reason I couldn't bring back.

The front hall's floor was made of high-quality black tile, and on the wall just inside the front door hung a painting I recognized. I didn't know the painting specifically, but I was positive it was a piece by a Quebec painter named Riopelle. It had the thick layers of paint in his style. Someone, maybe Riopelle himself, labelled the style "lyrical abstraction."

What the hell, I thought to myself, standing in this lovely room looking at the high-priced painting. Something was way off here. I hadn't been two minutes in the place, and already nothing squared with my expectations. Freddie Chamblis wouldn't hang a Riopelle on the wall of a house he owned. From what I knew of him, he would be a black-velvet painting type of person, or maybe he'd put up comic pictures of bulldogs. The other thing about Freddie, no matter what impression Sal and Franny had formed — I was betting a seven- or-eight-million-dollar residence like this one was way beyond his financial situation. He might earn a large buck in porn and conceivably more as an enforcer, but he wouldn't pull in mansion money. Something was screwy with the image of Freddie as the owner of the home I had just entered. I should have caught on to it earlier, not that there was any reason to reprimand myself now. Still, I silently vowed to build more common sense into sleuthing on the Flame case.

A hand-printed note was Scotch-taped to the closed door on the far left of the entrance hall: PRIVATE OFFICE. VIDEO PERSONNEL MUST NOT ENTER THIS PART OF THE HOUSE. The note wasn't signed, not by Freddie or anyone else.

I opened the door and climbed the flight of thickly carpeted stairs. At the top, a wide hall ran both ways, straight ahead and behind me in the other direction. The floor was covered in a carpet with an even thicker pile than the covering on the stairs. I had the feeling I might sink in up to my shins.

Nothing stirred on the entire floor. The air up there was still and silent. Whatever sounds the video crew might be making in the living room didn't carry to the second floor.

I took a few steps down the hall in the straight-ahead direction, glancing into the first room I came to on my left. It was a sitting room, furnished in masculine taste. A black leather couch and two matching black leather armchairs were the main pieces of furniture. Overhead hung a small black chandelier. Handy to the sofa was a coffee table in dark wood. Just one object sat on the coffee table, but the object, a book, was enough to knock me for a loop.

Edward Everett Horton's face beamed at me from the book's cover. I was staring at a copy of Annie's new Horton biography. Flipping the book open, I turned straight to the title page. Annie had signed it:

For Roger Carnale,

From one movie fan to another.

Best wishes,
Annie B. Cooke

Annie had dated it the previous Wednesday, the day of the book launch in New York. She had never met Roger, and her inscription was the kind of pseudo-personal thing an author would write for somebody she had never met.

"Find something that interests you?" a man's voice said behind me.

I turned around.

"As a matter of fact, yeah," I said, holding up the book. "The woman I live with wrote this."

"How nice for you," the man said. Medium-sized and balding, he looked in his early forties. If his comment was meant to convey disdain, it came across as half-hearted and maybe a little tired. But the tone of the guy's voice was precise and careful. The same two adjectives applied to the way he was dressed. He had on a dark blue suit, a white shirt, and a tie decorated with narrow, slanted stripes. The shirt's collar and cuffs looked starched. I couldn't remember the last time I'd come across somebody in a starched shirt for everyday wear. Maybe the guy had been to church that morning.

"Jerome Suggs Fed-Ex'd the book to Roger?"

The man nodded. "You must be Mr. Crang," he said. "The lawyer."

I took my turn nodding, "And you are Roger's accountant?"

"Jerome used Purolator," the man said. "Just to be exact."

"How about the accountant part, just to be exact? That's you?"

"I'm Arthur Kingsmill," he said. "And, yes, I'm Mr. Carnale's accountant, for my sins."

Kingsmill made no move to shake hands or to greet me as a

welcome visitor. I didn't suppose I was welcome. Taking the social initiative, I sat down on the leather couch. After a little hesitation, Kingsmill sat in one of the armchairs opposite me.

"Tell me," I said, "is this Roger's house?"

"Whose house did you think it was?"

"On that," I said, "I was misinformed."

"Maybe not entirely," Kingsmill said. "If you came for the waters, there's a very large swimming pool at the back."

Kingsmill smiled for the first time. It looked like he was out of practice with his smiling. I smiled back, letting him know I appreciated his small *Casablanca* joke.

"I can't help noticing the painting on the wall behind you," I said. "That's a Ron Bloore?"

"So I understand."

The painting was one of Bloore's white-on-white creations. It made a nice contrast with the sitting room's black furniture.

"So far, I've been in two rooms," I said, "and I've seen two paintings by Canadian artists who have terrific reputations."

"The paintings play a part in one of Roger's many schemes," Kingsmill said.

"What's the scheme? To build a nice collection?"

"Building the nice collection is only Part One."

"And the second part? Not that it's any of my business."

"It isn't," Kingsmill said. "But I'm feeling confessional. Roger intends to donate the collection, when it's complete enough, to the Art Gallery of Ontario for a sizeable tax credit."

"He seems to have a good eye."

"What he has, Mr. Crang, is a good advisor," Kingsmill said. "Roger hired a woman to tell him what to buy and for how much. This woman normally chooses the paintings for big law firms and the head offices of banks."

"Everybody interested in art has to start the learning process somewhere," I said, sounding like mister magnanimous. "I learned about Canadian art from Annie."

Kingsmill let my remark pass.

"As I'm sure you know, Mr. Crang," he said, "you're not supposed to be here, in Roger's house."

"Because I'm no longer Roger's lawyer of record?" I said. "Yes, I know."

"And you've been paid."

"That too."

"Are you going to tell me why you're in the house?"

I reached into my jacket pocket for Sal's contract, and held it up for Kingsmill's long range observation.

"I've been retained by one of the young women downstairs," I said. "She wants me to vet her contract. I came up here, looking for a desk to sit at while I checked it over."

Kingsmill's face registered distaste of a high degree.

"You don't approve of the porn shoot going on down there?" I said.

"Even if I didn't have a wife and two young daughters, I'd still consider the videos those people make shameless and dangerous."

"Roger doesn't feel the same way?"

"He goes down and watches the sex if he happens to be around, but what he likes best is the money a man named Chamblis pays for renting the premises."

"How much?"

"Ten thousand for each week they shoot."

"The payments are made in cash?"

"What else would they be?" Kingsmill said. "Roger calls it his pin money. It finances his lifestyle."

"The canes, the fedoras, the champagne?"

"Taken altogether, the things that Roger insists he can't do without run to a very pretty penny."

"Veuve Clicquot and the rest of it — Roger seems to go first cabin in everything."

"Unfortunately for our balance sheet, the ten thousand from Chamblis is a drop in the bucket."

"You're up against it at bill-paying time?"

I thought Kingsmill would probably avoid an answer, but before he could open his mouth, we could hear feet thumping on the carpeted stairs leading to the second floor, somebody moving very quickly.

"That'll be Mahuda," Kingsmill said.

"Who's Mahuda?"

"I've been told you met him the other day," Kingsmill said. "Roger's chauffeur."

The rushed footsteps reached the second floor, and turned down the hall in the opposite direction from the sitting room.

"Any idea what's he doing up here?" I asked.

"The servants' quarters at the far end of the hall are Mahuda's," Kingsmill said. "Roger likes him to be handy at all times."

"Lex Mahuda, that's his name?"

Kingsmill gave a small laugh. "Lex?" he said. "Is that what he's calling himself?"

"According to two of the girls downstairs."

"His first name's Anin," Kingsmill said. "I should know. I make out the pay vouchers around here."

"Lex is probably an affectation for his porn persona."

"That sounds like his taste."

Kingsmill stood up. He seemed restless, on the verge of tossing me out. Doing it politely but firmly, I had no doubt.

I stood too. "Before I leave, you don't suppose I could see some more of Roger's paintings?"

"As long as there's not much lingering, Mr. Crang."

"I'm assuming Roger's not around."

"He's out of the country."

"Manhattan?"

"Los Angeles."

"Ah, movie business?"

"Behind you, Mr. Crang," Kingsmill said in an insistent voice. "If you're content with two more pictures, they're through that door."

Before I made a move, there was another thumping of feet. This time, the thumps began in the servant's quarters and continued down the stairs to the first floor.

"Mahuda again," Kingsmill said. "Probably put on something sexy for the cameras."

"As long as it's white," I said. "He needs white to meet the wardrobe requirement."

"A codpiece perhaps?"

"Maybe not," I said. "The point of the movies is for the actors to take their clothes off."

"And in Mahuda's case, disrobing would reveal the codpiece's deception?"

"You're catching on, Mr. Kingsmill."

Kingsmill grimaced the way he had earlier. He walked across the sitting room, and opened the door into the room off the sitting room. It was a large office dominated by a beautiful partners desk that must have been a century old.

"Roger's?" I said.

"As everybody always says, nothing but the very best for Roger."

"So I've heard," I said. "Where do you work out of?"

"I have a very pleasant office down the hall," Kingsmill said.

The room we were in had other touches of a Carnale-esque nature. Two shelves opposite the desk held rows of his fedoras. On a shelf below the hats, another shelf accommodated several briefcases of different leathers and designs. And standing upright below the briefcases were racks of walking sticks, a dozen at least. Most were wood, some looked like they could be metal, the majority were round in shape, two or three gave me the impression they could be square from top to bottom.

A memory flashed through my mind, Wally Crawford's description of the weapon that bludgeoned the Reverend. Wally said it was probably square. Was that it? Or did Wally just imply something about the bludgeon striking with a straight-lined force? Not from a round weapon but from something more rectangular?

"The paintings are on the other wall, Mr. Crang," Kingsmill said.

My eyes went to the wall Kingsmill was pointing out, to a large painting of Second World War soldiers marching away from the fighting somewhere in Europe. It was by Alex Colville, and it was a beauty, probably from Colville's earlier years after he returned from his own service overseas.

Further over on the same wall, sitting above a side table, there was a small Albert Franck painting of a Toronto backyard in early spring when the cityscape looked dirty and desolate. I loved Franck's pictures. They were the most Toronto pictures I could imagine.

I stalled around for a while, gabbing about my enthusiasm for Albert Franck. Kingsmill wasn't much interested, but I kept up the line of patter, figuring I might spot something else in the office that offered hints about Carnale's business affairs. I'd already learned the guy might be spending beyond his means. Was there more?

Kingsmill went along with the stall for a few minutes until he ran out of patience. He steered me down the stairs, and waited in the front hall, standing at the foot of the stairs, tapping one foot, barely able to mask his impatience with my slow progress. I stopped at a small table against the wall close to the living-room door, though it wasn't serving as a living room at the moment. The small table displayed a lovely vase. I lifted the vase and placed Sal's contract underneath it.

I thanked Kingsmill, and turned toward the front door. Kingsmill vanished up the stairs. I hadn't taken more than a pace or two across the front hall when the door to the living room swung open with force. Sal and Franny came out in a big hurry. They were not quite dressed. Each had pulled on a thong, but both pressed the rest of their clothes to their bosoms as they tore into the front hall.

"Stop him, Crang!" Sal shouted. She was barely through the living room door, running and spitting at the same time.

Stop who?

Sal was first into the hall, Franny right on her heels, and three or four long steps back was Lex. Sal flew past me, then Franny at such a clip she dropped a blue sock and didn't bother to break momentum long enough to get it back.

Lex wore an angry expression and nothing else. Judging from the red swelling around his bare groin, someone had kicked him in the crotch. No wonder he looked pissed off.

"Crang!" Sal screamed, still in full flight, glancing back. "Do something!"

I pulled out my cellphone. By then, I was backpedalling like a mad man to keep a space between me and the hard-charging Lex.

Holding the cell in the camera position, I snapped pictures of the naked idiot.

He kept coming at me, still determined to get past me to the girls who were now almost at the front door. I didn't think Lex had yet caught on that I was photographing him in a state no man would want recorded.

Finally Lex got the point of my picture-taking. That flummoxed him. He didn't know what to do with his hands. First, he lowered both to cover his crotch, then he raised one to block his face from the camera. Lex was a man in confusion. He stopped running. He seemed to forget the girls. For a second or two, his anger had nowhere to go. The indecision didn't last long. He shifted his temper tantrum to me. He lunged forward and swung his right fist in my general direction. It was a lousy punch. I made an easy move to let his fist slip by. Lex lost his balance. I turned and was through the open front door before he straightened up.

I sprinted down the front walk to the sidewalk. Looking over my shoulder, I saw no sign of Lex. He must have given up pursuit of the girls and me. Maybe the earlier kick to the gonads had zapped his energy.

I slowed down to a trot, and caught up to the girls just as they reached Sal's Volvo. Both of them were still nude except for the thongs, still clutching the rest of their clothes to their breasts. I said

I'd drive. Sal managed to flip me the keys, and both girls climbed into the back seat. I drove down the winding street, not stopping until I reached a pond at the bottom of the hill. I pulled over and parked.

By then, both girls were dressed.

"I lost a sock," Franny said.

"Franny," Sal said to her, "it's not like we're going back for the sake of one damn sock."

"It's my favourite shade of blue."

Sal reached over to cup Franny's chin. "But, listen, thanks for kicking old Lex in the nuts."

"Franny did that?" I said. "She's the one responsible for all the red swelling around his privates?"

"That's my girl," Sal said.

"What brought it all on?" I asked. "Lex tried for the forbidden move?"

"A blow job!" Sal said. "He tried to stick his penis in my mouth! Even just a taste of it was disgusting. And, my god, humiliating!"

"His real name's Anin Mahuda," I said. "The guy who calls himself Lex."

My news brought Sal to a brief pause.

"Crang," she said, "are you telling me and Franny that for everything the two of us went through, this is all you learned? The idiot's name?"

"Freddie Chamblis doesn't own the mansion," I said. "Roger Carnale does."

"Who's Roger Carnale?" Franny said.

"Flame's manager," Sal said.

"The singer?" Franny said. "Oh wow, I love Flame's voice."

"Roger's probably the tall, well-dressed, polite, servant type guy you ladies have talked about," I said. "The one you said dropped into the video shoots now and then."

"Why didn't somebody tell me who he was?" Franny said. "I'd freak to meet Flame."

"So the day was worthwhile for you, Crang?" Sal said.

"Something funny's going on with Carnale's finances," I said.

"That's helpful in what way?"

"Always follow the money," I said. "That's what somebody mixed up in the Watergate scandal once said. That's my new plan with the Flame situation."

"What's the Watergate scandal?" Franny asked.

"It's totally old-timey," Sal said to Franny. "Crang's majorly big on old-timey stuff."

"Following the money makes sense as an investigative technique in any era," I said.

Sal looked at me as if she had another question. But she didn't ask it.

"I need to get home for a shower," she said.

I drove a block down to Queen Street, turned right, and pointed toward Lake Shore Boulevard.

"Crang," Franny said after awhile, "can you introduce me to Flame sometime after you've finished whatever job it is you're doing for him?"

"Be my honour, Franny."

I left the girls and the Volvo at Sal's condo, and walked home.

Follow the money? It wasn't such a bad idea.

CHAPTER THIRTY-FOUR

I was still in bed next morning, awake but not alert, when my cell signaled a long-distance call coming in. The bedside clock said 7:20. If Annie was phoning from Los Angeles, it would be 4:20 a.m. where she was. Ergo, the caller couldn't be Annie. The screen on my cell read "Hotel Bel-Air." Would the *Ellen DeGeneres* people put Annie up at a super chic place like the Bel-Air? Kingsmill, the accountant, said Roger Carnale was in Los Angeles. He was a guy more likely to book himself into the Bel-Air, whether his finances were shaky or not.

I answered the phone in a noncommittal tone of voice.

"Sweetie," Annie said, "you'll never guess what's happening out here."

"At this time of morning," I said, "nothing should be happening in Los Angeles."

"I flew in on the red-eye," Annie said. "Now I know why they call it that. My eyes look like a couple of tiny ball bearings except mine are pink, not silver. Also my sense of time is shot."

"But something's still happening?"

"Jerome's leading a small revolt of the troops against Carnale."

"What troops are there besides Jerome?"

"You're right, there's only one other," Annie said. "But he's crucial."

"Somebody I've never heard of?"

"Flame himself. Jerome's trying to line him up on the rebel side against Carnale. Nothing's set in stone, but it's the first time someone's even suggested Flame should question Carnale's way of doing business."

I made a whistling sound. "And the showdown's out there today?"

"They're going to meet with people from the movie company. That's when Jerome is set to make his pitch. Everybody's supposed to be in Los Angeles. Jerome's asking for something like a piece of artistic control over the movie."

"You think he has a shot at getting it?"

"One thing is for sure, Jerome's become much more realistic about the movie's budget."

"As evidenced by what?"

"Instead of Scarlett Johansson, he's lobbying for one of those English actresses who do an American accent like they were born and bred in upper New York State. I forget this girl's name, but she comes way cheaper than Scarlett, and she's got the chops."

"So now there's going to be a sit-down in Hollywood about all of this," I said. "My source tells me Roger has already hopped to the coast."

"And your source in this instance is who?"

I couldn't just tell Annie that the guy who brought me up to date on Carnale's travel schedule was Arthur Kingsmill, the accountant. She'd be motivated to ask a ton more questions about when and why I got on to Kingsmill, and all the rest of the tale. My immediate reaction was to get out front on the whole deal, and tell her on my own the entire story of the weekend's events. Not the part about the tussle on the roof with Freddie Chamblis, but everything else, especially the scene at the porn mansion which turned out not to be Chamblis's property but was, instead, Roger Carnale's. I got going, and talked for ten minutes straight.

"This means you've liberated Sal and her friend from the clutches of the pornography business?" Annie said when I finished.

"In effect."

"Now the only person you need to free up from the whole mess is yourself."

I skipped past Annie's remark. "Kingsmill," I said, "left me with the impression Carnale might be wanting for bucks."

"Maybe that's why Jerome thinks Carnale is likely to sit still while Jerome takes his run at Carnale's authority, if you can follow that thicket of my thinking," Annie said. "Normally, I gather Carnale would have popped a gasket at the temerity."

"That's about the size of it," I said.

"Usually I need to pry this kind of stuff out of you," Annie said. "Thanks for sharing, sweetie."

"You're welcome."

"But from what you said, you're not any closer to figuring out who killed the Reverend."

"I'm not as keen on Freddie Chamblis as the murderer, not like I was yesterday."

"Leave it to the police. It's their job, not yours."

Annie's voice sounded to me like it had run out of gas, and I told her so.

"I think I'm likely to be here three more nights," she said, pushing past the fatigue. "There's some rescheduling needed for my item with Ellen."

"Not because they're having second thoughts about the value of Edward Everett Horton as an attraction for Ellen's audience?"

"Just the reverse," Annie said. "It's because they're juicing the item up to a thing where Ellen and I exchange our own versions of Edward Everett's double takes."

"The way you did it solo at the book launch?"

"That's where the show got the idea. Someone who was at the launch told them I had a rubber face."

"In this case, it's a compliment."

"I took it as such," Annie said.

"You got the double-take routine routine down pat, sweetie," I said. "You can relax on that score."

"Relaxing is what I need to do right now, this very minute," Annie said, her voice falling away to practically zero. "Rest my little pink eyes."

A moment or two later, I hung up, but I had the feeling Annie might already be zoned out on her phone.

CHAPTER THIRTY-FIVE

Wally Crawford, ace homicide detective, had told me to meet him at ten that morning on the bench, next to what he called "the brick-laying chick." I knew he was talking about the sculpture outside police headquarters on College Street. The sculpture had baffled me from the time it was installed a few years earlier. It showed a life-sized female cop in full gear — a handgun holster on her left hip, cellphone, or maybe it was an old-time walkie talkie, baton, the whole set up. But the woman's right hand was lifting a small trowel of cement that she was applying to a wall of stone blocks. It was symbolic as all get-out, but the symbolism seemed forced to me.

I sat studying the thing for about five minutes before Wally walked out of police headquarters.

"Let's go for coffee," he said.

"You can't stand the sculpture either?" I asked, still looking at the brick-laying chick.

"That's why we're going to Second Cup," Wally said. "So I don't have to listen while you analyze the thing."

The local Second Cup was on College, a few steps past Bay Street on the west side. Cops liked to go there because it was handy and reasonably quiet. Wally and I picked up cups of coffee at the counter, large for him, small for me. We sat in a booth next to the window.

Wally pulled a package of fifty or sixty pages from a large white envelope.

"Interim report from Forensics on the murder of the Reverend Alton Douglas," Wally said. "The final report won't be much different."

"What's it say about the murder weapon?" I asked.

Wally leaned across the table. "You're asking a question before I even get started?" he said. "For crissake, Crang, I'm not supposed to show you anything in the Reverend's file, but here I am, and already you're making demands."

"And don't think I'm not grateful, Wally."

"But overanxious."

"Let's just say I'm keen."

"The reason I'm sharing information with you is I think you've got ideas about the killer's identity."

"You're not wrong there, Wally."

"In addition to that, you might even divulge some ideas to me."

"I like your choice of determiners, Wally. *Some* ideas."

"In grade school, when I went, the teachers said 'some' was a pronoun."

"It still can be, but nowadays, in the way you used it, they call it a determiner."

"Whatever, you won't share all your ideas with me. Just some. Am I right?"

"Right," I said.

"Okay," Wally said, flipping through the first dozen pages of the pile in his hand, "a single blow ended the Reverend's life. The killer swung a blunt object as he faced the victim. The object connected with the Reverend's left ear and kept going into his skull. On the way, it hit what's called the middle meningeal artery. That caused bleeding from a high pressure system, something you get in just 1 to 3 percent of cases. It happened in this one. We're talking about a catastrophic brain injury. That could have killed him, but he also could have suffered a cardiac death resulting from lack of oxygen. Take your pick. The Reverend was lying in his office dying and dead, mostly dead by far, for a while. All of it resulting from just one blow to the poor sucker's head."

"Whatever he'd done in his life," I said, "the Reverend didn't deserve that kind of suffering."

"Not a lot of actual suffering when you think about it in numerical terms."

"From the time he saw the perpetrator swing the blunt object until the object knocked him unconscious — what would that be? Two or three seconds?"

"Maybe quicker," Wally said. "But does any of this measuring of time make us feel better for the Reverend?"

"Not much."

"Maybe we should stick to business."

"For example," I said, "what do the Forensics people say about time of death?"

Wally didn't need to look at the papers in his hand to answer. "Not earlier than 10 p.m., not later than midnight. Most likely closer to the latter."

"That's last Tuesday night, right?"

"Correct."

"What time did the barista kid discover the body Wednesday morning?"

"Not that the time particularly matters to your detecting, but it was around 9:15 a.m."

Wally flipped through more of the papers in his hand.

"Are we getting to an extremely crucial detail?" I asked. "The blunt object that did all the damage?"

"This is the hard part," Wally said. "In more ways than one."

"What have you got?"

"The blunt object in question was primarily metal in makeup."

"Primarily?"

"Overwhelmingly," Wally said. "But there were traces of fabric mixed with the metal."

"Like what, the cloth was knitted or weaved into the metal somehow? Or around the metal? Is semantics the problem here?"

"Crang," Wally said, looking at me in a steely-eyed way, "I get the feeling semantics is always a problem with you."

"Can you simplify things for me? Is that asking too much?"

"The guys in Forensics say it was leather among the metal."

"That's the so-called fabric?"

"Leather is a chemically treated animal skin."

"I get it," I said. "Your Forensics experts detected the presence of the chemicals, which is how they could tell it was leather."

Wally checked through the last pages in the bundle from Forensics.

"All that's left of importance," he said, "is the shape of the blunt object."

"What's the shape?"

"Would you for chrissake wait until I finish what I'm saying?"

"Sorry, Wally. I seem to be in an eager frame of mind this morning."

"It's annoying the hell out of me," Wally said. He had slowed his delivery, either to tune me in to the deliberateness of his cadence or just to pay me back for irritating him.

"The killing object appears to have a straight line in its shape, you follow me? It wasn't a baseball bat or anything else that had entirely rounded contours. It would be shaped in more of a rectangular form."

"Like a two-by-four maybe?"

Wally shook his head. "There were no traces of wood in the head wound."

"Just indications of metal and a hint of leather, and the metal wasn't rounded. It was more like a bar in shape."

"You got it," Wally said. "And that's all you get."

He slid the sheets of paper back into the large white envelope.

"Now," Wally said, folding his hands on the table. "There's something I'd like you to get for me."

"A solution to the Reverend's murder. Right, I'm on it, Wally."

Wally shook his head. "Much easier than that."

"What?"

"You're going to ask your client to put something nice on each of my daughters' Facebook pages," Wally said. He took a card from his wallet. "On here, I've written their particulars, Fleur and Sandrine. Ask him, does he mind making each one different. So Fleur's isn't the same as Sandrine's and vice versa. You understand what I'm saying?"

At first, I wasn't clear who Wally was talking about. My client? Which one? Before I looked like a total fool, I realized we were on the subject of Flame, hero to Wally's two teenaged kids.

"These are your daughters?"

"My wife's French."

"Fleur and Sandrine."

"The wife's Babette but you don't need to bother with her Facebook page. Just the two girls. There'll be no trouble with that?"

"I'll speak to Flame's mother today."

"You're my guy on this, Crang."

Wally stood, and without another word, he walked away, carrying his large coffee, heading back to police headquarters.

My cup was still half full. I leaned back in the booth and thought about the blunt object that had murdered the Reverend. Before the meeting with Wally, I was thinking that maybe one of Roger Carnale's walking sticks was the murder weapon. Most of the sticks were probably wood, but there must be a few metal canes among his vast collection. But where did the leather fit in? I wouldn't know the answer until I got a long look at the collection in Carnale's office. No one was going to invite me to examine the sticks at my leisure. Getting in would necessitate a surreptitious entry to the Carnale mansion. I needed to bring Maury into the job. Talking to him might be a delicate operation all by itself, though, depending on how Sal framed her explanation to him of her adventures in the porn trade and my role in the adventures. Maury might think I'd betrayed him. Smooth relations with him might need a little fancy talking on my part.

I finished my coffee, stood up, and started out of the Second Cup.

"Sir," a girl said behind me. "You forgot your envelope."

The girl was wearing a Second Cup uniform. She was busy wiping down the table Wally and I had sat at. From Wally's side of the booth, the girl lifted the white envelope with the Forensics report in it.

I took the envelope from the young woman, put it under my arm, and said thanks warmly. The fifty or sixty sheets of paper were still inside the envelope. Had Wally forgotten them or had he left me the whole package deliberately?

Wally was a meticulous kind of guy. He didn't forget things. I felt pretty sure he intended that I should have the report and make whatever use I could of all the specifics in it. Maybe it was a bonus for promising to get Flame to write something on his daughters' Facebook pages. That made sense.

CHAPTER THIRTY-SIX

Mount Sinai Hospital was a ten-minute walk from Second Cup, west on College to University Avenue, then south a couple of blocks. The proximity gave me a chance to drop in on Freddie Chamblis, my would-be assassin. I'd written him off as the mastermind behind the blackmail plot. And I doubted he had any involvement in the Reverend's murder. But what about his attempt to drop me off the roof?

Freddie occupied a double room on the sixth floor. The room's second bed was empty, and Freddie, in his bed, was encased in plaster down most of his left side. He was hooked to one machine that provided his nourishment and another that removed his waste. A nurse, her back to me, was fussing with the hookups. Looking over the nurse's shoulder, Freddie spotted me standing in the doorway. His face went into terror mode. A lumpy sound came out of his throat.

"Don't even think about talking," the nurse said to Freddie in a voice sharp and impatient. "Your oral surgeon spent an hour stitching that tongue. We don't want to spoil his work, do we?"

The nurse, noticing where Freddie's eyes were focused, turned and saw me.

"No visitors unless you're a relative," she said.

She was middle-aged, and had deep black hair that didn't owe its colour to nature. She seemed tired and crabby. Maybe just crabby.

"I'm a half-brother," I said, still comfortable with the lie.

"Your mother married my patient's father?"

"That would make us stepbrothers," I said. "With us, it's the same mum but different dads."

The nurse frowned at me. What was this woman's problem? I checked out Freddie again. Terror was still written all over his face. Maybe the patient's attack of the jitters bothered the nurse.

"I think if you check Freddie's chart," I said to the nurse, "things will clear up about my identity."

"You can't just come barging into a patient's room," she said. "Especially one as badly injured as Mr. …"

The nurse had forgotten Freddie's name. She walked to the foot of the bed and flipped through the pages on the clipboard attached to the bed's railing. My name was probably on the first page where the patient's relatives were listed, but she went through the motions of studying each page.

After two or three useless minutes, she flipped back to the first page.

"Name?" she said to me.

"Crang."

"You say you're Mr. Chamblis's stepbrother," she said. "I'll give you ten minutes, but under no circimstances is Mr. Chamblis to speak."

"It's half-brother, but thank you."

"Thousands of dollars have gone into the tongue surgery."

"Got you."

The nurse patted Freddie's good arm, the right one, and left the room.

"Nice to see you looking so spry, Freddie," I said.

Freddie stared at me. His eyes were glassy, and fright still hung in the vicinity.

"Just a couple of simple questions, Freddie," I said. "Signals with your right arm ought to be okay for answers. First question, why did you try to kill me?"

Freddie kept staring. He moved his right hand in a squeezing motion. The squeezing probably indicated Freddie's state of hopelessness.

Freddie was right to feel hopeless. There was no way hand signals could answer the question I'd just asked. I looked around the room. A copy of *Maclean's*, with Justin Trudeau on the cover, sat on a chair beside the room's empty bed. I picked up the magazine, flattened Wally Crawford's envelope against it, and lay the combination of magazine and envelope on the right side of Freddie's bed. I put my pen in his right hand.

"You better not be left-handed, Freddie," I said.

Freddie shook his head, the first demonstration that his brain was functioning.

"To repeat," I said, "why did you try to kill me?"

Freddie went immediately to work with the pen. In answer to my first question, he wrote two words.

"Not kill."

"You thought I'd survive a fall from the twelfth floor?"

"Land on balcony," Freddie wrote. His handwriting was small and tidy.

"You were aiming to drop me on the balcony one floor down?" I said.

Freddie nodded.

"So I was supposed to end up in the same shape you're in right now?"

"Teach u lesson," Freddie wrote.

"A lesson about what?"

"Stay away from blackmail."

"You're the guy running the blackmailing of my client Flame?"

"No!"

"I like the exclamation point, Freddie," I said. "It indicates sincerity."

"Paid to teach u lesson."

"Paid? Who paid you?"

Freddie didn't hesitate with his reply. I thought he'd dodge a straight answer to a question like that, but his crash to the balcony must have knocked the prevarication out of his system.

"Carnale," he wrote.

"Roger Carnale wanted you to warn me off?"

Freddie nodded.

"He left it up to you to choose the place and means of doing the warning?"

Another nod.

"But not kill me?"

Freddie got busy again with the pen.

"Fuking no."

"Your spelling's disappointing, Freddie."

"Fuk u," he wrote again.

"How much did Carnale pay you?"

"Ten Gs."

"That's all I'm worth?" I said. "The same sum you pay to rent Carnale's living room for a week's porno shoot?"

Freddie did a mini-shrug with his right shoulder.

"What about the Reverend?" I said. "Did you whack him on the head?"

"No!" Freddie wrote, exclamation point once again included.

"Carnale maybe?" I said. "You think he killed the Reverend?"

"No idea," Freddie wrote. His handwriting was getting a little ragged.

"Your right hand must be tired," I said.

"Like a bitch," Freddie wrote.

"You didn't have to answer that one, Freddie," I said. "It was just me thinking out loud."

The crabby nurse walked into the room.

"Time's up," she said.

I looked at my watch. I still had three minutes left.

"Say goodbye to your stepbrother, Mr. Crang," the nurse said.

Couldn't the damn woman get my lies straight?

"See you soon, half-brother Freddie," I said.

Freddie made panicky motions with his right hand. I interpreted them to mean he wouldn't mind if I never again showed my face in his hospital room. Maybe I didn't need to ask Freddie any more questions. By my calculations, he had dropped all the way off my list of sure-fire blackmail suspects. Roger Carnale had taken over the top of the list. The guy was blackmailing his own client? It sounded nuts, but there had to be a halfway logical explanation for such a turn of events. I needed to have another chat with Arthur Kingsmill the accountant.

As for Freddie, the guy I'd fingered for most of the crimes, he was pretty much in the clear. He had pulled nothing heinous lately other than his try at dropping me on to the balcony. That was a rotten thing for the guy to do, but I was inclined to believe his answers to my questions. He was too terrified to tell me anything except the truth.

I collected Wally Crawford's envelope from Freddie's bed, and nodded farewell to the nurse, whose stern facial expression looked like it was cast in stone. Poor Freddie. Maybe it was punishment enough that he'd spend the next week with Nurse Crabby for company.

CHAPTER THIRTY-SEVEN

My next call was on Flame's mother. I was riding a hot streak with interviews, and I figured Alice Desmond would be super co-operative. When I reached Palmerston Avenue, walking over from Mount Sinai, Alice was sitting in one of the wicker chairs on her front porch.

"Hey, Crang," she said, a genuine smile on her face. "You back for another cup of coffee?"

"I'm here for favours," I said. "Two of them."

"I'm happy to do what I can, seeing as it's you." Alice had a book in her lap, one of Michael Connelly's Harry Bosch novels. "You got the interests of my son at heart, am I right about that?"

"Flame's the good guy in whatever's going on," I said.

Alice told me to have a seat. I liked the feel of the wicker chair. I could have sat there all day chatting with Alice about Harry Bosch and his affection for Art Pepper records. But it was better to get straight to business.

"The premise I'm working on goes like this," I said. "If I can prove who killed the Reverend Alton Douglas, the solution ought to get me the second blackmailer. From there, I'll be closer to recovering the eight million dollars."

"That's your premise?"

"You think it sounds too ambitious?

"I'm wondering, where do I fit into a case of murder and blackmail?"

I got out Wally Crawford's card with his daughters' contact information, and handed it to Alice.

"You'll see from the card Wally Crawford is a police detective," I said. "The two names on there belong to his daughters. He wants Flame to send his own personal salutations to each of the girls' Facebook pages."

"Sandrine and Fleur?"

"French names. Their mother's Babette."

"That's one of my favours?" Alice sounded reluctant.

"You can't do it?"

"Won't take me two minutes to get it done," Alice said. "But, man, I was hoping for something a little more, you know, mysterious? Cloak and dagger? Me playing the femme fatale or some such?"

"Let me explain about Wally Crawford," I said.

"Father of Sandrine and Fleur."

"And a homicide detective who's already done me the good deed of providing evidence pointing to the nature of the weapon that murdered the Reverend."

"My son sending a little something to Fleur and Sandrine is payback for this piece of evidence you're talking about?"

"It is."

"That makes the first favour sound more worthwhile," Alice said. "What's Number Two?"

"Some time tonight, I intend to put my hands on what I'm pretty sure is the object that killed the Reverend. When I do, I'm taking it to somebody who's in the private forensics business. The forensics guy, he'll compare the instrument with the information I got from Wally Crawford. If he gets a match, I'm pointed at the killer."

Alice straightened in her chair. She had excellent posture anyway. The straightening up made her look formidable.

"This catches your fancy?" I asked.

"The forensics guy you're talking about, who would that be?"

"Man named Archie Brewster."

Alice smiled. "I thought so."

"You know Archie?"

"I know *about* him. Anybody who's been around hospitals in the city as long as I have knows about Archie Brewster. The man's a legend. But I never met him. I'd give him a real friendly handshake if I did."

"Was it your hospital where Wally did his original neurological work?" I asked. "Where he was when he discovered the little gizmo that made him the big bucks?"

Alice shook her head. "Women's College was his. But everybody in every hospital admired Archie, him opening his own little laboratory. Archie stood up to the big boys, made himself into a legend like I said."

"So you underdstand what I'm trying to get done here?"

"I got enough of a grip on the things you're up to and where Archie fits into the whole deal."

"What about how Archie does business? You're aware of that? The way he accepts payment? The only way? This is where we get to the reason I'm sitting on your porch right now. The second favour."

"If he doesn't get paid in normal cash money," Alice said, "what other form of remuneration is there?"

"Bottles of wine," I said. "That's how he's paid. It doesn't have to be a lot of bottles. Doesn't even have to be expensive wine. Just as long as it's something that pleases him. Or surprises him. Both at the same time would knock his socks off. Especially if it's hard to buy."

Alice looked into my eyes for a couple of beats.

"My man," she said in a triumphant voice, "talking about wine, you have come to the right place."

Alice stood up. "Follow me," she said.

We went into the front hall and turned at the first door on the right. Alice switched on some lights, and we made our way down the stairs to the basement.

It was spic and span. The furnace and a new looking washer-dryer were down there. So were rows of cardboard boxes in the size that held wine and liquor. The boxes lined one wall, all laid on the side, about twenty of them. On an old carpenter's table next to the boxes, two fat wine bottles stood upright. Each had a label with a large-sized ace of spades.

"Armand de Brignac champagne," I said, sounding a little breathless even to myself.

"But you knew I had these," Alice said. She didn't sound like she was accusing me of anything. "That's why you came here."

"But so many bottles. I had no idea."

"With rap people, when they give presents, it's important they out-gift the last person."

"It was Jerome who first mentioned what was in your basement," I said. "The bottles of Ace of Spades. But he didn't mention the volume."

"The reason there's so many is we're not either of us drinkers, my son and me."

"Clearly."

"Last year, when word about the movie came from Roger Carnale, my boy and me opened a bottle to celebrate at dinner-time. Three hours later, when we called it a night, the bottle was still half-full."

"If you can let me have a couple of bottles at market price," I said, "they'll dazzle Archie, no question."

"*Two bottles? Market price?* Listen here, *I'm giving you a case.* Only way I'm gonna get rid of this stuff is handing it off to worthy causes. This here, Crang, what you're doing, it qualifies."

After I protested, the protests sounding more pro forma by the second, I lugged a case up the stairs to the front porch.

"Something about champagne," Alice said, "it weighs a ton."

"You're telling me," I said, feeling sweat prickling my arms and back.

"One detail you might clear up for me, Crang," Alice said. "Archie charges no regular fee for his services? Just the wine?"

"His lab doesn't have whatever official seal a place like that is supposed to get," I said. "That means lawyers who pay money for Archie's services, they can't charge it to Legal Aid or even to clients in some cases. So Archie does it free, except for the gifts of wine. Money's nothing to him anyway. Only reason he keeps the lab, it's because he loves the work."

"Man's a *generous* legend."

Alice and I chatted while I recovered from the climb up the basement stairs. I felt like I'd just done a couple of events in the decathlon. I asked Alice about the Michael Connelly book beside her. She said it was her first, and she was loving Harry Bosch. I recommended a couple other titles in the Bosch series.

After a while, I left Alice's porch, staggering a little under the champagne box's load, at the same time keeping a grip on the white envelope from Wally Crawford. I lugged my burden down to Dundas Street to hail a cab. Standing there, keeping a lookout for empty taxis, thinking about my visit to Alice, I knew I'd deliberately omitted one essential part of the story I told her. I didn't mention that the person I expected to prove guilty in the blackmail scheme, and just possibly in the murder, was the man who had created her son's career. Roger Carnale.

I tried to rationalize the omission. I hadn't proved anything yet. I hadn't pinned the blackmailing or the murder on Carnale or on anybody else, not beyond a reasonable doubt. Naming a name would come later, when I'd done more sleuthing. That was my excuse for keeping part of the story from Alice.

Besides that, I happened to be a person who dreaded delivering bad news until it was impossible to avoid.

CHAPTER THIRTY-EIGHT

Archie Brewster opened the door, and said, "What have we here?"

"Good things, Archie," I said, holding the box of Armand de Brignac in my aching arms. "They come in heavy bottles."

A few years earlier, Archie bought three row houses on an east-west street just north of the gay village in the Church and Wellesley neighbourhood. He knocked out the interior walls between the most westerly house and the one in the middle, and set up his laboratory in the enlarged space. The house at the east end Archie kept for his family's living quarters. He had a wife who worked in the labs with him.

I was now standing at the front door to the Brewster laboratory.

"Come in, come in, Crang," Archie said. "I'll get my people to carry the box. All the sweat on your face, you look like you've crossed hell's half acre."

"Some parts of the city, it feels that way."

Two young women in white lab coats picked up the box of champagne, and deposited it across the hall in Archie's office. Archie and I trailed after them. The decorating touch I always loved about the office was the absence from the walls of professional diplomas, scientific degrees, or anything else that mapped Archie's scholastic and scientific life. The man had no airs. Hanging on one wall was a wacky painting by a Canadian artist named Dennis Burton. It showed what downtown Toronto might have looked like if the province had allowed a six-lane road called the Spadina Expressway to blast into the city centre forty years earlier. It was a rare time in Toronto's history when good politics prevailed. The Spadina Expressway never got off the drawing board.

"This box of what I assume is wine, Crang," Archie said, "it's a kind of bribe? I ask because I don't have any work from you in the lab right now. So I'm drawing the conclusion the wine in the box is my reward if I jump a job for you to the head of the line?"

"Simple payment in advance, Archie."

"That sets a precedent. Nobody's ever handed me wine ahead of time before."

"It's a special champagne, and it happened to become available all of a sudden. I thought of you right away."

I was exaggerating like crazy, but if Archie didn't go for it, I had one more argument in favour of giving me instant service.

"Archie," I said, "this is a case where a fine young man is certain to be the victim of malign forces if I don't get speedy about helping him out."

"Malign forces? Jesus, Crang, you're really working me hard."

Archie reached into his desk and pulled out a box cutter. My optimism shot up. If Archie got a look at the Ace of Spades, I felt sure I'd be home free.

He sliced into the box with three smooth strokes of the box cutter. Archie was a practised hand at this. I watched as he lifted a bottle from the box. He examined the Ace of Spades on the label from every angle. Intrigue was written all over his face.

"I've read a lot about this brand," Archie said.

"In hip hop magazines?"

"In wine tasters' guides," Archie said. "What in hell have hip hop magazines got to do with champagne?"

"You don't want to know, Archie."

Archie was staring at the bottle, rotating it in his hands. "There's a big argument over this brand in champagne circles. On one side, the fussy people say it's a showoff wine; the other side says only snobs reject it."

"Who are you throwing your lot in with?"

"Haven't tasted it yet, have I?"

"Not ever?"

Archie shook his head. "This stuff isn't cheap."

"The nice young man I mentioned? My client? He wants you to have it."

"He's a collector?"

"You might say."

Archie put the bottle down on his desk. "All right, Crang, you talked me into a deal."

"You're going to have a taste now?"

Archie held up his right index finger. "One, I don't drink during work hours." He raised another finger. "Two, I drink champagne only with my wife." Another finger came up. "Three, these bottles need some chilling."

"So, shall we talk about the matter of my young man coming to potential grief?"

Archie laughed. "Don't be so damn subtle, Crang."

"Strike while the iron is hot, always my motto."

Archie heaved a sigh. "Have it your way, Crang."

I handed him the white envelope holding the papers from Wally Crawford documenting the Reverend Alton Douglas's murder.

"What's this writing on the outside of the envelope?" Wally said.

"It's about the guy who fell from the twelfth floor to the eleventh the day I ran into you at Fox's office," I said. "But he isn't the subject of the material inside the envelope. Forget that guy."

"How's he doing? The guy you're telling me to forget, whatever his name is?"

"Freddie Chamblis. He's under tender care at Mount Sinai. But, please never mind Freddie. It's this forensics report I'm banking everything on."

It was silent in the room for a few minutes while Archie flipped through the report's pages.

"This is official forensics stuff meant only for the cops," Archie said after a while. "Should I know how it found its way into your hands?"

"A Homicide cop I know thinks I can solve the case for him," I said. "But the report you're looking at represents only half of the material I'm asking your lab to work on."

"There's nothing in here about the weapon that killed the victim," Archie said. "Except for some speculation."

"That's the other half of the material."

"You're going to bring it to me, whatever information about the weapon you can get ahold of?" Archie asked, giving the pages in his hand a little shake to keep them straight. "At the moment, there's nothing in here that I can add to or object to."

"Tonight I expect to obtain by various means the implement that killed the Reverend."

"Which you'll deliver to me?"

I nodded. "You'll be able to compare it with the blow on the poor Reverend's head, and tell me definitively whether or not this is the weapon that did the terrible deed, am I right?"

Archie nodded his head. "I can do some other tests too," he said. "Take whatever fingerprints are on the weapon. Somehow you may come across somebody whose prints match up to what we find. And we can compare the blood on the weapon with the deceased's blood. See if they're the same."

"The Forensics people who did the report you're holding right now, they analyzed the blood, got the Reverend's DNA, all to your satisfaction?"

Archie tapped a finger on the report. "It's their usual beautiful work."

"So we're in business?"

Archie lay the report on his desk very carefully, squared it up with the edge of his desk, and said in a deliberate voice, "Just so I understand how far over the line I may be stepping in this case, could you give me some of the backstory? I'm not going to jump ship on you, Crang. I'll keep our deal. But I'd like to know more. Just think of it as humouring an old guy in a lab."

I took my time and told Archie the entire tale involving the Reverend Al and the guys in Heaven's Philosophers. I told him about Flame and his manager, Roger Carnale, and all the bad stuff I was beginning to believe Carnale had done. I left out the part about me in the shower stall while the Reverend had the piss to end all pisses. And I didn't need to dwell on the incident on the roof of Fox's building. Archie had already heard that part of the story shortly after it took place. With those two exceptions, I told him all the steps in the crime as most of them had happened. The rest of what I related to Archie consisted of my own deductions.

Archie was quiet for a few moments after I finished, leaning back in his chair, his gaze directed at the Dennis Burton painting, though I knew his thoughts were on something other than the Spadina Expressway that never happened.

"Follow the money, you say?" Archie said after a bit.

"Sounds like I'm dramatizing things, but, yeah, that's my *modus operandi* for the moment."

"Which leads you to finger this guy, Carnale?"

"He's the blackmailer for sure, and in my mind, the evidence is piling up that he was the guy who bumped off the Reverend."

"If he did the blackmailing, he was stealing eight million dollars from his own organization."

I was nodding yes in a rhythm timed to Archie's words. "Right, right. I figure he hired the Reverend for a fee to pretend he, the Reverend, was the blackmailer."

"And you yourself were window-dressing to the scheme?" Archie said. "Carnale hired you as a way of convincing everybody else that he regarded the blackmailing as a serious threat to his client, Flame?"

"The only place Carnale slipped up is he didn't count on my tenacity."

Archie smiled. "He didn't count on the Reverend changing his mind either."

"That was where my tenacity became Carnale's problem," I said. "He figured I'd fade from the case after the Reverend was murdered. And he definitely didn't think I'd still be hanging around after he alledgedly paid the eight million to the second blackmailer who was actually himself, if my deducing is correct."

"Which explains why Carnale hired the guy presently under tender care in Mount Sinai to throw a scare into you."

"This is how I figure it," I said.

Archie paused. "There's something about the money that's still a little off," he said. "I appreciate Carnale rigging a phony blackmail scheme because he needed money to pay the cost of maintaining his lifestyle. But eight million dollars? That's a hell of a lot of money over a relatively short period of time just to cover the cost of a big house in east Toronto and a bunch of fedoras and walking sticks."

"Maybe he's got a gambling problem."

"An eight-million-dollar problem? I don't think so. There must be something you're missing."

"You think my reasoning about the phony blackmailing is solid except for how I explain Carnale's need for eight million bucks?"

Archie, rubbing his jaw with his right hand, took his time about answering. "Yeah, I buy it with the caveat about the eight million."

"Is that begrudging approval I hear in your voice?"

"The story is a lot for a person to take in, you got to admit that. You've been at the thing for days. I'm brand new to what you've figured out."

"Assuming you might be right, I'd say the next step I need to take today is to have another chat with Arthur Kingsmill."

"I've forgotten, which guy's he?"

"Carnale's accountant. I'll get him to give me a complete explanation for the eight million — an answer to the question, how did Roger run up such a big debt?"

"You're doing it today?" Archie said. "Today, you're supposed to be getting me the instrument you think killed the Reverend."

"That's tonight. Obtaining the instrument in question is an after-dark operation."

"What time can you drop it off here? At the lab?"

"Probably not till two in the morning. But I don't expect you to work on my case at an hour like that."

"If you deliver it by two, I'll be waiting," Archie said. "If not by two, I'm going to bed, and you can bring it over tomorrow."

"Won't your wife object to you keeping late hours?"

Archie shook his head. "Once I've told her the story, she'll want to stay up with me."

"You're kidding."

"Not in the least," Archie said, standing up, ready to show me out. "My wife is a person who loves a mystery. Just like me."

CHAPTER THIRTY-NINE

I bought a falafel with hummus, pita, and all the trimmings from the food wagon parked next to Matt Cohen Park. It was almost three o'clock. I hadn't eaten since eight, and felt like a guy on a fast. I carried my Middle Eastern lunch across Spadina to my building and up the elevator, a cloud of exotic food scents trailing in my wake.

Walking down the hall, I could hear two voices coming from the open door of my office. One voice belonged to Gloria. The other, a man's, I'd heard before but couldn't place.

When I stepped into the office, Gloria was smiling at something the man with his back to me was saying. I recognized the back.

"Mr. Kingsmill," I said. "Convenient that you're here."

"Call him Arthur, Crang," Gloria said, still smiling. "He's in a desperate jam. But he's being brave about it."

Kingsmill stood up. "I knew I'd reached the end of my rope the minute you showed up at the office yesterday, Mr. Crang."

"It's okay if I call you Arthur?"

"Please do."

"Well, Arthur, you're planning to retain a criminal lawyer?"

"You think I should?"

"Depends on what you came here to tell me, but whatever you say, I can't represent you if the cops lay charges."

"Gloria explained why," Kingsmill said. "But I still want to get some things off my chest. After that, maybe you can give me a hint of advice about my bleak future."

"Good move, Arthur," Gloria said. "Crang's a wonder at advising people."

"The prisons are full of them," I said.

For a moment, Kingsmill's face froze.

"That's Crang's idea of a joke," Gloria said, patting Kingsmill on the arm.

I spread my meal on the desk. Gloria poured me a cup of the coffee she'd already made. The cups she and Kingsmill had in front of them were almost empty. Gloria topped them up.

"The last couple of days, Arthur, I've been working on a theory," I said. I was talking carefully because my mouth was half-filled with falafel and pita.

"*A* theory?" Gloria said. "Not just one. You've been working on half a dozen theories."

"Gloria's point," I said to Arthur, "is that some of my ideas about the blackmailing of Flame haven't panned out."

"Go ahead, Crang," Kingsmill said. "I have a feeling from the way things are happening, you're close to getting it right."

"This second blackmailer, the guy who is supposed to have collected the eight million dollars," I said, "he doesn't exist."

"You've almost there, Crang."

"Okay, he exists, but he's Roger Carnale."

"Now you've got it," Kingsmill said.

"The son of a bitch!" Gloria said. "He cheated his own client out of eight million?"

"Is it plain old greed at work here?" I said to Kingsmill. "Or is there something else going on?"

Kingsmill was shaking his head.

"Okay, another possibility," I said, "Carnale needs it to support his lifestyle. He got himself in hock to the tune of eight million bucks on fedoras and walking sticks, a bunch of other very expensive toys, and a multi-million-dollar house."

"Not quite, Crang," Kingsmill said, sounding sorrowful. "Roger spent the eight million all in one place. He needed it to cover a loss in a stock investment."

"Somebody talked him into a bad bet on the market?" I said, feeling outraged on Flame's behalf. "You're saying the entire mess of the last couple of weeks, a guy getting murdered, it's all about something as simple-minded and wrong-headed as that?"

Kingsmill made calming motions with his hands, letting me know that if I'd just shut up, he would explain what I was missing in the Carnale story.

"It all began about a year ago," Kingsmill said. "Roger got together with a man at the bar on the street level of First Canadian Place. Somebody had introduced Roger to this man earlier at a card game or some such affair. But it was in the First Candian bar when the two of them started talking deeply about investments. Roger decided this man was in the genius category at understanding the stock market."

"Is that a swindle I see on the horizon?" I said.

"I wouldn't be here if it were not," Kingsmill said. "Roger rolled the whole eight million over to the man he called a genius. The money was gone in an amazingly short time. Roger was devastated, as you can imagine."

"Am I going to recognize the name of the investment genius who brought on the devastation?" I said.

"I don't know why you would. But it's Sizemore."

"Willie Sizemore?" I said.

"Oh lord, one of the damn gang on St. Clair," Gloria said. She got busy on her laptop, scrolling down a list of names.

"An older man, this is the Sizemore I'm talking about" Kingsmill said, surprised at our swift reaction to the name. "Early seventies, grey-haired, oddly charming at times. You're both aware of him?"

"No criminal record," Annie said, looking at her laptop screen. "This is according to the profile I put together on the guy. But the Toronto Stock Exchange suspended Sizemore twice. He got his ticket back both times. Comes from a well-to-do background. Went to Ridley College, the boys' school over in St. Catharines. Some kid from the Weston family once whacked his head with a cricket bat by accident."

"You sure it wasn't Upper Canada College and a kid from the Eaton family?"

"No, no, Crang," Gloria said. "The *Westons*. You know, the bakery, Loblaws, Holt Renfrew."

"Where did you find this nugget?"

"A book of reminiscences by Ridley alumni. I thought it was a weird item about one of the Squeaky Fallis crowd. That's why I made a note of it."

"Willie Sizemore's shaping up as an all-round scamp," I said.

"He's very convincing," Kingsmill said. "Roger brought him around to the house when Sizemore was courting Roger's eight million. Then the money vanished, something followed by Mr. Sizemore's own disappearing act."

"This eight million," I said, "Roger couldn't have had money like that of his own just lying around."

Kingsmill squirmed in his chair. "That's the problem," he said.

I paused a beat. "I'm guessing it was Flame's money."

"Flame's?" Gloria said. "You're talking about the money Flame thought Roger Carnale was squirreling away for his future? Flame's nest egg? That money?"

"It's what I feel most guilty about," Kingsmill said. "I'm the one who wrote the documents we regularly sent to Flame. This was the paperwork that showed where his money was supposedly invested. For the last several months, they've been fraudulent, those documents. I concocted them on Roger's instructions. They're why I'm going to need a lawyer."

"Maybe not," I said. "Just bear with me for a minute."

"There's a legal way I can get out of this mess?"

"Never mind the legal part for now," I said. "Just answer a few questions. I need as clear a picture as I can get about the whole blackmail scheme."

Kingsmill gave a tentative nod.

"This sum," I said, "eight million, that's an accurate total of legitimate Flame money? It shouldn't be more? Ten million, say, or even higher?"

"Eight million is correct," Kingsmill said. "The money Flame earned has kept flowing in for a few years now. Roger thought he had a touch for investments, so it was he who moved Flame's money around himself for a couple of years. He earned a little more than he lost, but we're talking about tiny increments, far under what a legitmate investment house would have earned. The answer to your question is, yes, the total stood around eight million at the time the disaster struck. That was at the time of Roger's fatal drink at the bar in First Canadian."

"Answer this for me," I said. "When Roger lost the eight million to Willie Sizemore, it was then that, lo and behold, a blackmailer in the person of the Reverend Alton Douglas showed up asking the Flame Group for exactly eight million bucks?"

"I had no part in conceiving the blackmail idea," Kingsmill said, speaking quickly.

"Holy Toledo!" Gloria said. "So Carnale was able to say to Flame, sorry, kid, but the money I've been investing for you all these years is needed to keep somebody from publicizing a bunch of lyics you wrote a long time ago that could ruin your career today."

"You didn't know the Reverend Alton Douglas before all this unfolded?" I said to Kingsmill.

"Never heard of him by name until Jerome reported to Roger about this Reverend Douglas approaching him at the Air Canada Centre for the eight million."

"But you put two and two together?"

"It seemed obvious," Kingsmill said. "Roger must have set up the blackmail scheme with this Reverend."

"Any idea how Roger latched on to the Reverend in the first place?"

"The order of events is a little misty," Kingsmill said. "But everything seems to have begun with a club that has a silly name, which I can't quite remember now."

"Heaven's Philosophers," Gloria said. "The organization I mentioned on St. Clair. Except I don't think they'd like it if you called them a club."

"Whatever they are," Kingsmill said, "the people who belong to it don't seem to be upstanding citizens exactly."

"That part we already know," I said. I made hurry-up motions with both hands, urging Kingsmill to get on with the answer to my simple question. Did he know how Roger and the Reverend connected with one another?

"As I understand it from Roger," Kingsmill said, "it was his own messing around on the stock market with Flame's substantial sum of money that got Sizemore's attention in the first place. He arranged for someone else in the organization you mentioned, Heaven's Philosophers, to bring him together with Roger. This intermediary person operated some sort of gambling outfit, which happened to be another interest of Roger's. He was a fiend for card games. The intermediary's name was Gabriel, a pleasant enough fellow, badly overweight but for all of that, he had a style you'd have to describe as cool."

"Georgie Gabriel," I said. "Him we're already dealing with."

"Georgie and his father are giving Crang a hand," Gloria said to Kingsmill.

"And I know you're aware of this man Chamblis who makes the dirty movies in Roger's living room," Kingsmill said.

"Yes," Gloria said, "but he's not giving Crang a hand."

"What about Reverend Douglas?" I said to Kingsmill.

"The best I can do in fitting him into the picture comes from inference," Kingsmill said, sounding very earnest about his answer. "Gabriel the gambler often came by Roger's house on evenings when the two of them were going to play cards somewhere. On a couple of those occasions, one or the other of them, Roger or Gabriel, mentioned someone named 'the Reverend' in passing. It didn't mean anything to me then, but now I have to ask myself, who else could they be referring to except the Reverend Alton Douglas?"

"Now deceased," I said.

"Sadly, yes."

"So, at the time Roger got his open sesame into the Heaven's Philosophers gang through Sizemore and Georgie, he was meeting practially everyone in the organization. And it would't be out of the ordinary for him to come across the Reverend."

"I suppose not," Kingsmill said.

"Now move forward a bit in time, Arthur," I said. "After you realized Roger had cooked up something with the Reverend, you helped Roger rig the books to look as if the Flame Group had paid out eight million dollars to cover the blackmail?"

"Yes, but those papers were useless after the Reverend Douglas was killed. I ripped them up."

"But you prepared the same kind of documents," I said, "when the supposed second blackmailer came along?"

Kingsmill shook his head, and made gestures with his hands that said I wasn't to proceed so peremptorily. "By then," Kingsmill said, "the whole enterprise had become ridiculous. Roger was in a panic. He didn't want to waste this great idea of his for covering up the loss of Flame's investment money. He made a list of people he could pay to pretend they were blackmailers. I told him all he was planning was stupid and dangerous, and in the end, he decided that the non-existent blackmailer would be hidden behind an anonymous numbered company. That's the way he expressed the situation to Flame and Jerome, a few days ago. So now, as far as they're concerned. the eight million has gone to an unknown blackmailer."

"A numbered company is always a safe fallback position," I said.

"It probably is," Kingsmill said. "But I want you to know I refused to draw the fake documents that said as much."

"You put your foot down?"

"Which has made Roger very unhappy with me."

"I can imagine," Gloria said.

"As soon as he gets back from California," Kingsmill said, "Roger and I are supposed to have a special meeting."

"He expects you to provide the bogus documents or else …" I said.

"Or else what?" Gloria said.

"Or else I'm out of my job with the Flame Group," Kingsmill said.

I had finished my Middle Eastern meal, and took my time about cleaning my hands with the paper napkins the guy in the food wagon had given me. I flipped the balled up napkins into the wastepaper basket.

I turned to Kingsmill. "Maybe if things can be arranged to break the right way, you won't have to think about drawing up another set of phony documents."

"There's only one way that could happen," Kingsmill said, sounding doubtful. "We'd have to recover the eight million dollars."

"That's the part I think I can arrange," I said. "What I'm going to try, my basic idea, is to keep everything in house. That way, neither the police nor the courts will need to get into the act."

"I'm not following you," Kingsmill said.

"At this stage, you don't need to," I said, standing up. "Leave things to Gloria and me."

Kingsmill paused, and looked at me as I stood on my feet, looking in the direction of the door.

"You want me to be on my way for now?" he said.

"Gloria and I have telephone calls to make," I said. "They're at least partly in your interest."

Kingsmill brightened a little. Gloria patted him on the back, and Kingsmill finally propelled himself out the door and down the hall.

"Phone calls?" Gloria said to me.

"Damn right."

CHAPTER FORTY

"I'm calling Jackie Gabriel," I said to Gloria in the office. "You get in touch with Jerome on the Coast. Check if Roger's still there. If so, find out when he's coming back home."

Gloria picked up her cellphone, and went out in the hall to make her call. I did my phoning from my chair in the office, and a swift few minutes later, Gloria and I sat at the desk exchanging the results.

Gloria went first. "Carnale's still in talks with the movie people. Jerome and Flame are sticking right alongside him. They're winding things up Wednesday morning. Depending on what happens, Jerome and Flame may or may not head back to New York. No matter what, Carnale will be on a plane home. Gets into Pearson at 7:30 tomorow night."

"Things are clicking right along," I said, rubbing my hands together.

"What about you and Jackie Gabriel?"

"Got a meeting set up with him tomorrow morning," I said. "In the atrium of the cardiac wing at Toronto General."

"I thought you'd milked Jackie dry."

"Not concerning the eight million."

Gloria threw her hands up in the air. "Lord, Crang, everything concerns the blinking eight million," she said.

I poured myself half a cup of coffee.

"Let me ask you something," I said to Gloria, "Arthur Kingsmill, is he more a guy on the up and up than otherwise?"

"He completely unloaded to us this afternoon, don't you think? Open and honest in all his answers?"

"I agree," I said. "But does this mean we can trust him? In your opinion?"

"He seems like a good accountant who's learned a hard lesson," Gloria said. "Why? You've got something in mind for him?"

"I want him to draw up documents that wouldn't improve the present state of his relations with his boss."

"You could always get an outside accountant to do the job."

"That would only be spreading the mess around."

"Which," Gloria said, "should be avoided."

"Correct."

"My opinion, Arthur can be trusted."

"That's mine too."

"Gotta scoot," Gloria said, her laptop and cellphone packed. "My movie club's going to the new Steven Soderbergh at the Varsity."

"Nothing but girls in this club of yours?"

"Of course all girls."

"That's how you meet hot guys? At the movies with the movie club?"

"Are you kidding? We're serious about films. Guys would ruin everything."

Gloria kissed me on the forehead, and left. I had one more phone call to make. It was to Maury Samuels.

"You got yourself locked up in another cathedral, Crang?" he said when he came on the line.

"I hope you're free for a couple hours tonight, Maury. It's a house."

"You're forgetting, Crang, I only did hotels my whole career. Never went near a private residence."

"Even big ones? This house I'm talking about is what most people call a mansion."

"You wouldn't be referring to the place in the Beach where some asshole makes porn movies?"

I hesitated. Had Sal revealed to Maury something about her adventures in the skin trade?

Maury was still talking, "The house on a hill with a lot of trees? Just above the lake? Got a swimming pool in the backyard?"

"How come you know so much about a place I only just mentioned to you a matter of seconds ago?"

"I followed Sal there one afternoon." Maury's voice showed no particular emotion. Not jealousy or anger. "I saw some suspicious characters going into the place. That muscle guy, Freddie Chamblis, for one. A bunch of other guys of the same type, they were on the scene at this mansion."

"You were wondering what Sal was doing in company like that?"

"She told me the whole story last night."

"And?"

"And I'm cool with it," Maury said. "For crissake, Crang, what else am I gonna be? An older guy like me with a beautiful young thing like Sal? I get a big kick just hanging out with her. She says she feels the same about me."

"So this period of complete understanding you've entered into with Sal," I said, "does it mean you'll come with me on a prowl tonight at the mansion? I need to pick up one vital piece of evidence."

"A guy calls himself Lex, you know who I mean?"

"He's actually a chauffeur named Anin."

"He's somebody I got a bone to pick with. So this break-in tonight, you figure it might produce whatever it takes to nail Lex for something crooked?"

"The way I see the situation at the moment," I said, "Lex should go down alongside the man he chauffeurs for."

"Pick me up at midnight outside the Woodbine subway station."

Maury hung up.

I sorted through the papers on my desk. There didn't seem to be anything more that required my attention. I left the office and walked home. What I needed was a nap. Or a martini.

I ended up having both.

CHAPTER FORTY-ONE

Twenty minutes past midnight, Maury and I were standing on the sidewalk a half block from Roger Carnale's mansion. The only lights in the big house came from the second floor at the far end.

"Those are Lex's quarters," I said. "Where the room's all lit up."

"There's nobody else in the house you know of who might be tucked away, sound asleep?"

"The only other regular resident is Roger Carnale. Tonight, he's thousands of miles from here."

"Lex could have a broad in there with him."

"True," I said. "He seems to fancy himself a chick magnet."

"If a woman's spending the night, she better watch herself. Sal says he's what you might call overeager in the sex department."

I looked at Maury. "Sal told you about her offensive Lex experience?"

Maury didn't say anything, but he appered to be simmering at whatever thoughts he had of Lex. Both of us spent the next few minutes giving Roger's mansion a careful study.

"We could get on to the property from the rear," I said. "I noticed there's a porch off the living room. We could hoist ourselves from the porch on to the roof. Probably an open window up there."

Maury turned to me. “For crissake, Crang, you think this is *To Catch a Thief*? I don’t do roofs.”

“Then how do we make our entrance?”

“You never heard of the front door?”

We walked down the sidewalk to the Carnale porch.

“What if the door’s on an inside chain?” I whispered.

“I disabled the chain.”

“You did this when?”

“The time I followed Sal, I unscrewed the chain. It was part of me taking a look at the house’s general security,” Maury said. “I was on what they call a busman’s holiday.”

“But you were anticipating a future break-in?”

“I was thinking I might want to sabotage the porn operation they got in there. You could say I had Sal’s best interests in mind.”

“Very noble, Maury.”

“The house’s general security is shit, by the way.”

Maury reached into his jacket pocket and took out a ring holding several picks. The third pick he tried on the lock sprung open the door. We stepped into the entrance hall. The inside chain was no longer hooked to the frame on the wall. It hung loose, looking forlorn and useless.

“If we get separated inside here,” Maury said to me, “meet me back at the car. Whatever happens, the first of us who gets to the car waits for the other guy. Understand me?”

“Seems straightforward.”

Maury led the way across the entrance hall to the door that opened on the stairs to the second floor.

“Nice carpeting on the stairs and the halls upstairs,” Maury said in a lowered tone.

“You’ve really studied the entire layout, Maury?”

“Keep your voice down.”

I nodded.

“We’re going to the office off the hall to the left, correct?”

I nodded again.

"We're looking for a cane?"

I nodded. Much more of that, and I'd turn into a human marionette.

"You bring the equipment I told you to?"

"White latex gloves and a plastic bag," I whispered. It was a relief to talk again.

His quiz completed, Maury opened the door, and led the way up the deeply carpeted stairs to the even more luxurious carpeting of the second-floor hall. We proceeded through Carnale's sitting room into his office. Maury left the office door open a crack, and switched on a desk lamp. He made a careful check of the room.

All appeared to be in order. Maury took up a position by the door, motioning me toward the walking sticks stacked upright on the wall opposite the partners desk. That was the signal to pull on my latex gloves and begin the search for a stick that included metal as a significant part of its makeup. The search stretched over the next three or four minutes. I was conscious of the noise factor. If I wasn't careful, a stick could tip over and generate a racket of tumbling canes. I avoided that, but I still couldn't see anything except wooden sticks. Dark wood, light-brown wood, white wood, all kinds of colours and shades, but all of them entirely in wood. No metal in sight.

"I heard a door open down the hall," Maury said. His voice was calm. "Gotta be Lex."

"Oh, terrific." My voice wasn't calm.

"You duck out of sight for a couple minutes, Crang," Maury said, "I'll get the asshole back to his suite or some place else away from the office. Then you finish your search."

Maury started out of the office door. He stopped and turned back to me. "Gimme your cellphone. I want to see the pictures you took of Lex's swollen balls."

I got out my cell. "I don't know if they're swollen. Definitely red."

Maury cut me off. "Just give me the fucking pictures."

"Sal told you about me shooting the pictures of Lex?"

"Damn right she did."

I scrolled down the photos until I came to the Lex pictures. Maury took the phone from my hand, and walked out of the office door on his way to the corridor. I went around the partners desk and sat on the floor in one of the desk's leg spaces. The sight line was straight through to the wall on the other side of the office. I was staring at the section of the wall where Roger Carnale's collection of briefcases was on display.

Loud voices reached into the office from the corridor, Lex's voice and Maury's.

"How the fuck did you get in here?" Lex shouted. "Who are you anyway?"

"You practically invited me into the place, Lex." Maury's voice was controlled and matter of fact. "If you don't want people to come inside the house, you might think about locking the front door."

That brought silence from Lex's side of the conversation.

"Another thing, Lex," Maury said. "You got no need of that gun you're holding in your hand there."

A gun?

"I got the gun to protect myself till I phone the cops," Lex said. "They're gonna wonder about somebody breaking into the house in the middle of the night."

"Lex, my friend ..."

Lex interrupted Maury. "I'm not your fuckin' friend. And where in hell do you know my name from? I've never seen you in my life."

"That's funny, Lex," Maury said. "Because I know you intimately."

Another period of silence came from Lex's side of the conversation.

"How did you get these goddamn pictures?" Lex said.

Now I understood the latest silence. Maury was giving Lex a look at the red testicles I photographed.

"From Sal," Maury said. "I got them from Sal. You know her. Sal's the woman you sexually assaulted, Lex old pal. She's the woman who happens to be my girlfriend."

"Sal with the big tits?"

"You want to be a crude son of a bitch, that's one way of identifying her."

"She's way too young for an old guy like you."

"Ah, Lex," Maury said. "There's a lot you need to learn about women. So why don't you put the gun in your dressing-gown pocket, and we'll go downstairs to the nice white room where you make the porn videos, and we'll have a talk that's gonna help you a whole lot."

"The production people moved the movie stuff out, the white furniture, all that," Lex said. His voice sounded subdued.

"It's a nice room anyway," Maury said. "Let's continue our little chat down there."

Lex said something else, but the voices were fading. Maury and Lex must have been on the stairs on the way to the first floor. That let me get back to the search.

From where I was sitting on the floor under the desk, something had caught my eye. It was one of the briefcases stacked against the opposite wall. I stood up and walked around the desk to the row of briefcases. The one I concentrated on was slimmer than the others. Its leather was black. It was the briefcase Roger was carrying when he and Jerome first called at my office for the meeting that introduced me to Flame's blackmail problem. In most ways, the briefcase wasn't much different from the others in Roger's collection, except that it had rims around the edges. The rims gleamed in the light of the table lamp in Carnale's office. These rims were made of metal.

If I was surmising correctly, the instrument I was looking for, the thing that combined leather and metal in its makeup, wasn't a walking stick. It was a briefcase. It was the briefcase I was looking at on the shelf in the Carnale office. This slim black leather briefcase with the metal rims made a leading contender, maybe the only contender, as the weapon that killed the Reverend.

Wearing the white latex gloves, I slid the black briefcase off the shelf. I paid special attention not to jostle the rest of the cases. Careful in all my moves, I carried the black case over to the partners desk. In the desk's centre drawer, I found a magnifying glass. Studying the briefcase through the glass, I was able to see that the rim at one end of the case was speckled in tiny drops of something brown. Could the drops be dried bloodstains? I had no idea, but I knew a scientist who could come up with the answer.

I slid the black briefcase into the plastic bag Maury told me to bring. Carrying the bag, still wearing the gloves, I hustled silently down the stairs to the first floor. Judging from the tenor of the voices coming through the living-room's open door, Maury and Lex were having a brisk debate over a subject I couldn't make out. I wouldn't have been surprised if it was over women in general and Sal in particular.

I crossed the entrance hall, opened the front door, and made my getaway from the house. So far I'd committed no goofs. I hadn't dropped the briefcase, hadn't slipped on the tiles of the entrance hall's floor, hadn't let a door slam behind me.

I climbed into the Mercedes. It was 12:40. Only twenty-five minutes had passed since Maury and I sneaked into the mansion. This seemed to me a miracle of efficiency.

Ten minutes later, Maury got into the front passenger seat. He handed me my cellphone.

"This guy Lex isn't taking me seriously as Sal's boyfriend," he said.

"You sound insulted," I said. I started the car, made a U-turn and headed up to Kingston Road.

"He had the fucking nerve to tell me he was gonna take another run at Sal," Maury said.

"That's definitely insulting," I said.

"'Totally' is the word you're supposed to use," Maury said. "Not 'definitely.' You should've said 'totally' insulting. Which it totally was."

"Young people's language."

"Of course young people's language," Maury said. He sounded irate. "What other kind of people do you think I've been keeping company with lately?"

"I totally get it."

I took Kingston Road until I could merge into Queen. Traffic was pactically non-existent, and I was making such good time I knew I'd get the briefcase to Archie Brewster's lab ahead of schedule.

"You know what I'm gonna do before this thing is over?" Maury said.

"Kick Lex in the testicles."

Maury turned to look at me. "How'd you guess that?"

"Something in your attitude told me."

"The job Franny started on the guy's balls, I'm gonna finish off," Maury said with conviction. "I do that, you can bet Lex'll be inoperative in the sex department for the next couple years."

"Totally awesome," I said.

I pulled up at Archie's place at ten after one. Archie answered after just one knock on the front door.

"A briefcase?" he said, taking a look into the plastic bag.

Archie didn't invite me in. Not that I wanted to spend time in chit-chat. Maury was waiting in the car, and I was keen to get home.

"Very ingenious," Archie said, still checking out the briefcase. "And not hard for us to work with. I'll phone you later this morning."

"You're going to start the matching job right now?"

"It's the least you should expect for all that Ace of Spades you gave me," Archie said. "Now, Crang, you'll excuse me."

Leaving Archie's place, I drove Maury to Sal's apartment. Then I went home, where I faced a choice between a martini and sleep. It turned out to be no contest at all. I lay down on the bed for a short, pre-martini rest, and fell into a sleep that didn't end until the morning sun shone through the bedroom windows.

CHAPTER FORTY-TWO

The first things I noticed, walking off University Avenue and into the Peter Munk Cardiac Centre, were the rows of empty wheelchairs lined up next to the main door. Cardiologists apparently didn't trust patients with weak tickers to get around the building on their own two feet. The second thing I noticed was the atrium on the ground floor, which soared three or four storeys high. It brought a hushed atmosphere among all us visitors and patients down at ground level.

It was just before 10 a.m., a time that put me a couple of minutes ahead of the schedule set by Jackie Gabriel, but Jackie and Georgie were already sitting at a table in the only commercial outlet in the atrium. The outlet was a Starbucks.

"You want a tea, Crang?" Jackie asked me. "Iced chai tea latte. I never had it before, but it ain't bad."

Before I could say I'd rather eat ground glass than consume a Starbucks product, Jackie had dispatched Georgie to the counter for my treat.

"You're here for a checkup, Jackie?'I said.

"Yeah, but don't ask me what's getting checked up. I lost track a year ago and never caught up."

Georgie returned with my iced chai tea latte, the same drink the other two had in front of them.

I sipped mine.

Jesus, the thing was so sweet I thought my teeth might fall out.

"Hell of a smooth taste, don't you think so, Crang?" Jackie said.

"Got something going for it, Jackie," I said. "I just can't put my finger on what."

My answer seemed to satisfy Jackie. Georgie just grinned. I noticed he was taking his time getting through his own latte.

"You called the meeting, Crang," Jackie said. "What's it all about?"

"Willie Sizemore," I said. "The cricket bat he got whacked with years ago? It's acting up again."

"You know what?" Georgie said. "I heard Willie talking about the cricket bat the other day. But there was something different about the story. Willie said the school he was at was called Lakefield, wherever the hell that is, and it was a guy from English royalty that whacked him."

"Lakefield's up near Peterborough," I said. "The only royalty at Lakefield I ever heard of was Prince Andrew. But he's about twenty years younger than Willie."

"It was another royalty than him," Georgie said. "Willie said this guy was a cousin of the Duke of Kent, something like that. Anyway, Willie wound up with the same dent in his head he's always had no matter who did it."

"Forget the goddamn cricket bat," Jackie said to me. "Answer me this, Crang, there's some guy you know, Willie took him for a few bucks? Is this what your problem is?"

"Eight million."

Georgie made a whistling noise.

"Guy stupid enough to let Willie talk him out of that much might deserve whatever happened," Jackie said.

"I can't argue with that, Jackie," I said. "But the trouble I'm having, the money he lost belongs to somebody else."

"Who're we talking about here, Crang?" Jackie said. "You're friends with the guy who lost the eight million to Willie or with the guy who the eight million really belongs to?"

"Guy number one goes by the name of Roger Carnale," I said. "He's the sucker Willie Sizemore scammed, but I'm not friends with him."

"I know that guy," Georgie said, speaking brightly. "Carnale."

"Somebody told me you know him," I said. "Where do you know Carnale from?"

"He's played cards in some of the games I set up," Georgie said. "I had a nice thing going on Friday nights up in Woodbridge. This guy Roger was a regular there for practically all of last year."

"Am I wrong in guessing he was one of your bigger losers?"

"A loser, yeah," Georgie said. "His type of guy I see a lot of in card games."

"What's the type?"

"The one where the player is very successful in whatever his regular job is. He thinks the success is gonna carry over to blackjack, poker, whatever. This type of guy figures it's automatic he'll win because he knows how to win at business. But he's wrong about that. With cards, you need a whole different touch. Different psychology, you know what I mean?"

"I'll take your word for it, Georgie," I said. "I got an aversion to gambling myself."

Georgie leaned back in his chair. "Oh shit, you know what?" he said. He looked stricken, as if a deeply unpleasant thought had hit him. "It just dawned on me."

"What's the problem, kid?" Jackie said to his son.

"I'm the one who introduced this Roger guy to Willie Sizemore."

"This was during your card games?" I said.

"Not during," Georgie said. "Nobody talks serious when a game's actually on. It was when we took a break from playing. Those Friday nights, they were social evenings too. We left the cards for a half hour, drinks were on the house, everybody mingled a little. Willie was there. Roger had already asked me if I knew anybody in the investment business. So, this one night, I introduced Roger to Willie."

"A case of feeding the lamb to the wolf," Jackie said. "On a platter."

Georgie turned to me. "I wouldn't have done it if I knew you were involved with Roger."

"Wait a minute, Georgie," Jackie said. "Let's hear the rest of the story. Maybe you don't have to apologize."

"Roger Carnale is in the artist management business," I said. "That's 'artist' singular because, as far as I know, he just has one client." I paused for dramatic effect. "Either of you gentlemen ever heard of Flame?"

"The hip hop guy?" Georgie said.

"Good for you, Georgie," I said.

"Hip hop for crissakes," Jackie said. "Doesn't anybody listen to Vic Damone no more?"

"Remember that we're talking about today's music, Jackie," I said. "Today, Flame makes more money in a month than Vic Damone made in any year of his whole career."

"I only heard of Flame," Georgie said. "I never actually saw him sing or whatever."

"This guy Roger manages the other guy, Flame?" Jackie said. "That involved him looking after the big money you say Flame earned? I've got this right?"

I nodded.

"And eight million of Flame's dough that Roger was looking after got conned out of him in one of Willie's bogus stock deals?" Georgie said.

"I think we all understand the circumstances we're dealing with here," I said. "Roger lost Flame's money to Willie."

Everybody went silent for the next few moments, each of us thinking over the way future responsibilities might unfold.

Jackie looked at me. "You want me to get the eight million back from Willie, am I right?"

"That's the idea,"I said.

"Same as I did two other times."

"Restore it to Flame, its rightful owner, the man who earned it with his talent and hard work."

Jackie switched his attention to Georgie. "What's your feeling, kid?"

"Crang's the guy who got me Fox, who's a hell of a lawyer for getting right on top of things," Georgie said. "I owe Crang for that. Plus, if I hadn't introduced Roger to Willie, this kid Flame would still have the eight million."

"I'm thinking the same thing," Jackie said.

I said to Jackie, mustering my most sincere tone, "Flame and I would appreciate it if you scared Willie into returning the money."

"All it takes is a phone call, Pop," Georgie said to his father.

Jackie nodded, but didn't immediately agree to get on Willie's case.

"I've been wanting to ask you since I heard about your past experiences with Willie," I said to Jackie, "what's the magic to retrieving the money Willie suckered out of people?"

"This is beauty," Georgie said to me, answering for his father. "You ever heard of Paulie Profundo?"

"Not a chance I'd forget a name like that if I'd ever heard it."

"His nickname back in the day was Basso Profundo," Georgie said. "This is the story Pop's been telling me since I was a kid."

"A natural nickname for a guy named Profundo," I said.

"Basso, yeah," Georgie said. "He came from the Brooklyn mob. He was the number one enforcer type guy. So when Willie took Pop for the hundred grand twenty years ago, Pop went down to Brooklyn and asked Basso as a favour to come up here and speak to Willie. That's all he needed to do. Just speak to Willie. Not beat him up or anything involving blood."

"Basso was a man who made a large physical impression?"

"No, as a matter of fact, he was a smaller guy," Georgie said. "But he was so crazy he could scare the bejesus out of anybody. You remember Joe Pesci in *Goodfellas*, Pesci's ranting and raving like he's gonna tear the other guy's head off? That was what

Basso was like in real life, a complete over-the-top-menace type of person."

"The characters Pesci played in movies got actually murderous from time to time."

"Basso never did."

"I can understand why Willie might have yielded to Basso Profundo's threat and returned the hundred grand of yours he scammed," I said, turning to Jackie. "So do I understand correctly you brought Basso up here the second time you wanted to get the two million back from Willie for your friend?"

"That time," Jackie said, "all I had to do was mention Basso's name to Willie. He gave back the money the same day."

"The power of the man's name was enough?"

"I couldn't bring Basso up here in person that time on account of he was dead."

"But Willie wasn't aware of Basso's deceased status?"

"He wasn't."

"But what about right now? Today? Does Willie know the man he feared above all others is no longer around to terrify him?"

"He knows."

"Listen, Jackie," I said, "why are we talking about Basso Profundo if the man isn't going to be of any help in recovering Flame's eight million?"

"Basso's got a son carrying on the family tradition."

"The son's as effective as the father?"

"Even more ferocious," Jackie said. "Calls himself Profundo. Just plain Profundo. That's very popular these days — entertainers and athletes and so forth with just one name. Madonna, Ronaldo, Pele going back further."

"Liberace."

"Not fucking Liberace, Crang," Jackie said, showing a little temper. "You want me to help you, you better take this thing serious."

"Believe me, I would appreciate you interceding with Profundo," I said. "You need to bring him up here?"

"The name's enough," Jackie said. "But he charges a fee for us using his name."

"That's like a copyright payment," I said. "Though I don't know if copyrighting what is essentially a piece of extortion is entirely legal."

"Who cares, legal or not legal," Jackie said. "It'll cost you ten thousand. That would be my guess."

"Seems a fair price."

"You want," Jackie said, "I can arrange that Willie pays the ten grand."

"He's probably earned a lot more than that out of the eight million he's had his hands on the last little while, even if it wasn't doing anything except collecting interest."

"Probably," Jackie said, sounding mildly pissed off. "But so what? The eight million is what's important here. Am I right?"

"Right as rain, Jackie," I said, my hands up in a defensive signal.

"Pop," Georgie said, his hand on his father's arm, "don't get worked up. You're gonna be seeing the heart doctor in a couple minutes."

"Get me one of them wheelchairs," Jackie said.

Georgie got up and walked over to the rows of wheelchairs by the door.

"Georgie'll deliver you the eight million any time tomorrow," Jackie said to me.

"Tomorrow?"

I thought about the timing for a moment and the place for the money's delivery. While I was thinking, Georgie came back with a wheelchair.

"Let's make it nine Wednesday night for Georgie to come around with the money," I said to the two Gabriels. "He can bring it to Carnale's house in the Beach."

I gave Georgie the address.

"And whatever form the reimbusement's in," I said, "make it payable to the Flame Group."

"No problem," Jackie said. "Pleasure doing business with you, Crang."

"Pleasure's all mine, Jackie."

"Just to show we're on good terms, Georgie's gonna order you another one of those nice iced chai tea lattes."

"No need for that, Jackie. Please."

Jackie waved off my objections. Georgie wheeled his father away, and as they passed the Starbuck's counter, Georgie stopped long enough to put in the order for more of the dreadful tea concoction. The damn stuff tasted like it was made from a blob of chemicals. I waited until Georgie and Jackie disappeared into an elevator. Then I got up and beat it out the University Avenue door.

In the background, I could hear the barista at the counter calling, "Somebody for this iced chai tea latte?!"

CHAPTER FORTY-THREE

I was in the office making enough coffee for one cup when Archie Brewster's wife phoned. Her name was Ruth, and she had a chipper voice.

"Archie asked me to call you, Mr. Crang," Ruth said.

"He's still busy in the lab with the project I brought in?"

"He's busy grabbing forty winks is what Archie is," Ruth said. "We finished the job for you. Now he's catching up on his sleep. It was very exciting, comparing the metal work on the briefcase with the wound on the deceased man's head."

"And the result was what?"

"I worked alongside Archie all night, but I react differently than him. I get so pumped up I might not sleep for days after we're done."

"The metal grooves in the briefcase match the marks on the Reverend's skull?"

"Reverend? Was the victim a man of religion? Archie didn't say anything about that."

"Ruth, what was the result of the matching process you and Archie performed?"

"I hope this Reverend wasn't killed because of his religious beliefs. There's such a lot of that in the world today."

"No, it wasn't a religious killing. Nothing like that. But what I am interested in is the nature of the killing instrument."

"Oh, yes, of course," Ruth said. "Archie has done a full written report. It's waiting here for you to pick up."

"I can hardly wait to learn the result."

"Archie wrote the report before he settled down to his sleep."

"I can just bet it was exciting to reach a conclusion, whatever it might be."

"The report isn't very long, only four parts," Ruth said. "And of course I contributed my few paragraphs. They're in part four where we present our final result."

"Which is what, Ruth?"

"Pardon, Mr. Crang?"

"The conclusion you reached, what is it?" I realized I was shouting.

"The briefcase is what killed the poor man. Didn't I say that? Not a doubt in the world about the weapon."

I thanked Ruth, and told her I'd come by the lab in about an hour to pick up the report and the briefcase.

My coffee had gone lukewarm in the time it took me to winkle the test result out of Ruth. I made a fresh cup, sipped from it, and phoned Arthur Kingsmill.

"You have news for me, Mr. Crang?" Kingsmill's voice had a guarded sound.

I mentioned the guardedness to him.

"Of course I sound that way," Kingsmill said. "People pay accountants to project a sense of defensiveness. I'm not having second thoughts about what I told you and Gloria. I'm just nervous about whatever it is you're arranging for the next steps."

"If you'll join in a meeting at Roger's house, nine tomorrow night, I'll do my best to see you emerge from it a happier man."

"Let me judge that, Mr. Crang."

"I want you to draw up a document for Roger to sign. In it, in this document, he surrenders all his signing powers in the Flame Group's financial dealings. You with me on this?"

"You've got the leverage to make Roger actually sign such an extreme document?"

"Leave that part with me, Arthur."

"This puts the Flame Group in a position where it's financially moribund."

"Moribund, huh?"

"Well, who's going to sign the invoices and other documents that go in and out of the business?"

"Alice Desmond."

"Flame's mother?"

"The very woman," I said. "I want you to draw up another document that gives Alice all the signing rights that Carnale used to have."

"I can't believe this," Kingsmill said. "But supposing I prepare such a document, it needs to be signed in approval by two people who are designated to okay such major changes."

"Both of them friendly to Alice, I'm sure."

"Flame and myself."

"See, I was right" I said. "Who could be friendlier?"

Silence once again came from Kingsmill's end. But I was willing to take the non-reply as his agreement to what I was asking for.

"Excellent, Arthur," I said. "Now on another matter entirely. Is Lex the chauffeur on the premises at this minute? I'm assuming I reached you in your office at the Carnale mansion?"

"Anin Mahuda isn't here," Kingsmill said. "Or Lex or whatever you want to call him. I'm alone at the office. You need to talk to Mahuda? He's at a Cadillac dealer in the west end getting the car detailed. That'll take all afternoon. Mahuda wants the car looking smart when he picks up Mr. Carnale at the airport at 7:45 tomorrow night."

"What I want, Arthur, is to avoid Lex today," I said. "I'll be driving over to Carnale's place an hour or more from now."

"Is there a serious reason why you're coming here?"

"I want to drop off something I borrowed from Roger's office. That's reason number one. And, number two, I need to make sure you're okay with the program."

"You *borrowed* something?"

"Okay, I *swiped* it. But this is the object that clinches the case against Carnale."

"Oh lord, why did I mix myself up with you?"

"That's a laugh, Arthur. You got yourself in a pickle and virtually begged me just yesterday to extricate you. Which is what I'm in the process of accomplishing."

Kingsmill had no answer to that.

I hung up, and sipped my coffee. It had gone lukewarm again. Damn, I definitely wasn't leaving the office until I'd enjoyed a jolt of caffeine. I made another cup, and thought about the errands and chores I needed to get done. Pick up the briefcase from Archie's lab. Put the case back in its regular spot on the shelf in Carnale's office. Invite Flame's mother to the Wednesday night session at the Carnale mansion. Set up one more meeting with Wally Crawford.

I checked my watch. It was just past one o'clock. I had plenty of time and a cup of hot coffee in my hand.

What more could a man on a mission ask?

CHAPTER FORTY-FOUR

The sun was dropping in the sky, and the time was coming up to 6:30. I sat with Wally Crawford in the same booth at the Second Cup where we met a few days earlier. Wally wore a beaming expression, the sort of look Homicide detectives didn't usually display to the civilian world.

"My girls are ecstatic, Crang," he said.

"Fleur and Sandrine."

"Flame went way beyond anything I hoped for."

"A generous guy, no question."

"You know what Flame did for the girls?"

"I'm sure I'm going to be thrilled," I said. I was feeling a tad impatient. The afternoon of driving out to the Beach, getting stuck in traffic on Rosedale Valley Road, spending an hour with the nervous Arthur Kingsmill guaranteeing he was onside for the Wednesday night meeting, getting stuck in traffic on Rosedale Valley Road on my way back from the Beach, all of this had put me on edge.

"On each girl's Facebook page," Wally said, "Flame left a personal message with a piece of a new song on each one."

"Sounds nice," I said to Wally. "Really, it does."

I imagined me as a teenaged kid if I got something personal from my favourite singer, from someone like Sarah Vaughan. But what would qualify as personal back in those days of no technology to speak of? Undoubtedly something that involved the mail. Maybe a signed note and Sarah's version of "Tenderly" on a 45 rpm, all in a large envelope with a lot of stamps on it. That would have thrilled fourteen-year-old me.

"Here's the essential thing," Wally said. "Each girl's package is different from the other."

"Variety is the spice of life, that's what you're getting at?"

"The point is, it indicates Flame's thoughtfulness. For each girl, he gives a different message and a few bars of a different new song."

"So Flame has come through big time as far as Fleur and Sandrine are concerned?"

"They're the envy of their friends on Facebook."

"That makes you a hero in your daughters' eyes?"

"I'm riding high."

I leaned forward over the table. "With all of that in mind, where do you and I stand in the matter of giving and receiving favours? In your view?"

"Even Steven," Wally said. "I leaked you the medical report on the Reverend Alton Douglas, and you delivered Flame's incredible presents for my girls. We're square."

"That's where I disagree."

"Thought you probably would."

"The favours in this particular matter," I said, "are part of a flowing entity. It's not one for you and one for me and then, wham, bam, we're done."

"Given that attitude, the way I see it, you're going to ask me something that'll mean I have to cut corners. In other words, I'm going to run the risk of my ass getting booted sideways by my superiors."

"Let me just get back to the flow I was speaking of."

"My guess is you flowed over to Archie Brewster's lab and showed him the medical report on the Reverend."

"You have anything against Archie?"

"I got a ton of respect for Archie and his wife, even if the wife is a screwball and their lab isn't technically legit."

"Not a screwball, Ruth Brewster. More a person who's tardy at getting to the point."

Wally drank from his cup of coffee. So did I, even if the cup was probably my fifth of the day.

"What you should know," I said, looking Wally in the eye, "is that Archie and his good wife have identified the murder weapon."

Wally held my gaze for a moment or two. "That's impossible unless you gave them an instrument of some kind that you aleady suspected of being the murder weapon."

"I admit to that."

"You were being a bit of a snake in withholding information from me."

"I can think of other ways of phrasing my actions."

"You'd prefer to leave 'snake' out of the defintion?"

"I was proceeding with caution," I said. "That's what I was doing when I took the object in question to Archie."

"Without telling me, you snake."

Wally was wearing his cop stare, but I thought he was kidding. Maybe just a little.

"Where's the murder weapon at this moment?" Archie said to me.

"Restored to its owner's office where it normally sits."

"Nice move, Crang," Wally said. "This means, as long as nobody says otherwise, the weapon in question has never left the owner's possession."

"Archie and his wife aren't going to say otherwise. Neither am I. Nor can I think of anyone else who might utter a peep about the weapon's recent movements."

"All of which," Wally said, "sets the stage for me to take out a search warrant and seize the weapon as soon as you tell me what it is and where it is."

"It's a briefcase," I said.

Wally flipped his hands in the air. "A briefcase's too soft on the edges to do the damage I saw on the Reverend's skull."

"A briefcase with metal edging."

Wally paused. "Maybe I'll withdraw my doubts."

I took a notebook out of my jacket, wrote Carnale's name and address on one page, ripped out the page, and handed it to Wally.

"Who's this Carnale?" Wally asked, reading from the page. "A mobbed-up guy?"

"He's Flame's manager."

"Oh shit, you're not gonna tell me Flame's involved in a murder."

"He's a victim in the story," I said. "The manager tried to dupe him out of eight million bucks."

"Where's the money come into the murder story? It's part of the motivation?"

"Roughly, yeah," I said. "But let's you and I concentrate on the briefcase."

Wally looked again at the piece of paper. "The briefcase is the reason I'm going to this address, wherever it is."

"Out in the Beach," I said. "Come there tomorrow night at 9:30. You'll walk away with the briefcase and the killer in cuffs."

"It's going to be a civilized business, this meeting of yours? The alleged killer — when I show up, he'll come peacefully?"

"I think the murder was probably committed in a moment of madness. The killer isn't normally a violent person."

"Should I be wary of any resistance at all?" Wally said. "This Carnale guy doesn't pack a weapon?"

"Only person who's got a gun is the chauffeur."

"A chauffeur? What kind of gun?"

"A handgun. Not that I saw it myself, but he was waving it around when he thought somebody had broken into Carnale's house."

"Was he right about somebody breaking in?"

"Technically, yeah."

Wally gave me more of his stare. "Just to be safe," he said after a moment, "I'll get some backup, and I'll wear my vest."

"It's bulletproof, that kind of vest?"

"Bullet-resistant is the correct phrase."

"Resistant? You mean there's a chance the vest won't stop the bullet altogether?"

"Hell of a long shot."

"To coin a phrase."

"I suppose it is."

"Anything else you want to ask?" I said. "It's all clear?"

"I don't suppose Flame's going to be there? At Carnale's place?"

"He'll be either in New York or Los Angeles," I said. "But I invited his mum over to the meeting."

Wally perked up. "Flame's mum? My girls are gonna love the idea of me meeting Flame's mum."

"All kinds of strange perks in this case, Wally."

"Isn't that just the truth."

CHAPTER FORTY-FIVE

I made a martini, sat down at the dining room table, and phoned Annie. It was 8 p.m. my time, three hours earlier in L.A. I was banking on Annie taking a breather after taping the *DeGeneres Show* that afternoon. The phone rang three times in Annie's suite. She picked up on the third.

"You knocked them dead, sweetie?" I said.

"All I have to say, doing the skit, we went a little crazy with the kidding around," Annie said. "Everybody told me it was what they hoped for, both Ellen and me breaking up. Ellen said so. But I'm reserving my opinion until I actually see it for myself."

"Which is when?"

"My plane gets to Pearson 9:30 in the p.m. on Thursday. You and I can hold hands, and watch the disc they gave me of my segment. It's in my handbag right now, and it'll stay there while I do a couple of interviews tomorrow."

"Wednesday night," I said, "I'm bringing down the curtain on the entire l'affaire Flame."

"Oh god, Crang, please tell me you don't have something crazy in mind."

"What's your idea of crazy?"

"A scenario where somebody wreaks physical havoc on you."

"Relax, kiddo. A Toronto Homicide detective will be on the premises."

"What premises?" Annie said. "Not our house?"

"Carnale's place I told you about. In the Beach."

"The mansion where the porn movies were made?"

"That's the location."

"From where you rescued Sal and her friend from the clutches of the evil pornographers."

"Franny's the other girl's name," I said. "But all this still leaves me with the main event."

"Blackmail and murder," Annie said. "They'll be on tomorrow night's agenda?"

I brought Annie up to date on very recent events, ending with the bombshell news that I'd probably be unmasking Roger as the leading suspect in the Reverend's murder.

"Oh my god, Roger really could be an actual killer?" Annie said, sounding semi-stunned. "I had dinner with the man last night, Flame and him. Thank heavens I didn't know what you think, murder-wise. I would have been so nervous I'd have blown the whole deal."

"How did the dinner come about?"

"Both of those guys have moved into suites in my home away from home, aka the lap of luxury, the Bel Air. Both Flame and Carnale are on the premises, but it was only Flame I had the dinner date with. Then we're just starting our appetizer when bloody Carnale walks in, and takes a seat at our table."

"He horned in on you guys?"

"Not even Flame liked it, but you know him, always the gentleman. It wouldn't occur to him to give Carnale the boot from our table."

"Any indications from Carnale that you were dining with a guilty man?"

"He was subdued, but then I've never seen him in anything like what I'd call a voluble state."

"You got an opinion how things are between Flame and Roger?"

"All I know for certain," Annie said, "the movie stuff is supposed to be thrashed out once and for all at a final meeting with the Hollywood studio people late tomorrow morning. As of the dinner last night, Roger was still resistant to Jerome's promotion into a higher role as executive producer."

"He offer any reasons for his stand?"

"Personally, I think he's glad to let Jerome have free reign on the creative side, but Roger doesn't like him calling some of the shots on the accounting end, as Jerome would if he were executive producer."

"Listen," I said, mustering my most serious tone, "it's for sure Carnale stole Flame's eight million and I'm about 90 percent sure he's the guy who killed the Reverend. Given all of that, it would be a whole lot healthier for the movie's chances of getting made if Jerome ascended to the executive producer's job, and Carnale was eliminated from any role among the people who make movie decisions."

"Otherwise, if it's all true about Carnale, and he remains still more or less in charge out here, the movie people might rightfully get the impression they had a sinking ship on their hands."

I paused at my end, thinking things through.

"Crang?" Annie said. "What's with the silence?"

"How do I get to speak to Flame?"

"Right now?"

"If not sooner."

"He's in his suite. I saw him in the lobby when I came back from the taping with Ellen."

"Can you scamper over to his place and ask him to phone me?"

"Hang up, sweetie, and stand by."

I stood by long enough to finish my first martini, but not long enough to make a second. The phone rang.

"Mr. Crang?" Flame said in his silky baritone. "Two people said I needed to speak to you."

"Who besides Annie?"

"My mother. She told me you'd be taking her to a meeting at Mr. Carnale's house tomorrow night. What's this all all about, if you don't mind me asking?"

"Potentially, tomorrow's meeting will produce good and bad news for you and your immediate career. I can't tell you what's involved until the meeting's done with. But I've got an approach worked out, and if you give me an okay to push ahead, I think I can get the best result possible."

"This is mysterious stuff, Mr. Crang," Flame said, sounding as phlegmatic as ever. "Neither Mum nor me have ever even been in Mr. Carnale's house."

"It's a mansion in the Beach."

"Mum'll love that."

"Swimming pool out back."

"Olympic size?"

"Nothing less for Roger."

"Mum's a fool for swimming. You tell her about the pool, she'll pack her bathing suit for tomorrow night."

Admirable as I found Flame's sanguine attitude, I needed to get him off the domestic stuff and back to business.

"In the meantime," I said, "I've got one piece of advice I'm offering for free."

"Let's hear it."

"At tomorrow's meeting with the movie moguls out there, I think you should come out strongly in favour of setting up Jerome as executive producer of your film."

"I've already arrived at that point of view," Flame said. "But how do I handle announcing it without Mr. Carnale going ballistic?"

"I got a suggestion."

"Let's have it. I can use all the help I can get."

"What you say around the board table, you say you think it

would serve the interests of the Flame Group best if Roger were spared the worries of the film in order to concentrate on his duties to your career as a concert performer and recording artist."

"Mr. Crang, you talk bullshit with the best of them."

"Comes in handy in my line of business."

"So I tell everybody at the meeting it would be better for all concerned if Jerome relieves Mr. Carnale of burdens connected with making the movie."

"You might add something about Jerome's great ideas on the creative side."

"That'd be the truth, especially now that my man Jerome's got off his Scarlett Johansson kick."

"We see eye to eye on this, Flame?"

"We do," Flame said, "as long as you understand you've got to tell me what comes out of this meeting tomorrow night as soon as the thing wraps up."

"Your mother's got your cell number?"

"Sure she does," Flame said. "But I'll give it to you."

I wrote down the number on the kitchen notepad.

"You said there was bad news coming for me," Flame said. "I've already had a man murdered who was maybe blackmailing me, not to mention eight million dollars of my own money disappearing into the hands of another blackmailer entirely. How much worse can news get?"

This was the first sign from Flame I'd seen of anger or dismay or whatever he was expressing.

"I mentioned there was good news coming too," I said. "I'm banking on the good far outweighing the bad."

"The way I figure it," Flame said, returning to his imperturbable self, "as long as I concentrate on the music, I'm going to feel okay."

"Keep thinking that way till tomorrow night," I said.

I hung up and made a new martini. Things seemed as set as I could get them on the Hollywood front. Should I alert Jerome to what was in the works? It might be wise. On the other hand, I felt talked out for the day. I'd settle for something to eat. The refrigerator had nothing except organic peanut butter and twelve grain bread. They'd have to do. Plus some frozen yoghurt in the freezer. And a banana in the fruit bowl.

I ate, drank, and went to bed with more Jane Gardam.

CHAPTER FORTY-SIX

I sat with Flame's mother in the Mercedes. We were parked on a street just up the hill from the Carnale home, by now a familiar view for me. The time was close to 8:30 Wednesday night.

"That's a swimming pool, it looks like, behind the tall fence out back of the house," Alice said.

"A very big pool, I understand."

"I swim at the public sports centre near my house three days a week."

"No doubt accounting for your excellent figure."

"But it's a battle, you know, with all the seniors at adult swimming times."

"I imagine, the menace of pool overcrowding."

"The seniors are the worst, zigzagging out of their lanes and into mine."

"An aquatic traffic jam."

"And here's Roger with a pool all to his own self. You'd think he'd invite me over to do my lengths in his empty pool. Thoughtless, that man."

Down below, Arthur Kingsmill approached the house on foot, coming up from Queen Street. He must have taken the Queen streetcar from wherever he lived. Under his arm, he carried a thick file of papers.

"Should I know that man?" Grace said.

"You've never met the Flame Group's accountant?"

Alice shook her head.

"Arthur Kingsmill," I said. "He's prepared the papers I told you about."

"Meaning I'll have the authority to sign all the expense sheets that come into the Flame Group?"

"And you give the approval or otherwise to all the payments that go out."

Alice was quiet for a moment. "Crang," she said after a bit, "Roger must've done something awfully dreadful for you to be making all these manipulations with the way my son's money comes and goes."

"My guess is we're in time to rescue the situation, Alice."

Down below, Arthur Kingsmill took a key from his jacket pocket and unlocked the Carnale front door. He went in, closing the door behind him.

No more than a couple of minutes later, a car pulled into the only empty parking space on the street within close range of the house. Two men got out of the car. The driver was unmistakable in the overweight person of Georgie Gabriel. But who was the other guy?

Georgie was supposed to be accompanied only by eight million dollars in the most easily transportable form. Since he carried a battered old briefcase in a small size, I assumed it held a certified cheque or a bank draft for the eight million. But there was no reason for Georgie to bring along a second guy.

The two stepped clear of the car, and started up the walk to the house. The second guy was grey-haired, slightly stooped, and nicely dressed in a tan summer suit.

"Who do we have here?" Alice said.

"The one with the briefcase is a gambler named Georgie Gabriel," I said. "He's the one bringing the good news. The second ..."

"Yes, who is he?"

"... Holy shit."

"Somebody you didn't expect?"

"Pardon my language, Alice."

"Heard a lot worse in operating rooms," Alice said. "And that's just from the surgeons."

"The older guy is a crooked stockbroker named Willie Sizemore, and he wasn't on the evening's guest list."

Georgie knocked on the Carnale door, and almost immediately Arthur Kingsmill opened it. I couldn't make out much of Kingsmill's facial expressions, but his body language told me he wasn't thrilled to find Willie Sizemore on the doorstep.

After a small show of hesitation, Kingsmill stepped aside, and the three men disappeared into the house.

"Everybody arrived now except for Roger?" Alice said.

"And his chauffeur."

"But you and I want to be in there before Roger and the chauffeur get here?"

"That's the idea."

"So what are we waiting for?"

"Give it a minute to make sure there are no more surprises."

The idea of Roger as the killer was giving me a sudden case of second thoughts. I had no doubt he had done all the heinous things with Flame's money, but did he have the look of a man who murdered someone? He came across as too mild and ordinary for the role. On the other hand, did killers as a species even have a look? Well, yeah, sort of. Freddie Chamblis had the appearance of someone who wouldn't think twice about taking another guy's life. No matter what he said in the hospital about only intending to drop me on the balcony, maybe his real intention was to shove me all the way to my demise on Centre Street. And if he did, I reminded myself, Chamblis was acting on Roger's instructions. That would have made Roger as guilty of murder as Freddie was. So why was I feeling squeamish about implicating Roger in the real killing of the Reverend?

"Get a grip," I said to myself.

"Anything bothering you, Crang?" Alice said.

"I'm peachy."

Alice and I got out of the Mercedes, and walked down the hill to Carnale's house. Arthur Kingsmill answered after my second knock.

"We have an unanticipated addition to the group," he said even before I introduced Alice.

"Willie Sizemore," I said. "I doubt he can disrupt our plan."

"He says he's come to apologize," Kingsmill said. "He keeps talking about a cricket bat and a blow to his head."

"I've heard versions of the story," I said.

I presented Kingsmill to Alice, and asked him to tuck her away in a room close enough for her to hear what was going on in the living room but out of sight.

"The kitchen," Kingsmill said.

"My plan," I said, speaking to both Alice and Kingsmill, "is for Roger not to know Alice is in the house until I've told him about the document he's going to put his John Henry on. That's the one where he surrenders the Flame Group's signing responsibilities and so on. Once that's done, I'll bring Alice into the room."

"That's a good strategy," Kingsmill said. "Roger will probably be less embarrassed and more willing if Ms. Desmond isn't present when his perfidy is revealed."

"Perfidy, huh?" I said.

"Good word under the circumstances," Kingsmill said. "And I'm not forgetting I was part of it."

"I'm still in the dark," Alice said.

"Not for long," I said.

I turned to Kingsmill. "You put the briefcase somewhere in the living room?"

"On the bottom shelf of the bookcase beside the fireplace."

"Good man," I said. "Stout fellow. Sound chap."

Kingsmill led Alice down the hall to the left, past the closed door to the living room, and further on to what I assumed was the kitchen area. As soon as they were out of sight, I opened the door ahead of me, and stepped into the living room.

The first thing that registered, even before I checked out the two guys in the room, was a large and lovely painting by Graham Coughtry. It was on the far wall directly in front of me, one more in the Carnale collection of Canadian artists. The painting was in pale oranges and greens, two figures colliding sensually in midair.

I swung my gaze around the rest of the big room, which seemed to be divided into two sitting areas. One was grouped in front of the fireplace, a dark maroon leather sofa and three armchairs, also leather and dark maroon. The other area, closer to the window looking into the backyard, consisted of two sofas covered in flowery designs, a couple of straightbacked chairs, and a substantial coffee table with bowls and a vase on it. The vase held a nice arrangement of pale blue flowers, which I couldn't identify.

"Hey, Crang." Georgie Gabriel greeted me with a big smile.

He and Willie Sizemore were admiring the view out back. Georgie held up his battered briefcase. "Got the goods," he said.

Willie came toward me with his hand out. "Mr. Crang," he said. "I believe we met at Heaven's Philosophers. Sizemore is my name. Call me Willie."

"Interesting to find you among this company, Willie," I said.

"I came here to explain myself," Willie said. His voice had a wheedling tone.

"Start with this one, Willie," I said. "Where did you get the whack on the head from the cricket bat? At Upper Canada, Ridley, or Lakefield? And was it from a member of the Eaton family, the Weston family, or British royalty?"

"You get directly to the point, Mr. Crang."

"We don't have much time tonight, Willie."

"My parents sent me to all three schools at different times."

"The schools asked your mum and dad to move you on, did they?"

"There might have been some of that, but all of it happened long after I got the hit to my head," Willie said, one hand fingering the gouge near his right temple, "I had trouble focusing on my studies."

"So, which one of the schools did the whacking happen at?"

"None that you mentioned," Willie said, stepping up the wheedling. "Before I went to them, I was at a small boarding school called Harrington out towards Lake Huron. Not on the level of UCC or Ridley. But it was at Harrington where a boy struck me with the bat. He was the scion of a family in photo engraving."

"Not much of that going on these days. Photo engraving."

"Why I asked Georgie to bring me along tonight, Mr. Crang," Willie said, "I want to let Roger know how sorry I am about the misunderstanding over the eight million dollars."

"I'm sure Roger will be glad to see you, Willie. He might take the opportunity to put his mean chauffeur on your ass."

Willie looked from me to Georgie and back again. "Maybe this wasn't such a good choice, coming here," he said.

"On the contrary, Willie," I said, "You being here, I think it'll turn out to be beneficial to the cause I represent, namely Flame and his mother."

"I've never met those two people, Mr. Crang, though I'm sure I'd be pleased to make their acquaintance."

"The feelings might not be mutual, Willie," I said. "Not when they hear from your own mouth that their eight million dollars found its way via Roger Carnale into your bank account. The beneficial part, it drives home the message Roger's not the best guy to choose investment destinations for Flame's money."

"Speaking of which," Georgie said, holding up his briefcase. "Certified cheque. Eight million. And we're letting Willie here keep the interest the eight million earned while the dough was in his hands."

Willie had the good taste to look sheepish. "I should emphasize, Roger went into our dealings with his eyes wide open," he said. "It was a matter of him encountering a little bad luck in his investments."

"Bad luck?" Arthur Kingsmill said, coming up behind us. He was speaking to Willie. "What Roger encountered was a bad hat in the person of yourself."

"You're supposedly an accountant, Arthur," Willie said. "That means your duties include preventing activities you've always accused me of."

"There's no *supposedly*, Sizemore," Kingsmill said. "I'm an accountant. About that there's no doubt. But you, you're nothing but a charlatan."

I spoke over Kingsmill. "Gentlemen, I've got an agenda for tonight, short but sweet, and I don't want you people squabbling before Carnale even gets here."

"Why don't we all have a drink?" Georgie said. "There's wine and other stuff on the table over there. Vodka, I notice. Scotch."

Georgie was pointing to a table against the wall, close to the door to the kitchen.

"I thought it might help smooth the way," Kingsmill said.

"Thank you, Arthur," I said. "Good planning."

For the next few minutes, the four of us helped ourselves to drinks. The vodka was Stoli. I poured some into an old-fashioned glass, which I filled with ice cubes from a silver bucket. Peace and calm had descended on the room. It was an atmosphere that might encourage a more productive exchange of information.

We sat in the area with the two sofas done in floral designs. Everybody took a sip from their drinks. Then second sips all round. We looked at one another. Then looked away. Nobody spoke. Nobody exchanged information with anybody else.

"The collegial approach to our relationship doesn't seem to be working any better than the argumentive style," I said.

Everybody sipped again from their drinks.

In the stillness, we heard the front door open. That was followed by footsteps coming into the front hall. Then came the sound of keys being dropped in a bowl. A voice spoke. It was Carnale's.

"Anin, I'll be up in the office," he said. "You want to see why all the living room lights are on. While you're at it, make me a scotch and water. I'm beat."

None of us in the living room moved or spoke.

Somebody, almost certainly Anin, whom I couldn't help thinking of as Lex, dropped suitcases in the entrance hall. He walked across the hall toward the open living room door.

Lex got two steps into the room before he noticed the four of us sitting on the sofas, drinks in our hands. A startled expression made a brief appearance on his face. It was followed by a pleased smirk, the look of a little kid who'd discovered something secret and naughty. He turned his head toward the entrance hall.

"Mr. Carnale," Lex said, "you want to come in here and see what the fuckin' cat dragged in."

CHAPTER FORTY-SEVEN

Carnale didn't react as gleefully as Lex did to the personnel that made up our little group of visitors. From the moment Carnale laid eyes on us, the air began to seep out of the man. It seemed to me he sensed exactly what lay in store. Lex got his boss a scotch and water. Carnale, sitting not very straight in one of the straight-backed chairs, clutched the drink in his right hand. He took a generous swallow. It didn't appear to buck him up much. Lex, who had set himself up in a position behind Carnale, was looking increasingly bewildered by what was going on.

I was sitting in the sofa closest to Carnale, Georgie beside me.

"Roger," I said, looking Carnale in the eye, "let's begin with a little show and tell. Georgie here has something to show you. The part I'm calling 'tell,' you ought to be able to figure out for yourself."

Georgie opened his briefcase, took out a cheque, and passed it to me. Very impressive this cheque was, the numerals in extra large type, one *8* and six *0*s. The certification was stamped across the cheque. The signature at the bottom of the cheque was flashy and indecipherable but was attributed to the president of a numbered company, which was no doubt Willie Sizemore's covering corporation.

I handed the cheque to Carnale. His face showed no emotion,

unless defeat qualified as an emotion. He had no doubt figured what the cheque was all about in the instant Georgie produced it. But as soon as he saw it up close, the eight-million-dollar sum on the cheque's face payable to the Flame Group, he knew how thoroughly he'd been nailed. He gave the cheque a long stare, maybe hoping to detect a flaw in it, something technical that would get him off the hook. When he spotted nothing out of place, he gave the cheque back to me.

Carnale looked at Willie.

"I'm ashamed to admit you tricked me out of such a large sum, Sizemore," he said.

"A misunderstanding entirely, Roger," Willie said. "If you'll let me explain …"

"Save it for later, Willie," I said.

Willie tried to speak again, but Arthur Kingsmill, beside him on the other sofa, put a warning hand on Willie's knee.

"Roger," I said, "you concede you turned eight million of Flame's earnings over to Willie Sizemore?"

"The way you put it is too simplistic to even begin to cover the situation," Carnale said.

"Yes or no?"

"Yes, with an explanation."

"Next," I said, "you organized a bogus blackmailing scheme with the Reverend Alton Douglas as your front man?"

Carnale paused, "Do I need a lawyer?" he said.

"Nobody's talking criminal charges," I said. "The people who know about your dirty tricks are pretty much all in this room, and none of us has the faintest intention of bringing criminal charges against you or against anyone else" — I aimed a stern look at Willie Sizemore — "in connection with the eight million dollars."

"I thought it'd be best for the Flame Group in the long run," Carnale said.

"After the Reverend died," I said, "you put together a second blackmail scheme. That second one's in the process of winding down right now, in this room, with the return of the eight million. For that, we can thank Jackie and Georgie Gabriel."

Willie began to clap his hands, beaming at Georgie. Nobody joined in the applause. I shot Willie another of my stern looks, and he cut his ovation short.

"I'm authorized to speak for Flame in what comes next, Roger," I said to Carnale. "Flame is willing to make you an offer. You stay on the job, managing Flame's career in music. Flame and everybody else who knows the hip hop business accepts that there's nobody better at guiding a client's career in hip hop. You got the contacts and the right instincts. That's why you're getting a break on the fraud you tried to pull. You'll get paid a decent salary, the right benefits, all of that. The one restriction, you won't handle Flame's money on your own. Arthur has a document for you to complete. It's a waiver of all your signing duties in the Flame Group."

Carnale got an indignant expression on his face. His confidence might have been staging a small return. "Without me running the entire financial side," he said, "who's going to read and sign the contracts and every other piece of paper that comes through this office?" He turned his head in Arthur Kingsmill's direction. "Not Kingsmill."

"I'm the person who'll sign, Roger," Flame's mother said, standing in the doorway from the kitchen. "For the time being anyway."

Everybody turned to look at Alice. She was apparently shocked enough at what she'd already heard that she couldn't wait for me to summon her to the living room.

At the sight of Alice, Carnale took a few seconds to reorganize his thoughts.

"Alice?" Carnale said. "You're part of what's being done to me?"

"Done to *you*!" Alice said. "What have you been doing to *me* all these years? The first thing, you stole those nine pages of lyrics out of my house."

"That was a long time ago," Carnale said. "I knew it would hurt Flame's reputation if anybody else got hold of them."

"Probably so," Alice said. "But then you turned around and used them yourself to harm my son."

"But that was only money," Carnale said.

"It was *his* money," Alice said. "Not *yours*."

I made a motion to Kingsmill, who handed a document along with extra copies to Carnale and a pen to sign them with. The pen was a gorgeous Montblanc. What lucky guy owned that? Kingsmill caught my admiring glance. He mouthed, "Carnale's." Kingsmill clearly loved what was about to happen, his domineering boss taking a great fall and signing the document that measured the tumble with his own pricey Montblanc.

Once he started signing, Carnale wasted no time in getting through the original document and the copies. As he finished each piece of paper, Kingsmill slid it with the others into a large file folder. While all this was going in, I strolled over to the bookshelf, picked up Roger's briefcase with the metal corners, and carried it back to the group.

"That went well," Kingsmill said to me, *sotto voce*. He held the file folder with all the signed documents.

"It was the easy part," I said. "Getting Flame's finances straightened around."

"Aren't we finished?" Kingsmill said. "Or are you implying there's a hard part still to come?"

"I am."

"What is it?"

"Murder," I said.

Kingsmill looked properly shocked.

"Roger," I said, speaking loudly enough to get everybody's attention, especially Carnale's. "Roger," I said again, holding up the briefcase for his inspection, "this is yours, am I right?"

"I own eight or nine briefcases," he said.

"But only one with metal edging?"

"I suppose."

"This, Roger," I said, hoisting the briefcase a little higher, "is an instrument of death."

Damn, I thought to myself, that sounded melodramatic and pompous. From the looks on the other people's faces, mostly of bemusement and bafflement, they agreed I'd hit a wrong note.

"What I mean," I said, "is this briefcase was used to kill the Reverend Alton Douglas two weeks ago last night."

"Don't be ridiculous, Crang," Carnale said.

"I had the briefcase tested by a private forensics lab. There's not a doubt, Roger, somebody swung it at the Reverend's head."

I was back in stride and seemed to have regained the group's confidence.

"This," I said, once again holding up the briefcase, "is a murder weapon. The question is, who handled it on the fatal night? I think the answer must be evident to all of us here."

"Crang," Georgie said in a voice just above a whisper. Georgie was sitting on the edge of one of the sofas, to the right of where I was standing. He pulled on my jacket as he whispered my name again. "Hey, Crang."

"Georgie," I said, dropping my voice to Georgie's level, "I'm reaching the climax here."

"I know," he said. "That's why I need to speak to you."

"Soon as I'm done."

"We better speak right now," Georgie said, "or you're gonna make an ass of yourself."

Georgie's usual facial expression included a grin. At that moment, he wasn't grinning. He was dead serious.

I excused myself from the rest of the group, and led Georgie over to the door to the entrance hall. I intended to give him a small blast for wrecking my big scene, but Georgie spoke first.

"Carnale didn't kill the Reverend," he said. "He couldn't have. At the time you say the murder was going on, he was with me hundreds of miles away."

CHAPTER FORTY-EIGHT

Georgie and I continued the conversation out in the entrance hall, the door to the living room closed behind us.

"We were comped by this casino in Atlantic City," Georgie said. "They do that with big-time players, which Roger was for a little while."

"No insult intended, Georgie," I said, "but how did you qualify for the freebie?"

"I'm what they call a friend of the casino. What that means, I steer the big players from up here down to their particular joint. And just so you know, it ain't easy to insult me."

I smiled, and got on with the grilling. "For this jaunt, you left Toronto at what time?"

"Noon Tuesday — in one of those little Gulfstreams the casino leased for me and Roger and three other players I didn't know. We stayed in the same hotel in Atlantic City, Roger and myself. He played blackjack till around midnight. We had something to eat and went to bed. Next day, Roger was back in action, more blackjack. He lost a ton of money, and the Gulfstream flew us home that afternoon, the Wednesday."

"The impression I'm getting, Roger was hardly ever out of your sight?"

"Only way he could have done the murder is if he flew home after I fell asleep around 2 a.m., bopped the Reverend, and was back in bed in Atlantic City before I woke up around eight."

"Not a chance Carnale killed the Reverend," I said.

I knew I couldn't let the confrontation with Carnale just dribble away, not tonight when I'd organized everything to reach a grand finale. He may not have been the killer, but he owned the briefcase that did the job on the Reverend. That ought to lead somewhere useful. The briefcase was all I had to work with.

Georgie and I went back into the living room. Everybody seemed to have fresh drinks; even Alice had a glass of white wine. She and Kingsmill had their heads together over the documents that gave Alice the signing power in the Flame Group. Everybody else was sitting or standing silent, even Willie.

"Roger," I said, once more holding up the damned briefcase, "this is the weapon that killed the Reverend."

"You don't need to tell me again, Crang," Carnale said. "But, if you listen for a moment, I've been thinking about the situation."

"Never mind thinking," I said. "Just answer my questions."

I didn't have much in the way of questioning, but I didn't want Carnale taking control of the conversation.

Carnale still insisted on talking to me. "Georgie told you I was with him in Atlantic City at the time of the murder. Am I right?"

"Roger, will you just let me ask the questions," I said. "Who had access to the briefcase while you were away?"

"That's not the only thing you should be concerned about, Crang. It's not only a matter of the person having access to the briefcase."

I paused, wondering whether Carnale was on to something interesting, "Just this once," I said, "I might listen to you, Roger."

As I was speaking, Lex made a small movement. Lex had been standing behind Carnale all evening, just to Carnale's right, never budging, hardly noticeable, the only person in the room without a drink. Now he stepped closer to the chair Carnale was sitting in. He placed his left hand on the back of the chair, as if he were reaching out for aid or protection.

Well, damn, I thought, *Lex*! This idiot must be the guy who had the briefcase on the night of the murder. It made sense. He had plenty of access to the briefcase. He could have carried it with him across town to see the Reverend on a Carnale errand. He got in a disagreement with the Reverend, and impulsively whacked him with the briefcase.

"Lex?" I said to Carnale.

"I gave Lex, as you call him, more properly Anin, I gave him an assignment," Carnale said. "The Reverend phoned me on the Monday to say he wasn't going through with our agreement about him pretending to blackmail Flame. I told him I'd pay him fifteen thousand dollars in cash right away if he'd rethink his decision to cancel our arrangement. When I hung up, I had the impression he might be coming around to what I said. I gave Anin the fifteen thousand dollars to deliver Tuesday night. I said I'd deal with the Reverend as soon as I got back from Atlantic City on Wednesday."

I looked at Lex.

"I didn't kill anybody," he said. His lips were quivering. I couldn't tell whether it was from fear or rage.

"Did you deliver the fifteen thousand dollars to the Reverend?" I asked Lex.

"He wouldn't take it, but that doesn't mean I hit the guy."

"Were you carrying the briefcase at the time?"

"That's what the fucking money was in."

Carnale said to me, "Later on Wednesday, when I heard about the Reverend's death, I asked Anin for his version. He told me it must've been somebody else who came into the Reverend's office after Anin left. He insisted it was this other person who killed the Reverend. Obviously, now that we all know about the briefcase being the murder weapon, Anin's story has to be a lie."

"Why doesn't anybody believe me?" Lex said, his voice shooting up the register. "I didn't kill the man!"

Carnale, sounding cool and confident, said to Lex, “You’ve placed yourself in the Reverend’s office with the briefcase that killed him. What else are we to think? You must have struck him dead.”

“On the surface, Lex,” I said, “it doesn’t look good.”

I was going to add that Lex might have an innocent explanation for everything that happened in the Reverend’s office, but I didn’t get a chance to finish what I wanted to say.

Lex had moved from behind Carnale’s chair. He was standing closer to the centre of the room, halfway between the sofas and chairs where we were sitting and the arrangement of leather furniture by the fireplace. As Lex stood there, his right hand was going into the belt under the back of his shirt. When he brought his hand out, it was holding a large-sized gun.

“Oh, Jesus, Lex,” I said. “The gun’s a mistake.”

“Nobody believes me!” Lex said in a kind of shriek, waving the gun as he spoke, not focusing it in any particular direction. “I didn’t kill that guy!”

“POLICE! PUT THE GUN DOWN!”

Everybody turned to the doorway. Wally Crawford was crouched in it. In his left hand, he held out a police ID card. His right hand was pulling a gun out of a holster on his right hip, but the gun got tangled in the lining of his jacket. The gun came out in a lurching motion.

The room filled with a roar. It was a noise that didn’t come from Wally’s gun. It came from Lex’s. When I looked in his direction, Lex was staring at his gun as if it were a strange object he had nothing to do with.

“I didn’t mean to shoot!” he said in a small voice. He was looking at me as he spoke.

I turned back in Wally’s direction. He was falling to his left. His gun fired as he fell. It made a sound much more muted than what came out of Lex’s gun. The bullet from Wally’s gun zipped past me and into a corner of the Graham Coughtry painting. Glass from the framed painting flew into the air.

Alice rushed to Wally's side. "I'm a nurse," she said. She got Wally on his back and opened the left side of his jacket. Wally's gun had fallen from his hand. I got the impression Wally hadn't meant to fire any more than Lex had.

"Fuck, that hurts," Wally said.

"Now isn't that fortunate," Alice said, as she pulled back Wally's jacket. "You're wearing a bulletproof vest."

I thought about telling her the term was bullet-resistant, but didn't bother. Whatever it was called, the vest had done its job. I could see the bullet from Lex's gun mashed into the part of the vest where it covered Wally's shoulder. The bullet was almost unrecognizable as a bullet, now flattened in the shape of a tiny plate.

"Where the hell's the other car?" Wally said to Alice.

"Lie back now," Alice said. "What other car?"

"Emergency Task Force guys. They were supposed to help me make the arrest."

I looked around for Lex.

"He went out the front door," Kingsmill said from behind me. "My advice is you should leave Anin to the police. He's still got the gun, Crang."

"I can't believe how sore the damn bullet makes my shoulder feel," Wally said, trying to sit up.

Alice pressed him gently back to the floor. "Give the soreness a few minutes and it'll be manageable," she said to Wally. She eased the suit jacket off his left side.

I hustled across the living room and out to the entrance hall. I was carrying the briefcase. It was a piece of evidence I intended to hang on to until the case was done. I opened the front door.

"You're a fool if you're going after Anin," Kingsmill said, still behind me. "That man's a proven killer, and he's armed."

"So you keep telling me."

"Why are you ignoring my advice?"

"Lex says he didn't mean to shoot Wally," I said. "The odds are he isn't going to shoot two guys he didn't mean to shoot on the same night. He won't even think about pointing his gun at me."

"Don't say I didn't warn you."

"It's a deal, Arthur."

"What?"

"Next time I see you, I won't say you didn't warn me."

CHAPTER FORTY-NINE

Lex hadn't gone far. He was still on Carnale's street, just a half block up the hill. He was sitting on a low brick wall across the front yard of a neighbouring mansion. He looked despondent, his hands anchored beside him on the brick wall, his head hanging almost to his knees.

"Where's the gun, Lex?" I said.

"In the back of my belt." He was practically whimpering.

I fiddled the gun out of Lex's belt and stuck it in the briefcase.

"We need to move, Lex," I said. "Emergency Task Force guys'll be here any minute."

"Emergency Task Force?"

"First thing they do if they think you're armed, they'll blast you to smithereens."

That got Lex in motion. Together we walked briskly up the street. My Mercedes was in sight a short block away.

"Is this some kind of trick, Crang, you being all friendly?" Lex said. "You messing with me on purpose?"

"You think I might be somehow getting payback for your attempted sexual damage to my friend, Sal?"

"Her damage? What about her friend kicking me in the crotch?

That's what I call real damage! My balls are still so big and sore I have to wear extra-large underwear."

"At the moment, Lex, none of that is a motivator with me."

"Just answer me this," Lex said, "how come you haven't dragged me straight back to the cop I shot by mistake?"

"I don't think you killed the Reverend, Lex. But I think you know who did the deed."

Lex had no answer to that. We got in the Mercedes, but before we pulled away from the curb, a cop van came down the street in a rush, stopping in front of Carnale's house. Five people piled out of the vehicle. All five were dressed in black gear, helmets, bullet-resistant vests in the super deluxe size, loose pants, and heavy boots. They carried guns with what looked like enough ammunition to start a Mid East war. They trotted into Carnale's house, shouting all the way.

"Jesus," Lex said. "I wouldn't have stood a chance."

"A real possibility, Lex."

I drove down to Queen, heading west to Woodbine Avenue, then south on Woodbine to the roadhouse-style restaurant with the big parking lot on Lake Shore Boulevard. I parked in the lot.

"Are you nuts, Crang?" Lex said. "I don't feel like eating."

"The parking lot's a good place for a private chat."

"What about?"

"Somebody must have been with you when you called on the Reverend," I said. "Who was it?"

"I went by myself."

"Somebody else was already in the room with the Reverend?"

"He was alone."

"Don't make this so hard, Lex," I said. "With the first two possibilities eliminated, I'm saying somebody came in while you and the Reverend were talking."

Lex stretched out the time it took him to answer. "You're right," he said in something close to a whisper.

"This was somebody known to you?"

Lex shook his head. "Never saw him before this one time in the Reverend's office."

"The Reverend knew him?"

"Yeah, but I could tell he didn't like the guy."

"Now we're getting somewhere," I said.

"I'd like to know where it's getting *me*."

"Here's the big question, Lex. This guy's name, you catch that?"

"Robert."

"No last name?"

"Robert's all the Reverend called him."

"Describe Robert."

"Big guy. A lot older than me, but still built like a horse. He wasn't a guy I'd want to tangle with, which is something I definitely did not do this one time I met him."

"Speaking generally, Lex, were you aware what went on day-to-day in the building where you got together with the Reverend and this Robert?"

"I knew from Mr. Carnale the place was a front for different criminal stuff."

"Did Robert appear to be one of the people doing the criminal stuff?"

"How am I supposed to know that?"

"Here's one way, Lex. When Robert came into the Reverend's office was he deferential or did he act as if he owned the place?"

"He was like a bully. Very rude and demanding."

"You're doing wonders, my man."

I got out my cellphone and scrolled through it until I found the photos I took at Heaven's Philosophers. I put on screen the shot that included Squeaky Fallis with two other guys.

"Recognize anybody, Lex?" I said, handing him the phone.

"The guy in the middle, that's Robert."

"Robert Fallis, nicknamed Squeaky behind his back."

"Oh yeah, the high-pitched voice," Lex said, pleased with himself. He handed the cellphone back to me.

"What business did Squeaky have with the Reverend on the night we're talking about?" I said.

"The eight million dollars, what else?" Lex said. "I got the point right away, the Squeaky guy wanted in on the money the Reverend was supposed to be getting out of the Flame people."

"Did Squeaky know about the song lyrics that were at the basis of the blackmail?

"No," Lex said. "But I told him."

"*You* told Squeaky? Right there in the Reverend's office, *you* told him all about the song lyrics?"

"He started yelling and screaming at me. I never heard anything like it in my life. This big guy saying he's gonna put my head in a vise if I didn't tell him right away what he needed to know about how the blackmail thing was supposed to go down. All he'd heard up till then was basically that somebody could score eight million bucks. He said I should tell him the rest or he'd do the thing with my head."

"Several of your bodily parts have come under serious siege in recent times, Lex," I said. "From your skull to your testicles."

"You can understand why I gave him the answers he wanted. All about the song lyrics, the whole story as far as I knew it."

"Then what happened?"

"Oh shit, man," Lex began. "It was the worst."

"Under duress, the Reverend offered to show Squeaky a copy of the lyrics?"

"How'd you know?"

"Informed guess," I said. "What came after that?"

"The Reverend was as scared as me. He unlocked the drawer in his desk, and shuffled through a bunch of papers in there. He got very frustrated. Said he couldn't find the pages with the song lyrics. He kept saying he was certain he put the lyrics in that particular drawer."

"That didn't please Squeaky?"

"He went bats."

"Be more exact if you don't mind, Lex."

"First he pulled all the pieces of paper out of the Reverend's drawer. They were blank, every one of them. That really pissed the guy off. He threw the papers all over the place."

"Then he turned violent?"

"Not yet. He made the Reverend open all the other drawers in his desk."

"Came up empty again?"

Lex nodded vigourously.

"After it was abundantly clear the Reverend didn't have the song lyrics," I said, "how did Squeaky react?"

"The briefcase was sitting on the Reverend's desk," Lex said. "Squeaky kind of swept it up with his hand, and all in one motion he bashed it into the Reverend's head."

"Just one blow?"

"The thing that amazed me, there was hardly any blood. But I knew the Reverend was dead anyway. The briefcase hit him, and he dropped to the floor. He just lay there, nothing moving. He was totally gone."

"What about Squeaky?" I said.

"He got even madder. It was like the Reverend had personally offended him by falling down dead."

"So Squeaky threw up his hands and walked away?"

"First he told me if I said anything about what happened in the Reverend's office, he'd personally rip my head off at the neck. I was scared shitless. I'd just seen this guy murder someone. I figured I was lucky he didn't whack me out too. What I did then, I picked up the briefcase with the money in it, and went home. I've kept my mouth shut until this minute."

"That might work in your favour, Lex," I said. "Or maybe not."

Taking a chance that Gloria would be reachable somewhere, I punched in her number on my cellphone.

Ha, she picked up.

"What's up, Crang?" she said.

"In the file you put together on Squeaky Fallis," I said, "you got a home address?"

"No time for the little social amenities?"

"The file handy to you right now?"

"Oh, we're in a rush, are we?" Gloria said. I could hear the sound of clicking on a computer keyboard. Neither Gloria nor I spoke.

"Here we go," Gloria said. "It's a house in the Playter Estates. The man appears to live there alone. Anything else?"

Playter Estates was the name of an older upscale neighbourhood east of the Don River and north of Danforth Avenue. It was only about fifteen minutes away from where Lex and I were parked. Gloria gave me the number on Playter Boulevard.

"If you're about to do something completely idiotic," she said, "then hang up right now. I don't want to be walking around with information that Annie might need to dig out of me one day."

"Thanks, kid," I said. I clicked off the phone, turned on the Mercedes's ignition, and pulled out of the parking lot and back on to Lake Shore Boulevard. I wasn't wasting any time.

CHAPTER FIFTY

I drove across town to my office. Lex went silent the whole way, no doubt wrapped up in thoughts about his own fate. My phone beeped twice on the drive, but I didn't answer either. I parked on Robert Street around the corner from the office.

"Be right back," I said to Lex.

"What crime can the cops charge me with?" Lex said, coming out of his trance.

"Accessory after the fact to murder."

"That's because I didn't go to the police right away and tell them what Squeaky Fallis did to the Reverend?"

I nodded. "But if you agree to testify in court for the Crown when they prosecute Squeaky, the cops'll likely give you a break."

"That's what I was thinking."

"You might get an even bigger break if you help me seal the case against Squeaky."

"That's what you're planning right now?"

"And I can't do it without a strong hand from someone else. You're elected, Lex."

Lex thought about what I'd said. "One thing I don't get," he said, "why are you going to all the trouble?"

"I owe it to the Reverend."

Taking the Carnale briefcase with me, I went up to my office. First thing, I checked the two phone messages. One was from Wally Crawford. He wanted to know where I raced off to. And was I, by any chance, in Lex's company? Wally sounded sarcastic and impatient. I'd phone him later. The second message was from Archie Brewster's wife, Ruth. She had the results from the other tests on the briefcase. Number one, the blood on the metal corner of the briefcase matched the deceased Reverend's blood. And, second, the lab had found fingerprints from six different people on the briefcase's handle. None of the six matched any other prints they had on file of people who were even remotely connected to the case. The lack of a match wasn't surprising since the Brewster lab, unlike the cop facilities, had a limited store of prints. They didn't have Lex's prints or Carnale's in their records, and those two guys would definitely be among the six. I was betting that one remaining set of prints would belong to Squeaky. If all went according to my plan that night, Archie Brewster's lab could make a comparison next day, and prove that Squeaky at some point handled the briefcase.

Still in the office, I opened the desk drawer where I stored a digital recorder that was good for clandestinely recording conversations with people who didn't know they were getting caught on tape. The digital thing once belonged to a client of mine. This guy suspected his wife was cheating on him with his best friend. He taped a conversation with the friend who admitted he'd been boffing the wife. My client went home, and played the tape for the wife. Then he killed her. The client was now doing life in Kingston Pen. He had no further use for the digital thing. I fitted it into my shirt pocket, which happened to have a button-down flap. The flap ought to hold it in place while I carried out the plan I had in mind. That done, I got the copies of the Flame song lyrics out of my file cabinet, put them in the Carnale briefcase, and went back to the Mercedes.

"Now we call on Squeaky," I said to Lex.

I drove east on Bloor, across the Don Valley viaduct, and on to Danforth Avenue.

"What am I supposed to do when we see the guy?" Lex said.

"You're the muscle," I said.

"I told you, Squeaky's an animal. No way one person can handle him."

"A young and fit guy like you, Lex, you ought to be able to stand up to him long enough for us to get our business done. Besides, consider the odds. Two of us against one of Squeaky."

I turned left off the Danforth, and worked my way north on Playter to the number Gloria had given me. Squeaky's place was a stolid looking detached house, built of stone and brick. It showed no particular flourishes of beauty, and its front garden was home to more invasive weeds than flowers, not to mention a raggedy maple that looked half-dead. But the place was loaded with possibilities, and would probably go for two and a half million if somebody gave it a cosmetic fix up.

The room at the front on the first floor, probably the living room, was lit up like it was Christmas. I could see one large figure — Squeaky? — walking back and forth at irregular intervals, bending over from time to time, then straightening up.

"What do you suppose he's doing in there?" I said to Lex.

"You mean Squeaky?"

"I assume that's him."

"He's shooting pool."

I watched a bit more. "Good spotting, Lex."

"Remind me again how I'm supposed to handle myself?"

"Keep your mouth shut. Follow my lead. Be prepared to spring to our mutual defence. You think you can handle the assignment?"

Lex paused.

"If you can't do it," I said, "the cops aren't likely to be happy with you."

"Yes, sir!" Lex said as smartly as he could manage. "Don't worry about me! I've got your back!"

Lex was giving me everything except the salute.

"Very impressive, Lex," I said.

CHAPTER FIFTY-ONE

Lex and I stepped out of the car in front of Squeaky Fallis's house, Lex carrying the Carnale briefcase. Both of us trotted along the front walk to a half-dozen stone steps leading up to a stone porch. The top step had planted containers at either side. I rang the doorbell. Loud chimes came from inside, followed shortly by the master himself appearing at the door.

In a black T-shirt and jeans, Squeaky looked even more imposing than I remembered. In one hand, he held a glass with a light-brown liquid in it. It was probably scotch or rye, and the slight sway in Squeaky's posture might have been evidence he'd consumed a few.

"Well, shit," he said in a manner I'd call scornful. "Two dumb fucks on my front steps."

I gestured at the plants in the containers. "These aren't dumb fucks on your steps, Squeaky," I said. "They're zinnias."

"Nobody calls me Squeaky," he said, snarling a little.

"My apologies, Mr. Fallis," I said. "But you mind if my colleague and I come in for a little conference?"

"I know who both you guys are," he said. His expression turned wily. "And I can't think of any reason why I should talk to a couple of retards."

"How about if I said we might discuss matters to our mutual benefit?" I said. "Eight million dollars' worth of benefit?"

Squeaky, clearly a man who could change his attitude on a dime, pulled back the door, and ushered us across the threshold. The front entrance led straight into the living room where the pool table took up half the space. It was a room that smelled like I imagined an old-time pool hall did with its reek of ancient cigarette smoke.

"You're the lawyer on Spadina," Squeaky said, pointing a finger at me. "And this other guy drives the rich bastard that manages the singer who's supposed to be so shit hot."

"Crang and Lex," I said. "At your service for the moment."

Squeaky had his eye on the Carnale briefcase Lex was carrying. It was hard to tell from his deadpan expression whether he recognized it. If he didn't recall it, I might have a problem: how was I going to get a recording of Squeaky admitting to a murder when he couldn't identify the object he'd used as the murder weapon?

"You assholes want a rye?" Squeaky said. He stood at a sideboard on which there rested a bottle of Canadian Club, an ice bucket, and a double row of highball glasses. "Help yourself."

For me, rye had minimal appeal. I poured an inch of the stuff and drowned it in ice and water. Lex fixed himself a larger drink, and we sat on a brown leather sofa at one side of the pool table.

Squeaky leaned his bum against the table, and glared down at us. From my angle on the sofa, the guy looked ten feet tall.

"What eight million dollars?" Squeaky asked, speaking to me.

"The money that's up for grabs from Flame's people."

"Let me get this straight. You're the lawyer for the guy willing to pay the eight million to get back some dirty songs the moron singer wrote when he was a kid?"

"Astute job of condensing, Mr. Fallis."

"Why're you talking to me? I got nothing to do with the songs."

"But I do," I said.

I motioned Lex to hand me the briefcase. Inside were copies of Flame's lyrics. Also in the briefcase was something I'd forgotten until that moment. It was Lex's gun. I opened the briefcase at an angle away from Squeaky's sightline, took out the sheets, and held them up for Squeaky. He took the song sheets from me, and skimmed the lyrics for a few minutes.

"Even I can tell these things would piss the public off," Squeaky said, glancing down at me. "Not that I give a shit. But if your dumbass client thinks these are worth eight million, I'm not gonna argue with him."

"I believe we see eye to eye on the situation, Mr. Fallis, sir."

"So how come you're including me in a shot at the big money?"

"I can't openly blackmail the Flame people, not in my position as their lawyer."

"What about your pal here?"

"Lex? He hasn't got the gravitas for the role. We need someone who's going to be taken seriously."

"People take me serious or I yank their heads off," Squeaky said, sounding snarly again.

"So I understand."

"Something still smells fishy to me, you coming to my house with this deal," Squeaky said. The wary look had made a return.

"Number one," I said, "I expect to walk away with four million. Out of it I pay Lex his share. The other four million is yours. Money talks, right, Mr. Fallis?"

"What's number two?"

"The first time I made a move on the eight million, my front man lost his nerve."

"Your front man? You were in the deal with the minister? I don't believe it."

"You met the man, you must have noticed he had a little problem with follow through."

"What he had a problem with," Squeaky said, holding up the sheets of Flame's lyrics, "he couldn't find these goddamn songs when I asked him to gimme a look at them."

I propped the briefcase on my knee, a lame prompt maybe, but it might prod Squeaky into recognizing the murder weapon and blundering a frank answer to my next question. "So how did you handle the Reverend's failure to produce the lyrics?"

Squeaky took a big swallow of rye and water. He looked at Lex, then back at me. "You haven't asked Lexie here what I might have done to the Reverend?"

"As far as I know, Lex has no knowledge of what went on at any meeting you may have had with the Reverend. Unless Lex has been holding out on me."

"He hasn't told you anything about me and the Reverend?"

"Just that if you had an arrangement with the Reverend, it fell through. That was before the Reverend's murder ended the whole blackmail plan."

"And you're telling me you were partners with the Reverend?"

"Now I'm looking to be partners with you."

Squeaky pushed away from the pool table, and walked across the room to get himself another rye. I took a modest sip of my own, and thought about how things had gone so far with Squeaky. In general, not well. I'd wrapped myself in a network of lies that were supposed to coax Squeaky into an admission I'd catch on the digital recorder. That hadn't worked, and the main threat at the moment was that I'd get tangled in my own lies and give away the whole game.

Squeaky came back from the sideboard with his fresh drink.

"You want me to be the one that goes to the Carnale guy and tells him he better cough up the eight million?" Squeaky said. "Right so far?"

"I know you can carry it off."

"For that, I get half the payout?"

I hesitated.

"Hold off a minute, Mr. Fallis," I said. "I might have been hasty with my sum. Let's say three million for a half hour's work. That's all it'll take with Carnale."

"You welching on me?"

"Three million is more than reasonable."

"Four million is what you said. You came into my house, and practically the first words out of your mouth were 'four' and 'million.'"

Squeaky's face had turned flush red.

"Let's negotiate, Squeaky," I said.

Squeaky pushed off the pool table, and stood over me. At that moment, from where I sat on the brown leather couch, he looked like ten towering feet of fury.

"Never fucking call me that name!" he said, spitting as he talked.

"What's the matter with Squeaky?" I said. "It's a distinctive name. Makes you stand out."

Squeaky's rage was mounting. "You remember what I said I'd do to your head?" he said.

"Something unpleasant. But not nearly in a class with what happened to the Reverend."

"What *happened*? Nothing just *happened* to the fucking Reverend."

"It's still three million bucks, Squeaky."

Squeaky's face had gone such a deep red that it was beginning to resemble a giant plum.

"The Reverend pissed me off just like you're doing, Crang."

"And how did you react?"

"I made him pay, the dumb fuck!"

"What did he pay with, Squeaky? A flood of tears? You frightened him into weeping?"

"One fucking smack with that briefcase you brought in here. That's all it took. One smack, and the useless prick was gone. You want the same treatment? I can take you out the same way, Crang. Just like the Reverend."

I didn't say anything, and in the silence, a light seemed to come on in Squeaky's eyes. He had caught on. Squeaky was brutal but not entirely dumb, and in that moment, he realized something was wrong. He knew, and I knew he knew.

"On rethinking, Mr. Fallis," I said, "maybe we can go with the four million as your share."

I made moves to get up from the sofa. Squeaky reached out one meaty hand, and shoved my forehead. I sat back down.

"You gonna unbutton your shirt, Crang?" Squeaky said. "Or you want me to rip it off?"

"This old thing?" I said, fingering my shirt collar. "I got it on sale at Banana Republic last year. But it's kind of stylish, don't you think?"

"Don't dick with me, Crang," Suqeaky said.

"You're right, Mr. Fallis," I said. "Time to call it a night. I don't think we'll reach an agreement on our little deal just yet. But there's always another time. Maybe in a day or two?"

Squeaky put his glass on the edge of the pool table without taking his eyes off me. From the furious look on his face, I knew he was going to take a swing at me. I stood up, and got ready for him, raising my fists to waist level, prepared to block whatever kind of punch Squeaky threw. When the punch came, it was a looping left hook aimed at my chin. I caught Squeaky's punching hand on my right forearm, and steered it away from any danger to me or my chin. Squeaky followed with a straight-ahead right hand, I ducked and deflected the punch over my head. Another miss for Squeaky.

Two punches and I was still unscathed. But I knew this kind of stuff could go on for no more than another punch or two, me fending off Squeaky. His power was bound to trump my speed. Each of us in the room must have recognized the inevitable reality. Squeaky, Lex, and me for sure.

"Everybody freeze!" Lex shouted.

Both Squeaky and I turned in Lex's direction. He held his pistol in both hands, leaning forward, feet planted, shaking a little but aiming more or less at Squeaky.

"Jesus, Lex," I said. "Not the gun."

Lex switched his attention to me. His turn in stance meant the gun was pointed at my mid-section.

I reached out to push the gun's direction at another target, but Squeaky beat me to it. He swatted the gun out of Lex's hands. It flipped through the air, landing in the middle of the pool table.

Squeaky's ferocity seemed to have stepped up a notch. He threw another punch at me. This one had no loops that I could block. It came straight at my head. I made enough of a duck that the punch glanced off my noggin, and carried most of its power into my shoulder.

"The briefcase, Lex!" I shouted. "Use the briefcase!"

Squeaky moved in closer to me, within his best punching range. He set his feet and hands in position to fire another right cross. I raised my arms, all set to defend against Squeaky's best shot but not loaded with confidence about my success. Squeaky had a large rictus of a smile on his face. Confidence wasn't a problem for him.

Before Squeaky could land a punch that might polish me off, the room was filled with a sound like the crack of a baseball bat hitting a ball. The rictus slid off Squeaky's face. His eyes rolled back in his head, and he collapsed forward. I was the only thing in his path, and both of us hit the floor, Squeaky's formidable bulk on top of me.

"The briefcase hit him square!" Lex said in great excitement. "Is he dead?"

"No such luck."

"How can you tell?"

"I can feel his heart beating," I said, gathering myself to push out from under Squeaky. "And he's breathing regularly. I'm taking his breath right up my nose. Jesus, it's foul."

"It would've been weird if I'd killed him the same way he killed the Reverend."

"Ironic, yeah," I said, my hands just barely lifting Squeaky's left side. "Quit with the chatter, please, Lex. Go find something we can use to tie Squeaky up."

While Lex was gone, I shoved mightily at Squeaky until he rolled off me and on to the floor next to the sofa. He landed on his back with a heavy thud. Squeaky's breathing had grown loud enough to qualify as a snore.

I sat on the sofa, waiting to catch my own breath. When Squeaky tumbled on me, he had caught me in the diaphragm.

"There's no rope in the kitchen or the storage room," Lex said. He'd been gone only a couple of minutes. "Nothing that'll make knots."

I stood up, feeling not as shaky as I expected.

"Give Squeaky another hit with the briefcase if he comes to," I said. "I'll be right back."

Making as much speed as I could, I went up the stairs to the second floor. The master bedroom was at the front. Two doors led off it. The first was a bathroom. The second was what I was looking for, Squeaky's clothes closet. On the inside of the door, there was a tie rack holding a couple of dozen ties. The one with the lollipops stood out in all its pink and yellow glory. Every piece of neckwear belonged to the gaudy school of design. I scooped up an armful of the ties and galloped back downstairs.

"Tie his feet up really tight," I said to Lex. Squeaky was still out cold, but the snorts from his nose might indicate he was getting closer to consciousness. "Some of these neckties are silk and slippery."

"You mean the guy might be able to slide loose of them."

"Not if we make them extra secure."

I tied Squeaky's hands, Lex did the legs, and when we were done, I went into the hall, got out my iPhone, and called Wally Crawford.

"You better have a hell of a convincing story, Crang," he said when he picked up. Wherever Wally was, it seemed absent of background noise.

"You in a hospital room, Wally? It's dead quiet at your end."

"I'm doing the search of that guy Lex's bedroom."

"The man himself is with me."

"Lex? You two are where?"

"In the home of the guy who killed the Reverend."

Wally went quiet for a moment. "Dear god, Crang," he said, "what in hell have you got yourself up to?"

"How about some congratulations, Wally? I've got the Reverend's killer on a recorder describing his crime. I got the only witness to the murder, my man, Lex, as it happens, waiting to sing for you. And if you take the killer's prints and compare them with the prints Archie Brewster took off the briefcase yesterday, you'll get a match."

"Aren't you just the busybody."

"You sound fresh yourself for a guy who took a shot to his bullet-resistant vest."

"Tomorrow my shoulder's gonna be one big bruise."

"Lucky for you."

"Luckier for your pal Lex. He could have been looking at life."

"You notice something, Wally?" I said. "I haven't identified the killer for you yet."

"It was my next question," Wally said. "Who is he?"

"The adorable Squeaky Fallis."

"You're talking about one of the guys from the Heaven's Philosophers bunch of low-lifes? He killed the Reverend?"

"So he says."

"And you've got him at whatever address you and Lex are at?"

"Squeaky's all tied up."

Wally paused again, maybe wondering if I was making a wisecrack. Wally gave a pass on whatever rejoinder he had in mind.

"Tell me the street and number of your location, Crang," Wally said. He had turned all business.

I told him the address on Playter. I waited while he wrote it down. Then he said he and his people would be over in no more than ten minutes. Just to make sure I understood what was ahead, Wally told me he'd be asking a lot of questions. Most of the questions would be for me.

"Something to keep in mind, Crang," Wally said on the phone.

"What?"

"You shouldn't plan on getting to bed any time before sun-up tomorrow morning."

Wally laughed, and clicked off the phone.

I sat down on the sofa to wait for the police. Squeaky snored on, not knowing the surprise that was in store for him.

CHAPTER FIFTY-TWO

It was raining softly when I woke up. The clock on the bedside table read 12:14. That was p.m. It was the beginning of the afternoon. I'd spent all the previous night over on Playter getting debriefed by Wally. When I wasn't in the debriefing, I was waiting. Cops were big on making people wait. Maybe it was necessary, and maybe it wasn't. Cops seemed to think waiting was a natural part of the process.

The way it went in the Playter sessions was typical police stuff. Wally would take me part way into my story. Then he'd say, "Hang on, Crang." He'd go into another room and confer with the Forensics guys or with his boss at Homicide or with a cop he'd sent on an errand. Then he'd come back to me. "Okay, Crang," Wally would say, "from the top once more. The guy you call Lex slipped out of the house after he shot me. At that point, where did you go and what did you do?" It was tedious, and then, finally, it was done, and just as Wally predicted, I arrived home at about the time the sun was coming up.

I rolled out of bed, pulled on jeans and a light blue shirt, and went downstairs. I drank a glass of orange juice and ate a toasted raisin bun followed by a bowl of Bran Buds with a banana sliced into it. All my breakfast usuals. But I was still hungry. I poached two eggs and ate them on toast. The eggs and toast got me closer to feeling well fed. I made enough coffee for three cups.

I felt good, even rested. I'd survived. I'd delivered the goods for my client in particular and justice in general. All was upbeat in my life — except for something tiny that insisted on niggling at the back of my mind. It wasn't major, just annoying. The irritation grew out of my connection to the Reverend's death. He died when Squeaky Fallis flew into a temper tantrum and whacked the Reverend with the briefcase. There was no doubt about those events. It was settled fact that Squeaky killed the Reverend.

But the source of Squeaky's fury was what was at the base of my problem, minute as it was. The circumstances that turned Squeaky into a raging fool began with the missing nine pages of Flame's song lyrics. The pages were supposed to be in the Reverend's desk drawer, but when the Reverend told Squeaky they were no longer where they were supposed to be, Squeaky went nuts and briefcased the Reverend. And where exactly were the pages at that moment when the Reverend revealed the bad news to Squeaky? They were in a file in my office. I'd lifted them from the Reverend's desk drawer a few days earlier.

My question to myself seemed to be this: did the presence of the sheets in my office drawer bring any responsibility for the Reverend's death home to me?

Rationally, I told myself, the answer to the question was all in the negative. I had been carrying out an assignment from my client, the Flame Group, when I retrieved the stolen documents from the Reverend. It didn't matter that the person who had done the stealing in the first place was Roger Carnale, who happened to be the executive director of my client. The documents still retained their stolen status until I completed the rescue operation.

I poured my second cup of coffee, and sat in the dining room watching the rain fall soundlessly on our back garden. It was a fine moment in my small world, apart from the one small irritation. Maybe, to make it go away, what I needed was some psychological reinforcing for my view that the damn niggle had no basis for its existence.

The doorbell rang. Who'd drop by at this time of day? Had to be Jehovah's Witnesses. I opened the front door. It wasn't Jehovah's Witnesses. It was Wally Crawford.

"When a cop comes calling on a guy," I said, "it usually means the guy's in trouble."

"All I know is you've been letting my calls go to message all morning."

"And you've got a major need to talk to me?"

"Preferably not out here in the rain."

I led Wally back to the dining room, and asked if he'd like some coffee.

"You got cream to go with it?" Wally said.

"I got milk," I said. "But why do you want to ruin the taste of a good cup of coffee?"

Wally insisted on the milk in his coffee, and when he got settled, he made a little speech.

"I'm on my way home to bed, Crang," he said. "But before I do that, I want to thank you for how you handled the Squeaky Fallis thing. That was nice work. A little crazy, but still the right result."

"You came here to tell me that?" I said.

"Sometimes cops like to reach out to helpful members of the public."

"That's cool, Wally."

"You're welcome, Crang," Wally said. "Coffee's not bad either."

"What about the Crown's office? They made up their minds what they're charging Squeaky with?"

"They don't figure they can prove intent. With all the evidence they got, there's nothing that shows Squeaky intended to kill the Reverend."

"It's going to be murder two?"

"Second degree, yeah."

"Squeaky got a lawyer yet, have you heard?"

"Not that I know of, but your sidekick from last night, Lex, he's got Pete Guelph acting for him."

"Pete? Man, he's good. What's the Crown charged Lex with?"

"Careless use of a firearm, which is as light as we could go for Lex."

"On the unofficial condition that he testifies against Squeaky?"

"Naturally," Wally said, wearing a small smile.

I smiled back.

Wally said, "I got one more thing you'll be interested in, Crang."

"It's all interesting, Wally."

"I've just been to Archie Brewster's lab."

"There's a breakthrough," I said. "As long as I can remember, Archie's only served your sworn enemy, the defence bar."

"It made no sense to ignore him on this case, not when he'd already done all the work on the briefcase."

"So you took him what? A set of Squeaky's fingerprints?"

Wally pointed at me to indicate I was right with my guess.

"Archie did a computer run with all the prints," Wally said. "His conclusion — there was definitely a set of Squeaky's prints on the briefcase's handle."

"Another nail in the case against our man Squeaky Fallis."

Wally gave me a thumbs up.

It was easy to see that the energy was draining out of Wally. He must have been up for thirty-six hours straight. He had deep purple lines under both eyes, and his skin was going a little waxy. After a few more minutes at my place, Wally ended the small talk and left for his home.

As soon as Wally was out the door, I put on my black San Antonio Spurs windbreaker with Manu Ginóbli's name on the back. I walked up the street to my Mercedes, and drove over to Yonge Street. I went north on Yonge until I got to Crescent Road, turned east and followed Crescent's snakey curves into deepest Rosedale, past the handsome houses and the beautiful gardens on my way to Annie's favourite grocery store, Summerhill Market. I bought a Summerhill frozen shepherd's pie, a couple of heirloom tomatoes, a plastic container of triple-washed arugula, a bunch of green onions, and for dessert a pint of Saugeen County yoghurt and a package of frozen wild Canadian blueberries. Everything qualified as what Annie called comfort food.

At home, I went out to the kitchen and did the prep for dinner. By the time I finished, the table was set, a bottle of Annie's favourite Côtes du Rhône had been opened, and two of her antique dessert glasses had been filled with yoghurt, sprinkled with blueberries and a shot of lemon juice, and were chilling in the fridge.

After that, I made a martini, and went out on the front porch to sit on the steps and watch for Annie's airport limo. I wondered about the niggle over the Reverend's death? Was it still lurking in the back of my mind? It was. Would I tell Annie about the niggle? Of course I would. But I needed to pick my spot. There was no sense in springing the niggle on her before she recovered from the promotion tour. I'd wait for her to settle into life back here at home. Then I'd get down to the irritating piece of business.

CHAPTER FIFTY-THREE

I was still sitting on the porch steps with my martini mulling over the Reverend's death when I looked up, and there was Annie stepping from the limo. She had on neither of the two outfits she bought for the book tour. Instead, she looked like the familiar Annie in casual clothes: jeans, a dark blue blouse, and a straw-coloured jacket. Plus a smile as wide as all outdoors.

We hugged, and kept on hugging until the limo driver cleared his throat. He'd carried Annie's two bags up to the porch. I reached into my pants pockets for seventy bucks.

"No way, sweetie," Annie said, opening her handbag. "Columbia's paying expenses all the way."

"They've changed their former skinflint ways?"

"Damn straight," Annie said, tipping the limo guy generously. "They've already got orders for more Edward Everett books from book stores, the chains, Amazon. My book's actually selling, Crang."

"The *New York Times* best-seller people know about this?"

"It's all because of the Charlie Rose–type attention. Going on his show, on *Ellen Degeneres*, the sales are a response to all that. They won't last."

"You scored a hit with Ellen?"

"We took turns breaking one another up. This was live on television doing the skit, me being Edward Everett and her doing the hotel manager. She'd crack up at me when she was supposed to be in character, and I'd do the same with her."

"Like Harvey Korman and Carol Burnett on her show in the old days?"

"Exactly like that. Ellen's producer told me it was great TV. I'll play the discs for you later."

In the dining room, Annie made wow sounds when she saw the garden in all its green beauty. I handed her a glass of Côtes du Rhône, and built another martini for myself.

"My god, Crang," Annie said, looking at the garden and then back inside to the meal I was getting ready, "I should leave home more often. Comfort food and great wine when I come back."

"There's something wrong with that equation," I said.

"Yeah," Annie said. "The thing about leaving home. If we could just think of a way to omit that part."

Annie sat down, and talked about Flame and Jerome.

"Jerome's now associate executive producer on the movie. Gives him a chance to put his ideas in action. The Hollywood people are apparently pretty impressed with the arrangement. Jerome's happy as a clam."

"He still out in L.A.?"

Annie nodded. "Flame's not going to tour again until after they shoot the movie this winter. Which clears Jerome strictly for movie stuff."

I put the shepherd's pie in the oven, and turned it up to 350 degrees.

Annie talked happily and at length about the movie, its filming schedule, its casting, its chances for box office impact.

When she slowed down, I poured her another glass of wine, and asked about Flame and his current whereabouts.

"He's staying out west too. But he's going to fly up here on the weekend. He told me to tell you he wants to have a little chat with your good self. He says he owes you one. There's something in there about you getting his mother a new job with the Flame Group. What's that all about?"

"It's about the end of the case," I said. "It's about nailing the guy who killed the Reverend."

"Okay, sweetie," Annie said, "let's have the rest of what happened."

I picked up the story where Annie's knowledge of events ended. She knew all about pretty much everything leading up to the details of the previous night's vigorous action. That was where I started, with the gathering at Carnale's house and continuing all the way to the tussle around the pool table at Squeaky's place. I left out nothing, only pausing in the narrative to serve the shepherd's pie, the tomatoes, and the salad.

"Bless you, Summerhill," Annie said. "Hmmm."

I talked while we ate, covering the part where Lex and I subdued Squeaky just after Squeaky confessed to killing the Reverend into my concealed tape recorder. I kept going right up to Wally's arrival with the other cops at the house on Playter. Then I stopped talking.

The finale brought silence to the dining room.

I helped myself to a half glass of Annie's Côtes du Rhône, and raised it to a small toast. I wasn't sure which person or event I was celebrating.

"What is it I'm missing?" Annie said. She was sitting very still in her chair, staring intently at me.

"Squeaky's in the clink," I said. "There's not much more to miss."

"You had a little hesitation in your voice, just before you said the policeman came over to the place where the bad guy was tied up with his own neckties."

"I did?"

"What are you not telling me?"

I got up, slid another bottle of Côtes du Rhône out of the wine cabinet, uncorked it, and poured some wine into Annie's glass and some into mine. Then I told Annie about the niggle on my mind, what it was and how it got there. Again, Annie hardly moved when I did my explaining. She didn't touch her wine glass. She just listened until I finished. It didn't take long.

Annie picked up her wine glass, and had a drink that was much longer than a sip.

"Taking all the pieces of chicanery into consideration," she said, "the thefts and the retrieval, the blowup in the Reverend's office, all of that, you're feeling a tad guilty and don't think you should be?"

"That would nicely sum up the conundrum."

"Then what applies here is the Law of Unintended Consequences."

"That's one of those laws — have I got this right? — it's really nobody's law, not a real law, more bogus along the lines of Murphy's Law?"

"Which says roughly, Murphy's Law does, anything that can go wrong will go wrong. Murphy's Law has been attributed to a bunch of different people, a couple of them actually named Murphy. But more generally Murphy's Law expresses a belief that many people accept, and they feel better about it when it's wrapped up in something called a law."

"But it's not really a law?"

"Right."

"The Law of Unintended Consequences is of a similar brand of home truth?"

"Economists have used this one forever as somewhat of a real deal," Annie said. "But to everybody else, it's a convenience — the same way as Murphy's Law."

"Not that I remember what it says. Maybe I never knew."

"The Law of Unintended Consequences, it's a kind of adage, an idiomatic warning. It tells people they shouldn't imagine they can control the world around them."

I thought about that for a moment.

"What you mean in the case at hand," I said, "is that I shouldn't suppose that any action I took, as I did for instance in liberating the lyric sheets from the Reverend's drawer, would prevent the world from unfolding in ways it was supposed to?"

"Your own version of the world's unfolding, if you could control it, wouldn't include a homicidal villain murdering a man you didn't think was particularly bad-hearted."

"Right. I didn't suppose Squeaky Fallis would create such havoc in a way that was so immediate to my own actions."

"And yet now, you with your talk of niggles, you're reacting as if you should have greater power over the unintended consequences."

"So, what then? I must be guilty of something?"

"Hubris, sweetie, nothing less than hubris. Or nothing more either."

"Excessive pride, well, isn't that the damnedest thing," I said. I was beginning to feel a little giddy, which was a big improvement over the niggles of unnecessary guilt.

I got up, walked around the table to Annie's side, leaned over and kissed her on the lips.

"That's what I've been missing," Annie said after a few moments.

I went up to the kitchen, and brought down the glasses with the yoghurt, frozen blueberries, and squirts of lemon.

"Dessert?" Annie said. "We hardly ever have dessert. Isn't this just the perfect world."

"Maybe not perfect for real," I said. "But sometimes it feels that way, which is good enough for me."

Both of us polished off our entire desserts.

Annie and I smiled at one another.

"The dishes can probably wait until tomorrow," I said.

Annie reached across the table. Hand in hand, we walked upstairs to the bedroom.

ALSO AVAILABLE FROM DUNDURN